HUNTED!

They were right behind us. I could hear the powerful engines of the swamp buggies. We ran down the narrow trail following the white of the limestone in the dark night. The airboat stood hidden in the cypress clump where we had left it. We both pushed the bow into the two-foot-deep water and sawgrass. I dove into the front. The Swamp Master leapt into the driver's seat and hit the start button, the engine hesitated, coughed, and burst into life. The Swamp Master slipped on his ear protectors and strapped himself in. I did the same.

I saw the two swamp buggies catapult over the spot where we had been hiding and shoot down the narrow path we had used. They crushed the grass on both sides of the trail. The huge spinning tires made deep bigfoot tire imprints in the mud of the swamp. They were moving at a hell of a clip, like insane giant insects. Each swamp buggy had two high-powered halogen headlights that rayed out a white intense light ahead of them. Above the drivers was a string of white-hot halogen jackrabbit lights that lit up the area all around them in a one-hundred-and-eighty-degree light storm.

They made perfect targets.

FALSE WITNESS

R. L. SMITTEN

LEISURE BOOKS   NEW YORK CITY

A LEISURE BOOK®

August 2001

Published by

Dorchester Publishing Co., Inc.
276 Fifth Avenue
New York, NY 10001

ISBN 0-8439-4903-1

Visit us on the web at www.dorchesterpub.com.

This book is dedicated to my wonderful daughter, Kelley,
a rare and precious jewel, full of the fire of life.
Her spirit has often been my inspiration
and I see the history of my entire family
shining in her marvelous blue eyes.

ACKNOWLEDGMENTS

I would like to thank Dick Gregorie, an assistant U.S. attorney in South Florida, who knows more about the crime situation in South Florida than anyone I know. He was the force behind the indictment of Pablo Escobar, the Ochoa brothers and Manuel Noriega. In my opinion, he should be the Drug Czar for the United States.

And Pat Sullivan, also an assistant U.S. attorney for South Florida, a true and patient American patriot.

Richard Barber, my literary agent, who has been patient and persevering in getting this book published and a great encouragement to me.

Jeff Lean of the *Miami Herald*, who is the best investigative reporter in South Florida. He is the author of *Operation Caribe* and the story "US: Building a Cuba Drug Case" published in the *Miami Herald* on April 8, 1993, two factual sources that were helpful in writing this book.

And my best friend, Gordon Badger, who always lends me his wisdom and sage advice.

Finally, my parents, who have always been there for me with their love and support through my entire writing career . . . and my life.

Thank you all.

ACKNOWLEDGMENTS

FALSE
WITNESS

Foreword

This book is a blend of fact and fiction. The story unfolded itself slowly to me as the web of deceit and trickery became larger and larger. Like so many criminal activities, this one is complex and includes a lot of behind-the-scenes players. It is also difficult to convey the real labyrinth of how the crimes are committed.

Stolen aircraft and aircraft parts is a huge business. It flourishes because it is new to law enforcement and is policed by an understaffed FAA group and a bewildered FBI. There is no doubt in my mind there are hundreds of unsafe small planes in the air because of these crimes, and many of the crashes are due to factors that have never been truly understood or explained.

There is also no doubt in my mind that Cuba is a giant "Illegal Free-Trade Zone" for a myriad of products, like guns and high-tech equipment. It is also the major hub for transshipping and assisting the drug-smuggling business, particularly into the United States.

R. L. Smitten

The U.S. embargo assures that Cuba has a free hand in continuing its illegal operation by promising "no interference." Castro has outlived eight Presidents and outside of China, he remains the best-known Communist dictator in the world. But it isn't Communism that has driven Fidel Castro; it is money and power, the same things that drive the rest of the world.

But I am not discouraged. It is my personal observation that there are still a lot of great Americans, loyal patriots in law enforcement, with a high sense of duty and obligation to their country. The wonder is how they keep their cynical sides from devouring their high sense of duty.

It is the politicians who are the real enemies, because many of them have the same basic objectives as Fidel Castro—money and power . . . as you will read in this book.

Richard Smitten
Fort Lauderdale, Florida

Chapter One

We were airborne. Miami disappeared quickly as the Everglades slipped under the plane's ample belly. Heat waves rose off the great swamp giving it the look of a mirage. We were flying low, fifteen hundred feet.

The plane was a Grumman Albatross, built in 1949, one of the last descendants of a proud line. They were impractical airplanes, amphibians, magnificent birds that could swim, waddle along on the land, and fly. They were noble, the end of an era, the end of the wartime forties.

She sat next to me, eyes down, studying the map, her blond hair compressed by the earphones, listening to the chirping air traffic. She slid her eyes over in my direction, locking with mine, her face reflecting the orange glow of the sun rising from the ocean. She gave me that slow, quiet, I got-a-secret sexy smile of hers.

"See any alligators?" I asked her.

"The only alligator I wanna see is the one they used to make my bag." She smiled.

We were south of Alligator Alley, about fifteen miles from Florida Bay. I did an instrument check. My heart stopped. The planes's right-engine oil-pressure gauge was reading red, forty pounds of pressure and falling. I looked out at the wing to see if the engine was spitting oil, but none was visible. She picked up on my vibes immediately, and spotted the gauge. She looked at me.

"Trouble, Francisco?"

"Could be a bad gauge," I said in as steady a voice as I could. I checked the water-temperature gauge on the right engine and saw it rising—trouble—oil pressure falling, heat rising. It wasn't the gauge. I banked the plane up slightly, changing the attitude, before I reached over and shut down the engine.

"I guess it wasn't the gauge." She smiled, putting her hand on mine. Her hand was cool and steady. She squeezed my hand and lifted the radio receiver. "Should I alert anyone?"

"Well, we still have one engine and the manual says that the plane will fly on one engine. Plenty of guys in the war flew these babies on one engine. But I think I'll head due south to Florida Bay just in case we have to land. We will be able to land in the water and wait for help."

Slowly, I banked the plane south and headed for the almost-visible open water of Florida Bay, the top of the Gulf of Mexico. It was shallow as it neared the Everglades, but deep enough for the plane to skid in safely. As the plane started to swing south, I heard it. There was a loud bang, like a shotgun, and the cowling flew off the left engine, bounced off the window near my head, and tumbled off into the swamp.

A black sheet of oil spread across the windshield in front of us, viscous and dark. The left engine had thrown a rod through the block, and ripped off the cowling. Oil streamed out from the engine; the propeller was still.

I reached forward and started the left engine. I had to have power or we would sink like a stone. The right engine fired into life. The plane fell about five hundred feet before she came under power, but there was no time, maybe a minute, maybe two minutes, before the right engine burned out. I had to land in the swamp. I had to hope there was enough water under the saw grass to support us, so we could slide on the surface.

I looked over at her, There was no fear in her eyes. She had confidence in me. She loved me—even in the face of death. She ripped the radio equipment off her head and leaned over and gave me a fast kiss on the cheek. She then calmly put her radio gear back on.

It's impossible to explain how long a minute or two can be to anyone who has not been down to his last minute or two. It grinds out slowly and precisely. It is the moment the Zen monks refer to when they tell people to get in the moment. It is the moment of illumination. Ironic, at life's end comes illumination. I had to clear my mind and focus on only one thing—landing the plane in the swamp.

The oil pressure was flat now and the temperature was in the red; only seconds left before the right engine seized and the propeller froze. We were down to two hundred feet and coming in at about eighty knots per hour. It would be like falling off a twenty-story building while driving a race car forward at eighty miles an hour.

The engine coughed and sputtered, then spat out a last gasp. We were down to a hundred feet, an airspeed of seventy knots. My hand was on the throttle, but it was no use, there was no power left. We dropped now. She put her hand over mine and squeezed, hard. The silence was all-encompassing. Through the oil-slick-black windshield I saw the saw grass coming at us like a great field of tall summer wheat. I hoped there was water under the saw grass.

We hit with a bang. I could hear and feel the belly of the plane as it bounced off the grass and mud. We started to slide through the grass, gliding and bouncing on the two feet of water that lay below the grass. There was a scratching, tearing sound from the friction of the grass as it rubbed against the fuselage of the plane.

Then I saw it like a grotesque, disfigured, crippled black hand sticking out of the swamp. The remnants of a tree felled in a great hurricane or a survivor from the fires that swept through the swamp after lightning strikes. We were skidding straight for it, and there was nothing I could do—nothing at all.

We hit it straight on . . . head-on. The tree crashed into the crotch on the right wing where the wing joins the fuselage. A tremendous smacking noise spun the Albatross in a complete circle and jettisoned us off. We slid fifty feet and stopped. The plane on Lillian's side was destroyed, stove in and battered. She was crumpled on the throttle levers. She was still in her safety harness.

There was blood everywhere. I did a fast check on

myself and found I was bleeding from the head. I checked her for bleeding. The blood looked like it was mine. I took two cleansing breaths to calm down. I had been in the Air Force in Vietnam—helicopters—this was not my first crash. I knew I had to fight off the shock and stay focused. I grabbed for the radio—it looked like it was working. I put out an automatic Mayday signal and left it on.

Slowly, I lifted her head. She moaned slightly—she was still alive. Her leg was crushed. Through the broken windscreens, I could smell the aviation fuel as it leaked out into the swamp. The engines were hot enough to ignite the fuel. I had to get her out of there. I had to cut away her harness. I needed a knife. I would have to pull her over the throttles, and take her out. Could I lift her by myself, and what about broken bones, internal injuries?

I stepped out of my seat and ran to the belly of the plane and my toolbox. There was a large razor knife in the box. I slipped it in my pocket and tried to open the fuselage door. It was crashed shut. I could make it out the busted windshield window, but I could never get Lillian through. And how deep was the swamp outside that door—Christ, what to do? I banged on the fuselage door, and used my shoulder, but it did no good. We were trapped inside a steel coffin.

"One problem at a time," I said out loud, verifying I was still alive. I had a severe cut above my eye and the blood was making it hard to see. I opened my luggage and found a shirt, cut the sleeve, wound it around the cut above my eye, and tied it. That would do for a while.

R. L. Smitten

I went forward with the razor-knife to cut Lillian free from her safety harness.

I worked around her legs with the knife as quickly as I could. One problem at a time, one problem at a time, I kept mumbling to myself as I cut away the harness. One of her legs was crumpled under the other. I could see that it was broken. She was free of the harness now. I would have to carry her, but how? The smell of the aviation gas was getting stronger. I had to think. I had to get her out of the seat, but then what? The goddamn door was crushed shut.

I had to slow down and think. What was there to think about? I had to act—do something. Then I heard it. It sounded like the high-pitched engine of an airplane. The noise was increasing. It couldn't be another airplane down here in the swamp. The noise was loud now, real loud.

A face appeared through the windshield at the front of the approaching craft. The man put his engine in reverse and stopped. He was big, with bright blue eyes, wearing a T-shirt cut out for his beefy arms. He had a baseball cap on that said REDMAN, and he was chewing tobacco—a slight dark drip could be seen in the corner of his unshaven mouth. I was glad to see him and his homemade airboat.

He held the controls at idle, took off his ear protectors, and shut down the engine. "Hey, you look bad, podner. I seen you crash. I was playin' with the gators and spearin' frogs over in the main canal. Actually, I *heard* you crash—one hell of a whack when you hit the saw grass—hell of a splash too. I think you got a real problem here with this fuel leak—and I don't mean a pollutin' problem. You got any passengers?"

"My wife."

He pulled the stern of the airboat closer and stuck his head in. "She don't look good. She alive?"

"Yes."

"You sure?"

"Of course I'm fucking sure."

"Hey, take it easy. I'm jus' thinkin' we ain't gotta lotta time here till we hit the goddamn danger zone with them hot engines and all that fuel floatin' around. Can you get her outta there?"

"The side door's jammed."

"Yeah, I see that the door's jammed. Like I said, can you get her outta there?"

"How if the goddam door's jammed?" I asked.

"Take it easy, I'll call home." He picked up the receiver from his VHF. "Swamp Master to Gator Heaven, do you copy?"

A voice crackled on the other line. "Hey, there, Swamp Master, how they hanging, big guy?"

"Never mind that bullshit now, honey. I got me a situation. Plane down here in the Glades—big fella, one of them amphibians—all tore up—guy looks okay, but his wife ain't. They need help. Where are ya, baby?"

"I'm in the truck with the kids."

"Use the mobile phone—that new cellular—and call everyone, the Marine patrol, the Park Ranger, the Highway Patrol, anyone you can think of, just call that whole emergency list on the dashboard."

"Where are you?"

"I'm a half mile east of the Miami Canal on Seminole Flats—can't miss us. Gotta go."

"I'll do it, baby. Bye." The line went dead.

"How about gettin' out through the front here, pod-ner?" He leaned over and pulled on the windshield cowling; some of the rivets had popped. "Tell you what. I'm gonna tie a chain around the brace here in the mid-dle that separates the two windshields, and I'll go like hell with the airboat, and I'll see if we can pop her outta there. I'm gonna be pissed if I pull my transom off— but I can't see nothin' else to do to get your woman outta there."

He smiled, spat some tobacco, and reached into the stern. He pulled out a chain and tied it around the brace, then tied it to a hook on the stern of his airboat.

"I'll give this here a try and see what happens." He started up the aircraft engine on the airboat. The pro-peller spun into life with a roar that filled the wide empty swamp with a cacophonous screaming sound. Birds rose from the swamp and flew off. He eased the airboat into gear and skimmed out over the saw grass leaving a splashing wake. He ran out the forty feet of chain. The chain tightened and the windshield strained; the plane lurched forward. I fell back against the pilot's seat. The plane slid forward about twenty feet sliding on the saw grass and water. The plane was finally sucked onto a mud flat. He circled around to examine his handiwork.

"About four more rivets popped, podner. Maybe we gotta chance. Now that you're up on this here mud, you're sucked right onto it. You ain't gonna move, so its either gonna pop out or I'm gonna lose the ass-end of the Swamp Master's pride and joy." He checked the chain. "Well, I can always build a new one, can't I." He smiled and let loose a final projectile of brown tobacco-liquid into the swamp.

He lined up his airboat and headed out for a second time. This time the plane was tight into the mud. The chain whistled as it tightened and finally grabbed the windshield. The windshield screamed a metal-on-metal scream; rivets popping like pellets being fired, it arched out of the body of the plane. It shot like a bullet, landing only feet from the airboat. He tossed the chain and spat his tobacco into the swamp, signaling with his hand that he would be coming in with the airboat.

I ducked down into the passenger side to start to lift her out. She was semiconscious. "Can you hear me, Lillian?"

"Yes," she whispered, in pain.

"Your leg is broken. . . ."

"My leg hurts, Francisco—it hurts real bad—like it's almost torn off."

"We're leaking aviation fuel. I have to get you out of here. Can you put your arms around my neck?"

"Yes," she said, looking into my eyes.

"Listen to me. Don't fight the pain, let it come on, let it envelop you. When it gets too bad, your body will shut down and you will go unconscious—just let the pain come and take you, honey. I'll be here and I'll see you through this; now put your arms around my neck." I knew about pain, all about pain. I thought I was through with it, but maybe you're never through with pain while you are alive. She did as she was told. I felt her fingers lock behind my neck. I never loved her more. "The pain will come like lightning when I move your leg. Let it come."

I slid one arm under the small of her back and the second arm just under her shoulders. "It's real important that you keep your hands locked behind my neck, honey." I kissed her gently on the cheek. "Ready?"

She nodded and I lifted. I could feel her hands stay locked as I lifted. There was no scream, but I could feel her hands go limp as the pain overtook her and knocked her out—some woman, this woman, my woman.

I lifted her clear of the seat and gently twisted her around toward the torn-out windshield. I stared into the bright blue eyes under the Redman hat. He was standing on the seat of his airboat. His huge arms were outstretched, palms flat, waiting for Lillian. His face was expressionless. He took her from me like he would a small child, and carried her to the front of his airboat. He'd spread some life jackets on the floor of the boat, and he set her down.

I slid down out the windshield and down the nose of the plane into the mud. I could see the hole in the block of the left engine. The fuel had stopped leaking, the plane had tilted on the mud flat, and the fuel level was equal now to the hole. I looked around at his outstretched hand. He pulled me into the boat. I sat next to Lillian. He tossed me two sets of ear mufflers, one for Lillian. I put it on her and checked her pulse as the engine roared into life.

He shouted over the engines before we put the ear mufflers on. He pointed into the swamp. "That's the Florida Marine Patrol's airboat on the horizon. We'll head for it and Alligator Alley." He slipped the airboat into gear as he slipped his ear guards on. The boat slid forward smoothly, skimming the surface of the swamp. Within minutes we were even with the Marine Patrol boat. The Marine Patrol officer looked into our boat.

His boat was gray and bigger than the Swamp Master's boat. Both boats slipped their props into neutral. The Swamp Master yelled over the noise. "Get an airvac to pick up these people at the Alley. This guy's shaken up, but looks all right; the woman is bad, busted leg and maybe internal stuff. I'll be at mile marker thirty-two in case you can't keep up with me." He winked. "When you get through, tell the airvac that we should be gettin' there when they arrive." He smiled and spat into the swamp, then jammed the boat into gear. The boat plowed ahead into full forward. I knew he was thinking of Lillian—faster speed, smoother ride over the saw grass.

She was white in the sunlight-shock. I looked for something to cover her. Swamp Master tossed me a jacket he had under his box-seat. I knelt beside her and covered her. She would be coming out of the shock soon. She needed a shot of painkiller and intravenous, and she needed it now.

I saw the cars shooting across the Everglades. In the heat mist rising from the swamp the cars looked like a mirage, as if they were slightly airborne skimming on top of the grass. But as we approached I could see the highway, Alligator Alley, come into focus. We skidded off the saw grass and into the canal that ran parallel to the highway. It was a man-made canal; the earth that had been removed from the canal was used to form the roadbed. A tall chain-link fence ran between the canal and the highway; the primary purpose of the fence was to keep cars out of the ditch. Many drivers fell asleep at the wheel crossing the Great Swamp; they say it is the hypnotic effect of the grass, sky, and colors, or the dead deep blackness of the night, that brings the deadly sleep.

We were pushing white-water onto the banks of the canal as we skimmed along. The Swamp Master was fishing inside his box seat with his free hand and steering with the other. He pulled out a large pair of wire-cutters. I saw the Marine Patrol airboat slip into the canal about a quarter of a mile behind us. He was catching us. The Swamp Master saw him as well. He looked into the sky for the helo, but there was nothing to see. I kept my mind in neutral. The situation was being taken from my hands, and I welcomed it. I saw the roadside rest station up ahead. The Marine Patrol airboat was only a hundred yards behind us now. The Swamp Master throttled down as we approached the rest stop from the canal side. He slid up to the bank and cut the engine.

"Keep the boat up against the side of the canal," he yelled to me, climbing the incline to the fence, wire-cutters in hand. He chomped out a clear line with the wire-cutters in seconds, and ripped out an opening with his hands. The Marine Patrol boat was into shore now. He secured his boat and ran to me. He grabbed the gunnel of the boat.

"Get back in the boat and get your wife ready!" he yelled. I moved. A dark shadow passed over me as the airvac helo barreled in to the cleared landing tarmac spot at the rest station.

The Swamp Master tossed the wire-cutters, and ran

down the embankment. He got to the Marine boat and stood next to the Marine Patroller, arms outstretched. "Give her to me." I lifted her from the bow of the air-boat and handed her to him. He ran up the embankment with Lillian in his arms. I went to get out of the boat, and my legs gave out. I crumpled into a heap. The Marine Patroller sprang over the gunnel and helped me back to my feet. "Let's go," he said quietly, and helped me over the side to the embankment. He slipped his arm under my armpit, and gave me support as we climbed the embankment. "Just shock, fella, that's all."

They were putting Lillian into the helo. I saw them pull the needle of morphine from her arm and set up the intravenous as she was slid into the chamber to hold her. I was helped onto the helo and quickly strapped in with a safety harness.

"We're good to go!" one of the paramedics yelled. We lifted into the air. I saw the Swamp Master shade the peak of his cap with his hand, and squint his eyes as he watched us rise into the morning sun. He spat some tobacco to the side and gave me a slight salute good-bye, the kind I had seen in Nam so many times when we ran the medevac choppers out of a hot LZ.

I tried to raise my arm to salute back, but couldn't. I was too weak. Shock had set in.

The helo followed Alligator Alley for ten miles, then headed south toward the Miami skyline. Lillian was out cold and in no pain. The morphine had done its work. A paramedic was lifting the cloth from my head wound.

"That's nasty," she said.

"Yeah," I said. "How's she doing?"

"Your wife, she's doing all right. Vital signs are

stable, but her leg is very bad and there may be internal bleeding. This will take stitches." She removed the bandage and placed a special tape on my head.

"What the hell happened?" I asked myself, feeling the tape bite-close my head wound. Lillian would never be the same—this I knew. "Both engines—Christ, a chance in a million that both engines would go like that. I'll think about it later."

Hialeah was passing below me. I saw the Hialeah racetrack slip underneath us. The pink flamingoes in the center pool were so used to air traffic that they didn't stir. The barns were empty and the stands deserted. It was a sad and desolate sight, like a party waiting to happen. What a mess this was. I had to stay focused on Lillian and stay calm.

We picked up the snaking Miami River, the rusty freighters from Central and South America, the old Haitian hulks loaded with bicycles and used tires. The fish houses, which were disappearing every year.

The Miami Medical Center jumped into view. The helo started a slow arch aiming for the bull's-eye target on the roof of Jackson Memorial. The pilot did a smooth job of centering us over the target. The paramedics were well trained. The one who had fixed my head gave me a signal to stay where I was—stay out of the way. Lillian was critical and they would move fast when we hit the ground. I saw a doctor emerge on the roof with three attendants wheeling a gurney. The wind from the rotors stretched out the doctor's gown, flapping it in the wind. He held his clipboard up to shade his eyes as the helo came down out of the rising morning sun. It was only seven o'clock. The whole thing had taken less than an hour . . . less than an hour to ruin years of work and planning. "Both engines, how the hell could I lose both engines?" The thought kept creeping into my mind.

The helo rocked on the landing pad and the engine died. The three attendants and the doctor ran across the roof. The paramedics moved with graceful efficiency. They had done the drill many times before. It's training and practice that makes a good team act like one person, a harmony of precision.

They gently pulled Lillian from her place in the helo and slid her directly onto the gurney. I heard the main paramedic as the gurney was wheeled off the roof. "Vital signs are low, Doc. BP seventy over forty, pulse fifty-three; we gave her a shot of morphine and a saline solution. Her leg is broken and it looks like possible interior bleeding."

When they hit the elevator, the doctor turned and his eyes caught mine. He had no expression, but I could read his eyes. "This is bad," his eyes said. "Very bad." It was something I already knew. But in his eyes was something else. "You were in charge, weren't you! The pilot! This should not have happened! This was one of those stupid human acts of carelessness, or recklessness!" The look was only a reflection of my own thoughts.

I was next. They wheeled out a wheelchair. I was already out of the helo. I waved it off. I could walk, goddammit. But my legs were too wobbly. I looked up at the paramedic as she wheeled me over to the hospital attendants. "Don't let them knock me out," I pleaded with her.

27

"I won't," she whispered to me as they approached. She took the attendant aside and whispered something to him, and they wheeled me onto the elevator. The elevator doors closed. I suddenly felt the bite of a needle before I saw the needle. "What's that?" I asked.

"Something to keep the shock from taking over," the attendant said, smiling. "Don't worry, Carmen told us not to knock you out."

The rest I don't remember. I awoke about four hours later in a cubicle in the emergency ward. The curtain was pulled.

I thought I was dreaming. When I awoke, I was looking into those bright blue eyes. He wasn't chewing tobacco and he had no hat on. His hair was blond and clipped tight to his head, military style. "Hey, the Swamp Master. How's my wife?" I asked.

"She's in the operating room."

"Operating room?"

"Yeah, they had to do some work on that leg."

"I never did get your name," I said.

"Sawyer, like in Tom Sawyer, only forget the Tom part. Sawyer Pinder is my full name."

I was still a little groggy. I felt my head where they had stitched it shut. "Well, I like Swamp Master. How's that work with you."

"Fine, ain't unusual that people like that handle."

"And yours?" A voice came from the top side of my bed. It was the Marine Patrol officer. A third man stood next to him.

"You mean you haven't checked out my ID?" I asked.

"Not without your permission, no, sir, we wouldn't

do nothin' like that." He smiled. "I caught this since I was first on the scene . . . well, first after Sawyer arrived."

"Francisco Cruz," I answered.

"And you are?" I asked the third man.

"I'm Bobby Day, with the FAA. Hey, that kinda rhymes, doesn't it?"

I knew this was not the first time he had said this. "Well, I know why you two guys are here. How come you're here, Swamp Master?"

"Well, I just dropped by to see how you was doin'."

"Sawyer here always seems to be poppin' up in the Everglades and the Keys. He's got a nose for trouble," Bobby Day of the FAA said.

"More like trouble has a nose for me. Well, my momma says we're part Iroquois Indian, but I think she got it wrong. I think I'm part Seminole. See, I got these kinda Indian instincts. Anyway, Mr. Francisco Cruz, I'm glad you're okay. I'll leave you now. I hope your wife is okay." He handed me his card. "Here, take this and call me if you need me—night or day." He put his Redman hat on and walked out, passing a doctor who walked in.

The doctor came to my bedside, checking the vital signs monitor. "You're doing fine," he said.

"And my wife, how's she doing?"

"Well, Dr. Bartlett is with her now. He's a great orthopedic surgeon. Her leg was fractured, so he's had to take some surgical steps. . . ."

"Anything else?"

"Some possible internal problems; we have an internist standing by after Dr. Bartlett is finished. We took

X rays, blood tests, the works. I'll tell Dr. Bartlett to come in here when he is finished."

"Can he talk to us okay, Doc?" Bobby Day asked.

"Yeah. He's okay to talk, but not for too long." The doctor swung the curtain closed as he left, enclosing us in a blue cloth cocoon.

"Mr. Cruz, can you tell us what happened?"

"I'm not sure. We took off from Opa Locka just after dawn on the way to Naples for a little vacation, and then we were going down to the Caribbean. With the Albatross we could land on water, so we thought we would just fly around the islands down south for a year or so." I sipped some water; my lips were parched, my tongue dry from the dehydration and the drugs. "The right-engine oil pressure fell first; we weren't in the air ten minutes. I had to shut the engine down; minutes later the left engine went. Looked like it threw a rod, oil everywhere and the engine just died. I turned the right engine back on, but I only had about two minutes of power before it seized on me. I was able to get some forward speed, so we slid into the swamp instead of just falling like a goddamn stone. Both engines . . ."

"How many hours on the engines?" Bobby Day asked. The Marine Patrol officer was taking notes, as was Bobby Day.

"A hundred and sixteen on the right engine and a hundred and twenty-seven on the left since the last major overhaul. The plane got an overall airworthy certificate before I took delivery on it two weeks ago."

"This was your first flight?" Bobby Day asked.

"Yeah, maiden voyage."

"Who'd you buy it from?"

"Florida Private Planes Inc., in Opa-Locka."

"Who provided the airworthiness certificate?"

"Same—Florida Private Planes Inc. You know them?"

"Yeah, I know them. Your license up to date?"

"Yeah, it's in my wallet wherever that is."

"Right here," the Florida Marine Patroller said, handing it to Bobby Day.

"Where'd you learn to fly?"

"U.S. Air Force, I'm checked out on helicopters and fixed-wing. I flew two tours in Vietnam."

"Your driver's license says here you live on Ocean Drive in Golden Beach—nice address."

"Yeah. What happened to the plane?"

"Do you mean, did it catch fire?" Bobby Day answered his own question. "No, it didn't catch fire. The fuel leak stopped when you tilted up on that mud flat and the Park Ranger had the tank drained. The plane is being guarded by some FAA types, so the human swamp rats won't strip it out. Hell of a salvage job to get it out of the swamp, but I got a big Chinook helo from Key West Naval Station on its way to crane it out. We'll take it to a hangar at Miami International to check it out."

"That seems like a lot of trouble," I said.

"Yeah, well, I have my reasons." He smiled, a plastic smile. "Logbooks, and papers?"

"Under the pilot's seat in a leather pouch. I had a hell of a time getting them from the seller."

"Florida Private Planes?"

"Yeah."

The curtain swung open enough for Dr. Bartlett to

appear. I could read his name tag. I could tell by his face it wasn't good news.

"Is that all?" I asked the two cops. I wanted to talk to the doctor in private.

"For now," Bobby Day said for both men.

Dr. Bartlett was young, early thirties, brown hair, brown eyes, pleasant forgettable face. He stood at the head of my bed. "Your wife has had a tough time. We wired her leg up and gave her a new knee . . . she'll have trouble walking."

"At the beginning?"

"Maybe forever."

"Oh, God."

"She almost lost the leg." He paused. "I almost amputated, but finally decided we could save it."

I had to hold back the tears. Lillian had been a model, a top fashion model, for years in New York. Her legs were her pride.

"You live in Golden Beach, don't you?" Dr. Bartlett asked.

"Yes."

"I used to live near there, had my practice near there in Bal Harbor. I've seen your pictures in the society pages of the *Miami Herald*."

"Yes," I answered. Christ, hours ago we were on our way to the Ritz Carlton in Naples, then down to the islands. "Doc! My wife, does she know?"

"No. She won't come around for several hours."

"I would like to be there when you tell her," I said.

"It's not a good idea, puts more pressure on her. She will immediately think a lot of wild thoughts, kind of like a whirlwind, a maelstrom of the mind. Her life will pass before her; then she will start to adjust or go into denial, compensate somehow—it's the way the mind works—survival techniques.

"It is after the whirlwind passes that you should see her, give her a few hours, Mr. Cruz. I will come for you. It will be many hours from now. I will give you something to sleep. Don't fight it. Sleep Mr. Cruz. It's what your body craves after the shock. You will be little good for her if you are not rested."

"All right," I said. Minutes later, a nurse showed up with two red pills. I fell again into the dark cavern of sleep.

My sleep was restless. I moved in and out of sleep and wakefulness. I was inside the chapel wearing my seminary tunic. The tunic was tight on my growing body; the buttons that ran from below my neck down to above my knees compressed the black cloth on my body. We were saying our midday prayers, twenty young boys between eleven and fifteen, led by a priest who chanted in Spanish: the Act of Contrition, the Apostles' Creed, and the five decades of Hail Marys as we moved through the beads of the rosary. It smelled of flowers, soap, burning candles, old incense that hung in the air, and men. We were all lost in our thoughts.

I had gone to my father, an austere man of high principle who was later to become a doctor in Miami. He had graduated university in Cuba and practiced as a licensed doctor. In 1959 he immigrated, with the exodus—the wave of the Cuban middle class exiled by Castro into the United States. This was a wonderful asset to the United States and a devastation for Cuba, as the entire intelligentsia of the country of Cuba was expelled. Castro wanted no one left in Cuba who could organize and achieve a revolution against him. Eventually, he also got rid of Che Guevara, his trusted partner, by sending him away to dangerous places until he was finally killed. Castro left nothing to chance.

My father was stern but wonderfully fair. He treated my two sisters and three brothers all the same, sternly but fairly; he always acted like a stately padrone, like his father before him.

"Father, I want to be a priest," I told him as he read the newspaper one night when we lived in Cuba. He lowered the paper.

"Why would you want to ruin your life?" he asked, and raised the paper again.

"Why would I ruin my life?" I asked.

"Because you would have no life at all," he said, lowering the paper.

"But it's my life, isn't it?" I said.

"It's not your life yet. When you have reached the true age of reason and you have finished your schooling, then it will be your life." He raised the paper again, but then lowered it, folded it neatly, and pressed it on his knee. He looked at me. Said nothing.

"But I feel this thing, inside me. I feel a closeness to God, and when I am in church I feel . . . calm, a peace, a serenity that I don't feel anywhere else," I said.

"Everyone feels that in church. You are supposed to feel that in church. Francisco, you don't know what you really feel; your body is changing now and the signals it sends to your brain are not to be depended on. They will deceive you, these feelings that now rage in

your body. It is nature stirring you on to manhood."

The next day I went to my mother, who was always singing. She had the voice of an angel. I would sing with her often. Forever after, I never felt self-conscious when I sang. It was natural to me, like being with my mother. And my voice never let me down—it was always there for me, always ready to make music, like a songbird. We would sing together like two happy songbirds, and I would help her do her work. I would work with her in the garden picking tomatoes and peppers, skinning the vegetables, grilling them. We would nibble, and I would work with her as she cooked dinner every night for eight people. She would make the salsa for the rice and black beans from scratch. The cooking aromas would fill the air. I would help mix the salsa for the black beans. I would slice the Cuban bread she would buy fresh from the baker, and guava rolls and sugar cookies for after dinner. We would sing and we would work and the time would fly by. My brothers and sisters hated this work, but I loved it. I loved being with her, singing and working, making meals, the smells, the colors of the vegetables, the making of the salsa, the black bean sauce, her joy in serving her family. I just loved watching her. I never got tired of watching her, her smile, her long dark hair, her smiling fiery black eyes.

She would just smile at me, never say anything about the songs, the songs we chose to sing. It was our way of secretly communicating.

She asked me what was wrong when I fell silent and sad and I would no longer sing with her; I finally told *her I wanted to go into the priesthood. She wiped away my tears and said nothing.*

She had a private talk with my father, who later said to me: "Francisco, I think you are going to grow up to be a man who takes no advice and has to learn by his own experiences. If this is true, then you are going to have a rocky ride, but I will not stand in your way. Give your life to the priests, if you must."

"I will give my life to God, Father." I said.

"We will see what becomes of your life, my son," he said with a wry, kind smile and a tousle of my black hair.

For three years I stayed inside the Jesuit seminary walls on the Isle of Pines. I studied the Gospels and the teachings of the Church, Saint Thomas Aquinas, Saint Ignatius Loyola, and I learned of solitude and the power of prayer. I learned from books of humility and human folly and sin. I did not truly understand these things. Not until I went home in my third year to visit my parents at the finca on the Isle of Pines, and I met her.

It was then I learned of sin.

"It's time," Dr. Bartlett said, shaking me awake, leaning down into my face. "You're doing well, I checked your head wound. We would like to keep you here for the night for observation."

"Lillian?"

"Mr. Cruz, I told her about the leg several hours ago. I'm afraid it was a great shock to her."

"I want to see her."

"Of course. I have a wheelchair here."

"No, I'll walk." I got out of the bed and almost fell to the floor. Those damn pills.

"Use the wheelchair," he said, slipping it under me. He nodded to the nurse, who wheeled me down to Lillian's room. She was in intensive care. Her blond hair was pulled back, accentuating her high cheekbones, straight aristocratic nose, and strong chin. Her blue eyes looked at me, crinkling slightly at the corners. I could see them mist over as she tried to hold back the tears. I was wheeled in next to her. I held her hand.

"Don't, Francisco, don't blame yourself."

"Lillian . . ."

"No, I know you, the way I know myself, better maybe. You blame yourself, but it wasn't your fault. It was a mechanical fault, a mechanical problem. Nobody could have done any better. I have been flying with you many times, so I know."

I sat there looking at her. She always surprised me. She continued. "I know Dr. Bartlett told you about my leg." The leg was in traction with a full cast. "I will be in this cast for several weeks."

"Lillian, we will work on it together."

"I know you're there for me, Francisco." She looked away, wistfully; her resolve to be brave was faltering slightly. She looked into my eyes. "All of a sudden I miss the house now and the ocean. I want to go home, Francisco."

"It won't be long."

"Dr. Bartlett told me"—unstoppable tears began to fall from her eyes—"he told me that they actually considered amputation. How horrible, how truly awful," she said, and took her pills from a cup that the nurse handed her. "Thank you," she said to the nurse, who walked out. "Sleeping pills."

I squeezed her hand. She took the pills and her composure returned. She wiped her eyes with a tissue.

"So you see"—she tried a smile—"it could have been worse, Francisco. My legs made me a lot of money, didn't they?"

"Yes, they did. They are famous legs and a famous face."

"Not famous anymore, Francisco. I haven't modeled in years and you know it."

"Well, famous to me then." I kissed her eyes dry. "Always famous to me."

"I can't imagine having only one leg, so whatever I have I will be happy. I've had such a blessed life, my children, my family, you—you gave me back my life, Francisco. After Richard died I didn't want to live and you brought me back—you walked me back from my grave a step at a time. So you see, whatever I have is fine. I have you and I have my life. Our romantic adventures will just have to wait a while."

I saw her hit the switch on her intravenous, which would allow the morphine to drip into the saline solution. The pain must have been awful, but she never let on. I squeezed her hand tighter. I looked at my watch.

"I know they said ten minutes, but just please stay with me until I drift off. I don't want to talk anymore. I love talking to you, but I think I need to rest now." Her eyelids became heavy. I knew it was the morphine, not the sleeping pills. I sat there and looked at her. She was a classic beauty, the kind of beauty that God hands out to few people. I knew that it was her inner spirit that magnified her natural beauty, lent warmth to what could have been icy cold. She was icy cold when I first met her after the death of her husband Richard.

I owned a chain of Cuban restaurants in Dade, Palm Beach, and Broward Counties and one in Key West. They were called Hola Havana—Hello, Havana. We served home-style Cuban food.

The original restaurant in Little Havana on Calle Ocho in Miami was now really a nightclub-restaurant. It had started out small, as a restaurant. I opened it back in 1976, just after I returned from Vietnam and the service. I had saved up five thousand dollars, and I borrowed five thousand from my father. I used mostly my mother's recipes and some family friends. I had twenty tables and a small bar. I could serve fifty people. Now, I could serve 250 people, and I had a decent bandstand and a dance floor for the Friday and Saturday night shows. On Wednesday I had a "social club" night when all the Cuban musicians were welcomed to the club to jam for free drinks. I called it the "Miami Social Club"—after the Buena Vista Social Club in Havana. We sang any and everything on Wednesday night. I had the greatest musicians in Miami. Over 800,000 people had left Castro's Cuba for freedom—plenty of great musicians. We also had great visitors from the rest of the United States, Europe, and the Islands attending on a Wednesday night jam. We sang everything, from the songs of Gloria Estefan and the Miami Sound Machine, right through to the songs of Ricky Martin. On Friday and Saturday it was more salsa and mambos, like the soundtrack of the movie *The Mambo*

Kings—a lot of festive dancing, handsome people, dressed to the nines. They moved on the dance floor with the great grace and elegance of old Hollywood movies. These people knew how to move their bodies to the tropical rhythms of Havana when it was the Paris of the Western Hemisphere, and they had taught their children. Saturday night it was young and old alike, a great big extended family of people who knew how to live. I loved singing to them. They danced each with their own style, but somehow, on occasion, it was coordinated so it seemed to me from the bandstand as if they were one body. One massive body of humanity moving, swaying, gyrating, in love with their "aliveness." Their pure joy in simply being alive filled the room and made it heady, like sweet sex.

Those thoughts all blended together in my mind, and sometimes made we so weak I would have to sit down.

Lillian and Richard came often to my club. It was there where I first met her. Lillian was gone now, almost asleep, drifting off into the land of Morpheus. I signaled my nurse, who wheeled me down to my room. I had decided to take the doctor's advice and sleep in the hospital. I would check on Lillian in the morning and then leave. I was in no condition to drive to Golden Beach, and I didn't want to call anyone to drive me.

Lillian had loved her mother very much, but it was her father that she adored. They lived in Asbury Park, New Jersey, right by the ocean. Her father was Greek. His name was Costa Elides, and his father was from Athens; so was his mother. He had started with his father's produce market. It was in the days when supermarkets were just being invented. He started with the produce market and built it up into the first supermarket on the Jersey Shore. It grew to a chain of three hundred stores before it was sold out.

On the days when she would visit her father, she would get so excited she would be unable to sleep the night before. She loved the original produce market where he started. She was high-spirited, and deeply beautiful. She would run through the market, her blond hair flying behind her, stopping to take deep breaths, inhaling the delicious ripe-fruit odors; apples, bananas, oranges, melons; then she would run to the produce section and smell the radishes and the lettuce and the tomatoes; she would dash to where the potatoes and yams and sweet potatoes were and take a deep breath.

Then he would magically appear, always at the right moment. He was so handsome and tall, dark hair, darker eyes that would flash with pride when they saw her. He would say, "Lillian, why you running all the time? Walk like my little lady." And then Lillian would bolt off to go to the apples or the grapes and take one for herself and one for him. Or she would dart to the flowers and get a flower for each of them.

She did this all her life. He hated the office. He loved the people who shopped at his stores. She would find out what store he was in and go there, and as she got older she would drive herself to the store to surprise him, and he would always find her in the produce section and they would have their little game.

After he died, Lillian would sometimes find herself in the produce section of supermarkets wherever she was. She would inhale the delicious aromas, but her father would never come to her, not anymore. She missed the safety of holding his hand, and the big smile, the special smile that was reserved for her.

Her morphine dreams pumped up by the pills took her back to the beginning, to the original produce market where she would slip away from her mother. But in her dream now she couldn't run like she used to. She had only one leg that would work. She couldn't run anymore. Why not? What would she do?

Then he appeared from around a corner, with his apron on, and his full head of dark hair and those liquid-black sparkly eyes. He bent down and picked her up and carried her wherever she wanted to go. He never noticed her bad leg. He never said a word. He carried her to the flower section and got each of them a blood-red rose. Then they went looking for her mother. She forgot about her leg, and felt safe again in her morphine dreams, with her arms around his neck.

I left the hospital the next day just after dawn and rented a car. Lillian had been asleep when I left. She seemed fitful in her dreams. I was very restless. There was something bothering me that I couldn't identify. I drove up I-95 to the Miami Beach Causeway exit, then took the causeway over to the beach. Our house—actually it was Lillian's house, left to her by her late husband, Richard—was located on Golden Beach. Golden Beach is about ten miles north of South Beach—which is really the old Miami Beach with a trendy new name.

It was a mansion that cost over fifty thousand dollars a year just to keep going, but Lillian loved it and she had the money to keep it up as it should be kept up. Or at least this was what she used to believe. She had been defrauded out of millions by her dead husband's ex-partners and some bad real-estate and stock-market investments. She was waiting for a final statement from her accountant as to what was left in her estate. I was afraid it was going to be a lot less money than she thought.

There was one permanent female employee in the house, Merisol, a Cuban who had come with the house. Merisol was very protective of Lillian, and I would have to tell her what happened—something I was dreading. The driveway gate slid open with the automatic gate activator. I disarmed the security code and entered the house.

Merisol was standing at the top of the stairs, hair wild, long flowing green nightgown, holding a forty-five. "My God, Mr. Francisco, you scared me. You are supposed to be in Naples."

"Merisol, put the gun down before you shoot yourself, or me."

"I don't wanna shoot nobody. Mr. Cruz, you don't look so good."

"I know." I felt the bandage on my head. It had taken ten stitches. She placed the gun on a small table. "Mrs. Cruz has been hurt."

"Oh, my God."

"The plane crashed in the Everglades. She's all right, but her leg has been hurt. She's going to need you in a few days, Merisol."

"I will be here for her," she said, tears forming in her eyes.

"I know you will. I don't feel like talking anymore right now. I'll fill you in later."

"A Mr. Day called last evening and left his number. He didn't say who he was."

"Okay, I know who he is. I'll call him."

"Is Mrs. Cruz in the hospital?"

"Yes. She is going to need some medical equipment here at home, a traction bed and some other stuff. We'll look after it later. I'm going to my room now, Merisol."

I left and went into the master bedroom. It was a big room; the king-size bed looked like a single bed. The en-suite bathroom was also large, with a Jacuzzi tub and two very large closets with dressing rooms running off the bathroom. My clothes did not come close to filling my closet. Lillian's closet was full. I could smell her fragrance the minute I walked in. It was Bal à Versailles perfume. A flood of memories hit me.

I ran the Jacuzzi, very hot. I undressed and emptied my pockets out on the dresser. I read the card Sawyer Pinder had given to me.

Sawyer Pinder
Rodeo Rider and Deep Sea Diver
Builder of Air Boats and
Licensed Private Investigator
954-463-7916
Also expert fishing guide
Everglades City, Florida

I had to smile. I lowered myself slowly into the steaming water. I checked the temperature—106 degrees. I had a hangover from the pills and the shock. I was still groggy.

I checked my watch; it was nine o'clock, almost exactly twenty-four hours since we had been rescued. The surging hot water felt soothing. I drifted in and out of sleep. The ringing of the phone by the tub woke me up.

"It's Agent Bobby Day of the FAA." There was a pause. "I was sorry to hear about your wife's broken leg, Mr. Cruz."

"Thanks. Call me Francisco," I said.

"I'm standing here next to your plane in the Miami Airport. Do you feel like talking?"

"Sounds ominous. Wait a minute." I climbed out of the filling tub and slipped on a robe. I took the portable phone out onto the balcony. The surf was quiet. I saw a flock of seagulls working a breaking patch of bait. The big fish were underneath driving the bait to the surface. The bait was trapped in between the birds and the predators below. I leaned on the railing, letting the salt air waft over me. "Okay, Agent Day, what's on that mind of yours?"

"Well, I never like talkin' too much over the phone. I found your logs where you said they would be. We got ourselves a little situation here that is disturbing."

He was starting to annoy me. "Can you be specific?"

"Look, I need for you to come down here so I can explain better. I never trust phones anyway. I know you must be a little shaky. How about I send an FAA investigator from Miami to drive you down here."

"No, I'll need a little time to get oriented, but I'd prefer to drive myself."

"As you wish." There was a pause. I heard him talking to someone else. "Could you bring your papers with you. Ownership, stuff like that?"

"Yeah, I'll be there in a few hours, say by noon."

"Fine, we'll be here."

"Who's we?"

"My boss is here. Chief Inspector Harold Greene."

"All right. I'll be there."

I went in and slipped into the steaming Jacuzzi. I was still somewhat in shock, and knew I wouldn't think as clearly as I should. They'd probably figured that out too. Keep me off balance, make sure my answers were not rehearsed. I had learned a lot in the military. While I was in Vietnam I was put in the "Special Ops" unit for a year. I was a flying chauffeur for a bunch of wild-ass bad boys. CIA spooks going into Cambodia and Laos trading cash for ears and heroin. I remember one flight where we landed in a camp of Chinese Mungs—mercenaries. I sat at the table in the glow of the camp-fire where these two spooks in Hawaiian shirts passed out hundred-dollar bills for ears. Maybe, that was what I didn't like about that guy I saw with John Harrison before I took off from Opa-Locka—that Hawaiian shirt.

I remember every mission. The first one I flew up river into Cambodia was the biggest shock. The spook I flew in asked the leader of the Chinese Mungs: "These ears here are only from Viet Cong that you killed, right?" The Mungs smirked and raised and lowered their heads, staring at the U.S. currency, the green-backs, in the spook's hand. "Only one ear from each Viet Cong, right?" The Mungs raised and lowered their heads again, still staring at the U.S. currency in the

46

spook's hand. "Okay, then," the spook said, and peeled off hundreds of hundreds.

The ears were placed in gunnysacks. I noticed right ears and left ears, adult ears and children's ears. The ears were like receipts to the higher command. They included each ear in the overall body count that was published every month.

Madness disguised as war!

As the hot water seeped into my tired pores, I saw again the black oil form patterns on the windshield. Snaking around in dark intertwining viscous patterns, driven by the wind. In my mind, I felt the impact when we hit. That dark skinny tree looming up, sticking out of the swamp like an open fist. The impact when the tree hit her side of the plane. My head was spinning, aching.

Forget this. I climbed out of the tub and walked back out onto the balcony. Everything leading up to the crash was so clear in my mind. Buying the plane was supposed to be the culmination of our dream. We took off from Opa Locka Airport outside Miami an hour after dawn, into the rising sun. We smiled at each other like kids with a secret and we kissed in celebration.

It was so vivid in my mind. Just the two of us, heading out to a new life. It was so placid at the start. We flew due east into the soft southerly trade winds of the ocean, then a wide U-turn that brought us back over the Miami skyline and into the Everglades, the Great Swamp. As we banked into our turn, I could see the beach line snake off under our wings, a white thread-thin line running south from Miami, skimming Biscayne Bay and the scattered islands of the Florida Keys.

R. L. Smitten

Our destination was Naples, Florida, for some quiet R and R, then down into the Caribbean for the winter. We would figure the rest out later. We were both tired, life-tired, tired of people, tired to the bone. But not tired of each other. We were in love and we wanted a new private life.

What the hell had happened? The plane had been checked out and overhauled by Florida Private Planes Inc., the company we bought it from. It had a full airworthiness certificate, inspected from prop to tail. What did the FAA want? Did they know something?

I looked out to sea. The bait had cleared out. The birds were gone. I wondered what happened to the bait with the fish under them and the birds above. Somehow I was beginning to feel trapped like that bait, and I didn't know why.

Not yet.

Chapter Two

I took the Ferrari to go see Bobby Day, the classic 328
GTS that I had bought when I opened my last restaurant on Clematis Avenue in Palm Beach. Lillian never
liked the car. She said it reminded her of the *Magnum
P.I.* television show, and she wasn't a fan—too flashy
for her. It started right up, and I headed down Miami
Beach to I-95, where I would open it up a little on the
way down to Le Jeune Road and the Miami Airport.
My dark blue cotton shirt was tight to my body. Clinging in the heat, it brought back memories of my tunic
when I was in the seminary.

*It was in the third year of my time at the seminary. I
was fourteen, big for my age and strong. I played soccer
with the other seminarians and we exercised every day.
Battista was the dictator in charge and Cuba was wide
open for fun and pleasure—the tropical Paris of North
America. My parents had me home for a two-week hol-*

iday period in August. They had a finca on the Isle of Pines. It was owned by my grandfather and had been in the family since the 1850's. By this time my father was a respected surgeon in Havana. We were very proud of him. He was a kind doctor available for all the people.

But he never put his arms around any of us and just told us he loved us. He was not that kind of man. He was stern and full of duty, honor, and integrity. When I brought home A's from school he would just look at me, smile, and say: "That's good, Francisco," as if that was what I was supposed to do—bring home straight A's—no praise for my hard work—no praise, ever.

The finca was located on a hill where you could see the ocean, the sand, and the waves breaking. The finca had workers who grew corn and sugar. We would swim in the fresh mountain stream that slowly drifted down the easy grade to the ocean. Sometimes my brothers and sisters would drift along with the stream all the way to the ocean and swim right into the breaking waves, yelling and screaming when we got to the beach—for no reason but that we could.

Sometimes we would walk in the beautiful fields. My brothers and sisters would all play together. I was the youngest and the boy, so I had a special place in the family that I loved. They would protect me from all others, but tease me sometimes, make fun of me because I was in the seminary. They would sometimes build a confessional out of old plywood and scrap lumber and kneel down in the confessional, saying, "Forgive me, Father, for I have sinned," and then they would tell me the most outrageous disgusting sins, like *how they had killed little babies . . . and worse.*

My brothers would line up to confess, telling me of all the hundreds of women they had had sex with in the slowest, most graphic, and most pornographic words and gestures, and then ask for a serious penance. I would command them into silence and tell them to say a million Hail Marys.

My sisters would tell me of the impure thoughts they had had, but they would never get too specific, except to say they wanted to murder their brothers when they teased them.

My brothers would whisper these gross sins that they had told me into each other's ears, and fall over on the beautiful grassy fields and sprawl, and roll, and giggle. It was wonderful.

Nevertheless, my sisters were very proud of me in my black tunic with the buttons down the front. They would tell me the biggest problem I would have when I was a priest would be to resist the women who would tempt me, trying to touch my pee-pee. I told them, "God would give me strength," and they would laugh and say, "We'll see, handsome Francisco! We'll see."

When we went into the village, my sisters would hold my hands and kiss me and tell all the shop owners these incredible tales, about how they were all having this wild orgy-affair with this beautiful, pure-virgin priest, a stranger who had come to visit. But my family was well known and no one believed them.

In fact, I was a virgin. I had some nocturnal emissions, which we were warned about at the seminary— how the devil would send us women in our dreams, succubus demon-dream women to corrupt us. I kind of

*enjoyed my dreams, but I never told anyone. I con-
fessed them to the priests every Friday like the other
boys. I got my penance, said my prayers, and asked
God for forgiveness.*

In my second week at the finca *I took off on my own
for a long walk. I carried my missal with me and
stopped to read out of it every once in a while. In the
afternoon of my first day, I wandered past a cottage
where a woman was stacking the corn for the animals.
I had seen her in the town. She was a gorgeous woman,
long, beautiful, silky black hair and sparkling black-
shiny-coal eyes. She was strong, with ample breasts
and a slim waist. She wore no makeup, only a long
flowered light blue dress that went to her ankles.*

*She called to me. "Hey, Mr. Priest." She smiled and
waved for me to come to her with her free hand. She
held a stack of dark crimson grapes from her garden in
the other.*

*"I'm not a priest, at least not yet, and my name is
Francisco," I said, walking toward her.*

*When I got to her she smiled, a beautiful smile.
"Well, how about I call you Father Francisco."*

"If you want to," I said.

*"Come into the back," she said, opening the gate.
"Will you help me for a minute?"*

*"If you want," I answered. It was all I could think
of to say. I followed her.*

*She stacked the grapes on a wooden table and sat
down for a second on a bench. The house she lived in
was right there. "Here, try one." She plucked some
grapes from her bunch. I opened my mouth and she put
them in one at a time. She wiped a spot of juice from*

my mouth with the hem of her dress. She was rough in raising the dress. I could see the smooth light brown-ness of her thigh and the beautiful curve of her leg.

She smiled at me, and said, "Look all you want." She smiled.

I quickly looked away. She smiled again.

"Father Francisco, I've just moved that ladder over there so I can stack the rest of the grape vines on top of that arbor. I want you to hold the ladder so I don't slip. I have to take that small stack and put them up there."

I nodded.

She said, "Well, come over here, come along, Father Francisco, don't be shy."

I stood there holding the ladder as she climbed. It was steep. When she got to the top I looked up. She wore nothing under her dress. It took my breath away. I had never seen anything like it. She got to the top of the ladder and stretched to place the grapes on the ar-bor. Her legs parted. I could see the darkness of her womanhood.

She must have known I was looking, I thought, but I couldn't be sure. When she came down to get another bunch of grapes, I twisted my head and looked away. But I couldn't help looking upward each time she as-cended the ladder.

Finally, she was done. She climbed down and asked me, "Would you like a glass of cold wine in the house?"

"Yes," I said, and followed her into the modest farm-house. She told me to wait on the couch, and walked back in with a tall glass of white wine with ice cubes

in the glass. "This is a sacrilege putting ice in this magnificent wine, but I won't tell anyone if you won't. Will you tell anyone?" she asked.

"No, I won't tell anyone," I stammered.

"Good. I know that you are too young to drink, but I want to be able to trust you to remain silent . . . so this will be our first test." She got up from the couch and turned on the radio. She smiled down on me. "Now, I must go and do some chores, but I will return shortly. Will you be all right?" she asked.

"Yes." I watched her leave.

I got up several times to see where she was. She had disappeared. I sat transfixed by the music on the radio, but in my mind I saw her on the top of that ladder, moving around.

She returned after about thirty minutes. She went in the kitchen and got herself a glass of wine, cooled by ice. She returned and placed it on the table. She motioned for me to stand. She looked in my eyes for a few seconds. Her dark eyes glistened with a deep, living, natural passion. She placed her hand under my chin and kissed me lightly on the lips. I could smell the grapes, the soil, the country air, and her warm, sweet breath.

She unbuttoned my tunic, one button at a time, taking her time. She slipped the tunic off my shoulders and removed the belt from my trousers. She unbuttoned the fly and my pants slipped to my ankles. She knelt down and helped me slip out of my pants. She did the same with my underpants.

She caressed my erect member and stroked my raging testicles. She placed my manhood in her mouth and teased me at first by nibbling; then she moved up and down on my staff.

I exploded.

From that moment on I was her slave. I spent every possible minute with her. Her husband was away in the Army, and so we had the run of the house. We used every bed, every table, every rug; we even did it on top of the raw sugar cane stacked in the fields, clattering them as we made love. We showered outdoors under the garden hose, and we showered together in the main bathroom in her house. Her name was Maria, and I never saw her again after that summer.

I returned to the seminary and told the Monsignor of what had happened. I told him everything. I cried, and cried. I felt guilty, and worthless. I had violated everything I had said I would uphold. He told me it was not uncommon and that I should not be so hard on myself. What I could not bring myself to tell him was that she returned to me every night in my dreams, and sometimes not in my dreams—in the day, in my imagination, and I would handle myself.

My life had changed, and she had changed it forever. Six months later I left the seminary.

I was still stimulated by thoughts of her, Maria. I took a deep breath to calm down and rearrange my mind. I exited I-95 and took Le Jeune Road, the service road that spanned the Miami Airport. I drove past the old hangars that housed the second-rate freight carriers that ferried cargo to Central and South America, old Boeing 707's, planes that were taken out of service by the regular airlines, depreciated airplanes that were tired and worn out, but could still carry freight. These planes were often driven by burnt-out military or defrocked airline pilots, a wild and motley crew.

I finally arrived at the unmarked FAA hangar, reserved for postmortems, autopsies on crashed airplanes. I parked and walked to the door.

Investigator Bobby Day opened the steel door before I could ring the bell. The place was covered with surveillance cameras.

"Thanks for coming so soon, Francisco." He walked me through the empty office area. It was Saturday. I walked behind him into the huge hangar, and saw the Albatross in a corner. I saw what was left of the Value Jet airplane that crashed in the Everglades and killed so many people. Exploding oxygen canisters in the cargo bay was the official cause. It was awesome to see the twisted and ripped metal; my imagination soared when it came to what the falling plane must have done to the screaming people on board.

The Albatross was twisted and crushed on the one side, but it was still in one piece. A tall gaunt man stood next to the plane, smoking a cigarette. I could tell by his yellow fingers and teeth that he was a heavy smoker. He was easily six-three, and couldn't have weighed more than one-fifty. He was gray, his skin color, his hair, his eyes. The "grayman," I thought to myself.

"This is Chief Inspector Harold Greene, my boss, and chief enforcement officer for the FAA in the South Florida district." Harold Greene extended a bony hand. I shook it, and contemplated those yellow fingers. He nodded, and said nothing, so I said nothing.

"I hope all the fuel has been drained," I said, breaking the silence, referring to his lit cigarette. Harold Greene dropped the cigarette and twisted his toe on it, killing it.

"It has been," Greene said.

"I'm impressed at how fast you got the plane out of the swamp and over here."

"Military help, good training for the Key West Chinook rescue squad. They lowered a cable and plucked it out of the mud. We gave it a high priority."

"Why is that?" I asked.

"Florida Private Planes, that's where you said you bought this, right?"

"Yes."

"John Harrison, was he the seller?"

"Yeah, what an asshole," I offered. "It took me a year and a court order to get the goddamn plane from him. I paid him, but he didn't deliver the airplane until I beat him in a legal suit," I said.

"Maybe you would have been better off if he never delivered. Any idea why he didn't deliver the plane to you?"

"Not a clue. You got any ideas?"

"None that we want to talk about yet."

"So what's up."

"We checked the logbooks against the identification plates and they match."

"So?"

Greene finally spoke up. "You know how similar a car identification is to a plane ID?" I nodded and remained silent. He continued. "The identification plate don't mean shit. Like a car registration on similar cars don't mean shit."

"It's the VIN number on a car," Bobby Day offered. "And the stamped number inside the engine with an airplane."

"So?"

"Well, your numbers don't match up; the identification plates match with the logbooks, but the numbers on the engines don't match the ID plates."

Slowly, it was seeping into my brain. "So I got different engines."

"Yeah, and different props; check the numbers yourself."

I took the logbooks and specification sheets and checked them against the numbers. They were different. I saw that one of the props had the paint newly sanded off. "What's this?" I asked.

"One of our FAA mechanics noticed a slight bulge over the new paint on the prop. It's a weld."

"A weld?"

"Yeah, you got a welded prop there."

I knew what a welded prop meant. It meant that the prop could come apart at any time while in use; props were never welded. "Florida Private Planes responsible?"

"We think so," Investigator Day offered.

All my life I have had one tragic flaw. I know what it is, but that doesn't mean I can do anything about it. My anger, my red blazing-hot killing primitive fucking anger, maybe it's a Cuban Latin-blood thing. I tried with all my might to suppress it. My hands trembled slightly in anger as I handed back the logbooks and the spec sheets. I had to think. I knew nothing was ever as it appeared, and that first thoughts blended with anger are often incomplete thoughts, dangerous thoughts. Stay calm! Stay calm!

I needed time. I thought of Lillian, lying in a hospital only five miles from this hangar. She would never walk properly again. I had to reach down, deep down, and stay quiet. I thought I would faint from my rage. My head suddenly ached, and I felt nauseous, sick to my stomach, but I didn't show it.

They escorted me into the office and the conference room. Now that they had leveled me with shock and anger, I was sure they would try to con me into something. All I knew was that I had to be careful, very careful.

I followed them into the conference room, a gunmetal gray room with spartan government-issue metal furniture that was scratched and dented, tired through use. It was as if they were saying this was a no-frills operation, no waste here in the FAA.

Bobby Day picked up the banner. "I have talked with Inspector Greene and we have agreed that we will give you a briefing on the following conditions: that you will tell no one else; that you understand—"

"Stop there. Don't tell me anything," I said, head down, clasping my hands together hard in my lap. "Not one fucking thing."

"I don't understand," Inspector Greene said, lighting up a cigarette.

"Blow that smoke in another direction, will you please?" Inspector Greene went to the far side of the room. Blow that smoke right up your own ass, was what I wanted to say—don't blow it up mine. I was no stranger to working with the government. "What can't you understand? It's my problem—I'll deal with it," I thought, but did not say.

Inspector Greene spoke in a slightly louder voice. "You're sure that you don't want us to fill you in on what's going on?"

"I prefer to figure it out for myself. I like puzzles, puzzles that destroy my wife's ability to walk properly and almost kill us both. Puzzles where I pay over a quarter of a million dollars for an airplane that is basically worthless. What is it that you want from me?"

"A little patience. I want you to listen to me, Mr. Cruz," Greene said. "Maybe we can help each other."

"Please, save that for some regular civilian who believes the government is here to serve the people, not the other way around. All my experiences with the government have been bad. I served in Vietnam for the American Air Force. That was enough."

"Well, maybe it would be better this way," Greene added.

"What way?" I asked.

"No briefing. What are your immediate plans, Mr. Cruz?" Greene asked.

"Rest, and help my wife. What plans did you have for me?" I said, relenting.

"Well, we thought you could stir up the waters a little for us at Florida Private Planes."

"You looking for me to stir up the waters?"

"Yes, help us out in our investigation," Bobby Day said.

"Go undercover for you? Is that it?" I said, relenting again.

"Well, yes, it's a thought we had," Inspector Day said.

"How can I go undercover? My plane just crashed. What do I do, go in and say, 'Hey thanks for that piece-of-shit-plane you just sold me that almost killed me and thanks for hurting my wife. You guys are great, just fucking great. And forget about our legal battle for a year for me to get the goddamn plane. Oh, yeah, and thanks for relieving me of that quarter million bucks.' "

"Well, Mr. Cruz, you asked why we yanked that plane out of the swamp so fast. We did it to avoid press coverage. See, when we heard it was a Grumman Albatross that was in trouble, we figured it was a Florida Private Plane airplane."

"Why would that be?"

"Harrison has a fleet of them. He has thirty of them still left, parked down in Homestead. He brings them up to Opa-Locka, two or three at a time, and cannibalizes them to make one look good enough to sell."

"To assholes like me."

"Something like that. Anyway, we took over your Mayday call, and when we heard you were down and safely rescued, we stifled the information to the press and the media."

"Keep the press away—so nobody knows?" I asked.

"Yes, we had that big Chinook on the scene the same day pulling the plane out of the mud. We announced it was a rescue exercise. No crash was reported," Greene said, dropping his butt in an ashtray next to a sign that said, "No Smoking inside U.S. Government Facility—Thank You."

"So this is an accident that never happened. You

guys took a lot on yourselves, didn't you? What about my insurance carrier, how do I make a claim now for an accident that never happened?"

"We'll help you with that," Day added.

"I'm sure you will. What else will you help me with?" I asked.

"It's your help we need, Mr. Cruz," Day said.

"How long you been checking out Florida Private Plane?"

"Almost two years now," Day said.

"Two years and you need me?"

"We haven't been able to get a man inside," Greene said. "We need hard evidence, and we know that you're licensed for helicopters and small, fixed-wing airplanes, and that you were trained by the Air Force in Vietnam," Day said.

"So, you want me to make up a story, and go in wired and make a deal with these assholes so you can nail them," I said.

"Yes," Greene said.

"What do I get out of this?"

"Revenge for what happened."

"I don't need you to get revenge," I said.

"Well, if you want to do it on your own, that's fine." Greene lit up again. "You'll of course be the prime suspect and risk the wrath of the law. Let the law work for you, Mr. Cruz, not against you."

"And I'll mostly be fucking up what looks like an already fucked up operation you guys are running," I said. "My experiences with the U.S. Government have not been all that great, thanks."

"Is that a no?" Greene asked.

I thought as fast as I could. "What's the plan?" I asked.

"Well, Agent Day here goes in as a French Canadian drug dealer, and you are known to them as a wealthy businessman married to a wealthy woman. You already purchased one plane from them; now you want a plane for business purposes. They do not know if you are in the business or not—your nightclub may just be a great cover story for you. You can infer to them that you have a good cover story with the nightclub; you're using the plane as a water bomber for putting out forest fires in Canada. Tell them you want them to modify the fuel tanks and the cargo hold of the plane—this is another violation, an FAA and a DEA violation—to modify the interior of an airplane and falsify the documents."

"And Mr. Day here, what's his cover?" I asked.

"I'm the pilot and the smuggler who will actually fly the Albatross to Colombia, pick up a load, and land the plane on one of the hundreds of lakes around Montreal. *Sacre bleu, Monsieur,* it is a good plan, *qui?*" Day said in a perfect French accent. He smiled. "I speak French, Francisco. I lived in France for three years, my dad was with the State Department. The devil's in the details, right, Francisco? We don't want to get caught out on a little thing like not being able to speak French after we tell them I'm a French Canadian."

"How do we get around the fact that I got a defective airplane from them that could crash any minute."

"You tell them that you immediately resold the plane for a profit to a buyer in South America who wanted it for drug runs and was using it in-country to fly in the jungle and land on lakes. Pick Venezuela, lots of jungle and lakes there. If the plane crashed, who the hell could figure out what happened, or care? Just another dead doper," Greene added.

"It will add to your credibility and show you're pleased with them because you made a profit on the transaction," Day added.

"You guys just come up with this plan this morning, and get it approved by your superiors?" I asked. "It is approved, isn't it?"

"Well, we have been thinking about it for a little while. Yes, it's approved," Greene said.

"How long would it all take to set up?" I asked.

"Not long, say a week. You have to get on tape that the plane is going to be used for a dope run and that it has to be modified for that purpose. We get them for the FAA violations and conspiracy to smuggle a controlled substance. The DEA will be in on the raid with us and they will prosecute the drug stuff. It carries a more severe sentence than the FAA stuff does and prosecution is faster and easier. The system is set up for it."

"So, I go in and say, 'Thanks for the nice profit I made on Albatross number one,' and introduce my French Canadian business associate, Mr. Day. I tell them I'm a businessman and Day is the pilot-smuggler. We want to buy Albatross number two and have the belly of the plane modified to carry cocaine to be picked up in Colombia and dropped off in a lake someplace around Montreal. Is that it?"

"Yeah," Greene said, "and with a modified Albatross you will be able to fly at least a thousand keys—at today's prices, that's about fifteen million dollars wholesale."

"So, they'll jack up the price of the plane."

"Yes, expect to pay a lot and don't argue. Their greed factor will go through the roof, and they may actually piece together a decent aircraft because they won't want the Canadian gangsters coming after them if the plane falls apart," Day said.

"Like mine did," I added.

There was no response to my comment. Greene finally broke the silence. "Well, Mr. Cruz, how about it?"

"I'll let you know by tomorrow," I said.

"Let Mr. Day know," Greene said, emptying the nearly full ashtray in a scuffed steel waste bin. The ashes puffed up out of the bin in a small cloud; the ashmotes lingered and danced in the bright Miami sunlight, before filtering back down to the basket and onto the grey linoleum floor. I noticed a few ashes landed on the tips of Greene's dull black policeman's shoes. He wiped them on the back of his pants.

Day walked me to the car. "Nice car," he said as I slid behind the wheel. "Nice expensive-looking undercover car" was what he meant.

"Just like *Miami Vice* . . . thanks," I said. I looked him in the eye. "If I go ahead, I'll want something in writing."

"No problem." He smiled.

"Yeah, no problem," I said. "No problem at all . . . right!" I headed for Jackson Memorial Hospital.

They had moved her from the post-operation room to a private room on the top floor that overlooked I-95. If you looked far enough east, you could see Biscayne Bay in the afternoon sun. Her blond hair had been done and she was awake. Her leg was in traction, and I could see her intravenous still had the painkiller trigger. She smiled when I walked in.

"You look good," I said, leaning down to kiss her. I checked the bouquet of flowers on the table beside her.

"Thanks for lying and thanks for the beautiful flowers," she said.

"Your hair looks good," I said, stroking her forehead.

"I had the hairdresser come up first thing this morning. Just because I feel like a wreck doesn't mean I have to look like a wreck." She covered my hand with her own. "Francisco, are you all right? You have that look."

"What look?"

"That Spanish hot-blood look, that deadly preoccupied look, a darkness in the eyes."

"I'm sorry," I said.

"What's bothering you?"

"Nothing."

"Don't nothing me—just tell me. I have a right to know. We're partners in life, aren't we?"

"Yes, we are. You have plenty to think about, Lillian."

"You don't want to burden me with any more than I have. Is that what you're saying?"

"No, that's not what I'm saying."

"Is it about the accident?" she asked. Her instincts were impeccable.

"Let's make a deal. I have some things I suspect about that airplane, but they are not clear yet. When I clear them up, I promise—you will be the first to know."

"Okay, I'll accept that for now." She smiled, "Francisco, I need you to help me get out of here."

"You haven't even been here for a day yet."

"I want my home and my things around me." She looked pleadingly at me. "Merisol will take better care of me than any nurse."

"That I won't argue about. I've already taken steps."

"What steps?"

"I got Merisol to order a bed like this one, with the traction setup and intravenous poles and other hospital stuff. I called the doctor's office for a list."

"Francisco, you're wonderful, When can I go home?"

"We haven't even talked to the doctor yet."

She squeezed my hand and small tears oozed from her eyes. "My mother always taught me that there was always some good in the bad—some good that we didn't see when the bad was happening to us, because we were so consumed with the problem we couldn't see beyond—see to the good." She let go of my hand and reached for a Kleenex. I handed the box to her. "So, Francisco, my darling, I want you to tell me where the good is here. Where is the good hidden?" She dabbed the tears from her eyes.

"I will when I find it, darling."

I left to find Dr. Bartlett. He listened and told me to call him later that afternoon about Lillian's release.

I cranked up the Ferrari when I reached I-75, and then onto Alligator Alley, for some 140-miles-an-hour therapy. You could see for miles in both directions on the new four-lane highway that crossed the Everglades from Fort Lauderdale to Naples, a little short of a hundred-mile strip of road. It was just one long flat sprint, a strip of concrete that ran over a primeval swamp. Tall waving yellow brown saw grass with white slowly moving cotton-ball clouds hanging out of a crystal-clear blue sky. The sky looked the color of Sawyer Pinder's eyes. A pair of eyes I will never forget, looking in at me through where the windshield of the Albatross had been. I had called on my cellular phone when I left the hospital and asked the Swamp Master, Mr. Sawyer Pinder, to meet me at his home in Everglades City.

The meeting with the FAA had been a total setup. I hadn't figured it out until the Ferrari hit one-twenty. Those bastards must have had me under surveillance from the beginning. From the first day I walked into Florida Private Planes I was under surveillance. They didn't know if I was a crook or a good guy. They must have run a background check on me months ago when I first appeared at the Opa-Locka Airport.

They may have even had me locked on the tracking radar beacon with the Albatross from the moment I took off. They may have put a transponder on my plane to track me, and then removed it when they got the plane to Miami after the accident. And most of all, there was a good chance they let me fly an airplane off the tarmac at Opa-Locka that they knew was defective—maybe they even knew that Lillian was with me. Was I just too goddamn paranoid?

"Assholes. They're all government assholes, and don't ever forget it," I yelled out above the silence of the lazy, hazy, swamp. The swamp was deceiving, it looked calm, tranquil, but underneath the surface life was teeming, planning, multiplying, fucking, killing, eating, defecating, sleeping—doing all the things humans do.

I needed an inside man. I needed insurance. I needed a man like Sawyer Pinder to cover my back. The cutoff to Everglades City is at about Mile Marker 61 at Highway 41. A winding road takes you about thirty miles into the Everglades National Park and Everglades City, where the Everglades meets Florida Bay and the ten thousand islands, mangrove islands, all born from a little floating mangrove root that I always thought should be the state root-flower of Florida since it built most of the peninsula that is now called Florida.

I vaguely knew Everglades City from the days when I used to do a lot of light tackle fishing for tarpon, snook, and redfish. I had stayed at the Everglades Rod and Gun Club, a genuine historic Florida hotel. Pinder had given me directions. Go left at the convenience store and go until you hit the water. Look for the Swamp Master's airboat dock.

I saw the sign over a rickety dock surrounded by stone crab traps. The smell of creosote hung heavy in the air, from dipping and curing the new traps before the season began. That smell was overpowered by the high-octane fuel used in the airboat engines. The sign was hand-painted and explained that the Swamp Master specialized in Lycoming, Pratt and Whitney, and Grumman aircraft engines.

Two men stood with the Swamp Master at the end of the dock watching an aircraft engine propeller spin; a fourth man sat in the driver's seat of the airboat accelerating the engine. The airboat was tied to the dock. The propeller wash was leveling the saw grass that stood on the edge of the canal behind the boat. I could see the pilings on the dock strain as the boat tried to set itself free. All the men wore ear protectors. I parked the car and saw a pair of ear protectors on a bench. I slipped them on my head and watched.

The driver gradually slowed down the engine, the noise abating like the end of a long scream. I put some money in the Coke machine and got nowhere with it. After slapping it a few times with my open hand, I sat down and waited. The airboat was very beamy and looked like a homemade job. I saw the men try to give the Swamp Master some money, and he turned them down. He spotted me at the table by his workshop and waved. I waved back. The two men on the dock boarded the airboat, and then reached into an Igloo Cooler and pulled out a plastic bag, which they handed to the Swamp Master. He looked at the bag and smiled, a big grin followed by a black arching wad of chewing tobacco, which landed in the water.

The two men strapped themselves into the airboat and yelled something at the driver, who signaled the Swamp Master to release the stern lines. The Swamp Master stood as the boat left, then walked down the dock to where I was and tossed the plastic bag on the worktable.

"Frogs' legs." He smiled. "My favorite seafood, even though they ain't technically seafood—they are to me. How are you, Mr. Francisco Cruz, what do you go by, what do people call ya?"

"Francisco works fine."

"Okay, that there standin' on the dock was more Pinders from over near Flamingo City, quite a ways from here. They was havin' some engine problems, but we got it squared away, fuel flow, just needed some expert tweaking, that's what I'm good at Francisco, tweakin' shit."

"Well, your timing's pretty good too, as far as I'm concerned. I just wanted to thank you for what you did for us. I thought maybe . . ."

"Hey, it's nice of you to come out here to thank me. No problem, and I see you're drivin' this here fancy I-talian car and you got nice clothes and you're reachin' for your wallet, but don't even think about offering me no money. What I did for you I did for free. It goes in my karma book as extra points, and I need 'em, believe me."

"I see you were in Nam." I pointed to a picture of him at an Air Force base with a bunch of mechanics and pilots.

"Yeah, I was a mechanic at first, on the U-21's and the helos. We lost so many pilots in those early days they had to train me as a pilot, but I didn't get much combat air time before my tour was up. I joined. I wasn't drafted."

"I came in out of school."

"Yeah, you look like an officer. They had to make me a chief warrant officer to get flying status, but I only joined so's I could learn how to fix engines. I'm a Florida boy—come from here, love it, but there ain't a lot of employment opportunities around here in the Great Swamp. So, I got to see the mysterious Orient, and learn how to fix plane engines, even fly a little. And in the war I got to witness some of the stupidest shit that man could perpetrate on himself."

71

He got up and went over to the Coke machine that had eaten my quarters. He simultaneously banged both sides with the palms of both his hands, and a Coke came flying out. He did it a second time, and handed that can to me and spoke.

"Wasn't really too mysterious, the fuckin' Orient. Just a bunch of wild-ass slanty-eyed motherfuckers tryin' to kill everything in sight. I never figured what the hell we were doin' there in that stinkin' jungle, in the middle of a goddamn family feud.

"Hell, I coulda' stayed right here in these Everglades; the Sawyers and the Pinders still are real fractious with each other. My family were among the original settlers here, and in the Bahamas after the Revolutionary War, loyalists—we were called fuckin' loyalists. I guess we remained loyal to old King George. We're all real pure English stock. Probably includin' a little inbreeding that happened along the way and a lot of boredom, mix it with poverty, smugglin', lack of formal education, and alcohol and pot on occasion, the ravages of Mother Nature on occasion, and you got the right mix for some real eccentric Great Swamp behavior, if you know what I mean. How's your wife doin', Francisco?"

He sat down and pushed his Redman hat back on his forehead, tipped his head, and swallowed the Coke in one gulp. He waited for me to speak.

"Not good. She may never walk properly again."

He dropped his head and stared into my eyes. His eyes directly matched the sky over his head. They were English eyes, unreadable, bottomless. "That was a pretty rare plane you were flyin', that Grumman Albatross. You know that singer Johnny Buffet, he has

72

one. He's one of them sissy gentleman flyers. Only kidding. He's actually a licensed pilot, but I hear he flies with a real pilot, know what I mean."

"Is that your way of asking me if I'm a gentleman sissy flyer, who flies for a hobby, and who maybe doesn't know how to fly a big lumbering clumsy bird like that Grumman Albatross?"

"Now, don't you be gettin' all edgy on me. I was just makin' conversation."

"Sorry, I'm a little defensive."

"I can understand that." He patted the bag of frogs' legs. "Wanna have dinner with me and my family tonight?"

"Sure. Thanks," I said.

"Good." He started to lock up the shop. "Better put up the roof on that Ferrari, case we get some rain. I can smell a little rain in the air."

I did as he suggested, and we climbed into the Swamp Master's airboat and headed down the river. The noise was still loud even with the ear guards on. We rounded a bend and I saw a new well-built home sitting up on concrete stilts. A brand-new pickup truck and a brand-new Suburban were parked under the house. He parked at the dock. Two small children ran down the stairs, across the lawn, followed by a black Labrador. The children, a boy and a girl, jumped into the Swamp Master's arms. A woman appeared on the raised porch of the house, a beautiful Oriental woman, dressed in a colorful batik shirt and jeans. The Swamp Master saw me staring at her.

"Surprised, huh?" he said, and spat out the plug of

chewing tobacco. "She hates this Redman. I'm tryin' to quit."

"We hate it too, Daddy. Ugh!" the girl said, taking hold of his hand. She was startling in her beauty; light sloe brown eyes, pale bronze-brown perfectly smooth skin, white teeth, broad smile as she looked at me. She was eight or nine years old. The boy was younger.

"This here's my daughter Mary Magdalene Pinder and my son Joseph Pinder." I shook hands with them both as we walked to the house. "See, my wife, Mai Lynh, was an orphan; her parents were killed in the French Indochinese war. She was brought up in a Catholic orphanage, so we named the kids for saints. She speaks great French as well as English, spent a few years in France learning with them educated Frenchies in Paris."

I could see he was proud of her. I could only imagine what happened when the Pinder family first laid eyes on the new Mrs. Mai Lynh Pinder. But who would argue with the Swamp Master?

She walked down the stairs to greet us. She disappeared in the great bear arms of her husband. "Mai Lynh, this here's a friend of mine, Mr. Francisco Cruz; he's the fella ran into trouble in the glades."

"Francisco, just call me Francisco."

"I will." She smiled. She was exquisite. "Will you be able to join us for dinner?"

"Yes." I said, following everyone up the stairs into the house. It was hard for me to picture her driving a pickup truck and talking on a CB radio. Life was strange.

"Froggy legs," he said to Mary Magdalene Pinder,

tickling her and waving the plastic bag, when we were inside the house.

Mary Magdalene screamed, "Aahhgg, poor little dead froggies!" She ran to turn the television on. She was followed by her brother.

The meal was incredible. Mai Lynh cooked using a wok. The frogs' legs were lightly sauteed and cooked with fresh crisp vegetables, including fresh garlic. The colors of the meal were red and green mixed together with the white meat from the fresh frogs' legs. I watched the Swamp Master play computer games with his children and help his wife with the dinner. There were many sides to the Swamp Master.

We used the road to return to my car. We took the brand-new Suburban. "Nice car." I said.

"What you mean is, 'How can the Swamp Master afford this brand-new forty-thousand-dollar automobile,' isn't it?"

"Maybe."

"Well, let's just say I put away a nest egg in the eighties when it was wild and woolly back here in the swamps and a person who could pilot a small fixed-wing aircraft was in high demand. Now, I make my living fixing airboats and workin' the Great Swamp here."

"There's something I would like to talk to you about," I said.

"Shoot."

"I would like to hire you. Your card says you have a PI license."

"Yeah, I do. My cousin Billy Pinder runs the main private investigation stuff here in Everglades City at his insurance agency, and I run my license through him. We mostly use it to check on people who come pokin' around down here." He smiled as we bounced along the unpaved road back to my car. "It was great during the wild and woolly days." He smiled.

"Well, I been asked to go undercover and check out the people who sold me the Albatross, Florida Private Planes, in Opa-Locka."

"Undercover? Who asked you?"

"The FAA, two investigators." We wheeled under the Swamp Master's sign and he pulled up next to my car. We got out and he went over to the Coke machine. He slammed the sides with his open palms, twice. He walked back with a frosted can of Coke in each hand. "Too cold. That damn machine has a mind of its own. But it's been around here so long it's like family. All the damn kids know how to rip it off, but I figure, what the hell is a few cans of coke." He took a long swig and sat at the worktable. "After they took you guys off in that helo, I watched that Chinook come from Key West and pop your plane out of the mud and carry her off like a mangled bird—seemed like awful fast action for them pencil-dick-brain FAA bureaucrats."

"Well, it was. The engines had been switched and a lot of the electronic gear had been swapped . . . including a welded prop," I said.

"So, Francisco, what is it you would like the Swamp Master to do for you?"

"When I was last at Florida Private Planes, I noticed they were advertising for a mechanic. You licensed?"

"Yeah, last time I looked, but I ain't used it on legitimate airplanes in about five years."

"I wouldn't worry about legitimate airplanes in this case."

"So, if these guys fucked up your airplane, then they were the cause of your wife's problems. So, maybe we're dealing with revenge here."

"Maybe," I responded.

"Well, revenge means emotion and emotion means double trouble as far as I'm concerned—cloudy thinking leads to disaster. Didn't they teach you that in Nam? Besides, if these FAA boys want you to go in there and they'll back your play, why do you need my help?"

"I like to cover my bets."

"What you mean is, you don't want to get fucked up the ass here, right?"

"What I mean is, I like to cover my bets. I like insurance when I'm out there."

"How long we talkin' about?"

"Couple of weeks. You check it out from the inside and report to me."

"Three hundred dollars a day is what I get. I won't charge you expenses, since Florida Private Planes will be payin' me about fifty bucks an hour, if they hire me."

"So, that's a yes?"

"Yeah, I'm a little bored with spearin' frogs and hanging out here fixin' engines. I could use a little shot of the city life. You okay with the terms?"

"Yeah, can you start tomorrow?"

"Providin' they hire me, you got a deal. Now, what the hell am I exactly supposed to do?"

"Cover my back, find out what is going on in there

from the inside. I don't like walking into minefields, even if I know where the mines are."

"All right you got yourself an employee—Swamp Master, PI."

We shook hands. I gave him all my phone numbers and got up from the table. He walked me to the car. "Hey, I should be drivin' this here red fuckin' Ferrari, like that Magnum fella on the TV, since I'm on the job now."

"Too obvious." I smiled and slid into the front seat.

As I pulled out onto the road that would take me to Alligator Alley, I looked in the rearview mirror. The Swamp Master was just standing there, his arms in the pockets of his jean coveralls, looking up at the sky, like he wished he was up there flying around with the birds.

She was being led up to the coffin by her mother, who wore a black dress and a veiled hat. Her mother rarely wore black, and never wore a hat. They were hand in hand, but she was lagging, and her mother was lightly pulling her toward the open casket. The casket was silver with shiny wooden handles; men stood around the casket, men dressed in black suits, about to become pallbearers. Her mother's hair was pulled back severely, showing a shock of yellow against the black. She gently lifted the veil. They both looked down at her father at the same time.

The smell of funereal flowers was pungent, almost acrid, not like in the produce market, where they were sweet and natural, blending with the other smells of the market. At first her eyes refused to focus, refusing to let the angel of death into her heart. Her father was dark against the white damask cloth of the casket. Dark hair, dark suit, tanned skin, tanned hands folded on his chest, still handsome, like he was in a peaceful sleep.

He'll never wake up now! she wanted to scream. How would she be safe now that he was gone? Who would always be there for her, who would look at her with those adoring eyes, who would accept her always as she was . . . as she really was? Her mother was a black blurr next to her as she dipped into the casket to kiss her husband's lips, good-bye, good-bye, sweet love. Her mother surfaced, and now she knew it was her turn to kiss her father good-bye, good-bye forever. She released her mother's hands and grabbed the cold wooden handles on the side of the casket for support, to keep her legs from crumbling under her. She used all her will, her strength to keep her eyes open. She kissed his lips. The lips were cool and inanimate; a gasp escaped from her lips. For a second she thought she had breathed life into him. But that was not to be. She rose and felt her mother's arm cross her shoulders and steady her as she took the single step down from the casket. A Greek Orthodox priest stood now at the head of the casket. His face showed no expression, like the face of all mankind enduring all that God hands out. It was the priest who moved to the side of the casket, made the sign of the cross, and lowered the lid on the casket.

He was gone, her father was gone forever.

Suddenly she was back inside the plane. Francisco was fighting to control the landing. They bounced up off the slick wet swamp, maybe twenty feet up in the air, hit again, bounced again, shorter this time, then they slid, like she used to in the skating rink when she missed a turn, slid on her rump. She saw the knurled hand that once was a tree, maybe burned out by lightning or killed in a hurricane, its limbs hardened by the sun, and the rain, and the wind, turned into steel fingers spreading from a steel wrist of a trunk. The tree was heading straight for them, no, they were heading for the tree and the tree was not heading for the plane, the tree was heading straight for her. She looked around and could only see the great empty swamp; she thought of a world where there were no people and she was suddenly lonely, alone . . . abandoned.

The impact was a loud screech as the tree-fist smashed like metal against metal all around her a collapsing metal cocoon. She could feel the skin of the plane move, contract, and envelop her. Her leg was immobile, unmovable, she tried to pull it free, but it was too late, the leg was twisted like a piece of taffy in a machine. The pain was great, very great . . . oh, God!

"Lillian, it's me, Francisco, wake up, darling, wake up." Her eyes came into focus slowly. Her lips were parched and trembling, her hands shook. "Just take deep breaths, don't try and speak."

Gradually she came down. A nurse poured some cold water and helped her drink it. I knew it was the morphine in her system, but that was needed against the pain. Two nurses came in with a gurney. Dr. Bartlett followed.

"Darling, the ambulance is here."

"Ambulance?"

"Yes. You're going home."

"Oh, Francisco, I had this awful dream, so awful, and now you are here to take me home. I'm so glad."

"Mrs. Cruz, I think it's a little early to be going home, but your husband insisted, and he has hired a private nurse for a while. You are to do everything the nurse asks of you. Okay?"

"Yes, Doctor."

The paramedic team was very efficient. They had her out of the room and into the ambulance, even with her leg in traction. I followed the ambulance to Golden Beach in the Ferrari. All I could think of was her pain and the fear, and the fact that it was all so unnecessary. The bastards had sold me a defective aircraft, and they just didn't give a shit about what happened. I gripped the steering wheel and caught up to the speeding ambulance, then released the accelerator. I had to control my anger. I had to use the energy of my anger, channel it, and not let it cloud my judgment. I had to rise above it.

I also knew it was a murky swamp whenever the United States Government was involved. I had flown CIA operatives into Cambodia and Laos during the war. I had a friend, a pilot like me, who claimed he was flying regularly into North Vietnam to meet with an NVA general who sold opium to the CIA operative who was his passenger for cash, and the opium was then taken back to the USA and sold through the underworld. It was all done with the blessing of government officials—passes, diplomatic pouches, packed in body bags with no bodies, special airplane clearances to take off from Vietnam and land in the good old U.S.A. I was an ex-Cuban, so they used me a lot. They figured if I said anything, they could just arrest me and treat me as they wished since I was a naturalized citizen. I was no stranger to the complexities and the intrigues of dealing with the government and clandestine operations.

We used to go to China Beach down near Danang for R and R every couple of months or so. It was there that I met Lieutenant George Baker, an Annapolis graduate, a career officer. He was a Tomcat pilot off a carrier in the North China Sea. He told me that the carrier pilots were always given very specific targets in their raids on North Vietnam.

He was the wing commander on a five-plane squad. Their target was a train yard just outside of Hanoi. His wing man, his best friend and classmate, went in first, and picked up a Russian SAM missile that went right up his afterburner. The plane blew up in front of Baker.

Lieutenant George Baker lost it. He called off the rest of the mission and decided to attack a forbidden target, a target that was off-limits, the two mud dredges at the mouth of Hanoi Harbor. The dredges worked twenty-four hours a day to keep the harbor from silting up. If the harbor silted up, the Russian ships couldn't off-load; none of the Navy fly boys ever understood why we didn't take the dredges out, why they were a restricted target.

Lieutenant Baker and what remained of his wing went in for a rocket attack. They flew through a fierce triple-A barrage. They turned the two dredges into two twisted masses of molten steel. When Baker landed, the captain of the carrier had him on the carpet at attention standing in front of him in ten minutes. The captain asked Baker why he had taken out the dredges. Lieutenant Baker told him about losing his best friend and having flown over those dredges for months and seeing the endless line of Russian freighters, none of which were ever sunk in the mouth of the harbor . . . that he simply lost it. He was enraged and decided to take his revenge.

The captain dismissed him and sent him to China Beach to cool out and wait. Just before he left China Beach, he got his orders to return to the United States. Shortly afterwards he received a phone call from his air commander, who told him he should consider himself lucky that he didn't receive a court-martial.

Baker told the air commander to go fuck himself. He welcomed a fucking court-martial. He couldn't wait for some asshole officer to have to get up in court and explain why the fuck the U.S. Navy never took those fucking dredges out. Well, he got the dredges, but he lost his career, and his best friend. "Fuck it!" were his last words to me.

And I got an education in the United States Government—watch your back—always.

The flashing lights of the ambulance shone blue and red on my windshield. The screaming siren rang sharply in my ears. I was helpless to do anything for her, except make her comfortable. I remembered that old Greek saying Lillian said her father had taught her: "Revenge is a dish best served up cold." Could I remain cool, under control?

All I knew was that for Lillian I could try.

Chapter Three

Running keeps me sane. I once tried to figure how
many miles I've run in my life, but gave up. I had taken
up martial arts while I was in Vietnam to keep me calm,
keep my red temper under control. The running got rid
of my natural aggression, and the martial arts chan-
neled the aggression that was left over into productive
activities—at least that's what I told myself. I would
run on the beach for forty minutes, then practice Tae
Kwon Do for forty minutes.

I had been with Lillian for a week, helping her get
adjusted. The nurse remained. She would stay for another few days, then Marisol would take over. This was
provided the healing process took hold and no more
operations were necessary.

This morning was one of those wonderful summer
days when you could feel the heat rolling in as the sun
rose and the sand heated. I could feel it on my bare
feet. I ran usually a little after dawn and watched the

red ball rise out of the ocean. The trade winds were from the southeast in the summer, a steady reliable wind. It was in my face now as I headed back up the beach, to what I always referred to in my mind as Lillian's estate.

Her former husband, Richard, had built it for her, but Lillian told me he really built it for himself. He did the basic design and architecture, and she planned the interior. The house was as close to the ocean's edge as Dade County would allow. It had double pilings and double all the hurricane requirements. Richard had wanted it to last a long time.

I left it the way it was. I told Lillian that it didn't bother me that she had lived there in that house with another man; all I insisted on was new mattresses. I still wasn't sure I had told her the truth about whether or not it bothered me. I wasn't crazy about living on the ocean for security reasons. I often thought about how easy the access was from the beach; invading houses from the sand was not a difficult stunt to pull off in Dade County, Florida.

The house had been burglarized once several years ago, by art thieves who took specific pieces of art, a Picasso, a Monet, a Dali, and a Wyatt. They used a knife to cut the canvases from the frames, and they beat the cops on the alarm system. They escaped out to sea, according to the footprints, minutes before the cops arrived. They were never caught.

All these thoughts ran through my head as I ran. It was one of the reasons I liked running. My mind went into "random mode" and I let it go. This was the reverse of how it would be for the rest of the day, focused and pragmatic.

I thought about the Swamp Master; he had been under for a week now, and he had called me twice. He'd asked to meet with me later in the day. I had agreed. I had also confirmed with the FAA that I would go into Florida Private Planes as a confidential informant for them.

After my run and a shower, I left for Miami to meet with Bobby Day of the FAA at Denny's restaurant; he was in his best French Canadian disguise, a plaid sports jacket, bright yellow shirt, green pants, and white shoes.

"Ah, Monsieur Cruz, *mon ami, bon jour.*"

"Well, that's about all the French I understand, *monsieur,*" I answered. "We can try Spanish, it's close to French."

"Maurice Geoffreon, no relation to the famous hockey player, Boom-Boom Geoffreon. That is me." He smiled.

"Nice outfit." I commented as we ordered coffee.

"Merci beaucoup."

"All right, how about giving me a little background on what I can expect going in."

"You got it." The accent disappeared.

"The leader and owner of the business is John Harrison. He owns or controls three hangars, and half a dozen different businesses. He also owns the Frat House, a strip club in Hialeah near the racetrack. He uses it to do business, get and pass information. Most of the girls are coke whores that he keeps supplied, so he ultimately gets the money that the girls get from the customers when the girls come to buy coke from him. He sometimes gives them an extra gram for 'special' information. There are a lot of pilots, cops, and smugglers that hang out in the club, perfect setup for him. He's made a fortune out of that club. Our primary interest is busting him on tampering with the planes, but the DEA is with us on any dope stuff we uncover; they'll take the kudos for the dope, and we'll take the kudos for the FAA violations."

"Which are?"

"We think they are running a number of scams. They are buying confiscated planes from the Bahamas, buying stolen planes, stolen parts. They also buy foreign planes, especially Colombian planes, ex-dope planes without proper papers, and they repaper them here in Florida and resell them."

"Like a giant stolen-car chop shop and junkyard all rolled into one, only for aircraft?" I said.

"Exactly, *monsieur*."

"So what's the play?"

Bobby Day, aka Maurice Geoffreon, spoke nonstop for a solid half hour. I stopped him when he started trying to rehearse my lines with me. We went to the washroom together, where he wired me up with a tiny state-of-the-art voice-activated tape. He then handed me a briefcase with a false bottom and a camera; he showed me how to trigger the camera, a super eight with a four-hour tape and a microphone of its own, which would act as video and a backup sound device.

We drove to the Opa-Locka Airport, an airport primarily for private and corporate planes. Down one side were parked all the private jets; next to them were the private propeller-driven planes. Hangars stood in a U around the landing strip. The small control tower was the focal point, the nerve center. The airport was located about seven miles north of Miami International, in Hialeah, a suburb of Miami.

We drove in two cars. Maurice Geoffreon, as he was now known drove a red Rolls Cornice convertible, a deeper red than the Ferrari. It contrasted nicely with his plaid sports coat, yellow shirt, and black Wayfarer shades. We made quite a sight as we pulled up to the office of Florida Private Planes, a good-sized hangar building painted dark blue.

We walked into the waiting room, and were greeted by ex-stripper Sally Carruthers, the secretary. I had met her when I bought the Albatross. John Harrison took one look at me and darted directly back into his office.

I noticed Sally was not nervous at all, maybe she was just surprised to see me . . . alive. "Sally, remember me?"

"Yes. Mr. Cruz with the pretty blond wife."

"Yes, that's right, the pretty blond wife. I forget sometimes how much women notice other women."

"Competition. One always has to size up the competition, don't they, Mr. Cruz?"

"You flirting with me, Sally?" I smiled at her.

"No, sir, no, sir, not me." She winked. "Just part of my old life."

"I would like to see John."

"Let me see if he's in."

"Tell him I want to talk some business."

She left to check. I had purposely not introduced Maurice. Maurice did not escape her notice, and he certainly did not look like an official, of any kind.

Shirley reappeared with Mr. John Harrison in tow. Harrison was tall and lanky, with a slow, down-South gait, like nobody should move too fast in this heat. His skin was blotchy-red with tinges of tan blended in. He was the kind of nondescript man that would easily blend into any crowd.

I gave him one of my best smiles. "Hey, John, how's it going?"

"Any better and it would be illegal." He said. "Real good. Real good." His smile reflected brown cigarette-stained teeth.

"Great, this is a friend of mine, Maurice Geoffreon, from Montreal."

"Montreal, huh? Well, we won't hold that against him. Come on in, I got a little company in the office, but that shouldn't matter."

We followed him into the office. The office was small and full of boxes of paper. Paper was strewn all over the top of the desk—memos, airplane diagrams, newspapers, magazines, and handwritten notes. There was a computer terminal in the far corner of the desk. The windows of the office looked right into the hangar and the repair shop.

There were a series of monitors on the far wall for the television surveillance cameras placed inside and outside the Florida Private Planes property—heavy security surveillance equipment, I observed. I looked for the Swamp Master with the mechanics, but couldn't see him.

Two huge men sat in the chairs in front of John Harrison's desk. I understood why he didn't mind seeing me. These men could be his bodyguards. Each man was at least three hundred pounds, and they seemed crammed into the wooden tub chairs that were located in front of Harrison's desk. They had fleshy, unshaven faces the size of large frying pans. They wore blue jeans with huge T-shirts with Pelican Air Lift Services insignia, a giant pelican in the shape of a helicopter carrying a beautiful naked girl below in a cargo net. They wore peaked caps with the same logo and insignia. They looked like an overweight wrestling tag team.

"This here's my two neighbors, Jumbo and Action Jackson. I call 'em the Jackson Hogs—if they were wrastlin' that would be their moniker—right, boys?"

The Jackson Hogs did not respond in any way. They just looked permanently mean.

Harrison continued. "They're in the helicopter freight and rescue business. Kinda like helicopter tow truck operators." I reached out my hand, as did Bobby Day. Action Jackson and his brother Jumbo remained seated as we shook hands. Harrison continued. "This here's Mr. Francisco Cruz and Mr. Montreal. Hey, I forgot your name already."

"Maurice Geoffreon, *bonjour*, nice to meet you," my partner, Bobby Day, answered.

"You was the fella who bought that Grumman Albatross, wasn't you, Mr. Cruz?" Jumbo asked.

"Call me Francisco; yes, that was me. I already resold it to a buyer in South America."

"You make a few bucks?" Action Jackson asked.

"Yeah, I made a few bucks. Actually, I had it sold before I purchased it."

"That's why you were in such a hurry to get delivery," Harrison added.

"You call six months to get delivery on a plane already paid for a hurry?" I asked, a burst of temper. I had to recover. I took a deep breath and leaned on a corner of the desk. I placed the attaché case on the corner and pointed the lens of the camera at the Jackson brothers and Harrison.

"Well, I admit we were not our usual prompt self on the delivery of that plane," Harrison said. "Nice to see there ain't no hard feelings. How can we help you?"

"Well . . ." I hesitated, looking at the Jacksons.

"Listen, Jumbo here and Action are as close to me as kin. We're like brothers, ain't we?" They nodded. "And they're two great airplane modifiers and mechanics. They heard it all, believe me."

"All right, Maurice, why don't you start."

Maurice moved over to the window overlooking the hangar. "I inspected Francisco's plane before he sold it. I am a Canadian businessman and I could use a plane like that Grumman Albatross you sold him."

"They're not easy planes to get," Harrison said.

"Rare, real rare, like hen's teeth," Action Jackson added, nudging his brother.

"Like a whore at a church picnic," Jumbo added; the chair shook, rumbled, as he laughed.

"I need it right away if you can get it. I can't wait six months like Francisco had to," Maurice said.

"Well, we might be able to find one," Harrison said.

"I'll need some modifications done to it," Maurice said.

"Like?" Harrison asked.

"Like extra fuel tanks to increase the range and the hold cleared out so it could carry extra cargo," Maurice said.

"How long a range?"

"Say, fifteen hundred miles."

"So, you could fly from Colombia to the Bahamas?" Jumbo asked.

"Perhaps." Maurice explained. "And I need signed-off T-33 forms for the FAA and the DEA, to go in the logs to note the modifications," Maurice added.

"So's it'll be legal and all that, huh?" Action Jackson said. These brothers were like a verbal tag team. "So the fuel modifications and any structural changes will be legal and in the logbooks? We do that all the time. We get paid, we sign."

"You got another story?" Harrison asked.

"A cover story? *Qui!*" Maurice was laying on the accent. "The Albatross will be modified and used as a water bomber to put out forest fires in Quebec and other parts of Canada. These type planes are already used for that purpose in Canada right now."

Harrison sat down behind his desk. I moved the attaché case as he sat down. I directed the lens into his face. He spoke. "Well, I can't sell this plane so cheap like I sold that plane to Francisco here. I could maybe come up with one, but it's gonna cost you more. And we're gonna need a substantial deposit."

"How much?" Maurice asked.

"Can't tell yet."

"There won't be any deposit," I added. "I gave you guys a deposit, then I actually paid for the plane, and you still jerked me around for six months. Not this time, this time it will be COD. Maurice is a friend of mine; you can either do this deal in a hurry or we'll go elsewhere."

"See, I knew it. Goddammit, I knew it, Francisco," Harrison said. "You still harbor resentment because we were a little bit late in the delivery of that airplane."

I was using all my strength now to contain my temper. Flashes of Lillian, who I had kissed good-bye in her painful sleep that morning, flashed though my mind. Her small body pinned in that airplane, the broken windshield, her tortured face as I lifted her out into the Swamp Master's arms. These images flashed through my mind.

"John, this is strictly business, not personal. No, sir," I said. "Not personal at all. You know I'm good for the money because I paid you the last time. Maurice is good for the money, I'll vouch for him. It's a COD deal."

"Can you pay in cash?" Jumbo asked.

"You want cash?" I asked.

"Who does not want cash?" Harrison added.

"We can pay in cash," I added.

"Good," Harrison added.

"How much?" Maurice added.

Harrison looked down at his desk and shuffled some papers, thinking. "Well, how about you give me some time to think about it, and we all meet tonight for a drink at my club."

"Where's your club?" I asked.

"The Frat House on Dixie Highway, near the airport here."

"What time?" Maurice asked.

"Let's say eight o'clock," Harrison said.

"Okay, we'll be there," I added.

We prepared to leave. The Jackson brothers stayed compressed in their tub chairs, but Harrison got up and walked us out to the cars parked in the hot midday Florida sun. I followed Bobby Day back to the Denny's parking lot where we had met that morning.

I gave him the wire and the attaché case. "Thanks," he said. "We'll wire up here tonight. We'll have to be sound only tonight. We did good today. I think we're gonna have a money-laundering charge, conspiracy to import cocaine, and the FAA offenses by the time we're through."

"Sounds good," I said.

"See you tonight," he said, and drove off in the afternoon sun.

I went back to Golden Beach and spent the day with Lillian. I read the newspapers to her and we watched the afternoon television shows together.

At seven that night I met the Swamp Master in the Hialeah Bowling Alley. It was busy and noisy, with a lounge that overlooked the bowlers. The Swamp Master, Mr. Sawyer Pinder, surprised me. He had gotten a haircut, was clean-shaven, and wore a well-pressed light blue sport jacket, a white shirt, and jeans, with white Nike sneakers. "You look good," I said, shaking his hand and sitting down next to him.

"This is my disguise. My city disguise." He smiled. "I save my Redman hat for the Great Swamp."

"That's your swamp disguise?" I said.

"No, that's the real me. That's the me that is sane and happy."

"I enjoyed dinner with you and your family. Your wife is quite a woman," I added.

"You don't know the half of it. You know who loves her most?"

"Who?"

"The Pinders, my goddamn relatives. When I first brung her over from Asia, I thought they was all gonna have a shit-fit. Well, she didn't brook no shit from any of them. Instead of tryin' to kill 'em with kindness, she just told each and every one of them she would simply kill them if they fucked around with her or her kids, or me, and she goddamn meant it. And they knew it. She can handle an AK-47 and any other goddamn weapon you might wanna name. Well, my kin just fell all over each other tryin' to get her to like 'em. Now we're just one big happy family and they're extra-protective, my kin that is, they're extra-protective of her and my kids. They keep a good eye on 'em all when I'm gone."

We ordered a couple of beers and the Swamp Master continued. "I went for a ride with those two human hogs, the Jackson brothers—whoppers, ain't they?"

"Whoppers, all right," I said.

"We went to a field near where the old Homestead Air Force Base was in Homestead. Four of us went—me, the Jackson Brothers, and another mechanic, Gene Santini, nice guy. Anyway, we go to this hangar which is called Coral Reef Air Services. I wondered what's their slogan. 'Try to wind up at the coral reef'?" The Swamp Master laughed as the beers were delivered. "So, it turns out to be another one of their operations, one of their companies, hell, they must have a dozen companies all interconnected like a spider's web.

95

"As we pull up to this hangar, looks ex-military to me, I notice that there are about thirty Grumman Albatross airplanes sitting off the tarmac in the scrub grass. All in various states of repairs. Kinda like an Albatross boneyard, like maybe you could make a couple of good airplanes out of the whole fucking lot.

"So, we park and Gene Santini and me, we're told by the Jackson Hogs to see if we can find certain engines; they give me and Gene the part numbers and the plane numbers. They are supposed to be the engines with the least hours. So Gene and me, we start lookin', climbin' through the Albatross junkyard, while the Jackson Hogs head straight for the damn hangar, unlock it, and head into the office. Ain't but a minute till I hear the air conditioner whirrin' in the office.

"I'm trampin' around the scrub checking engine parts for about half an hour when a Ford Crown Victoria pulls up, brand-spankin'-new car. One suit and a guy wearin' a Hawaiian shirt get out and go into the hangar office."

"Red? Was the shirt red—colorful?" I asked.

"Yeah, a real Hawaiian shirt, and the guy looked somehow familiar to me even though I was too far to eyeball him. They stay in the office for about an hour and then they fuck off.

"After about an hour we find five of the engines, but there are six altogether. But one is still on the list, Gene keeps lookin'. I'm dyin' for a drink, so I head for the hangar and I let myself in, only I don't go in the office, I go into the hangar. It's not busy, nobody workin', but it's equipped with all state-of-the-art gear for fixin' planes.

96

"Then, thank God, I spot a Coke machine, but on the way there is a little room, so I start to let myself in when I hear the office door open. I quick close the door just as both Jackson Hogs emerge into the hangar and Jumbo yells, 'What the fuck are you doin' in here?'

"I'll tell you, Francisco, you don't wanna be bracin' them two. They start walkin' toward me and it's like a tidal wave of human flesh crossin' the floor rollin' toward me. I ain't no shrimp, but there's somethin' real mean about them two fellas. I hold up a hand full of coins, prayin' they ain't seen me open the door to that little room. 'Coke,' I yell, 'just tryin' to get a Coke.' Action grabs my hand and checks my fist full of coins and smiles. He says, 'We got a refrigerator in the office. You shoulda knocked on the goddamn office door; you ain't supposed to be in here.' 'How was I to know that?' I ask. I follow them to the office and give the location of the engines. Then I see them leave a note on the chalkboard to have them planes we picked out brought in. They must work the place at night when it's cooler and they are not so visible—rats work in the dark, ya know. I'll tell you, Francisco, I was pumped up when they came across that hangar toward me."

We both took a sip of beer. I handed the Swamp Master his check. He stuffed it in his sport coat jacket inside pocket without looking at it. "I thought of maybe not chargin' you, Francisco, because of that karma thing, but after today I decided to take it, kinda like I need danger pay is the feelin' I got from these guys. They give me the evil-creeps. These are some bad dudes."

"What was in the room?"

"Shit, I almost forgot, the most important thing of all, that was why I was so nervous. There was two beautiful computerized engravin' machines, and I saw a number of plates. Even looked like some real Cessna plates."

"Plates, engravin' machines, you sayin' what I'm thinking you're saying?" I asked.

"Yeah, that's right, they was registration plate blanks I seen. I think they're forging registration plates for aircraft. And I noticed in the office a bunch of correspondence from the FAA, because I recognized the letterhead. I think maybe they do a lot of checkin' on ownerships."

"Why?"

"So's they can make duplicates. It's easy. Think about it with these small private planes. Just suppose that two planes carried the same numbers and papers, how would they ever get caught? Kinda like two cars bein' papered the same and carryin' the same license plates, what are the chances of them ever bein' pulled over at the same time and crossin' in the computer—there's even less chance with two airplanes.

"And lots of planes get destroyed and their papers are sold with the junked airplane or they are not reported as being destroyed—then steal a duplicate good plane and put the plates on. It's big business, at least a hundred grand a clip for these airplanes."

"And the Crown Victoria, the suit, and the Hawaiian shirt, what was that about?" I asked.

"No idea, none at all, and the car was too far away for a plate check." The Swamp Master finished his beer. "I'll tell you one thing, Mr. Francisco Cruz. I see where you're comin' from, and how you wound up crashed in the Great Swamp. Listen, I know you're upset about that pretty wife of yours, but I'll tell you right now— this is one fucked-up mess."

"That's a pretty concise way of putting it," I said.

"Put it any way you want it." He patted his pocket and the check. "Thanks. I'll call when I have news." He smiled and left.

I sat there for a few minutes listening to the falling bowling pins. I concluded the Swamp Master was right—this was a fucked-up mess, and I knew it was going to get messier.

I left the bowling alley and headed for the parking lot at Denny's on the Dixie Highway to meet Bobby Day in his Maurice Geoffreon disguise and get wired up. We had a cup of coffee together where he did actually rehearse me on my lines, explaining that we wanted them to say certain things that would indicate they were modifying the planes illegally, that the planes were going to be used for drug smuggling, and that they wanted to be paid in cash so they could launder the money and avoid taxes—a tall order, I thought. When the rehearsal was over, we headed for the Frat House strip club.

South Florida is the center for strip clubs in the United States. There are three levels. The first level is the "A" level, where there is a hefty charge for admission at the door and the nude tabletop or friction dances can easily run twenty dollars each. These places are called Pure Platinum, Miami Gold, and Solid Gold. The girls wear long evening gowns, are perfectly made up, and have perfect bodies. The age range is from eighteen to twenty-five, girls in their prime, the major leagues.

The second level is the "B" level, where the door charge is five dollars and the dances run ten dollars each. These girls are also beautiful, but the age range goes from twenty to thirty-five, the minor leagues.

The final level is the "C" level, where there is no door charge the nude dances are five to ten dollars each, and the age range is twenty-five to forty-five, the scrub leagues. In all these clubs drugs and alcohol are usually the fuel that drives these dancers forward, and allows them to get through a night of acting sexy when they don't feel sexy. To me it is kind of like the wrestling industry, good costumes, athletic ability, some acting skills, and nobody gets hurt, unless they go too far.

The Frat House was a "C" level club. The clientele were: blue-collar mechanics from the nearby airport, pilots looking for some fun, weekend warrior bikers, rednecks driving sporty new pickup trucks, and some Hispanic types—Cubans, Nicaraguans, Colombians— the standard Hispanic mix that dominates the Miami culture.

In all, a rough, tough motley crew of customers being worked over by a rough, tough motley group of burned-out dancers, interspersed with some beautiful young girls who wander in now and then on their downward spiral into the hell of drugs and alcohol and are usually hated by the other girls.

We wheeled into the parking lot at exactly eight o'clock. A huge long-haired biker waved us into the preferred parking, which was two dollars instead of the one-dollar charge for regular parking. He promised to look after the fancy cars.

Maurice had on a black shirt, his same green pants, and white shoes with no socks; he was a vision. Inside, the club was indirectly and softly lit, the overall light level low. There was one main stage built out of rough plywood painted black; a brass pole stood in the center for the girls to work with. A thirty-five-year-old cocaine-thin once-beautiful black woman was on the stage, totally naked, gyrating to an old Rolling Stones tune. There were two other stages, but no dancers. A wide circular bar faced the main stage, and a side bar was being set up by the bartender but had not opened yet. There were a few customers and a half-dozen girls sitting at the main circular bar. There were padded booths in the rear of the club with a PRIVATE VIP CHAMPAGNE ROOM sign in blue neon that kept flickering on and off. The room was curtained with a gossamer-thin black cotton cloth with a few holes visible.

Some girls sat in the booths talking to each other, waiting for the night to come alive. The club was open until four in the morning. There were two other stages, but no dancers. It was early.

Maurice lit up a cigar as we walked in, and filled the air with blue putrid smoke. "Please, Maurice, enough!" I said, and he put the cigar down in the nearest ashtray.

I glanced around, and saw the Jackson Hogs crammed into a U-shaped table-booth designed for four people. It was in the very back of the club. It had a small pin-white spotlight that shone down on the table. They were working on some papers. I was sorry now that we had not brought the camera along. We walked over to the table.

Jumbo and Action Jackson were dressed exactly the same as they were in the afternoon: size triple-X Pelican Airlift Service T-shirts and baseball caps—same naked girl in the cargo net. They looked up together, their massive bowling-ball heads on thick bull necks raising as one, gray ratlike eyes in small slits zeroing in on us.

"How ya'll doin'?" Jumbo asked.

"Grab one of them chairs in the corner," Action Jackson said. "And grab another one for Johnny."

It was surreal in the white light from the pin spotlight that shone down on us, a beacon on a dark grisly coast. I pulled my chair into the table; Maurice pulled in next to me. A cocktail waitress sidled up to us. She wore a white low-cut uniform that formed a high-cut V at her crotch. She had two holes the size of a quarters in her fishnet stockings, a used-up dancer.

"What'le it be, boys?" she said, chewing gum between words.

"Beer, Corona, please, with a lime," I said.

"Ain't got no limes," she said.

"Then I don't think I'll have a lime."

"And you?"

"Royal Crown and ginger ale," Maurice said in his best accent.

"French, huh? No Royal Crown, no ginger ale—how about a seven and seven?" she offered.

"Fine," Maurice mumbled.

"Your tab, boys?" she asked the Jackson brothers.

"Yeah, this here's our treat," Jumbo said with a

smile. "And don't seat nobody in this here section, babe."

"Right, like we're jammin' here," she said sarcastically.

"How's it goin'?" John Harrison said as he appeared in the light.

"Fine," I said.

He took the third chair and pulled it into the table. He mused through the papers sprawled on the table, and finally stacked them into a file folder. In the shadows behind him in the back of the club I noticed a man in the grayness. I could not see his face, but a light shone on his shoulder and chest. It lit up a red Hawaiian shirt. He sat alone, and I was sure he was watching us. I was also sure he was the man I saw at the Opa-Locka Airport that fateful morning I picked up the Albatross.

"Shall we get right down to business?" Harrison asked.

"That's why we're here," I said.

The waitress returned with our drinks. As she dropped my beer in front of me, her hand slipped into my lap and she squeezed my crotch and winked. I jumped slightly. "Jumpy, huh, handsome?" she whispered in my ear.

"Okay, turns out we can lay our hands on another Albatross, but like I said, the price will be higher since you got a special purpose for the plane," John said.

"How much more?" I asked.

"Tell 'em, Jumbo."

"Five hundred large." He smiled. "All mods included, extra fuel tanks, cargo hold increased, and all navigational gear workin' and the engines fixed up real good, and an overall air worthiness certificate."

"*Sacre bleu,* this is outrageous. Monsieur Cruz has told me he paid only two hundred fifty thousand."

"Yeah, but he also told you he sold it to some South American spic-doper for a profit, which therefore means we musta sold the plane to him for a bargain. The goin rate's five hundred," Jumbo said; he was the smarter of the Jackson boys. "Besides, why you even bargainin' for? This here plane's goin to be carryin' that white powder, and with the cargo bay fixed up, you can carry a thousand keys. Hell, I can't even add up that high."

That was the sentence we needed to nail them. Hell, we weren't going to pay them anyway; we were going to raid them. I drove the nail home. "Well, maybe you're right. Let me make sure I got it—you'll give us a Grumman with checked-out engines and navigational gear, a modified cargo bay, extra fuel tanks, and all the paperwork, including logs and clean bill of sale, and the proper FAA certificates for the modifications."

"Yeah, all signed off nice and legal. But we got one more little item," Harrison said.

"I'm betting it is not so little, Monsieur Harrison," Maurice said with a smile.

"On delivery, we need cash. We need you to give us two-fifty in cash, two-fifty in a bank check."

"Is this for the taxman's benefit?" I asked.

"No, Mr. Francisco Cruz," Action Jackson said. "It's for the Jackson brothers' and Mr. Johnny Harrison's benefit. We got a deal?"

"When, *Monsieur,* when can we expect delivery of the plane?" Maurice asked.

"One week from today, Maurice, one week from today," John Harrison said. "We'll put our best men on it."

"All right then, we got ourselves a deal," I said, holding up my glass. We all toasted.

"Now, if you boys want you can hang around here with the girls, any girl you should see that takes your fancy, you can be sure she will be accommodating," John Harrison said.

"And we got some private stock we can have here in an hour, black, Oriental, Cuban, Dominican—hell, we ain't prejudiced around here," Action Jackson said.

"Hell, when it comes to pussy we're the goddamn United fucking Nations," Jumbo added.

The two brothers laughed. "The United fucking Nations. Hell if that don't take all. Maybe if there was more fuckin' there'd be less wars. Maybe we should start promotin' pussy peace," Action said.

"We're already promoting that, right here at the Frat House," John Harrison said with a smile.

"Well, here's to more fuckin' and less fightin'." Jumbo laughed. "Worldwide pussy peace."

We all drank to that. Maurice and I passed on the two girls and left. We took a long roundabout route back to Denny's, as we'd agreed we would. We wanted to be sure we weren't followed. We wheeled into the Denny's parking lot and went in to have a coffee.

"How'd we do?" I asked.

"Good as gold. We got them to admit they were going to modify the airplane to carry dope, so that's conspiracy to import a controlled substance. We got them to admit they were going to modify an airplane and falsify the documents—that's a felony. We got them on money laundering and money structuring when they asked us for the cash and admitted they were going to use it to avoid paying taxes. And we know they will switch the engines and ID plates when the plane's delivered, so that's another felony," Maurice said with a smile as I handed him my tiny tape recorder.

He slipped the tape into his recorder and played it back. The quality was slightly fuzzy, but highly audible. He tested his own tapes, and they were also good.

"Great con men," Bobby said in his regular voice.

"I certainly was a first-class sucker."

"Hey, I didn't mean it that way." He smiled. "God, those Jackson boys are huge, aren't they? I bet they could be mean motherfuckers."

"Yeah, a couple of living nightmares. Imagine those poor dancers at the Frat House, if they have to service those monsters," I added.

"People will do anything for cash, and that white powder if they're hooked. That's my observation," Bobby said. "I was with the DEA before I moved over to the criminal side of the FAA."

"Got tired of the dope business?"

"Got tired of the players, heartless, soulless bastards destroying lives, driven by only one thing: money-money-money."

"That's what drives most of the world, isn't it?" I asked.

"Yeah, you're right. Maybe I just found it a little hopeless."

"Inelastic demand."

"What?"

"In economic theory it's called inelastic demand. That's where the demand never shrinks, even if the supply does—cigarettes, booze, dope, sex; people will always pay what they have to—so there is always a constant steady demand. Remember Prohibition? People get what they want and need. And law enforcement will always be climbing a steep slippery slope where the public stands at various levels on the hill, always ready to push them back down the hill. The public wants their pleasures and will pay dearly for them," I said.

"I didn't know you were a scholar of economic theory," Bobby said.

"I'm not, just a casual observer of human nature," I answered. "What's next?"

"Well, I'll take this back to my boss and we'll contact the DEA. I think we got enough here to do our thing."

"Do our thing?"

"Yeah, stage a raid when the plane is delivered—nail these assholes."

"That's it?"

"Yeah, pretty much, why?"

"Too easy, that's why."

"Well, you must have had a rough life. Everything's timing, you know, and you walked into a good timing situation. We been on this case for two years, so it's not like we made the case in three weeks. Besides, we got more guys like you."

"First-class suckers!"

"I told you not to be so sensitive; you're in good company."

"Wrong. I think I'm in bad company."

"Well, you certainly were tonight."

"Does it go beyond Florida?"

"The airplane tampering?" Bobby Day finished his coffee. "We think their tentacles go worldwide, but we haven't got absolute proof."

"I guess you need more guys to wind up in the ditch, have their wives hurt, or maybe their kids. Tell me something." I stared at him.

"Yeah, shoot."

"Why couldn't you have come to me and warned me before I took off?"

"No proof, real proof."

"So, you waited to get your proof. You needed me to crash." I left a dollar tip for the waitress as he grabbed the bill. "I guess we could say Lillian is your proof; by the time this gets to trial she should be just about able to walk—if she doesn't need surgery."

"Francisco, we can't change what is. So just cool off that Spanish temper. I can see where this might go. Leave it alone. It's under control." Bobby Day stuffed the small recorders and the tapes in his pocket.

I took the Biscayne Causeway to Collins Avenue and drove slowly back to Golden Beach instead of I-95. I needed to think. I needed to calm down. They had gotten to me, that strip club with those poor desperate women, kind of like slavery. And the Jackson boys— pure evil—with John Harrison the obvious brains. But there was something else that bothered me. I tried to black my intellect out and let my instincts take over. I took deep breaths and watched the ocean flash in and out of view as I rolled up the Miami coastline past trendy South Beach into old Miami Beach and the huge high-rise apartment buildings, then to the mansions of Golden Beach.

My instincts were dead or sleeping. I had no subliminal signals, no subconscious impulses. I knew why. In order for my instincts to kick in, my conscious thinking mind had to shut down. It just wouldn't shut down—too many vivid images, vivid faces, like the cocktail waitress grabbing my crotch; the Jackson boys, their massive bodies oozing out of the booth; John Harrison's smug, ultra-confident, arrogant face. Bobby Day dressed in that outrageous outfit and me sitting calmly, quietly while everything inside me was raging, a red rage that wanted to kill these men for what they had done to Lillian and me. Yes, me and Lillian. They were prepared to take our lives, prepared to see us die to increase their wealth.

Lillian was sleeping, a medicated sleep, when I got home. The nurse was asleep in the room next door. Her room had been wired so she could hear Lillian if she awoke. I was sleeping in the opposite room, so as not to disturb Lillian. She liked to leave the balcony doors open at night and let the trade winds blow off the ocean and waft through the bedroom. She said it calmed her.

The white gauze curtains were swaying slightly with the gusts off the ocean. Her blond hair was spread out on her pillow framing her face. Her face was light brown, as if she had a permanent tan. Her tan came from her Greek blood. Her high cheekbones and perfect nose came from her French mother, another beauty.

Lillian had a great childhood, a rich attentive mother and father, well educated, well traveled. A successful early career as a model. But her real torment began when she was a child. She lost all the men in her life; she was abandoned through death.

First her father. Then her first husband shot himself over a bad business deal, and Lillian had to go back to work again, which she didn't mind. Her second marriage was to Richard Barnes, a wealthy New York investment banker who accepted her children, showered her with love and material possessions; both men had kept her protected and safe. She viewed the real world of suffering, struggle, and strife from the penthouse and through the tinted windows of stretch limousines and private planes. Then Richard died, killed by a creeping cancer, using his last breath to tell her he loved her.

So, after Richard's death, she was not interested in any relationship. She did not want to be abandoned again. I stroked the wisps of her blond hair away from her face. For a second I thought she smiled, but I couldn't be sure. I pulled the white sheet up and walked out onto the balcony to look at the ocean.

I don't think she fell in love with me at first. I think she fell in love with my voice. I sang for myself, low and soft, into the southern trade wind.

The melody drifted off the breaking waves, and the words flew off with the trades.

I sang to her many times. I sang softly in her ear after we made love until she fell asleep. I sang on New Year's

Eve. I sang to her on her birthday. She never got tired of me singing to her.

I was the opposite of her husbands. I wasn't sophisticated, urbane, a man who devoted his life to business—no, I was life in the raw; my experiences had been real and I liked them real. My business, the restaurant business, was a people business; I did not want a layer between me and life. I believed that anyone who was with me should take the full ride with me. I knew that money could create a layer of safety from the world's evils and eccentricities, but I preferred to take it as it was.

I believe Lillian was curious, curious to see how the world really operated, how it got up in the morning, how it fed itself, how it struggled with the problems of life, how it fought, how it loved its children, how it made love, how it dealt with love taken, paid-for love, violent love, unrequited love, love stolen, deadly love, abandoned love.

What were songs about? Most were about these kinds of love, and I sang love songs. So I believe she fell in love with the songs, like Cyrano with his poems to Roxanne. I had the help of great song writer-poets, who wrote the magic lyrics and the perfect melodies; all I had to do was sing them. I had the easy job, because I loved to sing.

From the minute I saw her I always felt we were destined to be together. It was just an overwhelming visceral feeling, undefinable. Of course she was with Richard, and the two of them used to come and visit me at Hola Havana. I liked them both, and Richard's death was a shock to us all. He was in good shape, watched his diet, and seemed able to cope with his stressful life. His death rocked us all.

After his death I called her several times to see how she was. Finally, after a year she came to visit me at my club. She came with her sister, who was visiting. I sat with them for a while and we talked. She came back a month later. She told me my voice and the great atmosphere in the club quieted the angry spirits inside her. Then her visits became more frequent and we finally went out for dinner. It took several dates before I could get her to smile. I loved to be in her presence; even now, here on the balcony I was very happy to be with her.

I stretched out in the chaise lounge. I let the cool ocean breeze and the softly breaking surf sing me quietly to sleep.

I spent the next three days with Lillian. I read to her. She told me that both her mother and her father would read to her when she was a child, not just to put her to sleep. Sometimes they would read to her in the living room instead of watching television, or in their beach cottage on Cape Cod in front of the fireplace in the fall, when the chilly northern winds would sweep down from Canada and the snow would threaten to fall. I was happy to read to her. I knew it made her feel safe. We did not discuss her leg or what to expect when the cast was taken off. She made no reference to the accident and asked me no more questions about what I was doing.

On the second day I went to the club. It was being run for me by my close friend and manager, Jaime Ortega, another Cuban. I had known Jaime since I moved to Florida after the military. He had given me my first singing break at his night club, Club Mucho Salsa, in Coconut Grove. It was the first time I ever sang for anybody but my family and friends. I did well. Performing was easy for me because I knew I could always depend on my voice—if I wanted an A or and E flat, I got it. It's called perfect pitch when you can sing a note with no help, just call it up from your brain.

My restaurant-nightclub, Hola Havana, was located on Calle Ocho, Eighth Avenue, in Little Havana. We served four-star Cuban cuisine. I had put the recipes together when I was a boy, mostly from my mother and her friends. It had been a dream of mine to own a bar-restaurant-night club since I was a boy. So, wherever I went in my Miami Cuban world I collected the best recipes. People always gave me their secret sauce or spice or special seasonings for black beans and rice, pork, chicken, steak.

They always looked at me strangely, a young boy of thirteen or so collecting recipes, and as I grew up they finally smiled, shrugged, and wrote out their secrets. "What harm could it do?" the men said. "He'll never remember." And, "He's so cute." The women would say, "Give him the recipes." So, I saved these and they became the nucleus of the semi-famous Hola Havana menu. I always spent a lot of time in the kitchen, and sometimes I would bring in a guitar and sing with the kitchen staff—the famous "Guantanamera," and "My Way" in Spanish.

The large stage stood at the far end of the club, up against the wall. Two large permanent plastic palm

trees stood on either side. The stage was big enough
for a ten-piece orchestra and could accommodate a trio.
The small dance floor was in front of the bandstand.
There were about sixty tables and the bar sat forty people, enough for a total of 250 people. While I was to
be away on my trip, we had arranged for a variety of
singers to appear. But it was really Francisco's club, my
club, and people expected Francisco to sing.

It was Friday night when I walked in.

"Hey, stranger!" Jaime said, and gave me a big hug.
"How's Lillian?"

"Lillian's doin' all right," I said.

"Your guests are over at the corner table, best table
in the house, like you said." Jaime walked with me over
to the Swamp Master's table. He had called and asked
to see me. I suggested that we meet in the club. He
asked if he could bring Mai Lynh, his wife. He sat there
with her. She wore a beautiful tight black silk long
dress that accentuated her small but perfect figure. She
wore no jewelry and light makeup. She let her natural
beauty carry her. The Swamp Master had on a dark
blazer and a white turtleneck. He looked good, tanned,
fit, and healthy. I missed Lillian; under normal circumstances she would be sitting with them, and the four of
us would have made a powerful happy foursome.

"Hey, Francisco, how about singing a few tunes with
us tonight," Lyda Jones, the well-known black Cuban
singer, said. Lyda was tiny, but had one of those incredible powerful blues/gospel voices that knocks you
on your ass. A voice so powerful from one so tiny was
always a shock.

"Maybe later, baby," I said, and gave her a hug.

False Witness

I sat down with the Swamp Master and Mai Lynh and ordered a pitcher of sangria, the house specialty.

"Let's celebrate," Mai Lynh said, her dark eyes and light brown skin radiating against the black silk of her dress. The lighting was indirect and shone perfectly on her face. The Swamp Master was a lucky man and he knew it.

"We thank God and celebrate that we are alive, and that Lillian is alive," Mai Lynh said, lifting her glass of sangria.

"Thanks to your man here," I said.

"I know. He's my hero," she said, and took his arm. The bicep bulged through his blue blazer. He beamed with pride, as he should have.

"Dinner all right?" I asked.

"Tres bien," she said, and smiled.

"Well, you have to go a long way to beat frogs' legs cooked in a wok," I said.

"Garlic. I love garlic and this here Cuban food, podner . . . it's the best," the Swamp Master said.

The band struck up the first notes, and Lyda's voice lit up the room with "My Way." She dedicated the song to me. We sat in silence as the table was cleared and Lyda sang her song. When it was over I asked the Swamp Master, "How's the job?"

"Like I said on the phone—we need to talk." I looked at Mai Lynh. "Don't you be worried about Mai Lynh. I tell her ever' thin' that's goin' on. Besides, after Vietnam there ain't nothin' that would surprise her."

"Please don't talk about me like I'm not here. I'm here." She smiled, and pinched his cheek. "You see, Francisco, my family was all killed in Vietnam and I got

115

out of Saigon through the embassy on almost the last helicopter. I have even seen myself in the newsreels. I was on the carrier when they pushed the helicopters into the China Sea to make room for us on the flight deck. I have seen human folly, murder, and mayhem. But life is still good, because I love my life so, my children, my home, and my Swamp Master even more. I cherish the life I have," she said. "I have built a new family."

I wondered how she had the pull to get out through the embassy. I was over there myself at the time. It was almost impossible to get into the embassy, to get on the list of those who were to be evacuated. I had a feeling I would find out.

"So, I have no secrets from my wife," the Swamp Master said. "I've been there over two weeks now. The whole gang of mechanics, six of us, moved from Opa-Locka into the big hangar in the Everglades three days ago. Four of us are working on your Albatross. We had a hell of a job finding two decent engines. I worked on the port engine. We removed it from another Albatross and stuck it on the plane they are selling you. The starboard engine was slapped on by my new friend Gene Santini, hell of a mechanic. It's him who's goin' to sign the airworthiness certificate. He says he gets five thou for each certificate and an extra two thousand for each engine when he gets it runnin'."

"So they cannibalize the other planes?" I asked.

"Yeah, major chop shop for airplanes. But there's more."

"Go on."

"There were six more planes that come in while I was

there. They were ferried in from the Bahamas. All small planes, two engines mostly. The pilots who done the ferrying told me they was all confiscated planes with no proper paperwork or logbooks. Florida Private Planes bought all six planes for a hundred grand cash total and fifty grand in juice, cash vig for the right Bahamians."

"What are they worth?"

"Well, they was all tricked out for drugging, you know, expensive radar and radios, satellite navigation gear, extra fuel tanks, modified storage areas, seats removed—you know the regular drill for drug planes. I'd guess we're lookin' at least a million-two, a million-three maybe on a quick-resale basis."

"A quick profit of over a million dollars."

"Yeah, papered up with the right plates on the frame and the right plates on the engines, no problem. These guys are real pros. We're in there workin' on seven aircraft countin' your Albatross; we're lookin' at way over a two million large in profit for a month's work. The new planes are first class 'cause they got them before the Bahamians got a chance to fuck them up by leavin' them out in the weather and doin' no maintenance. I hear this is a regular thing. My friend Gene says this happens every few months, where they buy these confiscated planes, from Mexico, the Bahamas, Colombia, Canada, and even the U.S. Government. This is big business. I figure they push through at least a hundred planes a year—at least that's what Gene says. He says last year was their best year. He signed over a hundred and seven airworthiness certificates; figure it out that's over a half a million for Gene alone at five thou a pop for the certs and extra for signing off on the engine overhauls. He's gotta be makin' close to a million a year and he's only the goddamn chief mechanic. I'm gettin' a thousand-dollar bonus if we have your plane good to go by Wednesday. I'm puttin' the best in her, just in case you actually have to fly the fucker."

"How long has this been goin' on?"

"Years and years. Gene says he's been with them since nineteen-eighty-nine. Hell, Gene has houses here and in North Carolina, a big fishin' boat, his own Aero-Commander. He's livin' large."

"So who are the customers?"

"Dopers and regular citizens, like you. For the dopers, he recycles the goddamn old doper planes. Buys them out of confiscation and resells them back to the dopers who probably owned them before they were nabbed by the DEA, or whoever grabbed them. For the regular citizens, he takes the planes when he can't get a doper and he sells them modified back to normal specs."

"Don't remind me," I said. "What a money-making concept."

"Yeah, what's that commercial—the human mind is a terrible thing."

"To waste—a terrible thing to waste, darling," Mai Lynh said to the Swamp Master.

He smiled at her and continued. "No bounds to the criminal mind. I saw two rough-lookin' Colombians in the office, and Gene told me it was the Arango brothers, two big players with the Cali Cartel. Gene speaks Spanish, and was there when they were looking at two

Cessnas in the hangar. They were laughing because it was the third time they bought the same planes from these assholes. They said it was still cheaper than goin' to the open market for the planes, and they were ready to go dope planes, new numbers, new logbooks, new airworthiness certificate, long-range fuel tanks, extra radar, satellite nav, the works!"

"So that room you found in Homestead is where they're engraving the plates and forging the logbooks."

"Right, and they keep real tight security on that room. I was lucky to get a look when I did. They got an armed rent-a-cop twenty-four-seven on duty now, and picture ID's are needed to get inside the room."

Lyda was singing a medley of Diana Ross songs in Spanish, and the room was full. Business was good. I should have been making my rounds, meeting and greeting people, waiting to go up on stage and do the thing I loved to do—sing. Instead, I was sitting here listening to the Swamp Master as he told me of a major crime syndicate, a crime syndicate that had sold me a plane that almost ended my life. I looked over to the empty place where Lillian would have been sitting on this Friday night.

"There's more," the Swamp Master continued. "I seen a guy at the hangar I recognized. See, Francisco, I haven't told you everything, and since I'm taking your money for the PI stuff, I feel maybe you should know.

"I told you a lot of the people in my unit in Nam in the early days were killed, so they were short of people and they trained me as a fixed-wing pilot and boosted my rank. I flew a lot of VIP's around and stuff like that.

"What I didn't tell you was that I flew my second

tour for the company, for Air America, and I got extra pay and a bunch of perks, like a big expense account and some cash now and then. Anyway, I flew this colonel around the Nam for a week. Weird motherfucker, very gung-ho-type of guy. He was a Special Forces recon Ranger and a West Point grad. An oh-my-God-gung-ho motherfucker, real quiet, but very deadly.

"See, I'm in Vietnam, having a sleep one day on the wing of my plane, catchin' the rays and gettin some Z's and a tan. I'm sleepin', dreamin', and I get this weird feelin' in my fuckin' sleep. I still remember it. I open one eye and I see this guy standin' there, just standin' there watchin' me, not sayin' a fuckin' word. God knows how long he was standin' there. I got both eyes open now, and right away I know he's a fucking ranking officer. I don't know how, no insignia . . . but I knew. He scared the shit out of me. He's standin' there wearin' a Hawaiian shirt, real baggy, like at least one size too big for him, and he's a big guy, Bermuda shorts, long hair, tanned, black shades, like a surfer. But I could see he was wearin' a shoulder-holstered weapon under his shirt.

"I seen the way that everybody acted when he was around, like I mean, even the other spooks gave him a wide berth. He invited me out one night in Saigon to party. Well, I ain't never seen a guy party like this guy. He had one drink all night and said two words. We go to a whorehouse, he selects a chick, goes with her—does his business and is back in twenty minutes sittin' with me saying nothin', nothin' at all, through the whole fuckin' night. After a while he got to me.

"Anyway, he's always scared the shit out of me. You

know what? The asshole walked into the hangar yesterday with them Jackson Hogs and Harrison. They were lookin' over the Bahamian planes. And you know what else?"

"What?"

"He had the same basic fuckin' outfit on, different clothes, but a Hawaiian shirt, Bermuda shorts, tanned, black shades, sandals, and I could almost bet he had that same forty-five in a holster under his armpit. And he hadn't gained a pound, he's in shape, and like always, he never smiled, or had any expression on his face. He's one scary motherfucker."

"Did he recognize you?"

"You kiddin'? The guys got a hard drive for a memory. He don't say nothin', he don't talk so he can memorize everything, that's what I think. I was the first thing he spotted. He walks directly over to me and just stares at me like when I was asleep on the wing of my plane. Doesn't say 'Hi' or 'Up your ass,' just stands there starin' with those blue eyes and the slicked-back blond hair, like a fuckin' Nazi. Like he's waitin' for you to fuck up.

"So, I give him a big Swamp Master smile and run a bunch of bullshit swamp talk on him. He finally shakes my hand, says nice to see me again, and walks back to the Jackson Hogs. About two hours later Jumbo waddles his fat ass out to see me, and says he didn't know I was a pilot and would I like to fly your Albatross up to Opa-Locka for you to pick up, gimme a grand for the ferry. I say okay. I figure I'll test out my handiwork. See if I'm as good as I used to be."

I smiled at the Swamp Master. "You got a location for me on the hangar?"

"Yeah, I brung you a map to where it is. It ain't easy to find, it's near that weird airstrip in the Glades that nobody can explain why it's there."

I put the map in my coat pocket when Lyda yelled my name from the stage. "Hey, Francisco, come on up here and give us a song." The audience cheered.

"Swamp Master said you were a singer. How about no more business tonight. You sing. You sing," Mai Lynh said with a smile.

Who could resist? "After your next tune, Lyda," I yelled back. I slipped away to the quiet of the office and used the phone; it was ten o'clock. "Hi." I said.

"Hi," Lillian answered.

"Wake you?"

"No, I was hoping you would call."

"How you doin'?"

"I have my good moments," she answered.

"The balcony doors open?"

"Of course. Francisco darling; how's the Swamp Master, my other hero?"

"He's good." There was a pause on the line. "I'm doing a song with Lyda, our song. Maybe you can hear it on the wind. I'm sending it out to you."

She waited and said, "Why wait?"

"You want it now?"

"I always want it now from you. This leg is driving me crazy. You looked so sexy tonight all dressed up in that white suit and blue tie. Gimme what I want."

"All right," I said, "I'll take the phone to the stage."

I walked out to the restaurant and placed the phone

on the top of the piano so Lillian could hear me. The people gave me a standing ovation. I started out slow. Lyda slipped back with her background singers and I did my special English-Spanish version of a song I loved.

The notes drifted off into the night air. When I was finished I picked up the phone from the top of the piano. "Hi," I said.

She whispered, "Francisco, I love you, really love you," and hung up. I had to take deep breaths to compose myself before I could join Lyda in her great version of "La Bamba."

Chapter Four

It was two days later, three in the morning. I took my big old Jeep Grand Wagoneer, the car I originally bought in 1988. It was new then. I loved this Jeep, like an old pair of Levi's that you hoped would never wear out. The sun had faded the wood paneling, and the tinted windows had faded to a dark gray, but it ran great. I wanted a vehicle that would draw no notice deep in the Everglades.

I wore a black T-shirt and black jeans, black deck shoes and a dark baseball cap. I wanted to blend into the darkness. The Jeep windows were open and the warm air smelled of rotting mangroves and that pure ocean-air-high-ozone smell, not an unpleasant blended smell, a true smell of Florida. The impending dawn, and the blazing sun, would create new smells.

I got through Little Havana and onto the Tamiami Trail. The Trail led out from the center of Miami into the guts of the Everglades. I had a tape of Frank Sinatra singing duets with famous people, and had a slight fantasy about what it would have been like to sing with him, the master, just one song—too late now—those old blue eyes were shut down forever. I turned the tape up and sang "I've Got You under My Skin" with Frank and Bono from the Irish group U2. Another song that I used to sing to Lillian. The three of us sounded great; I replayed the same CD track several times as I cruised into the Great Miami Swamp. I concluded that we were good, but Frank was best.

The Tamiami Trail is still Old Miami to me, with motley strip plazas, broken-down cars and trucks, Cubans selling cold coconut milk from roadside tables, Cuban coffee shops with strong-looking Latin men sipping potent espresso from tiny cups, arms moving as they talked, eyes intense, arguing politics, freedom for Cuba from the evil devil Fidel, "Cuba Libre," checking the good-looking *chicas* and even some not-so-good-looking *chicas,* and dealing with other matters that raised passion, like women and family.

The Tamiami Trail eventually turned into a two-lane blacktop, a strip of asphalt laid on top of the limestone bottomland that forms the lower Everglades, the southern edge of the Great Swamp before the flowing water from Lake Okeechobee spills into Florida Bay and the Keys. It was quiet this night, with most of the stores shut and the roadside businesses empty.

I had a Glock 45 under my seat. I had a special-made metal holster that had to be flipped out from under the seat to get the gun out. It was well concealed. I liked the Glock, all plastic except the barrel, nineteen rounds in the clip, and no safety to worry about. It was the weapon of choice for many cops.

I drove westward on the Tamiami Trail toward the Everglades into the Miccosukee Indian Reservation. I passed the huge gambling casino complex that acted as the main portal to the Great Swamp. I entered the Glades. The saw grass flew past me and civilization disappeared. When I looked into my rearview mirror I could still see the slight glow of the Miami skyline in the blackness behind me. There was no moon. I followed the excavation canal that paralleled the highway.

I had asked the Swamp Master if I could come and see the operation for myself.

He told me there was a window of time of about one hour, from five to six o'clock in the morning, when the night-shift mechanics left, before the Jackson Boys or their friends showed up. The security guard was a rent-a-cop who caught about an hour of Z's during that time. The Swamp Master had stayed behind one night and observed this. We would have to move fast.

I entered the Big Cypress Swamp and drove for about three miles. I swung off and parked exactly where he had told me, at an airboat- and boat-launching ramp. He told me there were always cars parked there, night and day. The swamp was never silent from the roar of aircraft engines that powered the airboats. He was waiting, sitting on his fender. He was back to being the Swamp Master. He had on a pair of dark mechanic's coveralls, a black T-shirt, and a black CAT baseball cap.

"Welcome to the swamp." He twisted his head and shot some chewing tobacco into the canal behind him.

"What swamp?" I asked.

"The swamp we call life, podner." He smiled. "You ready to rock and roll?"

"I don't do rap, and I don't do rock and roll." I smiled.

"There's always a first time. You got somethin' to look forward to." He walked to the launching ramp, to where he had already slipped his airboat into the water.

"Different airboat?" I said. It was smaller that the boat we had used before.

"It's my cousin's, Jethro Pinder. He's familiar with the Big Cypress and was showing me around the other day, so I borrowed it. Smaller but powerful and shallow-running is better for what we want tonight."

"How far?"

"Only minutes. The hangar is about two hundred yards from the airstrip. You remember the scandal about this strip?" he said, handing me my ear protectors.

"Yeah, when it was finished the project was canceled; everybody stood there and pointed at each other. The city of Miami, the federal government, the state. It was going to be the airport in the swamp that relieved Miami of its tourist burden. The hub of all tourism. Turns out it only relieved the treasury of millions of dollars. Supposed to be used now for training airline pilots and private plane pilots."

"Supposed to be, but that was before simulators were invented." The Swamp Master hit the button on the electric starter and ejected the wad of chewing tobacco from his mouth into the black canal water. "It just sits here now like two miles of concrete road out in nowhere, goin' nowhere, doin' nothin', but it ain't completely inactive."

I strapped myself into the forward seat with the Swamp Master at the controls sitting about two feet above me in the stern of the boat. He revved up the Lycoming engine and we started to slide along the surface. At first there was a wake, but it disappeared as the boat rose. Even with the ear protectors the roar from the highly tuned engine was formidable.

We paralleled the Tamiami Trail, Route 41, for about two miles, then turned off sharply, using the air-rudders, two long wooden paddlelike panels that directed the airflow behind the engine. We entered a small estuary, hardly noticeable, unless you knew where it was. The estuary dried up quickly and we skimmed up onto the wet saw grass. The wind was intense in my face; we were doing over fifty miles an hour. I understood now why the Swamp Master had gotten rid of his chewing tobacco.

We were in a great flat expanse. I looked behind into the blackness of the swamp. To our left you could see what was left of the great stand of cypress trees that had been gutted at the turn of the century by expert lumber men who found their way down into the Everglades from the great logging states of Oregon and Washington. Hundreds and hundreds of wood-growing years gone with the bite of a saw, the slash of a blade that had no conscience.

Ahead of us I could see what I knew to be landing lights from the strip that we were heading toward. I gradually began to make out a small control tower rising thirty feet out of the swamp. The lights got more readable as we approached.

The Swamp Master eased us out of the saw grass and into a small snaking channel about the width of our airboat. He slowed us down to a crawl. The lights from the airstrip were fully visible now, maybe a quarter of a mile from where we were. He eased us up onto a hammock of limestone that housed about a dozen cypress trees with fingery roots that dug downward into the muck of the swamp.

He turned off the engine. "Pretty good footing from here on." He smiled, taking a new bite of his tobacco. "Don't be stepping on no water moccasins now here."

"You go first." I smiled back.

"They knot up this time and get to fuckin'. You don't want to step into one of them knots."

"Save the swamp lore for the tourists," I said.

"Let's roll," he said, moving fast, but not jogging or running.

There was no sound except the sucking noise our shoes made in the ooze. The Swamp Master kept us out of the real soft ooze. He must have reconnoitered this entire terrain before tonight with his cousin, Jethro.

Hell of a guy this Swamp Master.

The ground got harder as we approached the airfield and the hangar. The airfield had been a major first-class construction effort, must have cost millions. It was all graded so the rainfall would flow off into the swamp; millions of cubic feet of limestone must have been brought in by truck. I could feel the earth harden under my feet.

I noticed a large wire-fenced compound and about

ten big-wheeled swamp buggies. They were balloon-tired vehicles that looked liked fat beetles with six wheels for legs, with high-powered engines that drove them through the slick swamp at high speed. They stood quiet and still like waiting servants.

The Swamp Master crouched down a few feet ahead of me as we got to within fifty feet of the hangar. "Look, gimme a minute, I gotta check and make sure the guard is asleep, like he aughta be. Then I'll swing back and go in that door over there. When I do you follow. Got it?"

I nodded. He took off. He moved like a swift shadow blending into the dark blue of the hangar. I felt for the Glock 45 in the small of my back, plastic against skin. It was hot from my body heat. I was sweating slightly, from the heat and the adrenaline. I looked around quickly. The airstrip runway lights were on. Lights flashed from various locations, and I could see that the tower lights were on. A radio beacon flashed as the lights climbed red up the radio tower. The lights seemed weird and out of place here in this dark, primeval, black swamp.

The Swamp Master rounded the corner moving swiftly in the darkness. He was through the hangar door and inside. I followed. Inside was like being on the inside of a huge domed cave. Small lights were on here and there for the security guard to make his rounds. There were six small planes, the Albatross, and a Gulfstream 3 parked inside the hangar. I could see the strongly built steel-pipe triangles in front of the Albatross where they were installing the engines. The Gulfstream had a jet engine out, and the small planes were all being worked on. I took my small camera out of my pocket, but the Swamp Master whispered.

"Too dark, even with a flash." He looked at my camera. It was tiny in his meaty palm. "Nice little toy," he said, handing it back.

We moved over to the Gulfstream 3. "Rumor is that this was taken in a drug sting in the Turks and Caicos by the British police—Scotland Yard—which ain't just in Scotland, laddie," the Swamp Master said with a Scottish accent, and smiled at his little joke. "The port engine of this beauty is being overhauled properly, like I'm tryin' to do with your Albatross over there. This here Gulfstream is going to a big player in Venezuela. Rumor floating around here is that it's going for fifteen million, about five million off the book value. Rumor is Harrison and the Jackson Hogs paid two million for it. They are repapering it with the papers of a crashed Gulfstream 3 that went down in South Africa about two years ago. They bought the plates and logbooks for a hundred grand from the former owner."

"How do they find out about these crashes and match them up to the right planes?" I asked.

"Don't know. Maybe they got somebody inside the government, inside the FAA."

We moved quickly through the hangar, back to where we had come in. There was a door to a small room. The Swamp Master took out a set of lock picks. He smiled as the door opened.

"Another cousin?" I asked.

"Luther Pinder. He's the locksmith in Flamingo City."

"Christ, how many locks are there in Flamingo City?"

131

I asked as we moved into the small room.

"At least two hundred or so. That ain't all Luther does." He winked at me.

Inside was a computerized engraving machine and ID plates for planes and engines. The Swamp Master reached into a drawer that was packed with Cessna ID plates. "Here, these ain't no fakes, these come from the fuckin' factory. Take one for a souvenir."

I slipped the plate in my pocket.

The Swamp Master checked his watch. "We better bug outta here. That rent-a-cop does his tour every sixty minutes, so he's gonna be cruising by here in the next few minutes."

We split. The Swamp Master was careful to lock all the doors as we eased out the side door. We headed back to the hammock next to the landing strip before re-entering the swamp. We stopped at a limestone man-made berm outside the hangar. I looked over at the Albatross graveyard, over thirty Grumman Albatross aircraft in various states of disrepair. They looked like dead and crippled old birds, silhouetted in the night.

We both heard it at the same time. A plane, a big plane, was somewhere out in the blackness, somewhere very near us. We both surveyed the skies and saw nothing. The sound was the sound of prop engines, not jets, getting closer, moving toward us. There were no lights to be seen in the sky. It appeared as a dark fat bird coming out of a graying sky. It was low and near the end of the runway—no lights. We both knew what it was, a C-130 military cargo aircraft. It eased down on the runway and hugged the concrete—no bounce, it looked loaded.

As the plane taxied down the runway, three black Chevy Suburbans with black-tinted windows drove through the chain-link-barbed-wire fence at the entrance up near the control tower and the swamp buggy compound. They blinked their lights twice as they slipped through the open fence gate, and entered the concrete strip that led to the control tower.

The Suburbans waited in idle, their exhausts breathing gray fumes out into the swamp air as the huge C-130 lumbered down the runway.

The plane did a U-turn at the control tower and shut down all four engines. The ass-end of the plane, the single cargo door, dropped down to the runway as the three Suburbans rolled up, did a U-turn, and backed into the door, single file, one behind the other. The passenger doors on the Suburbans opened and four men emerged from each vehicle. They were all dressed in black, with black faces and black watch caps, except for one man, who wore a Hawaiian shirt, shorts, and a strapped-on shoulder holster. He was visible in the headlights of one of the Suburbans for only a second before the lights went off. Five of the men dispersed in all directions across the runway.

I took pictures with my small 35-mm camera and hoped for the best.

The man in the Hawaiian shirt walked to the open door with six men dressed in black. Lights were on in the cargo hold and six men were inside. The men inside were dressed in military fatigues and carried side arms. They all got to work immediately, except the man in the Hawaiian shirt, who stood by the doorway.

We could see that the cargo was wrapped in clear

plastic liners. It looked like a white substance—probably cocaine. The blocks looked to be about two kilos each—standard size. The men from the trucks moved fast. They dropped the two-kilo packs into black plastic garbage sacks, and carried them into the Suburbans. They were well trained, organized, and disciplined about their work.

The first shot came in just over my shoulder and below my ear. There was no sound. It made a puff in the limestone berm. The Swamp Master saw it also. On the second shot I saw the tiny flash from the suppressed muzzle. I pulled the Glock from the small of my back and spun around. The Swamp Master did the same. He pulled a .45 from his belt.

"Don't shoot," I said. "They're using night glasses and he's probably the only one that has us spotted. You shoot and everyone will know where we are."

We swung over the top of the berm and down the far side. Bullets bit the limestone as we vaulted the top of the berm. "They're all connected by radio," he said.

"Tell me somethin' I don't already know." We both heard them. Two swamp buggies fired up, breaking the swamp-silence. The gates in the compound that held them were opened.

"Shit, they got the goddamn big-foot swamp buggies fired up. Let's beat feet, podner, before we're dead meat!" He took off running full speed into the swamp. I was right behind him. The footing was decent but slippery. The Swamp Master moved fast for such a big man. Fear is a great motivator.

They were right behind us. I could hear the powerful engines of the swamp buggies. We ran down the narrow trail following the white of the limestone in the dark night. The airboat stood hidden in the cypress clump where we had left it. We both pushed the bow into the two-foot-deep water and saw grass. I dove into the front. The Swamp Master leapt into the driver's seat and hit the start button; the engine hesitated, coughed, and burst into life. The Swamp Master slipped on his ear protectors and strapped himself in. I did the same.

I saw the two swamp buggies catapult over the berm where we had been hiding and shoot down the narrow path we had used. They crushed the grass on both sides of the trail. The huge spinning tires made deep big-foot tire imprints in the mud of the swamp. They were moving at a hell of a clip, like insane giant insects. Each swamp buggy had two high-powered halogen headlights that rayed out a white intense light ahead of them. Above the drivers was a string of white-hot halogen jackrabbit lights that lit up the area all around them in a 180-degree light storm.

They made perfect targets. I had my gun raised. I had a perfect shot at the Hawaiian shirt, sitting next to the driver of the first swamp buggy.

"Don't shoot, for Christsakes, don't shoot, Francisco," the Swamp Master roared, and drowned himself out with noise of the Lycoming engine as he pushed the throttle full forward. The stern of the boat sat down deep in the mud, stuck; the suction held it until the straining force of the engine finally popped it out of the mud with a sucking sound. We rocked forward, the bow dipping suddenly, down deep into the swamp.

The big-foot swamp buggies were coming down the

trail now full tilt, lights flashing, like two wild-ass run-away giant bouncing bugs trying to kill us. I knew if they caught up to us they would just run right over this small airboat, crushing us like weaker insects.

The deck of the airboat bow was dug in, level with the water. Water started to seep in over the bow. I could hear parts of curses as the Swamp Master yelled over the roar of the engine. "Come on, you mother-fucker, get up, get up, get up, goddamn you, you son of a whore, get up." He backed the throttle off for a fraction of a second to rock the boat, and then plunged it forward. I felt the bow rise up from the swamp as he backed off, and we jolted forward. The swamp buggies were closing the gap, but we were up on the saw grass and the swamp water now. We left a churning white wake for the first hundred yards. The swamp buggies were fast. They entered the swamp two abreast in our wake. I could see red bursts as their guns spat at us.

"Hang on," the Swamp Master yelled as he started to veer to the right and then the left, snaking a serpentine trail through the grass. Our small airboat was faster than our pursuers, and the gap widened as we cut through the swamp. Ahead in the distance there was a big stand of cypress trees that the Swamp Master headed for. He moved in through the trees like an artist with a brush. The trees would stop the swamp buggies.

I knew that we would stay away from the canal that ran parallel to the Tamaimi Trail, because they might send cars out to patrol the highway. We hit open saw grass again and cruised for about ten minutes. The sky was turning gray with the approaching dawn.

The Swamp Master slowed down and slipped off his

ear protectors. "Mighty cranky, weren't they?" he said, taking a chew from his tobacco pouch. "I guess they didn't want us seein' what they was doin'."

"Would you?" I asked.

"Guess not. Sure looked like government-issue activity to me. You see the Hawaiian shirt?"

"Hard to miss," I said.

"Never seen nothin' like that out there before. Hardly ever any traffic out there since I been workin' there. Some touch-and-go, airline-school practice stuff, but little or no traffic. What the hell was that all about?"

"Beats me," I said. "Those guys were all well trained and disciplined, military style."

"I don't know how it ties in with Harrison and the Jackson Hogs."

"Well, Harrison and the Jackson brothers are strictly freelancers, not government types," I said.

"The Hawaiian shirt, the colonel, he's the dude that gives me the heeby-jeebies." The Swamp Master looked to the East and the rising sun. "Well, podner, when I fire up again we're going to head south, toward Luther's house near Flamingo City. He can come back and get the truck. He'll bring you back with some fishin' gear for your car, and if anybody gets curious, you can say you was fishin'."

"Will they send up planes after dawn?" I asked.

"No, too many airboats out here in the Glades for them to figure what's what." He smiled. "God, they was riled."

"Kinda like steppin' into a knot of those mating water moccasins you were talking about," I said.

"Kinda," he said, spitting some tobacco into the great

137

swamp, slipping on his ear protectors, and ramming the throttle lever forward. We were roaring off again.

We took shortcuts on the way back that saved about five minutes. We cruised into the airboat ramp. Luther was waiting. Luther cranked the compact airboat onto the trailer. He checked it out, stopping at the transom, fingering the wood.

Luther Pinder was what you might expect as a relative of the Swamp Master. He was laconic, taciturn, and demanded respect when he was moving around in the swamp, roaming his turf. Same intelligent blue eyes, light skin, and irreverent mouth. There was nobody there but us.

"Bullet holes in the transom. You boys had some fun last night, huh?"

"I've had better times," I said.

"I ain't gonna have no repercussions 'bout this, am I?" He smiled. "Sometimes, my cousin Sawyer, he don't fill in all the blanks—leaves shit out. He's famous for it."

"No repercussions comin' to mind," he said.

"I'm sure you're right." Luther took the final crank on the airboat, bringing it flush to the trailer hitch.

I drove back to Golden Beach in the inside lane going at the speed limit. I had a lot to think about, but thinking didn't make it any clearer.

There were two messages waiting for me when I arrived home. I called John Harrison back first, at Florida Private Planes.

"Hey, Francisco, how's it going?"

"Good, what's up? My plane ready?"

"Will be on Monday. We'll have it here for you ready to go."

"Paperwork?"

"All in order. We'll have the logbooks, airworthiness certificate, bill of sale, the works. How about you and the paperwork, the greenbacks?"

"I'll be ready. I'll go to the bank today and get a cashier's check for two hundred and fifty thousand and two-fifty in cash. That's what you want, right?" I asked.

"Exactly right. I'll see you and the Frenchy at two in the afternoon on Monday."

"I'll be there," I said, and hung up.

Next, I called Bobby Day, aka Maurice Geoffreon, the French Canadian, at FAA headquarters. I told him of the conversation with John Harrison and waited for a response. He called me back twenty minutes later. "I called Inspector Greene, and he said we should do it on Monday. He asked if you could get the cashier's check and the cash; we need some flash money and you can give the check and the cash back to the bank on Monday. If we do it, it will take too long to process the internal paperwork to get the money. It's already Friday. You got that kind of cash?"

"Well, between Lillian and me, we have that kind of credit at the bank. You sure it will not be at risk?" I asked.

"We're not going to give it to them. We're just flashin' it so they will produce the paperwork. Then we'll call in the raid."

"I need to see you this afternoon. I'll go to the bank and set it up then I'll drive to Miami. There's something I need to tell you," I said.

"Okay, I know Inspector Greene will be here, and so will I," he said, and hung up.

I checked on Lillian, who was sleeping, talked to her nurse, showered, and went about my chores. It was Friday; a lot was going to happen in the next few days, if all went as planned.

At four, we met in the conference room of the FAA building in Miami at the airport. Three men sat at the gray metal conference room table; Bobby Day, Chief Inspector Greene, and a third man who was introduced to me by Bobby Day.

"This is the director of the FAA for Southern Florida. Francisco. Meet Director Jerry Fitzgerald."

He was a well-built man wearing an unseasonable dark suit and a nondescript tie. He was in his late fifties, slim, in good shape. He struck me as an ex-pilot more than a bureaucrat. He had a full head of dark wavy hair and an easy smile. He extended his hand.

"Heard a lot about you, Mr. Cruz."

"Francisco," I said, shaking his hand.

"All right, Francisco it is then." He smiled. "Sorry to hear of your unfortunate experience with these people. We have had them under investigation for over a year now."

We all sat down. "Coke's okay?" Bobby said, pointing at the vending machine in the hall. We nodded and he left, to return with a several cans of Coke for each of us. "Sorry, no glasses today," he said, sitting down.

"A year, huh?" I said.

"A year. I thought you knew that," the director said.

"Then you know about their hangar in the Everglades at the airstrip you guys control?" I asked as we sat down.

"Yes. We know about the hangar, but we don't know much else about it."

"It's leased out to Florida Private Planes." Inspector Greene said. "Much like American Airlines or Delta would operate a private facility here at Miami International."

"Actually, we believe a lot of their work to alter airplanes is done there, but we have never been able to get proof," Bobby Day said. "They are very clever in the way they operate. They work mostly at night and we have no hard evidence of them doing anything illegal there. The planes they work on are immediately put into that huge hangar and the numbers all seem to check out on the aircraft that fly into the facility at Opa-Locka."

"What do you mean check out?" I asked.

"Well, if it's a 1967 Cessna 150 with the numbers N1265P, then we look it up in the FAA records and it always checks out," Inspector Greene said.

"Like, if I had a 1992 Cadillac Coupe De Ville license RAM 141, and I checked it through the Florida DMV and it checked out, I would have to assume it was okay."

"Yeah, that's right," Bobby Day said.

"What about other agencies being involved with Florida Private Planes?" I asked.

"What kind of other agencies?" Director Jerry Fitzgerald asked.

"There's so many, take your pick—FBI, DEA, Treasury, NSC, the State of Florida agencies."

"Well, DEA is in this with us on this investigation from the start, because the planes are being modified to carry drugs and they also are being sold to the public."

"Like me, the public," I said.

"I don't believe there are any other agencies involved with them," Bobby Day said.

"Just hold on a minute here," the Director said. "Do you think if another agency was using this facility, we might not know about it?"

"If that question is: 'Do I think the left hand of the government always tells the right hand what is going on?' I would have to say, based on my personal experience of the fucked-up way the war in Vietnam was run—not always—the right hand does not always know what the left is doing—that's my unfortunate experience," I said.

"Well, we have checked with the DEA and the FBI and they claim we're on our own on this, and I can't see the other agencies having any interest. The customers of Florida Private Planes, according to our surveillance, and the DEA surveillance, is mostly bad guys—Colombian dopers and their American partners," Bobby Day added.

"Do you know something we don't know?" the Director asked.

"I'm not sure," I said, flipping the blank Cessna factory ID plate on the table.

"Where'd you get this?" Inspector Greene asked, examining the plate. "This is the real thing!" He handed it to Bobby Day.

"It came out of a desk, inside a little room in the hangar," I said.

"How could you know that?" the Director asked.

"A little birdie told me," I said.

"You have a man on the inside," Inspector Greene said.

"I'll tell you if you can answer one question. I want you to find out who flew into the Glades airstrip today at around six in the morning—a C-130 landed there. I would like you to find out and I would like you to make the call to the Central Air Control headquarters in Miami from here, with me on the line."

The three FAA men looked at each other, and finally the Director spoke. "We have nothing to hide from you. I'll make the call; we'll put it on the speaker phone."

The pictures were passed around as the call went through. "Give me the Officer of the Day," Director Jerry Fitzgerald said. The speaker phone was activated. "Hello, this is FAA Director Fitzgerald, who am I speaking to?"

"Captain Morris."

"I need some information, Captain. Do you have the computer logbooks handy from last night's shift?"

"Yes, sir, what do you need?"

"I need to know if you have a C-130 cleared for landing in the Glades training strip," the Director said.

"No, sir, no traffic of that kind cleared for landing in the strip."

"Check again."

We waited. They continued to examine the pictures. The voice came back. "No, sir, nothing reported and

143

nothing in the hand-written log at the tower in the Glades."

I believed the report. I was thoroughly confused now. He hung up.

"Well, we checked," Director Fitzgerald said.

"All it means is that you don't have control of the airspace like you think you have," I said, "or maybe you do."

"Where is this taking us?" Bobby Day asked. "You going down some weird conspiracy theory line now?"

"I know what I know," I added.

"What about this Cessna plate and the C-130? What does it mean?" Inspector Greene said.

I had to make a decision to tell them, or not. I got up and looked out the window at the tarmac and all the private planes, tied down against high sudden winds. I thought of all the regular folks who loved to fly. I thought of their families and their blind faith in the system that was in place to protect their safety.

It was inconceivable that someone could corrupt the entire Military Air Control Center, a huge combined operation between police agencies and the military located in a giant war room in downtown Miami. This facility was designed to stop the flow of drugs into southern Florida, set up under George Bush's reign in his famous war on drugs of the late eighties.

It used AWAC high-level radar planes and every other high-tech military device in the U.S. arsenal. It was something else I would have to figure out later, or maybe it would come in with the net cast to get the Florida Private Plane gang of cutthroats—God only knows how many people they had killed or maimed with their operation, how many lethal flying accidents waiting to happen they had launched into the air.

But I still decided not to tell everything. "Let's just say that I got the Cessna plate from a confidential informant, like you guys would say. Let's just say that based on that plate you can get a search warrant and execute a raid; as a result of that search you can make a number of arrests on the spot. I would like to leave it at that."

"Well, whoever you have on the inside, you better tell him not to go to work on Monday," Director Fitzgerald said.

They took the next hour to brief me on the raid procedure.

Chapter Five

The rain rolling in on the ocean always thrilled her. She could see the dark storm clouds being driven by the gusting wind. Her bed was propped up, and she could see the edge of the Gulf Stream. It was that deep dark blue, like a painter's color, unique, made with special care, a color known to the mind of the painter, but one that he always had to search for. The Gulf Stream moved in closer to the coast here in Golden Beach, sometimes only three miles off the beach in front of her house.

Her husband, Richard, had explained it to her the first day they went out in his Hatteras. He had shown her on the chart how when the wind was right and when the time of year was right and the tide was right, that the great current of the Gulf Stream would meander in close to land. It carried the big predators in with it, the sharks, and other pelagic fish, that never stopped wandering, moving through the ocean cur-

rents, like the sailfish and the great bluefin tuna. The Gulf Stream current carried them close to land, too close, where sometimes they would lose their bearings, their course, like humans when they were all of a sudden put in dangerous and new places.

She knew Richard had gone out of his way to protect her from the unexpected, the fearful, the dangerous things in life that haunted so many other people. Her father had done the same thing as Richard. She knew this was a good thing. She knew it instinctively, yet she often wondered what it would be like to cross over to that uncontrollable, wild, dangerous side of life.

When she was a model she had seen many of her beautiful friends lured into that dark life—drugs, sex, awful cruel abusive relationships with men and other women. But she only witnessed it as an observer; she had visited the emergency wards and the police stations to help her friends, but it was always as a person removed from the drama.

Richard had loved to hear Francisco sing. He had taken her to Hola Havana every Friday, and sometimes on Wednesday when there was an "open mike" for anyone who wished to perform. They had seen Tito Puente and Celia Cruz there one night. Richard loved "Volare," "Guadalahara," "Spanish Eyes," "Lady of Spain," "Dancing in the Dark," and other American and Spanish songs sung in Spanish, Cuban style. He loved Francisco's voice.

When Francisco sang, he would demand silence at the tables without asking for it.

It had been a day like today, a Friday. They had been out in their seventy-foot Hatteras, just cruising in the

Gulf Stream, sitting on the aft deck having a cocktail, when the captain came off the bridge and told them of a storm coming in from the east, a dark foreboding clump of ugly weather. "Keep ahead of it and head us home," Richard had told the captain, who swung the stern around and headed the bow landward. The storm was full of lightning and thunderclaps that roared off the surface of the ocean like angry bellowing, blustering demons escaped from hell. Richard said nothing. He just held her hand as the storm came, chasing after them. Dark gray funnel clouds came down behind them and made tiny tornadoes, boiling the water where the funnels hit. The captain took the big Hatteras up to full speed, and was able to run just ahead of the pursuing blackness.

Richard tightened his grip on her hand. The only thing he said was, "I love you, you know that, don't you?" And she had placed her hand behind his neck and kissed him on the lips.

It was that very night that he had his attack. In their massive bedroom. The bedroom she was in now, watching the roiling ocean and the storm clouds rolling in. The nurse had asked to close the windows to the balcony, but she had said, "No, move me closer to the window, and please leave."

She could feel the temperature of the wind change as the cool rain hit the beach in front of her, pelting the sand. The wind turned slightly damp, then wet, and it felt good on her face, in her hair. She opened her mouth and took big gulps of the ocean air, like drinks of soothing life-giving water.

Richard had just collapsed in pain, doubled up, hold-

ing his stomach. They were dressing to go to Francisco's. Richard loved to dress up and so did she. They were a handsome couple and they liked showing each other off. He had just fallen to the floor on one knee, no warning. She went to call 911, but he stopped her. He told her to call Dr. Trueblood at home. He took the phone from her when the number was dialed and told the doctor to come immediately. "There is no need to call 911, darling," he said. He tried to rise. She had to help him into bed.

"You know I have never kept anything important from you," he said to her when he was settled.

"Yes, I know."

"Only this once, darling. I was diagnosed with cancer six months ago. It was inoperable and had spread through my entire body by the time I found it. Dr. Trueblood has been helping me, but there is really very little that can be done—only some help with the pain."

She sat next to him holding his hand, dumbfounded, unable to speak. She helped him undress and tried to get him comfortable in bed.

Then he said, "No, darling, I would like my robe. I want to sit in that chair on the balcony and watch the storm." They sat in silence holding hands as the storm that had chased them in from the ocean ravaged the beach. He broke the silence between them. "I have a request, Lillian. A request you may find strange."

"Anything," she whispered.

"I want you to call Francisco and ask him to come over here."

"Richard. I . . ."

"You said anything." He squeezed her hand.

She made the call, and Francisco was there thirty minutes later. Dr. Trueblood arrived just before Francisco, and gave Richard a morphine shot, a painkiller. Francisco arrived in his tux, it was almost nine o'clock and time for his first show of the night. Dr. Trueblood was asked to stay.

"Francisco, I am glad you came," Richard said, shaking his hand, sitting inside the bedroom now. The balcony doors were closed. "This is Dr. Trueblood." The two men shook hands.

"Richard, are you all right?" Francisco asked.

"No, I'm not all right and that is why I have called you." He smiled at Francisco. "I have always enjoyed your singing, Francisco. And I have enjoyed your company. You know that I have built up a large investment firm over the years and people think I am a good businessman. But really, I am no better a businessman than anyone else. There is one thing I am good at, and I realized it when I was young and was smart enough to follow my instincts; that's what I'm good at and what I intend to do tonight."

"Darling, maybe this is not the time. . . ."

"Lillian, this is the perfect time. And maybe the last time. Francisco, I don't only trust my instincts; sometimes I check things out, and you checked out very well.

"Lillian, would you take my black shoes out of the closet, the Ferragamos."

Lillian did as she was asked. Richard pointed to Francisco. "Francisco, please. Will you try them on?"

Francisco slipped into the shoes. "They're a little big for me."

"Are they comfortable?"

"*Yes, they are soft. They feel good.*"

"*I want you to do me a great favor. When I'm gone . . .*"

"*Gone?*"

"*Yes, let me speak. I've thought a great deal about this matter. As I said, I have always followed my instincts. I intend to do so now. My business associates will come after my estate when I have left. They are dangerous men and it is a very complicated estate. I want you to help Lillian. I want you to help her deal with these men and their regiments of lawyers. These men are smart and ruthless. I have taken steps to look after Lillian, but they will act anyway. There is too much money involved. I want you to help her and do what is necessary to protect her interests against these men. Will you do it?*"

Francisco slipped out of the shoes and into his own. He looked at Lillian, staring into her eyes, then he looked back at Richard. "Yes. I understand," was all he said. He walked over to Richard, shook his hand, and left the room, without another sound. He had seen death in men's eyes before.

Richard was dead and buried a week later.

And the men came for the money. They stole her racehorses. They stole the furniture from her penthouse apartment in New York just to let her know that they could. They took the two airplanes, the art, emptied the offshore accounts, and they tried to take the real estate. Lillian finally went to Francisco for help; at first she just went to hear him sing. He asked if he could help; she said no. Then she took him out to dinner and she asked for his help. Francisco helped, but it was a little too late, the pirates had looted the ship.

In time they fell in love and married. Francisco could never quite figure out that night, but he admired Richard for wanting to protect the person he loved the most . . . and for knowing what men are capable of in this life . . . and for being selfless. He was a man who stood tall, even after he was gone.

Together, they were still, even now, fighting to save her estate. The final numbers were yet to be reconciled.

That seemed like another lifetime to Lillian. She ran her hands through her damp hair, and used her hands to rub the windblown rainwater into her face. The storm had rolled past and the ocean was settling.

Francisco was up to something. He was keeping it from her. To protect her—all the men in her life wanted to protect her. She looked down at her leg in the cast and she could feel tears coming. No, she wouldn't have tears now—she wanted her life back—she wanted their dream back. The dream had been stolen from her.

Perhaps that's what Francisco is up to, she thought, perhaps he's trying to get our dream back. No, this was no time for tears. She wiped her eyes clear. She must find out what he was doing. She knew she could help him . . . she just knew it.

Bobby Day was standing next to his Red Rolls Royce convertible in the Denny's parking lot. He was wearing his best Maurice Geoffreon disguise. A plaid sports coat, yellow shirt, green pants, and white shoes. He was leaning against the fender with his face skyward catching the last of the afternoon rays. His Wayfarer sunglasses were perched on the top of his head.

"How are you this fine Monday, Mr. Francisco Cruz?"

"I don't think I'm as good as you," I said.

"Great day for a raid, don't you think?"

"Good as it gets, I suppose," I answered.

"You got the cash-ola?" he asked.

I patted my attaché case, then opened it as he peered in the passenger side of the Ferrari.

He whistled as he looked in. "Nothing like the green, is there—two-fifty?"

"No, there's nothing like it, except more green," I said. "Yeah, two-fifty and a cashier's check for two-fifty."

"I'm wired so we'll be monitored from the time we go in; let's roll," he said, getting into his red Rolls convertible. The top was up. I was sure the air was on full blast. It was almost four-thirty, but it was still hot, one of those shirt-drenching, run-for-the-air-conditioning South Florida scorchers.

We cruised through the Opa-Locka Airport past the Coast Guard and the Cuban "Brothers to the Rescue" hangar and into the Florida Private Planes compound. We pulled up to the front of the office. I could see the Grumman Albatross sitting on the taxi strip in front of the hangar. I couldn't look at it for long; all I could see in my mind was the wreck, my wreck, sitting in the FAA hangar at Miami International Airport, less than five miles from where I was standing.

The receptionist was waiting. A new girl from the last visit. She wore a tiny miniskirt and a halter-top. Her makeup was streaky and she was chewing gum like she wanted to squash the life out of it with her jaws.

153

She was most likely a dancer from the Frat House who had other duties to perform than her receptionist chores. She escorted us directly into John Harrison's office.

He was behind his desk. The two Jackson boys were stuffed into the tub chairs that faced his desk. Their eyes went directly to us and then down to the attaché case I was toting.

"How you boys doin'?" Action Jackson said with a beaming smile.

"We're doing all right," I answered.

"Right on time," Harrison said, checking his watch. It was two o'clock.

"We aim to please," Maurice Geoffreon said, in his best French Canadian accent. His clothes seemed even brighter in the well-lit-by-the-sun office. I pushed some papers aside and sat on the couch, placing the case next to me.

"You all want a drink—Coke or somethin'?" Jumbo asked, swinging the tub chair around to face me. I wondered where they got their blue-jean coveralls, what store sold such large sizes. They had huge white T-shirts on. The black lettering on the shirts said, "God is my copilot—I have no fucking fear."

"Okay, Coke's fine for us both," I said.

Harrison beeped the receptionist on the intercom. He told her twice. "And write it down!" Harrison yelled at her.

"Fuck you, John," was the response on the other end. Minutes later she walked in with two cans of Coke. She leaned over and put them on Harrison's desk. It was obvious when she leaned over that she wore no panties.

"I don't appreciate the sarcasm, boys," she said as she closed the door.

"That's Mitzi from New York, she can't dance either," Jumbo said, sipping his own Coke.

Harrison popped the clip on the two Cokes and handed them to us. "But she gives great attitude."

"Yeah, every afternoon about three," Action Jackson said, and they all laughed.

"You got the money, you bring the cash?" Jumbo asked.

"Yeah, I got it right here." I patted the case.

"Let's see the green," Action said.

I looked at Maurice, who nodded approval. I flashed the cash. Harrison got up from his desk, and came over to me. He fingered a stack of hundred-dollar bills, and then placed them back in the case. "Shall we go inspect the goods?" he said, walking to the office door.

We followed. The Jackson brothers wrestled their way out of the tub chairs, holding the arms of the chairs down as they rose to keep the chairs from staying attached to their bodies. The chairs fell off their bodies with a clumping sound. We walked past Mitzi, who refused to look up from her *Cosmopolitan* magazine as we passed into the hangar area.

The Albatross had been painted since I last saw it in the Glades. It looked shiny and new, not like the death trap it was. Inside, the passenger seats had been removed. This made for a huge cargo hold that could be easily converted back to a passenger-carrying airplane. Harrison showed us the extra fuel tanks that had been welded inside the airplane, and the thick rubber bladder tanks that could be filled for the flight to Colombia and then jettisoned into the ocean when they were emptied. I was sure this was all going down on the wire that Bobby Day was wearing.

"This here radar works good, and the single sideband radio is the best you can get. The radios all work. The satellite navigational stuff needs to be provided by you; we don't put that in," Jumbo said as we inspected the plane.

The appearance of the plane was excellent, "Looks great," I said. "Does it work?"

Jumbo and Action Jackson looked over at John Harrison. They were too large to fit into the pilots' seats. Harrison slid into the seat and fired up the port engine. Some black smoke came out, but quickly disappeared. The starboard engine fired into life with a puff of black smoke. Harrison revved up both engines. The sound reverberated through the hangar, like a powerful animal. The Swamp Master had done a good job; too bad he hadn't worked on the first plane. He had left work early. He was aware of the coming raid.

"You'll be getting a full annual airworthiness certificate, and engine overhaul certificates. This baby is better than new," Harrison yelled over the spinning propellers. He shut both engines down.

We walked back into Harrison's office. "Next, the paperwork, right fellas?" Harrison said, and opened the bottom drawer of his desk. He withdrew a large folder. First the logbooks, posted up to date. "Here we have a bill of sale and finally the airworthiness certificates and the engine hours certificates." Harrison laid out the paperwork on his desk. Maurice Geoffreon got up from the couch next to me and examined the papers now strewn on Harrison's desk.

"These look good to me," he said. "You know what you bought yourself?"

"It's you guys that bought something," Jumbo said.

"No, Jumbo, that's where you're wrong. It's you assholes that have bought something"—Maurice Geoffreon lost his accent, as he pulled his gun from his shoulder holster—"about fifteen years in federal prison. You're under arrest."

All hell broke loose. Three DEA and FAA SWAT vans screeched to a halt in the front and in the rear of Florida Private Planes. Twenty men leapt out of the vans dressed in black ninja suits, carrying automatic weapons. The girls in the office stared in shocked horror; even Mitzi jumped up as the assault team shot by her, and dropped her *Cosmo* onto the floor. Four armed DEA swat team members rushed into Harrison's office. The office was packed.

"Get up!" they yelled at the Jackson Brothers, who struggled to rise from their tub chairs.

John Harrison stood in disbelief, his jaw dropped. "Are you guys fucking nuts?" he screamed at the raiding SWAT team. "What the fuck are you doing here?"

"Shut up," the team leader said, and turned him face-to-the-wall. "Put your hands on the back of your head. Do it now!" Harrison did as he was told.

Jumbo and Action Jackson were struggling to extricate themselves from their tub chairs. They started yelling, "Calm the fuck down, you bunch of cowboy assholes!" Jumbo screamed.

"You seen too much fucking television," Action

yelled, finally popping the tub chair loose.

"Cuff those fat fucks!" the team leader yelled as he personally slipped the cuffs on John Harrison.

"Calm down, will you. You got them automatic weapons in our face—you think we're going to resist? Just take it fuckin' easy," Jumbo said.

"Shut your mouth! You just do as you're told. Put your hands behind your back." They were having a hell of a time getting the Jackson brothers' arms to meet behind their backs, then securing the cuffs around the Jackson brothers huge wrists. "Double-cuff those monsters." The other members of the team flipped over their handcuffs.

"What do you think you're doing?" John Harrison yelled.

"You're under arrest for illegally altering aircraft, and falsifying documents," Bobby Day said, smiling, "and for money laundering."

"Fuck you, you don't know what you're dealing with here," Jumbo said. "We're going to be—"

"Shut up, Jumbo!" John Harrison yelled. "Just let nature take its course here. Keep still."

I noticed, through the window, the three mechanics in the hangar being collected, handcuffed, and escorted out. I walked out into the office and watched as the SWAT team placed police tape in front of all the files and desks. Mitzi and the two secretaries had been taken to the parking spaces in front of the hangar. Their ID's were being checked and noted before they were released.

The two Jackson boys and John Harrison were marched through the office and into a waiting SWAT paddy wagon. They glared at me as they passed. I stared back. Just before they exited Jumbo stopped, turned, and said, "I wouldn't be gloatin' just yet, asshole. This ain't over . . . not by a long fucking shot. This ain't over, I assure you." The DEA agent pushed him forward, losing his hand in the flesh in his massive back. Jumbo Jackson remained unmoved. "Don't be shovin' me, we don't want no police brutality happenin' here," he said to the DEA agent, and finally marched off to the waiting wagon.

Bobby Day was all smiles. He checked his watch. "It's a little after six. Let's go to the Glades; they were supposed to wait until at least six to raid the hangar. We need to grab the mechanics when they show up for work. They'll make great witnesses at the trial."

We jumped into one of the black Suburbans with two DEA agents. Bobby Day put a flashing red and blue light on the roof and switched on the siren. We sped down the runway out onto Opa-Locka Boulevard, onto I-95, and raced down to the Tamiami Trail.

Ten minutes later we were doing ninety miles an hour along the Tamiami Trail. We passed the Miccosukee gambling emporium and entered the Everglades swamp. We passed through the Miccosukee reservation. On the edge of the Big Cypress Swamp we made a hard right, and followed the brand-new blacktop that paralleled the FAA airstrip. We entered the airstrip proper at the control tower turnoff. We passed the compound that held the government swamp buggies, and moved directly to the big blue hangar. There were four brand-new black SWAT Suburbans and a black paddy wagon. The agents were just finishing handcuffing the mechanics and helping them into the paddy wagon.

I walked into the immense hangar with Bobby Day and the two DEA agents. "Jesus, this place is huge."

Two agents dressed in black ninja jumpsuits ran over to us. One of the agents was an FAA agent. He had a fistful of ID plates. The other agent had an armful of logbooks. The first agent said, "This place is a real fucking factory, a chop shop for aircraft. This is a bonanza! I never seen anything like this. Look at that." He pointed at the Gulfstream jet. "That baby is worth millions."

"Where'd you get those plates and logs?" Bobby Day asked.

"Right where we were told to look." He pointed toward a small room. "That room right there. They were actually working on some plates. The engraver couldn't believe his bad luck. I guess he only comes here once or twice a month to engrave the plates."

"You guys sealing everything off?" Bobby Day asked.

"Yeah, we're leaving four agents here for the night, and tomorrow we start going through the records," the FAA agent said. "And we got the physical evidence right here." He waved his arm at the great expanse of the hangar.

Bobby Day and I walked through the hangar. It was a hell of a bust. There was a paint booth where planes were being repainted, and new false fuselage and tail numbers were being painted on. Engines were being replaced or stripped. Other planes had secret compartments for carrying dope being built in; hidden fuel tanks were being welded into the plane or put into the wings.

Avionics were being replaced, stripped, modified—radar, single sideband radios, advanced satellite navigation, and special radios that could intercept federal agency police calls were being installed.

Some of these planes were being modified for sale to the public, like my Grumman Albatross. Others were being modified to sell to sophisticated dopers, or maybe even for John Harrison and the Jackson Hogs to use for smuggling operations for their own account.

Jeff Bacon and his crew had eased into the hangar very surreptitiously. He had dressed in a casual way, as I had told him to. He came over to us as his photographer snapped pictures.

"Who's this?" Bobby Day said.

"Friend of mine," I said.

"Hey, Francisco, this is some operation." He stood next to me. His photographer snapped away.

I introduced him. "Bobby Day meet Jeff Bacon, a friend of mine from the *Miami Sentinel*." I had tipped off the press.

"Hi," Jeff said. "This here shutterbug's Billy Wright, famous crime photographer. That's one hell of an outfit you're wearing there, Mr. Day. Hey, Billy get a shot of this man's outfit."

"Save the picture for later," Bobby Day said, putting his hand up to cover his face. He was obviously shocked. "Nice to meet you both." Bobby finally forced out a smile. "I'm afraid you caught me kind of flat-footed here, Francisco."

"What's the problem?" I asked.

"Well, this is something we hadn't considered," Bobby Day said.

"You think the press wasn't going to cover this? I just thought I'd give Jeff a scoop, that's all," I said.

"We thought we would just issue a press release. Well, let me call Director Fitzgerald and Inspector Greene from the office here. You guys wait here." Bobby made off to the office in a fast trot.

Jeff Bacon pulled me aside. "Hey, Francisco, this is a hell of a story. We got pictures of that John Harrison and those two huge rednecks, the Jacksons. We even got a picture of that Mitzi chick, what a piece of work. Once we started taking pictures and interviewing people she was all over us, thought she might become famous."

Jeff Bacon was in his early thirties, trim, well manicured, highly intelligent—he loved his status as the chief investigative reporter for the *Miami Sentinel*. He was a regular at my nightclub, loved the pretty Latin ladies and the "thirties" atmosphere of the club. The days of Al Capone and the early splendor of Miami Beach—he loved the "Real Cuban" atmosphere.

I had called him over the weekend and we had met. I had explained the story to him, and given him the timing of the raid, the location, the players, and the details of the overall story. I still didn't trust the government. I knew they would have trouble with the coverage and public disclosure on the one hand, and on the other hand they would want the recognition for the bust—career-enhancing publicity. I was nervous about Bobby Day's reaction.

"Look Jeff," I said. "Has Billy here taken a lot of photos?"

"How you doing on the pictures, Billy?"

Billy Wright pulled a handful of shot rolls of film out of the pouch pocket of his safari jacket. They were in plastic canisters. "I got maybe six rolls, plus most of a roll still in the Nikon."

I could see Bobby Day racing out of the office on the far side of the hangar, heading toward us. I said, "Look, switch those rolls with unshot rolls. And give the canisters to Jeff if he asks. I got a bad feeling here." I had to go with my instincts.

"What?" Billy Wright said.

"Billy, just do what Francisco says. We got nothing to lose if we do it his way." Jeff Bacon was smart. He watched his photographer fumble with the rolls of film. He was switching new rolls into the canisters and taking the exposed rolls of film out.

"What the hell do I do with these?" Billy asked.

"Stuff them into your Jockeys," Jeff said. "Let's intercept him. Billy you stay here and finish doing what Francisco says."

I followed Jeff Bacon across the hangar floor. He took his tape recorder microphone out of his pocket.

"No notepad?" I asked.

"Yeah, I got one. Some people hate to be taped— insist on me taking notes. With the tape they can't say I distorted the news. I just play the tape back for them and tell them to fuck off."

We met about fifty feet from where we had been standing. Billy Wright was trailing. He had his back to us. I could see he was reloading his camera.

Bobby Day came running up to me. "Look, guys, my boss says no pictures in here. This is an active and secure police area and both my bosses have had bad experiences with the press. Are you recording me?" Bobby Day said.

"Yeah, I'm recording you," Jeff answered.

"Well, stop." He put his hand over the mouthpiece of the microphone. "Turn it off."

Jeff did as he was told. He was wasting time. "I don't understand. This is news and under the First Amendment I have a right—"

"Well, I'm told to ask you to leave here. This is a secure police location, in an ongoing police investigation, and I'm afraid I have to ask you to leave. The press may impede our investigation."

Bobby Day walked directly toward Billy, who had spun around and started to walk toward us. As he got closer he knelt down on one knee, and fired off about six shots of the three of us walking toward him.

"I'll need to take that film. This is private property and is a restricted police investigation. I have been instructed to take your film. And I want the film you shot up at Opa-Locka; the same thing applies there."

"Excuse me?" Billy said, dumbfounded. "You must be fucking nuts. I'm not giving you my film. Tell him that's the way it is, Jeff. This is my work and it's news."

"I want the film in the camera and the film you already shot," Bobby said.

"Look, you can't take that film. I'll have the *Sentinel* lawyers all over you in a matter of hours; the court will never let you keep that film," Jeff Bacon protested. He was smart; he knew he had to put up a fight or Bobby would be suspicious.

"Come on, what's going on here?" Billy said, pretending to protect his Nikon.

"Look, I'll get some guys over here in a minute, and we'll just take the goddamn film. We can fight about it later," Bobby Day said.

"No, let's give it up," Jeff said, "on one condition."

"Which is?" Bobby said.

"That you promise not to lose or damage the film."

"You got my word on that; now give me the film in the camera and the other film you shot."

Billy Wright fast-forwarded the film, and slipped it into an empty canister. When he was done, he handed the film to Bobby Day.

"And all the stuff you shot at Opa-Locka."

Billy looked pleadingly to Jeff for support. "Do what he says," Jeff mumbled.

Billy reached in the pocket of his safari jacket and withdrew a large handful of plastic canisters that contained film. He handed them to Bobby, who said, "Now, let me look in your camera bag."

Bobby went through the film in the bag, making sure the remaining film canisters were still factory-sealed. He handed the bag back to Billy. "Look, fellas, I'm just doing my job here. It's nothing personal."

"Just following orders, huh," Billy said indignantly, rearranging the contents of his bag. He was enjoying his role now.

"So," Jeff Bacon said, smiling for the first time in a while. "I guess this means an interview with you is out of the question."

"That's good." Bobby was smiling now. "I'm afraid—"

"You're going to have to ask us to leave," Jeff Bacon said, finishing the sentence. "Well, it won't be the first time I've been asked to leave somewhere. I guess that's part of doing a good job."

Bobby Day and I stood there in the middle of the hangar watching them walk away. When Billy Wright had passed safely through the exit door, Jeff Bacon waved me over. I jogged across the concrete hangar floor.

When I got there, Jeff said, "I just wanted you to know that Billy says to tell you he really enjoyed those film canisters rolling around in his Jockeys—he might just leave them there on a regular basis and tell his friends about them." Jeff smiled, "Thanks for the scoop," he said, turned, and walked through the door. Billy Wright was already sitting in the car.

I passed through the door and watched them pull away. Why didn't I feel more elated? I had done two terrific things today. I had busted these guys that had almost killed me, and I had kept my temper in check and not done anything stupid. So why didn't I feel elated, happy, satisfied, smug, any fucking thing? I just felt flat . . . and I had a grim sense of foreboding. I went back into the hangar and caught up to Bobby Day at the Gulfstream.

He was under the wing, where the missing engine was on a hoist being repaired. He was looking at the blades inside the engine. His green pants and bright yellow shirt contrasted with the whiteness of the airplane. He talked with his head stuck in the open mouth of the jet engine. His voice resonated, echoing, like he was inside a tunnel. "Francisco, I don't appreciate it that you called in the press and didn't tell us. I don't think that was your call." He pulled his head out of the open maw of the engine and looked at me. "No, sir, I didn't like that and neither did my bosses. Why didn't you tell us?"

"Because you would have acted just like you're acting now?"

"Which is?"

"You're acting like you don't like anything you can't control," I said.

"And you, Francisco, you like things you can't control."

"I have to like them because in reality I control very little."

"Bullshit. Now what were you trying to accomplish by calling in the media?"

"I think the public should know if there's a chance they could be up there in the air, like I was, flying around in an aluminum coffin."

"Please, that's why we're involved, that's the job of the FAA, to protect the public from just what you're talking about."

"Bobby, why don't you drive up to Golden Beach and give my wife that speech—tell her what a great job you did protecting her." He stepped down the ladder, out of the mouth of the jet. I continued. I was angry. "Look around you here, at this place. You're only here because I gave you those Cessna ID plates. And this is an airport facility controlled by the FAA, leased to a bunch of bad guys."

"Don't break your fucking arm patting yourself on the back. The FAA is basically everywhere where there are airplanes, so it's no surprise we are out here and these assholes lease from us. We are in thousands of locations and we're understaffed, overworked, and just as full of bureaucratic bullshit as any other federal agency. Just 'cause we called you in to help us out, don't think you're fucking Dick Tracy or some junior G-Man."

A thousand responses flashed through my mind, but I had been down this road before. Anger is a tool in the human arsenal of emotions like many others, one that I was familiar with. This venting was doing nobody any good.

I took a cleansing deep calming breath and smiled at him. "Look, you'll have to admit this has been a hell of a good day. So why don't we take 'yes, we did it' for an answer and pat each other on the back. This is a hell of a result, a bunch of arrests, hard evidence, broke up a major plane chop-shop operation, and stopped a bunch of dope planes from getting into the air."

He smiled back at me. "Right. Let's get those two other agents and head back to Opa-Locka. I got that great red Rolls convertible for one more night before I have to turn it in to the DEA confiscation unit."

"Well, I'll treat you to dinner at my restaurant tonight. We wouldn't want this great outfit to be put away without some more people seeing it," I said, fingering the plaid sports coat he was carrying on his arm.

"Well, that sounds like a deal," he said, patting me on the back. I patted him back.

The two agents, sweating in their black ninja jump

suits, climbed into the backseat of the Suburban. We backed up slowly from the hangar and passed the other law enforcement vehicles. Bobby drove very slowly, as if he was savoring this moment. The control tower loomed ahead. The three-story tower was made of plywood, and dark-tinted floor-to-ceiling windows made up the top floor.

He was standing outside, leaning against the wall next to the tower door. The sun was setting so the light was a yellow red from the sinking fireball. His hair was dirty blond, long, and slicked back with some kind of gel. His sunglasses were lifted from his eyes and propped on the top of his head, buried in his hair. His face was uncommonly handsome, tanned, full of angular planes, with a sharp hawklike nose. His eyes were blue with a wild, feral, look, and he didn't blink. His face showed no expression, but you knew his eyes missed nothing. He wore a red and dark blue Hawaiian shirt with tropical fish splayed all over in a blast pattern like they had been put there with a print-paint shotgun.

The wind was wafting in from the east, and you could see the faint impression of his shoulder holster under his shirt, if you knew what to look for. He wore white shorts and rope sandals. His eyes were on us. I could see a pair of high-powered binoculars in his left hand. He had been watching us during the raid.

"Who's that?" I asked.

"Don't know," Bobby said. "Never seen him before."

"Looks like a spook," I said.

"Spook?"

"Yeah, you're too young to know about Vietnam, but that's what we called Company men, spooks."

"CIA?"

"Yeah, CIA, NSC, who knew? And they all had Army ranks, officers, usually above a captain, so they could get Army personnel to do what they told them to do."

"You ever do any of that stuff when you were over there?"

"No." I lied, and thoughts of the Swamp Master entered my mind.

We were moving very slowly. I turned in the passenger seat to look back at him. He had moved off the wall and was turned, looking after us. His face was glowing in the setting sun. It was the face of pure evil. I shuddered, and turned back to face forward. I looked in the mirror. His gaze was on us, like an ice-cold blue laser. I shivered again and looked forward.

I did not look back in the mirror. I knew I would see him again.

Chapter Six

Anticipated feelings often contradict reality—I thought I would be elated as I watched Lillian read the story on the second page of the *Miami Sentinel*. The headline read:

MAJOR AIRPLANE FRAUD BUST IN OPA-LOCKA AND EV-ERGLADES.

There were pictures and a full story. It was front-page news, yet it wound up on page two. Jeff Bacon told me that it had been put on page two at the last minute—orders from the publisher. Lillian read the article carefully; it was her first knowledge of what had been going on.

"Seventeen arrests," Lillian said, looking up from the newspaper. "Are these two men as fat as they look in this picture?"

"Fatter." I smiled.

"And all these planes in this hangar were being altered?"

"Yes."

"Hard to believe that we would buy our plane from this group. So, our plane was a combination of a lot of other planes."

"Yes, there is a field full of them, and they just stripped the parts, like fishing in the junkyard," I answered.

"How could we get the airworthiness certificate?"

"Florida Private Planes was licensed properly with the FAA, and they have a licensed mechanic, so they could legally issue the certificates."

"So, it was all false, the logbook showing the engine hours, the identification plates—everything." She looked out the window from her bed, the ocean crashing on the beach as a storm formed out at sea. "Francisco, we were doomed, weren't we—that airplane was an accident waiting for its time."

"Yes, and according to the first glance by the FAA, there are over a hundred planes just like ours, with phony documentation."

She dropped the newspaper and looked at me. "Why didn't you tell me you were doing this?"

"You had your own problems, and I didn't know if it would succeed. Your job is to get better," I said.

"I hate it when you talk like that," she said. "My job is to get better—please! How patronizing. Why does everyone treat me like I should be protected. Richard, my father, now you—you all treat me like I was a precious orchid in a hothouse, tended by you, but not allowed outside, outside in the wild with the other flowers."

"I don't know, Lillian, maybe you bring that out in men."

"Orchids are very strong, stronger than people think. They grow in the wild and they withstand storms, lack of rainfall, blight, hurricanes, and they have been around for thousands and thousands of years."

"Lillian, it's possible for a woman to be too beautiful, you know. And it's a normal male instinct to protect his woman."

"Don't protect me anymore." Her voice rose, "Please!" Tears formed in her eyes. "Richard, and now you—protecting me from the world. Well, maybe I want to see what the world is like. And I hate it, Francisco, that you couldn't tell me what you were doing. You were in danger, real danger, and you thought I shouldn't know. You come to me now, now that it's over, and expect me to say: Oh, darling, you were so nice to keep this from me while you were doing it, thank you. And now I get to read about it in the goddamn newspaper."

"Lillian, I—"

"I know, you thought you were doing the right thing. Suppose I was reading that you had been killed or injured. Do you think this is what a relationship should be—one person telling the other person only those things he thinks she should know?"

"You were sick, hurt, recovering—"

"Suppose it had been reversed, with you strapped in this goddamn bed. Suppose I had gone out, and acted like some secret agent. Suppose I had tried to get revenge for what had happened to you, and I didn't tell you—the person who had been really injured. You

173

would like that? I think not—you would be scream-ing."

"I didn't think of it that way."

"Of course not. You think that women are delicate little flowers to be treated like special creatures—"

"Look, I'm not going to just sit here and take this—I did what I thought was the right thing," I said.

"Yes, you did—you did what *you* thought was the right goddamn thing." She bunched the newspaper into a big ball in her fist and threw it at me. "You're running everything. That's what you're really telling me, isn't it? You're in control. I get to see the parts of life that you think I can handle, and our partnership is not really a partnership. I get included on what *you* think I can handle. Francisco, I won't have it this way anymore. We're a team or we are not a team. We can't be a team if it's only you who decides when we should be a team."

"I thought I was doing the right thing."

"That's lame, Francisco." Her eyes were filling, glis-tening in the light. She wiped them with a Kleenex.

"What do you want, Lillian?"

"I want to live, really live. No veneer. No steel wall to protect me. I want to live the way everybody else has to live. I want to feel life—be truly alive in this world. That was what we were going to do anyway, go away and see the world—the real world—before the acci-dent, wasn't it?"

"Yes. We were going to travel the world, help people, and live life to the fullest."

"Well, maybe we can still do it somehow, Francisco. At least we can start right here, right now."

I got up and kissed her gently on the lips, and slipped

my arms around her, sat on the edge of the bed and held her close to me. I felt the cool ocean breeze waft in from the open windows; heard the quiet sound of the pounding surf.

"If you want to be a full partner with me, you have a deal," I whispered. I could feel her cool hand move up to the base of my neck. "From now on I will tell you everything—everything."

She brushed her lips against my face and spoke into my ear. "That's what I want, everything." I held her close.

The phone broke our solitude. I slipped my arms from around Lillian.

"Hello," I said.

"Hey, podna, how they hanging?" the Swamp Master said.

"Fine." I could hear the voices of his children in the background.

"Glad to hear it. I read the *Sentinel*. Nice picture of the Jackson Hogs and John Harrison. Seventeen arrests shoulda been front-page."

"Well, I'm glad its over. I still owe you the last payment."

"Nah. I got a good paycheck from them boys. I quit when you called me, got my check and cashed it. So, I'm right as rain on a summer day in the Great Swamp. How's about comin' out here, and we'll go spear some frogs at night."

"Sounds great," I said.

"Yeah, well you know where I'm at." I could hear one of the kids crying. "I gotta go now, settle a family matter . . . big fight over control of the new Sony Play Station. See ya."

"See ya," I said, and hung up.

The phone rang again just as the receiver settled into the cradle.

"Hello."

"Francisco, that you?"

"Yeah."

"Bobby Day here." There was a pause. "I need to see you."

"Why."

"I need to see you in person."

"Why in person?"

"I hate phones—that's why."

"You spend most of your life on a phone, don't you? You'll have to come to Miami."

"I'll be there at six. Where should we meet?"

"The Versailles restaurant in Little Havana, on Calle Ocho."

"I know the place."

"See you in an hour."

The Versailles in Little Havana is a landmark. It serves the finest Cuban food in Miami—as good as my place. When Reagan was President he ate there when he visited Miami . . . so did George Bush. The pictures are hung prominently to prove the point. It was a hot and steamy Miami day. The men stood at the coffee bar drinking espresso and talking politics as I walked in.

Bobby was already sitting at a quiet corner table near the kitchen. The smells were great: cooking meat, coffee, rice, and garlic. There was a large potted palm tree on either side of the kitchen doorway, both acting like sentries to insure a confidential conversation. He forced a smile when he saw me, but I could see he was grim and glum.

"Hey, Francisco—how's it going?" He was dressed in a navy blue blazer, white shirt, and blue jeans, the federal officers' casual attire. He dressed right for every occasion, not like your standard federal agent.

"All right," I said as I sat down. "I miss those green pants, and your plaid sports coat." I smiled.

"Well, I miss my white shoes the most; it's unlikely I'll get another chance to wear them," he said, signaling the waitress. "Drink?"

The waitress arrived. "*Café con leche* will work," I said. "What's up, Bobby?"

"Bad news. My boss, Inspector Greene, he came to me this morning and told me that all the charges were going to be dropped down to misdemeanors and pled out."

"All of them?"

"No. Some of them will be dismissed."

"What's going on here, Bobby?"

"Seems we raided one of our own; that whole setup was our own operation, an undercover U.S. Customs play."

"What are you saying?" I said, and then waited for the waitress to place the cup of coffee on the table. "You're FAA and DEA, and you did not know it was a Customs operation?"

"Well, not exactly."

"Not exactly? Please cut the bullshit and let me know what's going on here," I said.

"One week before the raid, Inspector Greene got a

call from Rick Jacoby at U.S. Customs, and Jacoby told him to lay off. He had heard through the grapevine that the FAA and the DEA were sniffing around Florida Private Planes. Greene told him to put the request for us to stop in writing—officially tell us that we should lay off and identify it as a Customs undercover."

"Lay off?" I said.

"More like 'fuck off,' but Jacoby wouldn't put anything in writing, so we just went ahead with the raid."

"So this turns out to be some kind of pissing contest—one of those mine-is-bigger-than-yours kind of arguments. And why did you come to me, enlist my help?"

"Inspector Greene got the call after you and I were already undercover—the boys at Florida Private Planes didn't know we were agents. They believed our story and we believed they were dirty."

"But if it was an undercover operation, why didn't they just bust us for trying to buy an illegal aircraft to smuggle drugs?" I asked.

"We don't know."

"This all stinks. I still don't get it. I bought a goddamn plane from Florida Private Planes. I paid real U.S. cash, and they sold me a mechanically fucked-up, illegally altered, but properly papered airplane."

"Francisco, I understand. Look, everybody's embarrassed here. The fucking DEA was out of the loop—just like us at the FAA."

"Who wants to be in their goddamn loop? These guys are modifying aircraft any way they want. There's dope smuggling involved. They're selling these fucked airplanes and making a goddamn fortune. You better explain this a whole lot better than you have so far."

"It ain't easy, my friend."

"You know it makes me want to puke. Try," I said.

"All right, it's a Customs buy-bust operation. You know how they work?"

"Tell me."

"Okay, a doper pilot gets busted by Customs for flying contraband for some asshole big-shot doper. He's given two choices—door number one is: go straight to jail for about fifteen fucking years and kiss a good part of your life good-bye. Or try door number two—come to work for the U.S. Customs as an operative, a CI, a confidential informant, an undercover asset—they got lots of different names for them. These doper pilots become part of a secret buy-bust squad, working out of a location like Florida Private Planes, and they set about working off their beef."

"I'm getting it. . . ."

"Yeah, so let's say, for example, you have to fly three good missions for us at Customs. You're a known dope-smuggling pilot, so you go to your regular sources, big-time dopers in Mexico, Colombia, Venezuela, Peru, Ecuador, and get a job flying dope for them. Then after they get the job the CI's, the assets, the operatives, the . . ."

"The arrested pilots—now are unofficial Customs agents."

"Right. They come to their handlers and give them the skinny, then a buy-bust is set up. They're supposed to fly in the dope to the U.S.A. with a transponder stuck on the plane somewhere, so it can be tracked in the air—they are given a clearance corridor so they can fly through the protective air screen, and when they land the bust is supposed to happen and arrests are made—simple enough."

"These pilots are Americans?"

"Yes, mostly, a few Jamaicans, Colombians, Mexicans—but very few."

"And in addition to working off the beef, do they get anything else?"

"Yes, they sometimes get money if cash and dope is grabbed in the bust, and sometimes they get the airplane that was used."

"With modified papers, logbooks, airworthiness certificates, the works—just like I got," I said.

"Yeah, we suspect that's the case, but we have trouble proving it. We also think this is nationwide, with these kind of operations in Texas, California, New Mexico."

"Border states."

"Yeah, border states."

"So, I get fucked twice," I said. "I buy the plane, almost lose my wife and my own life in the crash. I lose my money—then like an asshole I help you guys on an undercover sting against one of our own federal agencies—U.S. Customs—so I'm a two-time loser."

"Look, we really didn't know about it being an undercover operation."

"Bullshit. You had a warning from this Jacoby that you didn't heed. I want my money back from the U.S. government, the two hundred and fifty thousand I gave them for the original Albatross," I said.

"I know how you feel."

"Bobby, how could you know how I feel? My wife is

suffering every day—she's five miles from here bedridden and in pain. I go ahead and help you—hell, I even bring the goddamn flash money."

"Francisco, we made the raid, the arrests, we thought we had a legit case."

"It is a legit case, for Christsake; they modified those planes and—"

"There is a statute that Congress passed that allows the government to modify airplanes for undercover use."

"I'm aware of that statute, Bobby, but they are supposed to bring the planes back to the original condition, like they were before they modified them. Selling me a plane with switched, bad fucking engines, forged logbooks, a phoney ID plate, and a bullshit airworthiness certificate is not my idea of bringing the fucking plane back to its original condition."

"Hey, Francisco, I know you're upset."

"Upset? I get played for a fool by *everybody,* and you think I'm upset?"

"All right, angry."

"God, you feds all have ice water for blood. I want that fucking money back."

"Francisco, it is very difficult to sue the federal government."

"Criminally it may be an impossibility to sue, but civilly—just watch me, Bobby."

"Francisco, look, if you sue on a civil level—"

"Yeah, I know it will all come out—the whole stinking mess."

"So, just cool off. We'll talk tomorrow." He finished his drink.

I took a deep cleansing breath, trying to calm down. "Bobby, for what it's worth I think you are a stand-up guy, and I appreciate your coming here to tell me this yourself. I know it can't be easy."

"Like I say, why don't you just chill for a while and we can talk tomorrow."

"What will I know tomorrow that I don't know today?"

"I don't know, Francisco. I'm a little fucked up here too, my emotions are spinning. I spent a lot of time on this, time before you came into the picture."

Bobby paid the bill, and we walked out into the evening warmth. You could smell the ozone in the air from the ocean, and the quarter moon was visible in the early night sky.

"Francisco, there is one other thing."

"Yeah?"

We walked to where our cars were parked. Bobby spoke. "Rick Jacoby, the Customs agent, told Inspector Greene that a couple of guys evidently broke into the Everglades facility one night last week, took some Cessna ID plates. The surveillance cameras were evidently unable to record their faces, but the security people gave pursuit. Know anything about that?"

"Bobby, please, now you're starting to upset me. Did they also tell you about a C-130 landing in the dead of night with what looked like a huge load of coke?"

"No. They never mentioned anything like that."

"Selective memory."

"Francisco, I think maybe this is a real cluster fuck—what's going on here? You know what I mean?"

"Yeah, I'm familiar with the term—a bunch of feds all fucking with each other."

"Francisco, don't get caught in the cross fire."

"Don't make waves, is that what you're telling me?"

"You're a big boy. You were in Nam, right?"

"Yeah."

"So you got a taste of how complex the federal monster can get when it's unleashed."

"So, we just leave the playing field to the big players?" I said.

"You might want to think about it."

"I'll think about it, all right."

I got into the Ferrari. I had the top off. I drove home along South Beach—Collins Avenue. I remembered when Miami Beach was the winter mecca for New York with the big hotels featuring Jackie Gleason, Frank Sinatra, Jerry Lewis, and Dean Martin, and I saw that change when Las Vegas and Atlantic City exploded as pleasure centers. I watched Miami Beach then turn into old-age homes, mostly for Jewish people. The porches filled every afternoon with hundreds of old folks sitting in aluminum rocking chairs with nylon strapping, waiting to die.

Then the Mariel boat lift happened, when Fidel tricked Jimmy Carter and the United States into accepting thousands of people. Fidel emptied his jails, his mental institutions tossed out the last of the middle class that could give him trouble. My cousin Dario went to Key West with the money of three families, and a list of our relatives, sixty thousand dollars for forty family members—fifteen hundred dollars a head—the going rate to get a boat and captain.

Dario hired a shrimp boat with captain and crew. He came back from Mariel with the shrimp boat overflowing with people. Two insane men were lashed to the wheelhouse, plus ten prostitutes still working their trade on the boat, thirty handcuffed prisoners from Fidel's jails, thirty confused old and infirm people taken from old-age homes—people with no family, twenty scared orphaned children, two doctors, and four lawyers. And four family members who were actually on his list.

Many of the Marielitos, as they were called, the criminal element, when they were released from the Krome detention center at the edge of the Everglades, headed straight for Miami Beach. They went there to carry on their criminal enterprises of: robbery, assault, dope dealing, prostitution, home invasions, stealing cars, and other mayhem including murder.

No one was happier than the Miami Beach Police when Hollywood, the New York gay community, and assorted actors, actresses, super-models, and their agencies bought homes and businesses at depressed prices in what they renamed South Beach.

Within a few years the old folks disappeared as the price of the real estate climbed and the old art deco hotels got refurbished. It soon became a trendy destination spot to get a glimpse at the rich, the weird, and the famous.

I pulled into our driveway. It was about ten o'clock. I looked in on Lillian. She was sleeping. I would tell her what happened tomorrow. I was too uptight to sleep.

I walked into my closet and checked out my suits. I

loved the thirties, forties, and fifties. My suits were all custom-made by the best Cuban tailors. I kept my closet in perfect order. I had about thirty suits. All perfectly cleaned and pressed, hanging on wooden hangars. The suits had wide lapels and some were double-breasted. The legs were straight, with cuffed pants. I love shoes and boots. I guess maybe it's a Spanish thing. My shoes were made by Argentinians who lived in Miami. I also like Italian shoes—Ferragamo and Bruno Magli—and I had several shoes that were two-toned, white and black, brown and white, two shades of gray. The shirts were silk, linen, and Egyptian cotton, blues, whites, light green, subtle stripes, and yellows.

I checked my ties; they were wide in the style of the thirties and forties, which was now back in vogue. Each tie was individually hung on a small peg. I had several hundred. I collected ties. I had about thirty sports jackets and thirty pairs of slacks, hung by the cuffs on special hangers—no blue jeans, I did not own one single pair.

See, my major Cuban hero was Desi Arnaz. I never told anyone. I just kept it as my secret. His career was swallowed up and overshadowed by the *I Love Lucy* show, but before that he was a great Cuban bandleader and singer.

Desi also loved the ladies and they loved him. It was what eventually ruined his marriage with Lucille Ball. His energy came right out through his voice, and when he played the big conga drum he was as sexy as a Latin singer gets. The women would swoon when he sang. He was the Frank Sinatra of the Hispanic world. I had all his records and I had collected as much film as I could get on him. He was a terrific musician and a great performer. He was also a fabulous dresser. I secretly emulated him. I even copied his stage moves and the way he danced. Desi Arnaz was my little secret, and by my admiration for him I was in a weird way keeping him alive. He lived on through me. That was my attitude. My father loved him, and it was my father who started the collection of his records.

Above on the rack over the clothes I had about a dozen hats, mostly Panama hats.

At the end of my closet was my thirty-year-old black tunic from the seminary. I had always kept it as a symbol, a reminder of my time alone with God, and the disciples of God. I went to it and felt the material, rolled the black buttons between my fingers. Seminary life was perhaps the best time of my life. I loved the orderliness of the life—the routines, the discipline, the way we ate at exact times, the constant hum of prayers, the absolute stillness that can be made by forty men, silently praying, examining their lives . . . my sinful life, my spiritual life, my cultural life, my life looking only for peace and tranquillity . . . my days in the seminary.

The discipline of life in the seminary in Havana calmed me, soothed me, made me feel safe. Life was planned carefully, but at the same time I was totally satisfied. I was free in a way I cannot explain, not even to myself. But perhaps it was also because I was innocent. It was before women entered my life, and Vietnam, and business, and singing, and the pursuit of money, and that evil heady feeling of ego and power. The seminary was during my age of innocence. I wondered if it was ever possible for a person to prolong that age of innocence, and what good does it do a man to know so much of life, when knowing is never as satisfying as those days of innocence—maybe ignorance is bliss, like those days in the seminary.

I placed the black tunic back in the rack. I thought of Lillian and our discussion, about her wanting to know more, not to be protected and sheltered, to get into the essence of life, the reality of life—God made life so complex for us all. I thought. What was the reason?

I decided to go to the club. I needed to sing. I needed to exercise my voice, get into words and images, beautiful lyrics written by word masters, the poets of our time. And melodies crafted and constructed by people with music in their souls. That would bring me down, calm me. I did not want to think about what was going on in my life. My mind was racing, racing like a high-performance engine.

I took a robin's-egg-blue suit off the rack, a white shirt, a blue and white tie, and black shoes and belt—forty minutes later I was in the club. Desi Arnaz would have loved it. I wished I could sing with him, just one time, but that was not going to be.

It was a Wednesday night, the night of the open mike, and the Hola Havana night club restaurant was crowded, not packed, but full. I talked to Jaime Ortega, who was busy with the kitchen.

Our chef, Jorge, had become very temperamental since his wife left him. Jaime was in the kitchen reassuring him that his wife would get rid of her young lover and return to him—Jorge was waving his knife telling Jaime that he would cut the young man's heart out—or worse.

"Hey, Jaime," I said, interrupting. Jorge went back to cooking, stirring a big pot of black beans and rice. I walked with Jaime to the kitchen door. "Good house tonight."

"Yes, thank God in heaven, business gets better all the time. You know, many people come to hear you sing."

"It's nice to know that, Jaime."

"Well, it's true. You singing tonight? Billy's on the piano. We got a beautiful trio."

"Yes, I saw Billy. Jorge is still upset about his wife."

"Worse. It's getting worse and I think he's helping himself to the cooking wine."

"Maybe you had better get back to him."

"Jorge's still the best chef of Cuban cuisine in South Florida."

"Yeah, and he's like family."

"But his mother was Italian—what a combo—the Italian mambo king," I said, slipping through the waiters' door, out of the kitchen and into the club. Jorge, our chef, was a great mambo dancer, and if the music from the club was right he would mambo in the kitchen, grabbing the waitresses for a turn or two as they entered and exited. Everyone loved it, but Jorge was not doing the mambo now; his wife had run away with a handsome polo player from Argentina.

Hola Havana. I loved the sound of it. Billy Rodriguez was the house piano player. He was from New York, semi-retired. Billy had learned his music playing in Harlem. Billy had played at the Cotton Club. He had played with Duke Ellington, Billie Holiday, and Cab Calloway. Billy had been taught by his mother, and had played with the Count Basie band when the Count was Frank Sinatra's main band. Billie had played with Duke Ellington at Carnegie Hall and Billy Eckstein at the Plaza Hotel in New York. He had a great touch on the piano and could drift from the blues to the hottest Latin rhythms. The music lived inside him. He was a big man, a handsome mulatto, over six feet and trim as a soccer player.

The mike was empty, so I grabbed it. I began with a Cole Porter tune in Spanish. The trio was piano, bass, and drums. I held the last note, full and firm, an A, for an extra several beats. Billy stayed with me on the piano. The crowd stayed with me also, responding with applause at the end.

I broke into "Guantanamera," which is a love song about a Marine stationed at the U.S. Guantanamo base leased from Cuba. The Marine expresses his love for a Cuban girl who he can only meet at the barbed-wire fence that separates the base from Cuba. I played it to a special beat that the trio knew and I started slow, increasing the tempo and the volume. The crowd went crazy as I came to the end. Singing was my salvation. It calmed me and brought my thoughts together.

The stage lights were normal, so I could see clearly out into the crowd. People were dressed up—decked out. It was good to see in Florida, where cut-off shorts and T-shirts are the norm.

My eyes cruised the tables. It was a perfect Little Havana crowd, mostly couples, some families, average age late forties, lots of money, fun-loving, easygoing group, self-made successes, enjoying their largesse.

My eyes moved to the upper tier in the back row, to two men seated at the furthest table, under a small pinpoint-lit plastic areca palm. Their faces glowed in the flickering candle. It was him. Hair slicked back, off-white suit, opened collar, tasteful Hawaiian shirt of reds and oranges that contrasted with his tanned face, the angular planes reflecting in the light of the candle. He looked wolflike. His eyes and facial muscles gave off no expression. He did not blink as he stared at me.

His companion was a stocky man in a beige suit with a white shirt and a dark nondescript tie. His body was powerful. His suit was at least one size too small. He gave the impression of a man who was about to burst out of his clothes and pound his naked chest like a wild gorilla. His face was beefy and looked worn, like it had been in the sun too long, or out on the mean streets through the hail and the rain.

Jaime came up with a note in his outstretched hand. "From the gentlemen in the last row, under the palm tree."

I took the note, The printing was precise. It said: "Francisco Cruz, come and join us for a drink." It was not signed. My curiosity overwhelmed me. There was a couple I knew who sang mambo songs waiting to come to the stage. I handed them the microphone and smiled. "Billy, carry on with Lisette and Jose. I have to talk with someone."

I stepped off the stage and went directly to their table. The stocky man in the beige suit spoke first. "Hey, Mr. Francisco Cruz, how's it goin'? My name is Rick Jacoby, and this here's Mr. Burton." Jacoby extended his hand, without rising. I shook it. Mr. Burton made no move. "How 'bout you sit down, and join us for a drink."

When I sat, Mr. Burton extended his hand. "Michael Burton, call me Michael—all right if I call you Francisco?"

"Sure," I said, forcing a smile. His handshake was cool, like squeezing a bag of ice cubes. His eyes were blue almost black, bottomless and unreadable.

"You sing very well, Francisco," Michael Burton said.

"Thanks."

"Good food—just like Cuba in the old days. Nice place too, a supper club a man would be proud to own," he said. "You must make a good living."

"I've seen you someplace before, haven't I?" I asked Michael.

"Maybe," Michael said, looking me square in the eyes. "Can't remember where."

Rick Jacoby said, "I'm with U.S. Customs and we think maybe that you were involved with a little bust-out at Opa-Locka and down in the Glades, and we come here to explain some things to you, so you would understand better."

"Explain away, Mr. Jacoby," I said, holding onto my rising anger.

"Well, what you got involved in out there was an undercover United States Customs operation. It's an important operation to the U.S. Government that has been very productive in the war on drugs, and we need for it to continue in operation. So, Francisco, you will find out in a day or so that most of the people that were arrested will be released on lesser charges or just released period."

"And you didn't want things stirred up, like with the *Miami Sentinel* story."

"Something like that," Burton said.

"And you, Michael, you with Customs?" I asked.

"Indirectly."

Agent Jacoby continued. "Like I was saying, we got a lot invested in that operation, and so we figured you should know."

"How'd you know I would be here tonight?" I asked.

"We took a chance," Burton said. "We know Wednesday is when the mike is open to most people, and we figured you would be here to act as a master of ceremonies. Just a guess; besides, we were hungry for Cuban food." He smiled that feral smile of his.

"Am I under surveillance?" I asked.

"Not really," Burton said.

"Do you ever answer a question directly?" I asked.

"On occasion," Michael Burton answered.

"Well, I guess we're just lucky that we found you," Jacoby said.

"I guess so," I said. "So, what you're about to tell me is that it was an undercover buy-bust drug operation, and that's why you needed the airport location."

"Buy-bust? Where did you get that expression from?" Burton asked.

"I don't know, why?" I said.

"It's kind of an internal thing, a term used by people in our business," Rick Jacoby said, gulping the last of his vodka on the rocks. He signaled for another drink. He was built rock-solid. I guessed his height at about five ten and his weight to be over two hundred, but he wasn't fat. He was a compact mass of muscle and nerves. He gave off a kind of strange electrical, high-tension type of energy. His eyes seemed to dart from thing to thing, like a hummingbird looking for a place to rest, and his hands were never still, his legs seemed to always be in motion, even though he was seated. The opposite of Michael Burton, the exact opposite kind of energy. They made for a scary pair.

"That's not important, Francisco. What is important is that you fully understand you interfered with an essential sanctioned government undercover operation."

"Hey, listen. I was brought into this by another federal agency, the FAA, after my plane crashed, a defective plane I bought from Florida Private Planes, your fucking operation. A Grumman Albatross. The original engines had been switched, the logbook forged, the ID plate forged, it had a welded propeller that could have split off in flight, and the airworthiness certificate was falsely issued.

"So, please don't give me this stupid line of bullshit that I somehow interfered with you. It seems that you interfered with me." I paused to take a deep breath, to regain my cool. "You guys don't talk to each other? The fucking DEA and the FAA raid an undercover U.S. Customs operation—it's like the Three Stooges meet the Keystone Cops."

"We know you're emotional about this, Francisco," Burton said in a soothing, highly patronizing tone of voice. "No need to be insulting. We are aware of what happened to your wife and you have our sympathies."

"Look, if you are trying to somehow piss me off or

scare me or get me to disappear, all you have to do is ask me. Is that what you want? Is that why you're here?"

"I guess you could put it that way, Francisco," Rick Jacoby answered.

"And you, Mr. Michael Burton? Is that what you say?"

"Your absence would not be missed," he answered.

"Well, I'll tell you what. I really don't give a shit about your undercover drug buy-bust operation. That's your business, but what I do not appreciate is that you are selling fucked-up airplanes to guys like me, airplanes that are flying death traps. See, I happened to buy one of these death traps for two hundred and fifty thousand dollars and it crashed and almost killed my wife. Less that five miles from here my wife sits confined to her bed in great pain and may have trouble walking for the rest of her life. So, I naturally wonder: 'What's with you guys—coming in here? You got a hell of a nerve!' "

"We're trying to avoid any further trouble, Francisco," Michael said.

"And you, Michael, you don't look like a Customs guy to me. You look like a fucking spook, like one of those CIA geeks I used to fly around in Vietnam. You don't look like a Customs agent. How deep does this shit run?"

"Well, I don't know what a spook is, or what a Customs agent looks like, Francisco," Michael Burton said, "And we certainly did not want to upset you. We just wanted to give you a better understanding of what was going on, what you had inadvertently wandered into."

"I think maybe I know now exactly what I've wandered into," I said.

"I wonder if you really do know," Michael Burton said.

"I don't like the direction this conversation is going. What about my airplane and the money I lost?"

"What about it?" Rick Jacoby said.

"How do I get compensated, since the fraud was perpetrated under the auspices of an approved government operation."

"Francisco, all you have to do is fill out an official claim form for damage, injury, or death—its Form 1105. You send it to the Department of Justice, Torts Branch," Michael Burton said.

"What are you saying, you will hand-carry this through the Department of Justice, make sure I will get paid?"

"Can't say that," Jacoby offered. "Wouldn't be legit to do something like that. We can't interfere with the operation of another branch of the U.S. Government."

"I see," I said. "You wouldn't want to do anything that wasn't legit, would you?"

"No, sir, not us," Jacoby said with a big grin. "No, sireee."

"So, I sue the government, which is practically iron-plated and bullet-proof when it comes to civil law suits, and I spend fifty grand on lawyers, waste a year or two, and get nowhere."

"Hey, look here, Francisco, we didn't make the legal process, so don't be getting your back up with us," Jacoby said.

"I suggest you follow legal channels, Francisco."

Burton said, "It's always better that way."

"Better for who?" I asked.

"Better for whom?" Burton corrected my grammar.

"I think, it's maybe better mostly for you, Mr. Cruz," Jacoby said.

"There's one other thing, Francisco," Michael said. "It concerns a Mr. Sawyer Pinder, known locally as the Swamp Master."

"What about him?"

"The asshole got a job at Florida Private Planes as a mechanic and quit the day before the raid," Jacoby said.

"Why do you call him an asshole?" I asked. "You look like the asshole to me."

"Easy, easy there, Francisco. These are just probes for information. No need getting your back up like a scalded cat," Michael said.

"See, there was a break-in at the Florida Private Planes hangar in the Glades and some ID plates were stolen," said Jacoby.

"Breaking and entering is a crime, Francisco. Even worse if it's a federal installation," Burton added.

"So is falsifying documentation, altering airplanes, and smuggling drugs," I blurted.

"Smuggling drugs is what we are trying to prevent with this operation," Michael said. "Why do you say we are smuggling drugs?"

"Well, maybe not drugs." I quickly realized he was trying to trap me into saying something about the C-130 we saw unloading that night in the Everglades.

"Do you have any evidence to the contrary about drug smuggling?" Burton asked.

"Never mind what I have. You guys are going too far here."

"Well, if you do have any information of illegal activities, please let us know."

"You guys are over the top, out of fucking control," I said.

"I don't know what you mean," Michael said. "What we do know is that it was Sawyer Pinder that rescued you from the crash scene in the Everglades. It was on the police report, and we know you are married to a very wealthy woman."

The reference to Lillian took me to the top of my ability to control myself. Even though I knew they were trying to bait me, I still had to put my hands in my coat pockets to control myself. "I'm through with this conversation. I would like you to pay your tab, and leave my club," I said, rising to leave.

"We'll leave," Michael Burton said, standing. He reached in his pocket and withdrew a hundred-dollar bill. He slipped it under the candle and nodded at Jacoby, who immediately rose. Jabobi was a couple of inches shorter than me, but only inches from my face.

"You know, Francisco, you got a certain arrogance to you—like your some kinda big shot," Rick Jacoby said.

"And you, you asshole, coming in here to my club and fucking around with me, what's that?"

"Federal business, that's what it is, government business," Jacoby snapped.

"Consider yourself informed, Francisco," Burton said softly, leaning toward me.

"Informed? Warned, is that what you really want to

say—I should consider myself warned?" I asked.

"If that's what I wanted to say, Francisco . . . I would say it," Michael Burton said, "At this point it's information that we passed along to you. Information you may want to pass along to your friend in the Great Swamp."

"And what exactly should I tell him?"

"Tell him to enjoy his life with his Oriental Chink wife, and his half-Chink kids, and to stay in areas he is familiar with and close to his inbred swamp family, that would be best." He said this slowly in a precise way with no expression. His feral eyes were blazing. He turned, and walked toward the door, with Jacoby two steps behind him.

When they were gone I sat down. I was shaking, in no mood to sing any longer. What the hell was that all about? I thought to myself. And how about Lillian's safety and the veiled threats toward me and the Swamp Master.

What the hell was going on here?

The next morning I told Lillian what had happened— the meeting with Bobby Day and then seeing Burton and Jacoby in the club.

"So, what will you do now, Francisco?" she asked.

"I thought it was: What will *we* do now?" I said.

"Come here." She held out her hand. I approached. She slipped her hand around my neck and pulled me toward her, kissing me strongly on the lips. "I can see you are upset," she said softly.

"Yes, I'm upset, and I waited until this morning to think about it, until I calmed down."

"And?"

"Well, I think I should file a civil lawsuit and try to get our money back from the purchase of the plane?"

"Who will you sue?"

"I will sue the U.S. Government, Florida Private Planes, and John Harrison."

"Do you want to put the exact details of what happened in the lawsuit?"

"Yes, we must."

"It will be expensive."

"No more than fifty thousand dollars—fifty thousand to get back two hundred and fifty, that's not a bad deal. I have the money."

"And publicity, what about that?"

"The *Miami Sentinel* will get a hold of it."

"Do you think it was the government that got the story of the raid moved to page two?" Lillian asked.

"Maybe," I answered, and thought. "Probably they did."

"So, Francisco, isn't this a little bit like tempting fate—pushing them?"

"Do you think I should do nothing—they almost kill us—you're hurt—and the final insult is that we actually paid two hundred and fifty thousand dollars for the plane—we finance them to hurt us, and we do nothing—not one fucking thing in return."

"It was only a question, Francisco."

"I'm sorry," I said, going back to the side of her bed, holding her hand.

"You are a passionate man, Francisco. It is one of the many reasons I love you—one of the strong reasons."

"So?" I asked.

"So, do what your heart dictates—sue the *bastardos!*" She smiled, talking a deep breath of the fresh ocean air. The day was sunny and very warm. The bougainvillea were in bloom on the balcony, a blanket of bright purple that contrasted with the white of the balcony. The French doors were wide open and the wind was low, hardly stirring the curtains.

An hour later I left for Miami. I spent the day with my Uncle Roberto's son, my cousin, my best friend, and also my lawyer, Felix Rodriguez, a top litigator, a giant-killer. He was expensive, but not for me. He was the best litigator in Miami. He was born, like me, in Havana, and was fifteen years old when his family and mine made the exodus to the United States in 1958 when Castro took over. His father, my Uncle Roberto, had been a great litigating lawyer, and his grandfather had been a Cuban supreme court judge. Felix had gone to Harvard. He was a major figure in Miami politics, which were always in turmoil, and Felix was often in the center.

He was also active in national politics, a phone call away from the President. He was persuasive and could help control the Cuban vote. The Cubans of Miami often voted in a block. Eight hundred thousand votes was a powerful block of votes in the powerful state of Florida. It usually voted Republican. I figured he was my best bet, and we got along well. He was still handling some of our affairs, some of Lillian's problems with her late husband's estate.

Felix was a man of forty-two, jet-black hair slicked back, a solid-gold Rolex on his wrist, an impeccable dresser—always a Georgio Armani dark suit, topped off with a hundred-dollar tie, usually of bright colors. His designer eyeglass frames were gold with tinted lenses that changed color in the light, the brighter the light, the darker the lenses. His offices were on the penthouse floor of the Intercontinental office tower at the foot of downtown Miami, directly on the water, overlooking Biscayne Bay and Key Biscayne. To the south you could see the bustling port of Miami, the massive cruise ships, and Government Cut, the waterway that ran to the ocean and where South Beach started.

Felix was a strong Catholic and a devoted family man, married to a beautiful Venezuelan woman from a powerful family; he had three beautiful children and an eighty-foot yacht.

Two paralegal secretaries were parked outside his office behind massive desks, one on each side of the floor-to-ceiling double mahogany door to his office, and they were both always busy. I always thought one secretary was for lawyering and the other was for politics, but I was never sure.

The night before, I had worked for hours on writing up what had happened. I faxed this to him in the morning. He read it, called me back, and we had talked for an hour. So when I walked into his office in the afternoon, he knew the score.

"Ah, Francisco, my favorite friend, cousin, singer, also married to my favorite client." He shook my hand, and at the same time pulled me toward him and gave me a big hug. "How is Lillian?" he said, seating himself and motioning for me to be seated. He sat in a high-back leather chair facing two slim-backed computer monitors, two keypads. Behind him was a huge sheet of plate glass framing the waters of Biscayne Bay with its incredible mix of colors, blue, green, shades of turquoise, contrasted against the light blue sky and the white cotton-clump clouds. Somehow he gave the impression that this was all his, that he owned it and he turned his back on it, like it was nothing, like he should own it, like nobility. I loved Felix. He knew who he was, exactly who he was, and he knew it from the day he was born. I admired his clarity and wondered what had happened to mine.

"She's doing very well, her recuperation is under way. The healing process is up to God now," I said.

"That's good news. Francisco. I called our chief investigator, an ex-FBI big shot, and filled him in on what we discussed. He looked into it, and said it looks like a mess. It appears that they truly and stupidly raided their own operation."

"Well, I think that part is true."

"It's not uncommon, my investigator tells me, that one branch of the federal government does not know what the other branch is doing."

"Well, Felix, it's a little more complicated here. Prior to the raid, the FAA was warned off. Inspector Greene of the FAA received a call and was told to lay off by this Customs agent Rick Jacoby."

"And?"

"Well Inspector Greene asked for a directive in writing from Customs, a directive telling the FAA the details of the operation in writing, confirming that it was, in fact, an official operation. He never got it," I said.

"So, Inspector Greene, in return, ignored the verbal

request. This I have learned, Francisco, is something these bureaucratic people like to do to each other. They feel like bigger men when they belittle their associate agencies. Remember, we Cubans have a long history with the CIA and the NASA, a history that still goes on to this very day. After our Brothers to the Rescue plane was shot down by the Cuban MiG in 1966, we were told it would be looked after by the State Department. But instead, they lessened the U.S. sanctions and the Pope went to Cuba to play nice with Castro. So a Miami law firm, not us, sued and won. And some accounts of Castro actually got confiscated to pay the damage claims of Brothers to the Rescue, so sometimes lawsuits can work. But ultimately, it seems that the agencies within the U.S. Government often do exactly as they feel like doing."

"Felix, I believed I was helping expose this operation when I went undercover, and now it has all been reversed. Did you see today's *Miami Sentinel*—the U.S. attorney has dropped the charges against all the key players, and they have been released. You understand they are putting planes in the air that are the equivalent of flying death traps, dangerous to the pilot and passengers, dangerous to anyone on the ground."

"Our investigator says that this operation that uses Florida Private Planes as a cover has a high security clearance. He was blocked from getting any specific information. It is being run under the control of U.S. Customs, but it comes from a higher place."

"I want to proceed with a civil suit, as I indicated in my communications with you. Felix, I know it is very difficult to sue the government, but we have specific charges: illegal tampering with the plane, damage of property and personal injuries. We have physical proof that the engines were switched, the ID plates were false, the logbooks were forged, and the airworthiness certificate was completely fraudulent."

"All right, I enjoy taking on the U.S. Government. Any estimate on how many private planes out there are not what people think they are?"

"My friend, Sawyer Pinder, the undercover mechanic, says that South Florida is only one operation. He believes there are more, in Texas, California, and other states. He believes that there are hundreds of these planes in the air."

"Planes that were previously used by the government in undercover operations, then sold back into general service."

"Yes."

"All right, Francisco, we can prepare a suit in two days if you will help us and file it in the federal courthouse here in Miami by Friday. Is that what you want?"

"Yes."

"All right, we will name U.S. Customs, John Harrison, and Florida Private Planes all as co-conspirators. We will ask for one hundred million in damages. Do you want press coverage?"

"I think it would be helpful," I responded.

"I also think it would be helpful." Felix smiled and buzzed for his secretary. "You already gave us enough documentation to draft the complaint, so I will get started."

"Good, let me know when you want me and Lillian to sign."

"I will," he said, and walked me to the door. When we got to the door he stopped me. "Francisco, that C-130 that landed that night in the Everglades, the one you thought was loaded with coke, do you think it could have been coming in from Cuba?"

"I don't know where it came from. We tried to take pictures, but they are not good."

"Okay. I will come with Luz and my oldest daughter to your club sometime soon to hear you sing and eat your fabulous food. They both love the way you sing. My daughter says you are better than Ricky Martin—high praise. Maybe you will sing 'Mambo Number 5,' that is Luz's favorite. And our daughters who are in love with Ricky Martin—how about 'La Vida Loca' for them?" He smiled.

"I'm living 'La Vida Loca.' I don't have to sing about it. But I would be happy to sing 'Guantanamera,' " I smiled and paused. "Felix, is that where you think that C-130 maybe flew in from, our base in Guantanamo?" I asked.

"Like I said, Francisco, it was just an idle question."

"Right, Felix, except for one thing."

"Yes."

"You never ask idle questions—your time is too valuable."

He patted me on the back as I left. As the door closed I could overhear him give instructions to his secretary in Spanish to call Jose Ortega, the head of the Cuban Freedom Fighters. I wondered if it was connected to my visit.

The complaint was filed on Friday, and on Saturday my real problems began.

Chapter Seven

In Saturday's paper, the *Miami Sentinel,* this time we made the front page:

U.S GOVERNMENT ACCUSED OF SELLING DANGER-
OUS AIRPLANES

In a civil suit today, filed in Miami Federal Court by Francisco Cruz and his wife Lillian Cruz, the U.S. Government is accused of being a co-conspirator with John Harrison and Florida Private Planes in the sale of dangerous airplanes using false and forged logbooks, ID plates, and issuing fraudulent airworthiness certificates.

Felix Rodriguez, well known Miami lawyer and anti-Castro Cuban activist, represents the couple in their lawsuit. He claims in the lawsuit that the government has been using an undercover operation to hide their own illegal operations, which include the fraudulent sale of dangerous aircraft that were altered for undercover operations, and then placed back into service without restoring the aircraft to first-class operational status as they are supposed to do by law.

The U.S. Government is also being accused in the civil lawsuit of allowing their undercover operatives to personally profit through these sales. Mr. and Mrs. Cruz claim that they paid two hundred and fifty thousand dollars to Florida Private Planes for a Grumman Albatross airplane that had been used in an undercover operation where the aircraft was altered, and they were not told of this fact. They claim that the engines of the plane they were sold had been switched with another undercover airplane and false ID plates were placed on their aircraft.

Furthermore, the Cruzes claim that the logbooks were falsified and a bogus airworthiness certificate was issued. This, they claim, was done by Florida Private Planes Inc., with the full knowledge of the U.S. Customs Service personnel and the owner of the business, John Harrison.

Mr. Rodriguez, in his lawsuit, referred to a prior report in the *Miami Sentinel* of an FAA and DEA raid against Florida Private Planes only seven days ago where seventeen people were arrested and charged with similar crimes.

It should be noted that these charges were later lessened to misdemeanors or dropped completely and the people released.

Howard Blackstone, a spokesman for U.S. Customs, went on record with the *Miami Sentinel* today and said: "There is not a shred of evidence to substantiate this claim. The U.S. Customs Service had no part whatsoever in the sale of a Grumman

Albatross airplane to Mr. and Mrs. Cruz. The charges against the U.S. Custom Service are frivolous and without merit," Mr. Blackstone told the *Sentinel*. He also denied the accusation that Florida Private Planes Inc. of Opa-Locka was an undercover operation for U.S. Customs.

When asked about the prior raid on Florida Private Planes Inc. and the arrest of seventeen people for similar activities, Mr. Blackstone commented: "Those people were later released by the court and the charges were dropped or dismissed—this speaks for itself. It is an ongoing situation. I have no further comments."

The article was written by my friend Jeff Bacon. Felix and I had given him an interview over the phone the day before the suit was filed. Jeff was a top-notch investigative reporter, and there was a good chance the story would be picked up on the national wire service.

I handed the paper to Lillian, who read it and said, "Francisco, do you think we really will ever get our two hundred and fifty thousand dollars back?" She always went straight to the heart of the matter.

"We won't get it back if we don't try." I smiled at her and said, "You feel ready?" Today was the day for her to try and walk.

"Scared, but as ready as I have to be," she said.

I helped her to the side of the bed, gave her a kiss, and slipped a crutch under each arm. The nurse was on duty today and she moved into the other side position. We waited as Lillian slowly slipped off the bed and onto the floor. She grimaced in pain as her right foot touched the carpet. I moved closer.

"No, Francisco, I must try this on my own," she said to me. Ever so slowly she rose from the edge of the bed, and placed her full weight on the arms of the crutches. She stood now with her full weight supported by her one good leg and her crutches. She pushed down on the handholds and moved one crutch forward, then waited, then moved the second crutch.

With the nurse on one side and me on the other, she made her way to the French doors, which were wide open to the soft trade winds, the blue sky, and the azure ocean. She smiled as the warm ocean breeze caressed her face. The sun lit up the natural angular planes of her face. Her beauty was natural and pure.

She stood there for a few seconds, and slowly turned and started her careful walk back to her bed. As she approached the bed her shoulders and hands trembled slightly, her legs wobbled, but she did not falter. She turned again at the bed and we helped her slide up the crisp white sheets until she rested in her cluster of white pillows, her blond hair cascading around her face. She never looked more beautiful to me—brave and beautiful.

"I think I'll rest a little now, Francisco," she said. "Just close my eyes for a while."

"Didn't some famous Chinese man say the longest journey begins with the first step?" I said, pulling the sheet up.

"Well, it was a long journey, those few steps, wasn't it?"

"Yes," I said. "Now get some rest and I'll be back later."

"Francisco, you want to celebrate tonight? The article in the paper—maybe we will get vindication."

"Yes, and you walked today. How would you like to celebrate?"

"Maybe you could help Merisol cook us a special dinner, with some nice wine, and I could sit on the balcony, and after dinner . . ."

"Yes, what about after dinner?" I said, whispering as I moved closer to her.

"Maybe you could sing to me—just me—no music—just your voice and the wind and the waves."

"Yes. I'll see to everything. Now, get some sleep." I stayed with her until she drifted off to sleep. It was a pure sleep; the morphine and the wild dreams were gone now and nature had taken over.

I took a long run on the beach, down the surf line, where the sand was cool and firm. I could feel the wet sand sticking to the soles of my feet and squishing in between my toes. The pure ocean air filled my lungs. I ran down to the rock jetty. I sat and rested on a flat granite boulder, and watched the pelicans flock together to go for a feeding cruise along the breaking surf. When there were eight of them gathered, they headed south toward Miami, floating in unison like one bird with eight separate pieces, hovering about twenty feet above the breaking waves.

I needed some time to think; everything had gone so quickly: my going undercover for the feds—why did I do it? Was it an ego thing? The raid at Opa-Locka and the Everglades turned out to be for nothing. The visit from Bobby Day—to give me the bad news. The encounter with Michael Burton in the club and that whacked-out Customs agent, Rick Jacoby—why did

Burton bother to come and see me at the club and mention the Swamp Master, just to scare me? The meeting with Felix Rodriguez in Miami—his question about the C-130 maybe coming from Cuba lingered in my mind. Did he know something? Lillian starting to walk again—almost a miracle. A lot to think about.

What did I want out of this?

I started off wanting satisfaction for what had happened to me, or was it revenge that I really wanted? Was my temper, my anger out of control—was I screaming in my heart for vengeance for what had happened to Lillian and me? Or was it a higher motive, altruistic? What had happened to me could happen to anyone who was unlucky enough to have purchased one of these airplanes.

Shit, why do we do anything? Is it ever for one reason, is it ever simple? Well, now, I had thrown the gasoline onto the fire with the civil lawsuit. I had to see it through. It was my way—once committed, ever persistent—was this a flaw in my character or a fucking virtue—who knows—when does persistence turn into stubbornness? Why do I even ask myself these questions on such a beautiful South Florida day?

I took off down the beach listening to the tape in my Walkman. As fate would have it, the first song up on the tape was Frank Sinatra singing "My Way"—perfect!

I sang along with Frank as I ran the three miles home.

Lillian and I have a little secret code. When she asks me to help Merisol cook dinner, what she really means is that she would like *me* to cook dinner. I love to cook so it's something I welcome. I wanted a diversion, hoping that my mind would become clearer, and if I was making a serious life mistake I would get a strong signal to change direction.

I went to the grocery store and picked up fresh vegetables and a beautiful pork tenderloin. I stopped by the club and said hello to Jorge, my Cuban Italian chef. I had him scoop me out two quarts of black beans and rice and some of our famous salsa. I also had him give me a small amount of our special liquid garlic.

We talked briefly about his domestic disaster; his wife had now moved out of the house to live with her lover. I took a loaf of the fresh Cuban bread that was wheeled into the back of the restaurant twice a day by the baker next door. I took a healthy whiff of the loaf before slipping it into my bag—no smell like it.

Jorge was wearing Wayfarer sunglasses all the time so people could not see he had been crying, but everybody knew. He cut a hell of a figure, dressed in his whites, with his chef's hat and his black sunglasses. He was very Latin, handsome and passionate, so it was only a matter of time before he would find a new lover.

When I got home I saw that Merisol had set a beautiful table out on the balcony before she left for the day. I inspected it while Lillian watched television. She loved the news talk shows.

Proper presentation was important to me: fresh starched tablecloth, tall silver candelabras from Spain, silver wine bucket, small bouquet of fresh flowers as a centerpiece, and different wine glasses for each type of wine. The table was perfect.

In the kitchen I prepared the yucca first by steaming it, and started getting the plantains prepared for coating and frying. Eating well was like a ritual with me. My mother had been my inspiration, her joy in looking after the family: feeding them well, her easy smile, her natural beauty, her lilting voice as she sang at her work, the hours I helped her, the smells, the colors of the food, the sound of chopping vegetables; her careful choice of only fresh bread to go with the meal. It was a sensual experience that did wonders for my psyche; it calmed and soothed me.

The preparation and eating of fine food was a very sensual experience for me, a ritual, a romance; it was best slow and loving with the anticipation growing as the meal progressed. I would often fast before a great meal so I could feel the true essence, the flavors of what I ate. Today, I had eaten nothing after my run this morning. I was alone in the kitchen, which faced the pool and the ocean. I watched the fiery ball of the sun fall into the ocean as I worked.

Next, I prepared the pork tenderloin. The preparation was a family secret. I rinsed the roast with clear water and placed it on a white plastic cutting board. Next, I took out the surgical syringe and poured the clear garlic into it. Slowly and with precision I injected the roast with liquid garlic—the key was in injecting just the right amount. It took practice. I would do this procedure one more time, when the roast was half-cooked. I would remove it form the oven and repeat the procedure. The result was the best pork ever tasted by man or woman. Thanks, Mom, I said when I was finished. This little trick had made me a lot of money. No one knew why our pork was the best in the world.

I sang "Guantanamera" to myself in Spanish as I

cooked in quiet solitude, the smells wafting into the air, the plantains sizzling, the black beans and rice being warmed, the roast baking in the oven, the great smell of roasting garlic. When it was finished I prepared the plates on a tray.

I carried the tray up the stairs and out onto the balcony. The smells had permeated the house and preceded me up the stairs. I thought of passion, pure passion, the essence of real life is passion, I thought, as I climbed the stairs. I ruminated on how life would be so dead if there was no passion. "To live without passion for something is not to live at all. It is a lucky person who can live his passion," my mother used to say.

My real passion was sitting on the balcony waiting for me with a sly mischievous smile. Her crutches were propped on the arm of the chair.

"You were supposed to wait for me to help you," I said.

"I could smell the food, Francisco, and I didn't want to waste a minute."

She had poured the wine, a chilled-in-ice white California Chardonnary. I served her food and sat down. She raised her glass for a toast.

"Whatever is to happen, darling, it will happen to both of us," she said.

"Mi amor," I said as I sipped my drink.

We ate slowly and talked of things gone by. Time passed quickly.

I cleared the table and pulled my chair next to her.

"You promised," she whispered, nuzzling my ear.

I closed my eyes, felt her touch on my neck, smelled

her perfume, and music came alive from my mouth with the rolling sound of the ocean and the lilting trade wind.

I finished with the ocean as my bass line and the wind as my strings. We sat with her head on my shoulder, breathing softly. Silence never bothered us; we let it envelop us.

After a while she whispered in my ear. "I have another favor, darling."

"Anything."

"Can I sleep with you tonight?"

"Tonight, and every other night."

The two men parked just outside Everglades City, near the old fish house that was long ago abandoned. It was a short jog on the edge of the canal to Everglades City. It was late, almost five o'clock, an hour from sunrise. They each carried bags that were the size of gym bags and black, like the men's clothes and the watch caps they wore, which they pulled down over their faces like a mask.

They sat there for ten minutes using night glasses, looking for any sign of life. The smaller and quicker of the two men spoke first using only hand signals. He would go in first and give two flashes on his light if everything was clear. He took a Glock automatic out of his bag. He went off on a crouched run. Minutes later the signal was flashed and the larger man, carrying both bags, made a sprint across the opening to the small repair shop and pier.

He handed the smaller man his bag. They worked like black lightning. They had done this drill many times, in training and in reality. The smaller man had the detonation cord. He ran it like rope over and under the aviation and regular fuel tanks. The larger man slapped small thin fist-size packages of C-4 on the transom of five airboats sitting still pressed into the pier by the incoming tide. The smaller man took the last of the detonating cord and ran through the store. The larger man stuck a C-4 pack on the safe and another one on the cash register.

They picked up their black gym bags and were across the open field in seconds. They knelt down on one knee when they were halfway to the parked car.

"Do it. Let's do it now!" the smaller man said.

"No, let's wait till we are in the car and have it started up."

"We can't see from there."

"Christ, who wants to see? We've seen this a thousand fucking times."

"It doesn't get old for me." The smaller man lifted his watch cap mask off his face. His fierce expression proved he was not to be argued with.

"Okay, you weird little fuck. We'll do it your way. Who's first?"

The smaller man took a quarter out of his pocket. "I'm heads."

The coin came up heads. "So, it's me first."

The smaller man took his timer in hand and armed it. He pushed down on the red button. The detonating cord was visible as it went off just a fraction of a second before the fuel went sky-high. A huge red-orange billow that turned into black smoke in the night sky. The larger man pushed down on the red button he was hold-

ing. The airboats all went up and split into many pieces, disintegrating in the air as a shower of flaming parts flew in every direction like wounded fiery birds.

A second later the larger man said, "Let's go!"

The smaller man nodded his head in agreement, a huge smile of satisfaction on his face. They ran full speed to the car and sped off into the night.

Early Sunday morning the call came.

"Francisco, my shop . . . it's been blown up," the Swamp Master said after I answered. "They blew up my business. It ain't nothin' but fuckin' splinters, shattered airboats, and pilings with no planks, no dock."

"When?"

"Around dawn. I think they put C-4 charges under the high-octane aviation tanks and the regular gas I keep near the dock for the airboats and such. It's still burnin' like a bastard, fucking chemical fire."

"I'll be right there," I said, hanging up.

I took the Ferrari, got on the Turnpike to I-75, and headed straight for Alligator Alley, then south on 29 to Everglades City. I had this sinking empty feeling in the pit of my stomach. I made it in an hour.

The fire trucks were still there; some of the trucks had come all the way over from Naples and Marco Island. The place was flattened and still smoldering. They were spraying chemicals on embers and blocking off the canal with rubber floats and air blowers to contain the spilled burning fuel. The shack the Swamp Master called his business was literally blown away; only the foundation remained. The twisted, melted, and burned frames of airboats were strewn everywhere including the canal. Engine blocks were scattered on the road, and on the other side of the canal. In an open field, machinery, like drill presses and welding equipment, was twisted and congealed into weird metal sculptures. The plastic face of the Coke machine had somehow survived in one piece and lay on the road. Wooden propellers stuck corkscrewed in the ground like javelins impaled where they had landed.

Everywhere within a quarter of a mile the saw grass had been burned down to the nub. It was black and smelled stifling, the smell hanging in the air like clotted soot. The firemen were everywhere, some still in their full firefighting gear; many were sitting down, stripping off their equipment and clothing, sweat flowing from their bodies like rain. There was still much confusion as little patches of fire would suddenly ignite into life.

The Swamp Master sat on the tailgate of his pickup truck. His two children sat on either side of him; his wife sat perched on the side railing of the truck. No one was speaking. I came and sat down on the tailgate, next to his son. His son had his head leaning against his father's shoulder. There were tears in his eyes. I looked up at his wife. She wore a black headband and black kimono with a yellow dragon on the sleeve. She was barefooted. She looked down at me. Her eyes showed no emotions. She had long ago learned to keep tragedy deep within herself.

I sat in silence with the family. After a few minutes the Swamp Master started to speak. He spoke into the air in front of him in a slow and steady voice.

"Francisco, the noise woke me, like a pure blast of early mornin' artillery . . . incomin'. I popped up in my bed, like I used to years ago, a lifetime ago in Nam. All my instincts came to me immediately, like my memory of things gone by was takin' over. There was no disorientation. I was sittin' up, wide awake, like I had never been asleep in my life.

"I thought the house had been blown up. My first instinct was to see what I could do. But, in a millisecond I knew it wasn't the house. There was another explosion, a second explosion, not as big as the first. Turned out it was the regular fuel tanks, the gas blowin', and then some loud pops like AK-47's, pop, pop . . . the oxygen tanks goin' up, the weldin' tanks. I ran to the window and flipped the shade up and moved the drape over. Then I saw the airboats go up one after another like airboat hand grenades.

"There was a huge red-orange fireball with black smoke risin' all around; it hung out over the canal and the great swamp. Nobody had to tell me what that was. I seen enough high-octane aviation fuel go off to last a man a lifetime. I knew where it was comin' from, that it was my place. I run over to the night table and got this here Glock and two clips. I figured maybe we were next. Mai Lynh was already awake by now. She seen me run over to get the Glock and the clips, and she was up and outta bed—gone in a flash, to get the kids out of their rooms. We got into the truck and come over here.

"Our one Everglades City fire truck was already ahead of us, but it wasn't much use against a fire like this; the heat was intense, singed the paint right off the fire truck parked two hundred feet away from the fire, but the local boys did a good job of containin' it until the Naples crew got here and the Marco Island trucks arrived. They put the chemicals on the fire as soon as they got here, brought it down under control, and they let it burn itself out.

"The whole goddamn canal in front of my shop was on fire—the water was burning like a damn sheet of flame, creepin' down the canal toward my neighbors' docks and boats. Luckily, they was awake by then and able to move their boats and flammables off the docks, away from the blaze. They used fire extinguishers and garden hoses to keep the fire from climbin' out of the canal and up onto the banks, helluva mess."

The Swamp Master's little girl got up and walked behind him. She kneeled and put her small arms around his neck. She laid her head into the nape of his neck.

He put his arm around her small waist and went on, "I know who done this to me and why they done it. Now, I gotta deal with it. I never felt no threat for my family before this. I lived a kind of wild life, but it's *my life*, and since Nam I ain't never had nobody's life to think about except my own, where danger was involved. See, my family's always been safe—out of any danger zone. Now, it ain't sure. I don't like this . . . I don't like this at all.

"There will be an arson investigation, but it won't go nowhere. I got only a small insurance policy, so there ain't no motive for me to have done it, no life lost, only my property destroyed, so the arson investigation will go nowhere. These guys are real smart. They know exactly how far to go, and they know it ain't sophisticated around here like in Miami. We got no genius arson guys

that could spot the C-4 residue and the tiny detonatin'
cap. I'm sure it was triggered from a remote detonator,
not a timer—so they could see what was goin' on, in
case somebody wandered into the fire field by accident.
One of them was maybe here on the scene through the
whole fire, probably disguised as a fisherman, or an
airboat pilot. I'm sure in an hour or so the bastards will
be gettin' a full damage report in Miami. They're probably takin' pictures of us right now."

The Swamp Master went silent and then turned to
his wife. "Honey . . ."

"Sawyer, don't say it. Don't you say it, goddammit.
I'm not going anywhere." She paused for a few seconds
and then said. "But I will take the children over to
Granny Pinder's place in Islamorada for a few weeks.
But only to drop them off, then I'm coming back."

The two children looked up at their mother, but said
nothing. Mai Lynh slipped off the side of the pickup
and went back to face the Swamp Master. No words
were spoken as she reached in his pocket and took the
keys to the truck. The kids jumped off the tailgate just
before he slammed it shut. He opened the door and
helped them leap into the cab.

"What about clothes and stuff for the kids?" the
Swamp Master asked.

"Credit cards work in Islamorada, don't they?" she
asked with a slight smile, and slipped the truck into
gear.

"She ain't goin' near that house with the kids. Helluva woman," he said.

"Helluva woman!" I repeated.

We both watched as the truck departed; a soft cloud of limestone dust rose in its wake.

"Francisco, I can't take this no more, watchin' my place turned into rubble. Drive me to the Rod and Gun Club."

We drove slowly through the tiny town. People nodded and waved at the Swamp Master; everyone knew what had happened. I parked in the rear and we walked to the front and sat on the huge porch. It was a little after nine A.M., and the few guests were taking breakfast in the main dining room. The waitress came out, spun around on her heel, and disappeared into the hotel. She returned with a tray. On the tray was a bottle of Remy Martin cognac, cups, and a thermos of coffee. She placed it on the table and left without a word.

"Relative?" I asked.

"Through marriage," he answered, and smiled slightly. "Whadda you think, Francisco? You think everybody around here is related to me?"

"Aren't they?"

"No, this ain't no scene from *Deliverance*."

"Look, Sawyer, about the fire . . . I'm sorry—"

"It ain't your fault this happened."

"I'm not sure."

He poured the coffee, and a stiff shot of the cognac into each cup. He sat back and watched the water for a second. He spoke without looking at me. "Look here, Francisco, you believe in coincidence?"

"Slightly."

"Well, I been doin' a lot of thinkin'. You know, how maybe a man's life is ruled over a little, maybe destiny or fate or somethin' like that, predestination shit, and if he leaves unfinished business behind him in his wake sometimes it haunts him all his life . . . specially if it's bad business."

"It's possible."

"Francisco, let's just back ourselves up a little. You buy an airplane from a bunch of bad motherfuckers, the plane is a flyin' shitbox, a death trap, and you crash right in front of me while I'm out looking for good frog-spearin' grounds. I rescue your ass and together we save your wife from maybe death."

"For which I—"

"Never mind that now, you just listen to me. So, then you come to me and tell me that maybe these are bad dudes and that the FAA and the DEA have come to you to go undercover and bust these assholes. But what you don't tell me, because you don't know, is that these guys we are gonna bust are really federal agents themselves, at least some of them are federal agents—and the fuckin' idiot feds wind up bustin' their own undercover operation—right so far?"

"Yeah, right so far."

"So, I go undercover for you inside; I'm your insurance policy against surprises, to get some information for you. Then I discover that this is one big motherfucker of an operation, the fucked-up-planes side is huge, and God knows what else is goin' on in the dope smugglin' department. Anyway, I tell you about seein' a guy in a Hawaiian shirt. A guy who I chauffered around in the Nam, a guy who was a major spook. And I tell you this guy has no fuckin' nerves, he is a man without nerves, without a conscience, and he gives me the fucking screamin' meemies.

"And I don't know what he's really doin' there, because he comes and goes only on rare occasions, and when he shows, everybody falls all over their own feet tryin' to get in line to kiss his ass. I also tell you he recognizes me, but he don't make no strong reference to anything in our past. I figure that he figures I'm just fixin' aircraft engines with these renegades to make a fast buck, and that's why I'm with these guys."

"Sawyer, I know all this."

"Don't get impatient; you have a short attention span sometimes, Francisco."

"Thanks."

"Don't mention it. So, you and me, we go out and do a midnight creep on the Glades location, and we find out a lot of shit. When we are splitting we see a C-130 come in with what looks like a full load of dope, picked up by a bunch of ninja-black-ops-lookin' military-type dudes, and then we almost get our asses shot off."

"So far I'm with you. I remember almost getting killed, yes."

"Calm down. So now to the latest events—a major article comes out in the *Miami Sentinel* yesterday that puts all these players on the front page for two million people to read about. Not to mention the news stations who interview Felix Rodriguez. It even mentions the clusterfuck, where the government raid themselves, their own double-super-secret undercover operation. And then the very next fucking day they blow up my business."

"A warning?"

"Yeah, hell of a warning." The Swamp Master

Here's how it works:

Each package will carry a FREE 10-DAY EXAMINATION
privilege. At the end of that time, if you decide
to keep your books, simply pay the low invoice price
of $11.25, no shipping or handling charges added.
HOME DELIVERY IS ALWAYS FREE!
There's no minimum number of books to buy,
and you may cancel at any time.

AND AS A CHARTER MEMBER, YOUR FIRST THREE-BOOK SHIPMENT IS TOTALLY FREE! IT'S A BARGAIN YOU CAN'T BEAT!

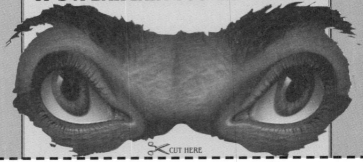

✂ CUT HERE

- -

Mail to: Leisure Horror Book Club, P.O. Box 6613, Edison, NJ 08818-6613

YES! I want to subscribe to the Leisure Horror Book Club. Please send
my 3 FREE BOOKS. Then, every other month I'll receive the three newest
Leisure Horror Selections to preview FREE for 10 days. If I decide to
keep them, I will pay the Special Members Only discounted price of just
$3.75 each, a total of $11.25. This saves me between $3.72 and $6.72
off the bookstore price. There are no shipping, handling or other charges.
There is no minimum number of books I must buy and I may cancel the
program at any time. In any case, the 3 FREE BOOKS are mine to keep—
at a value of between $14.97 and $17.97. Offer valid only in the USA.

NAME:_____

ADDRESS:_____

CITY:_____ STATE:_____

ZIP:_____ PHONE:_____

■ **LEISURE BOOKS,** A Division of Dorchester Publishing Co., Inc.

poured us each another drink, then he hit me with the punch line. "Look, Francisco, there's more here than what I told you." He paused.

"You been holding back—go on, give it to me," I said.

"After Nam I come home and there ain't no work and I'm pretty much a basket case—post-traumatic stress and just generally fucked up in the head. I start flyin' grass in from Colombia, Jamaica, and Mexico for various gangster types in Miami. The money's great. See, I come from a long line of smugglers here in Everglades City, kind of a family tradition. Sawyers, Pinders, been smugglers for hundreds of years.

"One day over Andros Island in the Bahamas, I'm carryin' a big load of pot, like several thousand pounds, and two Blackhawk helicopters drop out of the sky. They're on my ass like two big eagles after a rabbit. I have my copilot dump all the bales out of the plane over Andros, but these helos ain't leavin'. Anyway, they finally force me down at the airport in Marathon.

"They lock me up in Miami, and then the feds come on the scene and proceed to scare the shit out of me. They show me the entire episode on videotape, us pushin' the pot out, my flight plan from Jamaica. They tell me I'm lookin' at fifteen years of hard federal time—of which I will have to do a mandatory twelve years. I'm shittin' my pants, and then on the third day of bein' locked up who walks in?"

"The Hawaiian shirt."

"Yeah, Michael Burton, fucking super-spook. He, of course, remembers me from Nam, 'cause I flew him around on some of his black ops. By the way, this guy has been dirty for years and years. In Nam he was buyin' heroin and dealin' with the NVA with U.S. greenbacks. I could never quite figure it out, what the fuck he was doin', and I only flew him on a couple of missions—those guys never used the same pilots more than three times—SOP, standard operational procedure. So Michael Burton and me, we know each other.

"He tells me I can work off the pot beef they got me on in the Bahamas; it will disappear if I fly a load of coke in from Baranquilla, Colombia, to a secret airstrip in the middle of Florida, near Orlando. Only fly this one load and I'm clear—no charges. He knows I'm checked out on four-engine planes and flew C-130's for a while."

"Coke?" I asked.

"Yeah, coke. Five thousand kilos, twelve thousand pounds. This is in the mid-eighties when a kilo is goin' for from twenty-five to forty grand, not like today. So this is some real weight. He tells me that my entire flight plan will have prior clearance and there will be no interdiction action what-so-fucking-ever. You do the math on the low side, it's a hundred and twenty-five million dollars wholesale."

"Who was gettin' the money?"

"These guys are all weird fuckers who have been doin' weird shit all their lives. But Francisco, believe it or not, they ain't in it for the money—sure, they got money stashed for a rainy day or for high-powered lawyers if needed, but it ain't real money. They got maybe half a million or a million as 'fuck you' money stashed in case they have to beat feet someday."

"So, what are they doin' it for then, Sawyer?"

"Well, in those days, when I did my thing with them,

it was the days of the Contras in Nicaragua, and Salvador, and Guatemala—see, the Congress would not give enough money to the CIA to run their wars in these places. They refused to pony up the cash, so these CIA boys had to figure out another way to make the money to support their wars."

"So, they sold guns in Iran to free the hostages."

"And dope into this country to finance their private wars."

"So, they were patriots?" I said sarcastically. "Who bought the dope?"

"Who else, Francisco? Fucking dopers, narco-gangsters, that's who bought the shit. A whole big load of it went to California and Florida—great distribution points."

"So these guys went from black ops in Vietnam to the Contra wars—what are they doing now?"

"Who the fuck knows what they're doin'. See, it's always the same cast of characters who were trained in Nam, and it goes up very high in the current government. I know some of the money goes to campaign contributions and cash for expenses for big-shot politicians—lots of money—big money."

"After it's laundered."

"Of course after it's laundered. See, these CIA and NSA guys run their own world, and there are always corrupt politicians around who will put their hands over their eyes if they get enough money and cover their ears. And the big twist . . . the major reason why they really survive and prosper is that their motive ain't the normal motive."

"Which is greed."

"Fucking greed, that's the normal motive—money, greenbacks, cash, but that ain't what they are about. Now, Francisco, you're a smart guy . . . what trumps greed . . . what's a higher motive?"

"Power."

"That's right—power always trumps greed. This here is a power game, not a greed game. These guys like the Hawaiian shirt, Michael Burton, have wars to run, politicians to buy, elections to manipulate, nations to overthrow. And they know exactly how to do it, and they always keep people in positions of high fuckin' power and they stay hidden in the shadows. Believe it or not, you're right, they think of themselves as patriots. That's one of the reasons they're so fucking dangerous."

"So, is this some great big conspiracy theory you're tellin' me here?" I asked

"No, first of all, it ain't so big in terms of players, and second, it came naturally—it's a natural evolution. It was born in horror—it started in the very same fucking place where we both lost our life-cherries—where we went from boys to men—in one plane ride across the pacific from America to Vietnam. It was born there in those steamin', stinkin' jungles, and lives until today. Look at some of the players in the Iran-Contra mess— Oliver North, a Vietnam vet, a Marine colonel; General Segate; Casper Weinberger, the Secretary of Defense. All indicted on serious charges. And nobody goes to fucking jail. How does that work—figure it out. It's no big conspiracy, it's just common sense. It's a reality . . . only nobody wants to know about it."

"So you did it . . . flew the mission?"

"Yeah, I did it. Went like clockwork. After I landed

they slipped me five grand in cash. I rented a car in Orlando and drove home to Everglades City, a free man."

"They kept their word."

"Shit, yeah, wouldn't you? They get a free expert pilot to ferry in a hundred and twenty-five million dollars of coke and there is no record anywhere of the flight. And they could still hold the pot beef over my head for seven years, until the statute of limitations runs out. They know I can't say nothin'. These are smart fuckers, man, pros—it's what they do."

I finished my coffee and poured some more in both our cups. It was finally coming clear. I broke the silence. "So, they blow up your shop to show you that they can."

"Yeah, and they know I'll be tellin' you what I just told you, and that you should have sense enough to lay off on this. The lawsuit was not a smart idea."

I poured us each a good belt of the cognac.

The car pulled up right in front of the hotel and wheeled into the handicapped parking spot. A government-issued black four-door Ford Crown Victoria. There was one passenger. The door swung open and Rick Jacoby stepped out. He slipped on his suit jacket, and walked up the steps of the porch. He headed directly for us. The Swamp Master and I watched in silence as he walked to us.

He stood in front of us saying nothing for a few seconds. The butt of his shoulder-holstered gun was visible as the soft breeze blew his suit jacket open and shut.

I didn't acknowledge him. He spoke to the Swamp Master. "I'm Rick Jacoby, Miami Customs."

"So?" the Swamp Master said.

"I was in the neighborhood, and I heard of your misfortune."

"You call it a fucking misfortune?"

"What do you call it?"

"Never mind what I call it," the Swamp Master said. "Whadda you want?"

"I don't want nothing," Jacoby said. "I was just gonna offer my condolences."

"Look, unless there's something you want here, why don't you just leave—this isn't a good time, which any sensitive person would notice," I said.

"Oh, excuse me. I guess 'cause I'm not a singer, a sensitive artiste like yourself, you think I ain't a sensitive person."

"Get the fuck outta here," the Swamp Master said.

"Fuck you, asshole, I'll go wherever the fuck I wanna." He moved closer to the Swamp Master.

I was out of my chair and on my feet in one move. I kneed Jacoby as hard as I could in the nerve ganglia in his outer thigh. I felt my knee make contact with the bone. He crumpled onto the wooden porch; as he fell, I extracted the gun from his shoulder holster. I flipped the gun to the Swamp Master.

Agent Jacoby was almost speechless with the pain. I bent down close to his ear and whispered. "Listen, you asshole. You don't come to a man who is in pain and step on that pain. And don't bother insulting him or me again."

He spoke, gasping for his breath. "You've assaulted a federal officer."

The Swamp Master leaned down now and spoke to

Agent Jacoby. "I don't think that's what happened here. I think you slipped and fell on this slippery wooden porch, and when you did you lost your gun, which I now have in my hand. I'm connected to everybody here, one way or another, and they will all stand witness for the fact that you fell. Now, get up on your feet, you little sissy, take your piece, and get outta here. Tell that piece a shit you work for, Burton, that he should'na blown up my business. It gets a man mad when somebody just thinks they can shit all over him."

Jacoby, using a chair, slowly rose to his feet. He ripped the gun out of the Swamp Master's hand, and stuffed it in his holster. "You assholes will pay for this," he said as he limped down the front steps to his parked car.

The Swamp Master spoke first as the car disappeared. "They just want us to know they're in control now."

"Yeah." I paused, looking out at the channel in front of us. The tide was coming in from Florida Bay; the water was flowing quickly.

"Sawyer, why didn't you tell me this before, that you actually worked for Burton?"

"I didn't know where he fit into the whole thing; these guys are always operating under their own secret agenda; no matter what it may look like, it probably ain't that way. So I figure the fucked-up planes is not the major play for him."

"Is he CIA?" I asked.

"You never know. CIA, NSA, State Department, some weird military outfit, you just never know—these guys are like clouds in the sky, all different shapes, they come and they go, sometimes storm clouds, sometimes they look like friendly clouds, black clouds, white clouds, you jus' never fucking know. And they always got plenty of backup."

"So where are we?"

"Well, that article in the *Miami Sentinel* put them over the top. They hate the press—it's hard for them to control because some eager-beaver reporter sometimes forces his editor to move on a story, and before they know it the story is outta control and the spin guys get there with too little, too late. That civil suit scares them; it could all come out and they got real trouble stopping it. They want you to pull the civil suit, that's what this is all about."

"So it's threats," I said.

"Little more than threats . . . based on the job they done here today with me. Don't you think?"

"You want out, out of all this?" I asked.

"I don't know," the Swamp Master said as a stone crab boat, loaded with traps, rumbled down the channel headed for Florida Bay. "I gotta talk to my old lady after she gets the kids parked. I never know how she's gonna react, and every time I try to predict, I'm wrong."

"All right," I said, rising. "You wanna ride home?"

"No, thanks, I'm gonna finish this here cognac, maybe the bottle, and then I'm goin' for a long walk."

"See ya," I said. I was walking off the porch when I heard him call my name.

"Hey, Francisco, you're pretty fast for an old guy. That asshole gonna be limpin' for a week."

I didn't look back. I just raised my arm so he knew I heard him.

I knew that the scene with Agent Jacoby was a minor victory in what was going to be a long war. A war I didn't start, didn't need, and didn't want. I looked up at the clouds; no storm clouds, but I knew they were up there somewhere.

I did not withdraw the civil suit.

Chapter Eight

It was a week later, almost to the hour, when trouble struck again.

At nine on Sunday morning, I got the call from Jaime Ortega, my manager. "Francisco, you up?"

"Barely," I said. I had sung the whole night on Saturday, and helped Jaime close up the place and put the money in the safe.

"You had your television on?"

"No."

"Turn it on now, Channel Seven."

The picture came into focus in the hallways of the emergency ward of Jackson Memorial Hospital in Miami: about forty people, most of them on stretchers, all of them retching, looking gray, in obvious pain. I knew right away what it was when I recognized the faces of our customers, old customers who had supported me for years.

"Food poisoning," Juan Vasquez, the news anchor,

said as the picture flashed from the emergency room to a remote unit that was standing in front of Hola Havana in Little Havana.

"We have Tiffany Jackson in front of the restaurant and nightclub where the incident originated. Tiffany, what can you tell us?" The beautiful black reporter picked up on the beat. She started explaining how all these people were stricken within hours of leaving my restaurant, and the county health inspectors were on their way there to examine the facilities.

I had the phone in my hand as I was watching. I placed the receiver back into my ear. "Who's at the restaurant?"

"Jorge is there already, waiting in the kitchen to let them in. There was a cop on the door when he arrived who told him not to touch a goddamn thing. I guess they have some kind of a special response team for stuff like this. A kitchen SWAT team to track down the problem."

"Get over there, Jaime," I said, slamming the phone down. I was in my car minutes later. When I got there three satellite TV trucks were parked in front along with a police cruiser and three cars and vans from the Miami Health Department. I drove up in my old Jeep to avoid any notice. I slipped in the back after I explained I was the owner to the cop on the door.

Jaime was standing in a corner being grilled by the ranking member of the Health Department team. Jorge, my Cuban Italian chef, was running around after three inspectors speaking in English and Spanish at what seemed the same time. His reputation was on the line and he was fighting for his professional life. "Impossible. Impossible. Impossible that my kitchen could have one dirty thing in it."

A Health Department official scurried in and went over to the boss. He called the boss aside and whispered to him. Together they walked up to Jorge, who was now standing next to me. "Where is the salsa sauce?" he asked.

"It is not salsa sauce, it's salsa, you—you—"

I knew Jorge wanted to say, *"you idiots,"* or worse, so I stepped in. "In the walk-in cooler. It's my mother's secret recipe," I said with a smile.

"Anyone ever died of your mother's cooking?" the assistant said, not amused.

"I'll have to call all my brothers and sisters and see if they're all still alive."

"Well, before you do that, how about you show us that salsa sauce in the walk-in first. It's used with everything, right?"

"It's available to be used on everything, so, yeah, why?"

"Well, it appears to be the one thing in common that all the customers had last night." We walked toward the cooler.

"Does the lab know what it was?"

"The hospital lab says it's some mild form of botulism, some rare strain they are trying to isolate. They've been faced with this before," the health inspector said.

They went inside the walk-in with Jorge, and came out with a jar full of the salsa. One of the inspectors left with the jar in a labeled sealed plastic bag. The boss came up to me. "You're Mr. Cruz?"

"Yes."

"Well, I'm sorry, but we're shutting you down for a while, till we're able to do a full inspection and analysis of your premises, standard procedure in large out-breaks of food poisoning like this."

"If the salsa turns out to be the problem, then what?" I asked.

"We still have to do an analysis to find out how and where the botulism originated from."

"If you shut me down for more than a week, I'll be out of business," I said.

"Look, there's nothing I can do. If I don't follow the code on this, the county takes the heat, and in this case that means me. I'm sorry, sir, but you're shut down as of now."

"There is over a million dollars invested in this club."

"It's human lives we're talking about here, sir."

"It's about thirty jobs we're talking about also, and if the problem is the salsa, well, then we know what it is and we can isolate it."

"I already explained that—we gotta find out how it happened."

"Well, if you put me out of business, I guess it all becomes a meaningless question."

"Well, that's a question for your lawyers," the in-spector said. "Who are gonna be pretty busy with the lawsuits you are gonna get from last night's problem. You got insurance for this?"

"I don't think so. I'm not sure you can *get* insurance for something like this."

"Act of God," the assistant inspector said.

"More like the devil," I said. I was almost positive that my insurance did not cover this contingency. This could wipe me out, with lawyers' fees, judgments, and the business going under. I felt it rising up in me, all the anger that I had thought I had under control. I had a real dread, a feeling of dread that crept over me. I was afraid to think too much about what might have happened here.

I walked over to Jorge, who was staring down at his huge pot of black beans and rice. He was watching as it was being poured into the sink, disappearing into the maw of the garbage disposal spinning, churning it into oblivion. He was almost in tears. He took his work very seriously.

"Jorge, have you hired any new kitchen help lately?"

"One man, Jerman, a Cuban from Fort Lauderdale. He knows my cousin."

"He's the only one?"

"Yeah. Jaime told me maybe you would be back, to sing on a regular basis, and we would be packed like before. So we could use an extra hand."

"That's it, just him?"

"Yeah, that's it, only him."

"You know where he lives?"

"Yeah, pretty much. I can always find him. Why? Why you askin'?"

"Because, I want you to take me to see him."

"Why, why you wanna see him? He have something to do with this, ruinin' me, my beautiful food? People now think I serve dirty, poison food to my customers."

"Listen, Jorge. Don't jump to conclusions here. We'll just go and see for ourselves what's cooking."

"Francisco, I feel so bad for this happenin' to your place."

"Okay, Jorge, just stay cool and we'll get to the bottom of this. All right?"

"Yeah, you just let me know when you wanna leave and we'll go."

I went outside. I half expected to see a Hawaiian shirt in the crowd of spectators, but there was nobody like that. I looked for Jacoby also; he was nowhere to be found. But I felt their presence.

Jorge and I piled into the Jeep and headed south on I-95 to Fort Lauderdale. We got off on the Davie Road exit and went west to the town of Davie and the small enclave know as Fort Lauderdale's Little Havana. We drove in silence. Jorge knew enough to leave me with my own thoughts.

We drove directly to the house. It was the house of Jorge's cousin. The man we were looking for, Jerman, was living in the guest bedroom of the post-World War II tract house, a three-bedroom bungalow. A chain-link fence surrounded the house to keep the dog, a German shepherd named Gerta, inside. It was too hot and humid to get any response out of the dog. When we opened the fence, she barely opened an eyelid in the blazing sunlight. Jorge's cousin came immediately to the door, dressed in a white and green Dolphins tank-top T-shirt. He had his two-year-old daughter in his arms.

"Where's Jerman?"

"Jorge, you don't say hello to me, you just say where's Jerman?"

"I'm sorry, but we need to speak to Jerman. This is Francisco Cruz, my boss."

R. L. Smitten

Jorge's cousin just looked at me without saying anything. "He's in his room packing."

I walked past both of them and popped open the door to the guest room; it was the only closed door in the small house. Jerman was a small wiry man with little black marbles for eyes. His teeth were jagged and white against his dark skin. He needed a shave. He was stuffing clothes into his suitcase. I could hear Jorge and his cousin behind me. Jorge was explaining what went on in the restaurant. His cousin said they had watched it on the television news. He also said that Jerman had paid up his back rent and was going to Mexico for a while.

I walked into the small bedroom. Two very large suitcases were lying on the bed opened.

"Where you goin'?" I asked in Spanish.

"You're the singer, aren't you?"

"Sometimes," I said.

"He's the owner, you asshole," Jorge yelled, trying to squeeze past me into the bedroom.

I turned to Jorge and his cousin. "Leave us alone for a little while." I closed the door, locking them out, and turned to Jerman, who was shaking slightly. He was about five-six and 130 pounds, a little bigger than a jockey.

"Where you going?" I asked for the second time.

"Nowhere," he answered, lighting up a cigarette with a shaky hand.

"I'm allergic to cigarette smoke," I said.

"Hey, you're in my room, wait outside if you don't like smoke."

I reached over, pulled the cigarette from his mouth,

and butted it out on the top of his luggage.

"Hey, man, what you doin'?"

I slapped him very hard with my open hand and drove him on top of his luggage. The slap was like the sound of a cracked whip. His unshaven face felt gritty in my hand. He lay with his back in one of the open bags. I grabbed his T-shirt by the front, crumpling up the image of a dolphin, and pulled him toward me.

"Hey, you can't hit me like that, not in this country."

"Shut the fuck up and listen to me, you little weasel. You put something in the salsa, didn't you?"

"No way. I didn't do nothin'. Why would I do that?"

"When did you get here, to the United States?"

"I got here in 1980."

"You come from Mariel?"

"Yes."

"Were you in prison in Cuba?"

"Only for . . ."

The door behind me snapped open; the force pushed me to the side against the far wall as Jorge ran in with a kitchen knife in his hand.

"You Marielito scum. You ruined me! You ruined my boss's restaurant. You filthy son of a whore, you bastard, you . . ." Jerman was in the fetal position in the far corner of the bedroom in front of Jorge. The knife blade glistening silver in the sunlight coming through the window.

I rose to my feet as his cousin moved in behind him and slipped his arms around Jorge's neck and shoulders to prevent the stabbing. His cousin was a security officer for a bank. I stepped over to Jerman as he lay huddled and shaking on the floor.

"Who told you to do this?"

"Nobody, nobody tell me."

I slapped him again with my open hand. "You tell me, or I'll make sure Jorge chops you up in little pieces like hamburger meat."

Jorge's cousin yelled at the top of his voice, "Tell him, you little fuck, or I will let go of Jorge, and he will kill you and we will throw your body to the alligators."

Jerman looked up at me and the struggling men behind me. He started to whimper at first, then cry. "It was them, the government; since I come in from Mariel I have been under their thumb, since they catch me in a crime in this country. I give them killers I know from Havana, dope dealers in Miami, gun runners, Castro spies, counterfeiters . . . but it is never enough. Finally, they come to me and they tell me to pour a tiny bit of this liquid into some food. They say people will get sick, but no one will die. So, last night I done it."

"What else? What else did they promise you?"

"No more. If I do this thing there is no more bothering of me. I'm free to live my life." Tears were coming from his eyes. Slowly, Jorge's cousin released him from the hold. There was silence in the room except for the sniffling and whimpering of Jerman.

"There's more, there's always more with an informant like you. Rats like you always hold back something," I said.

"Money, they give me a little money and tell me to get out of the country for a while, Mexico or the Bahamas. They give me two thousand dollars."

"Where is it?" He pointed to his shaving kit. The money was in a plastic soap dish.

I put the money in my pocket. "There's one more thing. Where's the rest of the poison, where's the vial?"

"There's no—" he started to say, and I hit him so hard with my open hand that spittle and blood flew from his mouth, I was afraid I'd knocked him out. But I hadn't. He was tough.

He looked up at me with eyes bloodshot from crying. "It's in the shaving kit, in the toothbrush holder."

The vial was a small, black cylinder the width of a pencil, about an inch long.

I called a friend of mine in the Metro Dade Sheriff's office, and he sent a marked car down to pick up Jerman and the vial as evidence. Two hours later Jerman was in the Metro Dade County lockup, and the vial was in the crime lab being analyzed; the two thousand dollars was being held as evidence.

I called the Swamp Master later that night when I got home. I filled him in on the details. "I think I can get the Health Department to lift their closure order after they realize it was an isolated incident of employee misconduct."

"You think the press will give you decent coverage on the story?"

"Well, I'm trying to get Jeff Bacon at the *Sentinel* on the story, to get the truth out."

There was a long silence on the phone. I broke it. "Something wrong?"

"I don't know, Francisco. Look, I know these boys and they play real rough."

"I have proof, physical evidence of what happened. I have the vial. I believe it will carry the residue of whatever was put in the salsa," I said.

More silence. This time he broke the silence.

"What's this Jerman's bail?"

"It's high. Ten thousand."

"How long has he been in the slammer?"

"He's been in there since noon today."

"Call the lockup and see if he made his bail."

"He'll never make his bail, ten grand. He's got no family, no friends."

"Wrong, Francisco, he's got friends who are playin' for a lot more than ten grand here, podner. Call me back."

I called the Metro Dade lockup and found out that he had made his bail two hours after he was admitted. Nobody had to tell me who made his bail, and that he would disappear.

Lillian came into the library where I was making the calls.

"Bad news?" She asked. She was up to date on what had happened that day. She was walking with the aid of crutches.

"They released Jorge's cousin on bail."

"Surprised?" she asked, perching on the desk, still using her crutches for support.

"Surprised at my stupidity, maybe. I should have known that they just wouldn't sit around waiting for this to be dealt with by the courts. I should have at least gotten a written statement from him."

"They could say you forced him to say it, couldn't they, darling?"

"Yes. Every time I turn around here, and try to do the right thing, or think I'm making progress, the rug gets pulled out from under me."

"Darling, maybe we should just let nature take its course."

"Drop it. Is that what you mean?"

"I feel your temperature rising."

"I can't imagine why. I look at you, my beauty, with those crutches, and think of all the pain you've been through. I remember the crash in the Everglades and how we could have been killed. I remember going undercover for these assholes and then everyone is released. I recall perfectly the Swamp Master's entire business in burning rubble—my supper club is virtually destroyed. And it all started with the purchase of a plane that we paid two hundred and fifty thousand dollars for, for the privilege of living this nightmare! Why would I be upset?"

"Perhaps we should just cut our losses and let it go. We can concentrate on rebuilding the club," she said.

"You know, honey." I stood up and walked to her. "I'm so angry at this moment that I have nothing I can say. I'm afraid I will regret whatever I say. I don't even have the club anymore, where at least I could sing away my sorrows." I put my arms around her and held her to me.

"We have no sorrows, not really," she said, looking up into my eyes and kissing me sweetly on the lips. "We have our love," she whispered in my ear. It sent shivers cascading down my spine.

On Monday morning at seven I was on the beach running. I ran a full three miles south to the rock jetty and sat for a while and just let the trade winds sooth my troubled mind. The sun was just rising from its sleep in the ocean depths. The sand was getting warmer on the soles of my feet.

I ran back along the edge of the surf where the sand is firmer. I had no clear next move. The civil case was filed now and would stand on its own merits. Jorge's cousin's friend had disappeared. I had called Jorge. He told me that his cousin had received a call from Jerman, who called to thank him for letting him stay and tell him he could keep his belongings, that he would not be back to pick them up.

I spotted a flock of seven pelicans flying in a perfect V, looking for breakfast. They passed me heading south, as I approached the house. They were like old friends; seeing them made me feel better.

Our house stood on the beach behind several rows of sand dunes. The dunes were covered with rows of sea oats, sea grass, and sea grapevines with tough roots that dug deep to keep the sand from eroding after beatings by the strong trade winds and violent tropical storms.

I looked up at the second floor and noticed that the French doors that led to the balcony were closed. They had been open when I left, and Merisol had not yet arrived. I veered away from the surf line and headed up the thin trail between the dunes that led to the house.

I stopped suddenly, feeling the presence of danger, of people. The dunes were tall, well over six feet, and covered with the sea grass and sea grapes that made it very difficult to see over the tops of the dunes. I was halfway through them. The dunes gave off a slight sighing sound in the constant prevailing wind that blew in from the ocean. I looked back and visually followed my footsteps in the sand to the edge of the surf. The beach was deserted; far down the line there were a few surfers, but no other sign of human life.

I dropped to one knee and studied the crest of the dune in front of me and the thin trail that led forward through the dunes, into the first floor of the house. The trail disappeared on the crest of the hill.

I waited and looked up again to the second floor balcony off our bedroom. The windows were locked tight shut. There was nothing visible. What was going on here? I wished I had my gun. I listened as intently as I could; no sound but the murmured singing of the sea grass.

I rose to my feet. I had no choice but to go forward. I decided to break off the trail and go deeper into the dunes and approach the house from the southern side.

I crouched, and ran the fifty feet through the twisted tough roots of the sea grapes and the tall sea grass. I had to watch my footing to keep from falling. I climbed the dune on the southern side of the property line and eased down the far side, crouching in the cover of the sea grass.

I could see four men in black ninja suits hidden at the base of the dunes; they were waiting for me to emerge from the trail that led to the ocean. On the back of the ninja suits, written in clear yellow letters, was U.S. CUSTOMS.

I heard a noise from the balcony above me, and looked up at a man standing by the rail of the balcony. I was staring into the barrel of an M-16. The man removed his black ninja mask. I was looking into the face of Rick Jacoby. He slowly smiled and said: "You're under arrest, asshole."

My first thoughts were of Lillian and how Jacoby had managed to get onto the balcony. He had to have passed through my bedroom.

I saw the four ninja-suited men buried at the base of the dunes turn toward me at the sound of Jacoby's voice. They all stood, and raced toward me full speed. I rose from the cover of the dunes and put my hands in the air. The first man to reach me hit me full in the stomach with the base of his rifle. I doubled up. The second man took my feet out from under me with a side kick. The third man landed on top of me, his knee in the small of my back.

I sputtered and coughed as two men shoved my face in the sand, while two men each grabbed one of my arms and ripped them behind my back until my two hands met. I could hear the cuffs clicking shut and biting into my wrists, tearing the skin.

Rick Jacoby watched from above. "Don't be so nice to him, boys. We got ourselves a real dangerous person on our hands. Double-cuff him. I hear he knows magic tricks on how to slip out of handcuffs."

The two men with their knees in my back slipped on a second pair of handcuffs. The second pair bit deeper into my skin, then the first pair. They pulled me to my feet. I was standing now, face-to-face with the squad leader, who still wore his black face mask. I wondered how he could stand the heat in that mask. Then he hit me square in the face with his gloved fist. Things started to spin. I buckled, going down on one knee.

In my nearly unconscious state I heard Jacoby again.

"That's enough, we don't want him too badly marked up from resisting arrest, like he's doin' right now. Get him in the SWAT van and let's get outta here."

I was in and out of consciousness as they ran me to their van. I looked for Lillian, but it was hard for my eyes to focus. I felt my toes dragging through the hot sand by the side of the house, and then scrape against the bricks of the driveway, before they tossed me into the back of the van.

They took me to the Federal Correctional Center next to the courthouse in downtown Miami, fingerprinted me, and put me in the holding tank.

Two hours later, Felix Rodriguez, my cousin, met me in an interview room. He read me the charges: "Conspiracy to import cocaine, money laundering, and attempting to alter an aircraft against FAA rules." He read slowly in a serious monotone. "Francisco, the charges are signed by Rick Jacoby and they name John Harrison and Elmer and John Jackson as witnesses."

"This is total and complete bullshit—what evidence have they trumped up?"

"I talked to Robert Cohen, the assistant U.S. attorney on this, and he said that they have videotapes, with audio and other evidence. He claims you walked into a U.S. Customs undercover operation and you didn't know it."

"Felix, this is a total waste of time. All we have to do is contact Bobby Day at the FAA and he will explain everything. He will explain how I went undercover on the request of the FAA and he will show you the videotapes and that it was a sting operation against them."

"He has tapes?"

"Well, the FAA or the DEA has the tapes. It will clear all this mess up."

"Francisco, be careful here—you are dealing with sophisticated people who are angry and on full red alert against you. They are not going to overlook something like these tapes."

"All right, Felix, please just contact Bobby Day, he will straighten this out."

"The bond hearing is set for tomorrow."

"Lillian. How's Lillian?"

"She's upset, but fine. They served the search warrant by smashing the front-door locks with a battering ram. A full SWAT team invaded the house. They scared the hell out of Lillian and Merisol when they burst into your bedroom. She told them you were out on the beach for your morning run."

"So that's why they were waiting for me. They could have just knocked."

"They found your Glock in your night table, fully loaded."

"It's my house, for Christ sake. Besides, the gun is registered."

"Doesn't matter, Francisco, they are busting your balls with it anyway."

"So, Felix, what do we do?"

"I'll get a hold of Bobby Day, and prepare for the bond hearing tomorrow. If I can get him to appear on your behalf at the bond hearing, maybe we can settle this tomorrow."

"Felix, why do you look so worried?"

"Francisco, *mi amigo,* I have a bad feeling on this. The government of the United States is fully capable of bearing false witness if it is their interest. I have seen it many, many times. The man you referred to in the Hawaiian shirt, do you have his name?"

"Michael Burton, at least that is the name he uses. He had the rank of colonel in Vietnam." Felix scribbled down the name on his legal pad and rose. "Why, why do you have a bad feeling on this, Felix?"

"Because it's too stupid a move to arrest you like this if they have not thought of a clever plan."

"Rick Jacoby is a moron," I said.

"Perhaps. But that is a very complex and sophisticated setup out at Florida Private Planes."

"So?"

"So, smarter minds are at work here, Francisco. Remember, we of the Miami Cuban community have been trying to free Cuba since 1958, when Castro came to power, over forty years ago."

"It's common knowledge that the CIA put Castro in power," I said. "Then he turned on the United States and allied with the Soviet Union."

"That is how it appeared, and perhaps how it was for a number of years, before the Soviet Union abandoned him. Maybe now these people help to keep him in power, Francisco—perhaps he is useful to certain people in our government—perhaps they have common interests."

"Sounds scary," I said with a smile, to lighten things up a little.

Felix did not find it funny. "Maybe it will be scary to you, *amigo*," he said.

He signaled for the guard. "I will see you at nine

tomorrow, Francisco. I will be working for your release until we meet."

"And Lillian, can you arrange for me to see Lillian?"

"Perhaps after tomorrow."

He shook both my handcuffed hands and left.

After Felix left I was removed from the visitors' room. I was taken to the holding pod. I could see the guards in the computer control room looking at me, and talking with each other. They were trying to decide whether or not to admit me into the general population or wait until after my bail hearing. The pod is a semi-circle of ten individual cells with tables and chairs that are bolted down and placed in the center. The prisoners in these holding cells are left with their own clothes and not admitted into the general population until their bail hearing comes up before the judge or before they make their bail, if it was set when they were arrested. The pod I was in was full, twenty prisoners.

I sat alone at a table and ate in silence. There were four other tables where the men sat. Some sat alone as I did, others sat and talked. Two of the men were still hyped up on coke or speed and were running off at the mouth, but no one bothered me. The phone was at the far end of the pod near the cell door, and only allowed for collect calls. After dinner and an hour of contemplation I lined up for the phone. Prison life was new to me, but these people inside the pod seemed to know instinctively to leave me alone. I had been brought over in my running shorts and a T-shirt, no shoes. They had given me a green prison jumpsuit and a pair of sandals to wear to court in the morning. The sign next to the phone explained that you were allowed one call of fifteen minutes duration and you could only call collect.

There was a Cuban on the phone in front of me who was using up the last minutes of his call. He was speaking in Spanish, and I heard him say he would call right back. He hung up and started to dial again. I spoke to him.

"You had your call," I said.

"Yeah, and I'm having another one."

"Look, there's no one behind me. I'll do my call and you can go again."

"Hey, my woman, she's waiting for me to call back."

"Hey, my woman's waiting for me to call for the first time," I said. I clicked off the phone and yanked the receiver from his hand so fast that he stood looking at his empty hand. It was a direct challenge. We stared at each other for long seconds. Neither of us wanted a scene before our bail hearings in the morning.

"We will settle this some other time," he said, relenting, cursing me out in Spanish as he returned to his table.

I dialed the collect call and waited. "Hi," I said.

"Hello, darling, are you all right?" Lillian asked.

"Fine. You?"

"I talked to Felix. He brought me up to date."

"I think it can be straightened out tomorrow."

"Felix is trying to contact Bobby Day," Lillian said. There was silence for a minute; neither one of us wanting to say what we really felt. "The Swamp Master called and told me to tell you he would be happy to do whatever he could to help."

"There's nothing for him to do right now, but tell him thanks."

253

R. L. Smitten

More silence. "I'll be there tomorrow."

"Thanks."

"I know you don't want to talk right now, so I'll see you in the morning with Felix," Lillian said, softly.

"Okay. Love you."

"Love you too, darling."

The cells were small, eight feet wide, each with two beds. The mattress was plastic, no sheets, a single blanket, no pillow. Some men were released just before lights out, so I was alone in my cell. I lay on the plastic mattress in my shorts and T-shirt, the jumpsuit was laid out on the bed above me. The mattress felt cold at first, then soon became hot and clammy.

I stared up at the ceiling of my cell, into the blackness. I knew I could not start to review my situation or my anger would overwhelm me—my anger, or was it my pride, or was it my ego? Whatever it was, I wanted to keep it at bay—the wolf pack was alive now and roaming in my thoughts, wild, tortured, ready to tear my brain apart with recriminations and anger.

It was four in the morning when I finally fell asleep.

I was fed a breakfast of weak coffee, milk, and corn flakes in an individual pack, at seven A.M., then taken directly in a prison van to the courtroom at eight. We were all in full shackles, leg irons, and handcuffs linked by steel rings to a waist belt chain. We hobbled into court and were left sitting in the prisoners' dock. A single marshal sat in a swivel chair, reading the *Miami Sentinel*, occasionally glancing our way.

I saw Felix Rodriguez walk in with Lillian. Lillian was using her crutches, unaided. She made her way down to the first row and sat in the seat closest to the

254

aisle. I smiled at her; she smiled with her eyes. Felix pushed through the swinging door and took his position in the lawyers' section of the courtroom. He waved at me as he opened his attaché case and removed my file.

Next, I saw Rick Jacoby enter. I wondered who his tailor was. Every suit he wore was about a half-size to small for him, so he always gave the impression that he was bursting out—as if his thick muscular body wanted to pop out of his suit, like the Incredible Hulk. He was followed into the courtroom by Michael Burton, who was dressed in a bright blue Hawaiian shirt with wildly colored tropical birds festooned across his chest and back. He wore tan slacks and loafers with no socks. He slipped into the back aisle. His sunglasses were stuck into his blond hair and perched on the top of his head. His face showed no expression, but I could feel him gloating. Jacoby went to the witness row of seats.

Felix Rodriguez came toward me, nodded at the marshal, and whispered to me, "How you doin' Francisco?"

"I've been better. You scare me with that look on your face. Where's Bobby Day?"

"Gone."

"What do you mean, gone?"

"He's been transferred out of the country. He's in transit, unable to be contacted."

"What about Inspector Greene?" I asked

"Gone, he's been posted to Australia. He's also in transit."

"Great. So, we're fucked here."

"Yes, Francisco, for the moment we have a problem, a big problem. They claim to have video recordings of you from when you were in the offices of John Harrison and when you all visited some strip club. They were filming you while you were filming them. They also claim to have your bank records, which will show a sizable withdrawal for you to buy this airplane. The prosecutor is Leonard Cohen, a tough guy with political ambitions. You make good copy for the media mills: Little Havana nightclub owner, well-known Cuban name, married to a beautiful socialite—makes for good reading. He's hot to trot on your bones."

"Christ! How could this happen!"

"Look, stay calm, we're just going to go for bail here. We'll figure it out when you are home."

Leonard Cohen, the prosecutor, walked in with two other federal prosecutors, who were obviously here to arraign the other prisoners in the docket with me. Felix nodded at Cohen, then turned back to me. "Look, I'm going over to talk to Leonard before the judge comes to see what he's after here."

I watched as Felix approached Cohen. I saw Felix's arms start to fly and his mouth move like crazy. I knew we had trouble.

The judge came in and called the court to order. We were first on the docket.

The bailiff allowed me to stand to face the court. My chains rattled as I rose.

Leonard Cohen, the prosecutor, spoke first. "Your Honor, the government requests a bond of five million dollars."

Felix spoke up. "Your honor, this is absurd, preposterous, this man is a respected . . ."

256

"Save your breath, sir. Let's find out why Mr. Cohen is setting such a high bond," the judge declared.

"Mr. Cruz is a definite flight risk. He is a naturalized citizen from Cuba. He still has family in Cuba. He is accused of very serious crimes."

Felix spoke next. "Mr. Cruz is a respected member of the community, he is married, has a business in the state of Florida, and—"

"Save your expensive breath Mr. Rodriguez; the prisoner will be remanded in custody under a bond of five million dollars." The judge pounded his gavel.

I fell into my chair like someone had punched me in my stomach. Michael Burton had his sunglasses on now and was staring straight at me. His tanned face showed a slight expression, a fuck-you-Francisco expression. He had the power of the U.S. Government behind him. I got the feeling he wasn't through with me yet. All my anger seemed to well up and center in my hands. I felt that if I let my anger go I could break these chains with my bare hands. But instead, I sat quietly in the prisoners' dock looking straight ahead. I watched Lillian and Felix as they slipped out the courtroom doors.

I knew they were going to try and make my bail.

Chapter Nine

I stood there naked waiting for the search.

Prison life is like no other kind of life. It's unnatural to begin with, to lock men and women up in a small cell, humiliate them, anger them, and then sit back and watch what happens—try it with any animal and see what happens.

The Miami Correctional Center is right across from the Miami Federal Court House in downtown Miami. The building is a huge solid concrete high-rise slab, broken by a few perpendicular slits in the concrete. The slits let just enough light in to enable the prisoners to keep a dim recollection that there was a real world outside that grim building. A world they could remember, with a blue ocean, splayed green fingers of palm trees waving in the soft tropical trade winds, white sand beaches with breaking surf, and beautiful bikini-clad women strolling in the noonday sun. These memories were not to be stirred for pleasure; they are another form of punishment.

It was two days since my bail hearing. I had talked to Lillian on the phone and she was reviewing our financial position to try and raise bail. It was going to take a huge bite out of us financially. The government wanted more than just Lillian's house on the ocean; they wanted some cash as well.

I was in the holding pen and was waiting to go into the visiting room. The guards waved me forward.

The guard moved to face me. "Okay, you know the drill, convict—run your fingers through your hair."

I did it.

"Open your mouth and pull your ears forward."

I did it.

"Lift your sack."

I did it.

"Turn around bend over and spread 'em"

I did it.

"Okay, put your jumpsuit on and get in line by the door with them others," the guard said as he waved the next prisoner forward.

The metal door to the visitors' room was opened, and I entered. The visitors' room in the Miami Correctional Center is a large open room with chairs in the center for the waiting prisoners and tables with chairs, the legs screwed into the concrete rug-covered floor. Along the far wall are individual small rooms, fronted by glass for meetings with lawyers. I saw Felix in one of the offices and joined him.

He stood and shook my hand. "Francisco, you look well under the circumstances."

"I haven't lost my tan yet, Felix." I sat down. "How is Lillian?"

"She's walking better now; her doctor saw her today, and said her walking cast can come off on Friday. Has she told you?"

"No. I think maybe she wants to surprise me by walking in here."

"So, I ruined her surprise."

"Don't worry Felix, I'll act surprised."

"Well, Francisco, I'm afraid this thing gets darker and darker."

"What a surprise!" I said sarcastically.

"I finally got in contact with the two FAA men— Inspector Greene and this Bobby Day. They said that they are not allowed to talk about an ongoing investigation and that I should speak to the FAA attorney, Floyd Donaldson. He fed me the same line, that he was unable to discuss an open case with me—and since I was representing you I was off-limits and everything they had would be forthcoming with the Brady material in the natural course of the discovery process."

"Stonewalling."

"Yes, and I got the feeling this was being very well orchestrated, maybe from on high."

"Washington?"

"Perhaps."

"Look, Felix, I don't get it—none of this is that important, is it?"

"Francisco, I have a bad feeling about this; perhaps

you stumbled into something that is much bigger than you think it is."

"Do you know something, Felix? Something you're not telling me?"

"No, Francisco, I do not know anything that I have not told you."

"Felix, please don't play with me, here—this is my life and Lillian's life. Is the word *know* some kind of weird lawyer bullshit—like to *know* something is to have proof and to suspect something is not to really *know* it. You suspect something here, Felix?"

"Well, Francisco, since you put it that way. This man Michael Burton, he is known to the Miami 'Cuba Liberta' movement, but they have never been able to turn up any proof of his involvement."

"With Castro?"

"They doubt if it is Fidel himself; they think his brother Raul may be involved with this man."

"Dope?"

"They have never been able to prove it." Felix looked me directly in the eyes; silence enveloped the room. He continued. "There may also be stolen planes and plane parts involved somehow."

"Felix, how the hell would you know this?"

"My dear friend, how I know this is none of your business. But do you think we don't debrief the boat people that float up on the shores of South Florida from Cuba? You think some of these people that enter the United States weren't really our spies in Cuba to begin with? You think that we don't have a network of spies in Cuba who are preparing for the day when Castro is gone and the island is free to be reorganized?"

R. L. Smitten

"You gonna be the new president of Cuba, Felix, now that Jorge Mas Canosis is dead?" I asked.

"Be careful what you joke about, Francisco." He smiled.

"Who's joking, Felix. I was trying to get my vote in early."

Felix smiled. "It is unimportant who will become the new president of Cuba. What is important is that Cuba will someday soon be a free democratic society."

"Felix, you know sometimes I'm a slow learner; sometimes my emotions, my anger clouds my thinking. Let me just go off on some free-form thinking here," I said. "How about coffee first."

Felix nodded, and went to the coffee machine, I waited a few seconds to think before I spoke. He returned to the room, closed the glass door, handed me the steaming black coffee from the dispensing machine.

I began. "Castro has outlived eight American Presidents and the fall of the Soviet Union. He took over Cuba with the help of the U.S. Government, as we know he was originally sponsored by the CIA. He seized control and then told the CIA, thanks, but he was only kidding—it's Mother Russia that he really loves. He became a thorn in our side. He also pissed off the American Mafia when they lost their casinos and hotels, and they wanted to see him dead. The U.S. Government tried to kill him a dozen times, in a dozen different ways, and failed. Many people think he had a lot to do with the death of John Kennedy, since he was tired of being a target himself. He openly raped and looted his own country for personal gain, and is reported to have a personal fortune parked offshore of billions of dollars. So far, am I correct, Felix?"

"Yes, but most of this is now public knowledge."

"Let me continue. Our boy Castro knows he is getting older and Cuba is the last Communist state in this hemisphere, and outside of China and North Korea, anywhere else in the world that counts. But Castro is smart, and a student of history. He knows he can not withstand the coming tidal wave of democracy, a global economy, and a world of open information thanks to the Internet, and besides, his system of government stinks, as witnessed by the dismal shape that Cuba and Russia are now in—all this I know, what don't I know, Felix?"

"I will ask you a question, my friend. What provides power?"

"Money?"

"Yes, because with the money you can always have the power. But if you have the power and you don't have the money, well, then . . ."

"Your power is always in jeopardy and most likely short-lived," I answered.

We both sat in silence and finished our coffee. I broke the silence. "So, how specifically does this relate to me and Michael Burton?"

"We don't know exactly."

"How about un-exactly? You know anything un-exactly, Felix?" I asked.

"Nothing I want to talk about yet. Don't be upset, Francisco. I am not trying to be deceptive here, but we have no actual proof of anything. I do not want to tell you something that is absolutely wrong, have you go down the wrong trail, and get into more trouble. All we know is that the key to the puzzle appears to be this Michael Burton. Yet he eludes us."

"So, how do I stand right now, Felix?"

"Not good. We will get little help on discovery, the Brady material will be squeezed slowly out from the U.S. attorney. They will take their time, since they believe you will have a lot of trouble making your bail; they feel they will soften you up in here, break your will to fight . . . get you to plead out. It is standard procedure for the U.S. attorney's office."

"But Lillian . . ."

"Yes, they know Lillian is rich and can help you with your bail. They also know that she is also in serious litigation on the estate that she inherited from her former husband; most of those funds are being held in escrow or have disappeared, stolen by Richard's partners, and therefore no good for you."

"That's why they won't accept the house as collateral."

"Yes, they say they want some cash as well as the house. They are trying to leave you with no cash."

"Bastards."

"What, Francisco? You think they will play fair? Who plays fair in this world? And how do these men and women, the prosecutors, how do they get promoted?"

"Convictions and confiscations—that's how," I answered.

"Yes, they get no points for dealing in justice—justice does not make you the U.S. attorney—it's convictions and confiscations—big high-profile media cases like this one are what they dream of."

"So, where are we?" I asked.

"We are working hard to get your bail together, and I am doing everything I can to get the evidentiary procedure in place."

"Thanks, Felix. It's just breaking my balls to be in here. Any advice?"

"Take deep breaths." He smiled. "Lots of deep breaths."

We parted and I went back through the iron door that led to the cell blocks. There were over two thousand men locked in this concrete coffin, a place where you could only socialize with felons, convicted or accused. The *college for criminals,* I called it.

Back in the prisoner anteroom I took off my jumpsuit, socks, and underwear and stood naked with my fellow prisoners in the cold air-conditioning as the guards conducted their search of each and every one of us. My anger was almost overwhelming, my stomach was churning with bile, my fists were clenched, my breathing was short, my eyes focused. But there was nowhere to reach out, nothing to hit, no way to respond, and that was what they wanted. I had to keep my cool, my composure, as I ran my fingers through my hair, brought my earlobes forward, lifted my testicles, and turned around to spread my cheeks. Somehow, some way I would get even for this.

I took a deep breath. My time would come if I was patient—this I knew.

It was just past dawn when the Swamp Master kissed his wife gently on the cheek. He marveled at how peacefully she slept and how young she looked in slum-

ber. He backed the pickup truck out of the driveway and made his way down the road toward his dock. He had rented a trailer to use while his building was rebuilt. He had purchased a half-dozen airboats in varying states of repair. He was rebuilding them so he could rent them out and put them up for sale. He had launched his first airboat into the water two days ago. It was eighteen feet long with a Lycoming engine and his proprietary two-propeller configuration. He had tested it at the dock, but he had not yet gone on a test run.

He had been unable to sleep well, ever since the explosion, and he wished that Mai Lynh had gone with the kids, but there was no telling a strong woman like her what to do. Besides, the Swamp Master believed that deep down she maybe had a yen for the drama in life. It was common for those men and women who had lived through the war in Vietnam. The adrenaline highs were too high, never forgotten, never duplicated; the highs later in life were never as high and the lows never as low. He believed the same might be true of this woman who had lived through that tragedy and now shared his bed. Maybe it was one of the reasons he was so in love with her—she had deep dark secrets and so did he. He never wanted to hear hers and she never wanted to hear his. It was the fact that they each had those secrets that bound them together. Secrets born inside each of them in the same time and in the same place—but different and personal. How could she sleep so well? he asked himself with a smile. He marveled at the difference between the Oriental mind and his own. She looked so peaceful that morning, so like his babies.

He parked the pickup and rubbed his hand on the hood, sweeping off the beads of dew; the warm engine hood felt good under his hand. He rubbed his face with his wet hand, feeling the stubble of his beard. He then swept both his hands across the hood, rubbing the moisture into his eyes and hair. It felt good, pure, and cool in the early morning heat that was coming up out of the swamp with the rising sun.

He went to the new Coke machine and slapped the side out of habit, but nothing came out. He reached in his pocket, took out fifty cents, and waited for the can of Coke to come rolling out into his waiting hand. "Good as coffee in the morning," he thought to himself as he took a long swig. He walked the dock gingerly; all the boards had not yet been replaced from the explosion, so he had to watch his footing.

He sat in the driver's seat and checked the fuel. There was less than a quarter of a tank, but that would be enough for a test run out to Florida Bay and back. He looked out at the little river that led through the swamp, past Everglades City and into Florida Bay. He would cruise slowly till he reached the open water, then he would open her up. The wind sock on the end of the dock lay limp, no breeze, not a whisper. He released the dock lines and pushed the boat about a foot away from the dock.

He climbed in and strapped himself into the seat with an X aviation safety belt that was attached to the steel pipes behind his head. He put on his earphones to deaden the sound, and placed the key in the ignition.

He fired up the beast of an engine; it growled and rumbled first, then roared into life. Even with the sound-deadeners on his ears he knew the sound; he loved the sound, a primeval roar of a beast that he had built with his own hands.

He dropped the throttle back, slowly he engaged the clutch, and he inched forward, creeping, moving away from the dock and into the river. He noticed that the tide was going out, so it would be with him all the way to Florida Bay.

He pushed the throttle ahead slowly.

The power of the explosion was like the power of a jet engine. The roar was overwhelming, drowning out the engine. He was suddenly airborne, flying across the river, as a second explosion filled the air. He could feel a huge wave of heat as a fireball of aviation fuel chased him into the air like the ascending tongue of a red serpent.

Thoughts flashed through his head, his entire life whizzed by him, like snapping picture cards in slow motion: his life as a boy in the great swamp, his life in the bowels of Vietnam, his life as a smuggler, his beautiful wife, his amazing wonderful children. They would be taken from him now. His last thoughts were: "How the hell could they do this to me—blow me up twice?" And he knew the answer: "Because they were pros and they knew it would be the last thing I expected them to do."

Then everything turned white, then gray, then black—darkest black, black as the mouth of hell.

* * *

It was two days later that I heard this story. Lillian had come to the MCC to see me with the news that the Swamp Master had been blown up, but had lived. He was in Jackson Memorial Hospital and was in fair condition.

"I guess it was a miracle that he survived," Lillian said, "Mai Lynh called me with the news. It had something to do with his seat—his seat on the airboat that saved him."

"How was she?"

"Hard to tell, she is so stoic, inscrutable, but she had a real edge to her voice. I couldn't tell if it was anger, frustration, rage . . . I don't know. It was very strong, whatever it was."

"What did she say they were going to do?"

"She would not discuss the future. She said she would only discuss the present. It was how she got through her life—no past, no future—only the present. It was all you knew and all you could control. She does not deal in speculation."

There was a silence that came, a calm welcome silence between us. Lillian broke it. "You know, in a way she is right. The present is all we really have. I was just thinking of us crashing and being rescued by the Swamp Master and then his life begins to change."

"You think we caused his trouble—the trouble he has now?"

"I don't know. These chains of events that are somehow set into motion . . . I don't know, I just don't know. Look at us now, you in jail, the whole thing is incredible. What do you think?"

"I think sometimes there are things set in motion

over which we have no control, but perhaps they are meant to be."

"That sounds fatalistic." She smiled. "Darling, Felix called with good news. The government will accept the house and five hundred thousand in securities, which I will send them from my account at Morgan Stanley."

"That's good news? You are pledging your major asset and just about everything in your stock market account. I have trouble seeing how that is good news."

"Please, Francisco, don't do this. I want you home. We can get through this. We have gotten through everything else together. Come home to me." She looked at me with those eyes, sexy, soft, and sweet . . . all at the same time. "Look, I'm sorry. It's just that I'm . . ."

"Angry? Who wouldn't be, darling—just come home to me." She reached over and squeezed my hand. "My cast is coming off soon." She leaned across the visitors' room table and whispered in my ear. "And I need you." Her soft breath sent shivers down my spine and into my loins.

"I need you too," I whispered back. She took her hand, turned my head, and we kissed.

The next day Felix came with some clothes and got me out of the slammer. He took me to Coconut Grove Hotel. It's a beautiful hotel that overlooks Biscayne Bay. He stopped his Mercedes in front and handed me a key. "Penthouse, just go up—she's waiting."

I did as I was told, getting off at the top floor. I used the key and walked into a big one-bedroom suite. The view was beautiful. It overlooked the Coconut Grove Marina and Biscayne Bay. A sensational mixture of sailboat masts, coconut palms, tropical foliage, and the beautiful colors of Biscayne Bay. Lillian was waiting for me, wearing a white full-length dressing gown. She was standing, leaning against a chair. I went to move to her.

"No, darling," she said. She demurely moved the dressing gown to one side to slightly expose her leg. The cast was gone, but I saw the crutches in the corner. She saw me look at them. "Don't worry, darling, they're just for support until my circulation returns and I get full use of my leg."

I walked to her and held her in my arms. "I'm so glad."

"Yes, God was good to us. I prayed and prayed that it would be all right. The knee is good, only a small limp, which is nothing." She smiled.

We drank our champagne and I toasted her. "To you, my love—you with the great courage."

We ate a light lunch and then after lunch I kissed her and whispered, "Darling, how would you feel about . . ."

She put her finger to my lips. "Shsss . . . I'm reading your mind." She smiled. "Or maybe I'm reading *my* mind."

She took my hand and led me to the bedroom.

That evening I drove to see the Swamp Master in his hospital room in Jackson Memorial. He was sitting up in his bed reading an aviation magazine. A picture of Mai Lynh and the kids was propped up on the table next to him. He gave me a great big grin when I walked in.

"Hey podner, how they hangin'?"

"I think I should ask you that."

"I'm afraid to check them out—they might still be airborne." He smiled. "Any of them bad dudes in the slam try to make you their sweetheart?"

"No. I told them I knew the Swamp Master and he had cousins everywhere."

"Damn right."

"So, what saved your sorry ass?" I asked.

"My seat, believe it or not. You drove helicopters, right?"

"Yeah."

"Well, then, you know what you did with your helmet when you were flyin' "

"Sat on it like every other grunt in the war."

"That's right, 'cause you didn't want to take a round up your ass. Have one of them little bastards hidin' in the bush shoot your balls off with small-arms fire."

"So?"

"So, for some reason, I always made the seats of my boat triple-thick stainless steel. And I make 'em big. The assholes put the charge right under my seat. The explosion popped the bolts and sent me into orbit. I was still strapped into the seat when they pulled me out of the muck and mire of the great swamp. I coulda drowned from the muck, I went in so deep. One of the goddamn propellers stuck in the muck point-first only a foot from my head."

"So how come you're in the hospital?"

"Some tourist took a picture of me stuck head-first in the swamp mud like a human javelin with the saw grass all squashed down. It was the saw grass and the mud that saved me. The doctors took one look at that photo and convinced themselves I must have some sort of head damage. Hell, there ain't nothin' wrong with my head a couple of beers and a fast airboat ride through the swamp couldn't cure. They're just about done their probin' and testin'. Waste of money, I keep telling 'em. Lucky I got health insurance."

"So, you feel like talking?" I asked.

"Maybe."

"There's more going on here than I know, isn't there?"

"Yeah, podner, it's a knot of water moccasins all fuckin' each other."

"They fuckin' you too?" I asked.

"I'm a prime target for them."

"Because you flew for them?" I asked.

"Yeah, you could say that."

"What else could I say. What are you holding back."

"I knew we was in for big trouble the instant I saw that Hawaiian shirt."

"Michael Burton?" I asked.

"Colonel Michael Burton is his correct title. I shoulda split when I seen him out there in the Glades at the airstrip when he come up to me. He just figured I was up to my old tricks, was doin' my mechanic gig. But that night when we was out at the airfield and escaped with the airboat, he probably figured it was me."

"I don't get it. Why did he just blow up your shop and not go after you the first time?"

"Because he wanted to warn me off, but when you continued with the lawsuit, he felt that I was becoming a real threat to him."

"But I'm under indictment now and . . ."

"Hey, Francisco, forget it. These boys are playin'

chess all the time. They are always at least two moves ahead, and they think of every contingency."

"And? What am I missing?"

"Sooner or later I could have come up as a witness against them in your trial. They figure that maybe I saved some of them ID plates from the hangar in the Glades, maybe there are photos, and most important— maybe I'll rat them out on what I used to do for them."

"What you told me you did for them?" I asked.

The Swamp Master said nothing. He reached over for some water and took a sip from his glass. He put the glass back, then took the picture of his family from the night table. He looked at the picture for long seconds. He placed the picture back on the table. He looked me straight in the eyes and spoke.

"There's more, Francisco."

"Jesus Christ, there's always more, isn't there."

"Yeah, when you get in a game like this, there is always more."

"Tell me."

"Everything I told you was true. I just left out one part."

"And that's the part that they want to kill you for."

"Yeah. After they busted me in the Bahamas, I did fly just one big mission for them, but we made a stop on the way to the USA. I brought that C-130 into Cuba."

"Guantanamo?"

"No, it's very close to Guantanamo, but it's inside Cuban territory. It is so close to Guantanamo that you disappear on the radar screen. It looks like you landed in Guantanamo, but it is really inside Cuba. The entire operation is run by Raul Castro, Fidel's brother. It's a full airfield operation; there are hangars, a two-mile airstrip that can handle any plane. Planes are repaired there, modified there."

"Like Opa-Locka and the strip in the Glades."

"Yeah, it's a network with the hub bein' Cuba. The Colombians all use it, the Mexicans use it on occasion to service the East Coast and Europe. Every kind of drug is warehoused there; it's a free-zone port for any and all contraband. Only, it ain't free. Everything is charged for, fuel, fixin' the planes, warehousin'. Listen, Francisco, it ain't only drugs. There's a big business in weapons—gunrunnin' and high-tech military gear like computers, stolen cars. Now the Russians are involved as well. Ex-KGB guys bringin' in all kinds of weapons and technology from Russia for distribution elsewhere.

"Hell, Francisco, it's perfect. Everybody knows everybody from the Cold War days and the Vietnam days. Old enemies, now friends, lookin' for a war, supplyin' everybody from the IRA in Ireland to the Arabs in the Middle East, and all the while buildin' up their bank accounts. And who is the master of ceremonies?"

"Fidel."

"Of course Fidel. Look at that old fuck. He's brilliant. Who do you think is head of his security? An ex—Israeli—one of the Mossad chiefs, so we got ourselves a huge international cluster of the most giantest proportions of international gangsters doin' business from the world's perfect *contraband free zone*."

"And you saw it?" I asked.

"Yes, with my very own fuckin' eyes, and I recognized a lot of the other American pilots hangin' there, because of my shenanigans in Vietnam and my days of smugglin'."

"A lot of bad dudes all together, in one secure spot, well organized, well funded, well backed by a group of governments," I added.

"That's where you're slightly wrong, Francisco. It ain't the governments. It's rogue agents within the governments."

"But they represent their governments."

"Yeah. It's real complex, and no one really knows how far up it goes in any of these governments—like was Yeltsin or his daughter involved with the Russian gangsters and why did the new guy, Putin, give him a pardon."

"And the minute you say the whole government is corrupt, you get discredited and blown off as some kind of conspiracy nut," I said.

"Yeah, great opportunity for spin, spin, and fuckin' spin. Like the old Mafia guys—they always had other people do the dirty work, and on occasion they would have to sacrifice these people."

"Because basically it isn't true. It isn't the government," I added.

"That's right, always remember it's rogue agents and no one knows who's in it with them or how high up it goes along government lines. It's all being driven by these complex agendas—the Colombians, the CIA, the Russians, the Cubans, the Mexicans . . ."

"But underneath it is only two things that are driving this, money and power," I said.

"You got that right, podner. And that makes them all blood brothers in the end."

"And the party leader is Fidel."

"Yeah, and his surrogate is his brother, Raul. Sure, Castro was all indignant when it was plainly disclosed he was dealin' drugs. He said he didn't know nothin' about it, nothin' at all. And this General Ochoa and thirteen others were quickly tried and executed and then Castro announces the whole thing is behind him."

"When?"

"They were shot in 1989. It was all bullshit. Since the late eighties, early nineties, it's been impossible for the Cubans financially. Remember—the Russians were packin' up and busy going bankrupt. The sugar crop is shit, the world market price of sugar has been falling for a long time. The rest of the world is abandoning Communism, the Cuban people are discontent. How's the army goin' to get paid? How's Castro gonna keep a base of power? He knows his country is eventually gonna become democratic—then what about Fidel? He's gotta have some huge stash of money for when Cuba goes democratic."

"So you're saying it's the power, stupid!" I said.

"Of course, and you need the money to have the power, any kind of power; that's all he ever wanted— that stupid Communism crap was just used to get him to be boss—absolute boss, supreme dictator of ten million people, since 1958—what a fuckin' trip, the ultimate fantasy power-fuck, a forty-two-year orgasm of absolute power over an entire nation. He makes Saddam look like an amateur, because he's a hundred times smarter and he's been a constant thorn in the side of the United States and there is nothin' the U.S. can do.

"And it goes on to this very fuckin' day. Remember

when a lot of this came out in 1994, exposed with the Noriega trial that Cuba was the hub? It was made public that Noriega was goin' over there to Cuba on a regular basis, meetin' with Pablo Escobar, the Ochoa brothers, and Carlos Lehder. Christ, Lehder testified that this all happened and the rest of the Cartel was up to their eyeballs in Cuba. Hell, they even had pictures of them."

"In Cuba!" I said. "I remember a group photo."

"Just use your head, Francisco. Castro is not going to give up over a billion dollars in U.S. cash income every year, and the chance to pollute this country with drugs, not on your life—common fuckin' sense tells you that."

"And he's got powerful partners."

"The most powerful, the smartest, the richest kind of partners—why would he fuckin' quit. It's the perfect plan, and Guantanamo is the perfect cover. Planes flyin' in and out of Cuban airspace all the time, ours and theirs, some legal flights, some illegal. Rogue Customs and CIA agents in the game, rich Colombian and Mexican drug lords, now brown heroin's comin' in along with cocaine and pot galore—a huge drug-supermarket free zone—gimme a fuckin' break! What a business, cocaine, marijuana, and heroin, a tropical cash crop that costs shit to grow and process, there is so much profit margin that everybody gets a big hit, as long as it remains an illegal drug. A huge international business."

"All right, I get it. I'm a little confused about you and them."

"Hey podner, it's easy. Follow the action. You crash

right in front of me in the Glades and then I feel sorry for you. I could also use a few extra bucks, so when you ask me to go undercover as a mechanic in Opa-Locka, it sounds all right. Then they move me to the Glades operation.

"And then one day when I'm in the Glades hangar workin', I see this fuckin' Colonel Michael Burton and he sees me. The minute I lay eyes on him I know it's trouble. I shouldda just split right then, but I'm kind of disbelievin' that this could happen, him and me turnin' up in the same spot.

"But when you think about it, it makes perfect sense. South Florida, it's the cockroach corner for every doper and illegal aviation junkie in the United States. Why wouldn't he be here? It's where the action is—the illegal action.

"Francisco, why you happened to crash in front of me I'll never fuckin' know, never. My life has had many strange turns—like yours. Sometimes I feel I'm just livin' out a script that somebody else has written for me."

"And now? This very instant?"

"I'm fucked. That's a fact. See, at first they thought it would just blow over. They couldn't believe they were actually raided by their own sister agencies—the FAA and the DEA actually raids a rogue U.S. Customs and NSA-CIA undercover operation—a giant cluster fuck then occurs.

"So, they figure it all out and they figure they can handle it internally—cover it up, since they all have the same ultimate boss in Washington. But Francisco, you make a move they don't expect—you keep goin' after

them—goin' undercover, raidin' their Glades operation, filing a civil lawsuit, gettin' the newspaper to run
that story. Look, I'm a live eyewitness. I seen what goes
on in Cuba and sooner or later they think I'll talk, like
I'm talking to you here, and they just want all this shit
to go away."

"So, I'm probably next."

"Yeah, they wanted to discredit you, you got no credibility, because you're a crazy Cuban—that's how they
will explain you away. They set a huge bail on you for
extra insurance. If they can keep you locked up, you
got no chance of doin' nothin' more, and in about a
year or two your trial comes up and away you go into
the slammer, hard time in some federal institution. And
they got all the clout they need to take care of you."

"But I made my bond."

"Right, you're still bustin' their balls, and now you're
out on the street—my guess is you have an accident,
probably a car accident in one of them fancy I-talian
cars of yours. Or maybe you die of a heart attack from
a huge hit of adrenaline they inject directly into your
veins—they're creative when they want to be."

"You scared?" I asked.

"Look here, podner, I ain't never figured out whether
I might like to be scared—like why did I go to Vietnam
and then do the smugglin' and then workin' undercover
for you, or maybe I just like the action."

"An action junkie!"

"That what you think I am—like lookin' in a mirror,
huh, Francisco."

"We have wives, your children to think of here," I

said. "And what about Mai Lynh, what does she think?"

"Well, she heard the blast, and was there when they were pullin' my kisser out of the muck. She ain't too happy, but she's got that Oriental attitude." The Swamp Master went silent.

"Which is?"

"When trouble comes there are only two ways to go—accept the trouble and live with it, or take the trouble on—confront the son of a bitch."

"And how does she feel?"

"Well, she's at the lawyers' today switchin' all our assets into my brother's name in trust for our kids in case we don't make it. She says she don't want to go on with out me."

"Even with the children."

"Yeah, she says I got one of them extended families, the Pinders, where all the kids are welcomed no matter where they come from or what happens. She says she witnessed it herself. Twenty-four hours after they seen her, the shock wore off, after they seen she was an Oriental and all; they gave her a big hug and accepted her and later our kids, when they come along. She says it wouldn't be no good without me."

The Swamp Master looked out the window. He looked at me and rubbed his eyes slightly. "Can you believe that, Francisco, she says it wouldn't be the same without me, even over our kids. She wants to be with me over . . . nobody ever said nothin' like that to me before."

"What have you two decided?"

"Well, me, I ain't got much choice—she's right, it's

flight or fight for me. I can run like a motherfucker and hide in the Great Swamp or I fight the bastards. Problem is, I never was much good at runnin' and hidin' from nobody. And they went too far tryin' to kill me. Hell, I was pretty much resolved to just let it go. But I don't like it when they try to kill me. And right through me I'm a true American and I don't see much different here than that corrupt sorry excuse for a government they had in South Vietnam."

"And Mai Lynh?"

"She's a fighter, and there's somethin' I ain't never told nobody, didn't see no reason before."

"Christ, you never run out of surprises."

"I just started." He smiled. "See, Mai Lynh was in a Catholic orphan convent, like I told ya, but she run away to Saigon in the mid-sixties. She went to work in one of them boom-boom joints as a coochie dancer, and a hostess. You know. You were there."

"Yeah, I was there, all right."

"So, I met her in one of them joints. I liked her. So I set her up with an apartment. I was makin' great money flyin' them spooks around the Nam. Some of that ear money never made it for buyin' ears, or maybe sometimes them spooks only paid fifty dollars an ear to them Chinese Mung mercenaries, not a hundred, and kept the rest for themselves. Anyway, I was doin' good, getting big tips from the spooks to close my eyes. And I really liked her and I didn't wanna catch no diseases."

"Then you fell in love."

"I guess it's we—we fell in love."

"But maybe you wondered if it really was 'we.' Now,

today, you finally know for sure it was real—it was *we*," I said.

"Maybe, never can tell," he said, looking away for a second time, wiping his eyes for a second time. "Can't never tell," he whispered.

"So, you got a plan?" I asked.

"We got a half-assed plan."

"You're lookin' for the other half."

"You could say that."

"Well, I don't have the other half, not yet," I said.

"They really busted your balls on the bail, huh?"

"Yeah, five million dollars for what should have been a hundred-thousand-dollar bond tops," I said.

"I guess Lillian loves you, proves it with cash on the barrelhead." The Swamp Master smiled. "So, right back at yah with the love stuff. In case you didn't know she loves you, you know now," he said with a big Swamp Master grin. "So, we gonna' be victims, or victors?"

"Take a guess," I said, smiling back.

"Francisco, I gotta' get out of here. I'm all right now, just a little headache that comes and goes. They can reach out for me here anytime, if they want."

"Where's Mai Lynh?"

"On her way."

"You got a friendly doctor?"

"Yeah, Jedadiah Sawyer, he's my—"

"Cousin, I know."

"No, he's my uncle, Uncle Jed."

"Well, get him on a fax machine to get you released out of here."

The Swamp Master picked up the phone. He was a

man of action. Mai Lynh arrived and we helped him out of the hospital. We helped him into a sitting position in the bed of his pickup in a wheel chair. I followed in my old Jeep as Mai Lynh drove.

When we hit the Card Sound Road that led to Key Largo, I could see the Swamp Master turn his chair around and put his face into the wind, like a dog when he pushes his mug out the window of a moving car. The Swamp Master wanted to feel the wind, and smell the salt air-water coming in from Card Sound. And he wanted to look at his beautiful wife, her silky black hair snaking black strands against the glass behind her head as she drove down the unlit blacktop road that coiled through the Upper Keys. He wanted to know he was alive, really alive.

We pulled down an unpaved road in Tavernier to a trailer park on the Atlantic side. "Pinder Village— Trailer Park and R.V. Center."

We were greeted by two of the Swamp Master's relatives. They quickly ensconced him and Mai Lynh in a trailer by the ocean. As I left, the security gate was closed behind me. I noticed that the Swamp Master's relatives both had pistols stuffed in their waistbands. These people knew everything that went on in their family. They took no chances; they had been doing dark deeds in the night in Southern Florida for hundreds of years.

After talking to the Swamp Master I was slightly paranoid. I asked Lillian to meet me at the nightclub, which was still shut down. Maybe they had wired our home when they were in there with the warrant to arrest me. I could take no chances.

I told Lillian everything as she and I sat at the best table in the house, at the foot of the darkened stage. The electricity was still on. I had opened us two bottles of cold beer I had taken from the bar refrigerator. She sipped her glass as I talked. I brought her completely up to date.

"So, we wandered into a knot of water moccasins doing it to each other, as your friend would say," she said when I finished.

"An evil that was born in Vietnam, lived through Iran-Contra, the Colombian drug wars, and the evil continues to prosper now as it twists and turns and re-invents itself. A bunch of rogue agencies with tentacles of power that reach God knows where."

She polished off her small glass of beer and extended her arm for a refill. I poured in silence.

"So, what is the Swamp Master's half-a-plan?" she asked.

"I didn't ask." I smiled. "I thought I would leave him alone for tonight. I could tell that Mai Lynh wanted him to herself."

"And you wanted some time to dream up your half?" She smiled.

"How about our half, darling. That was our deal, wasn't it?"

She stretched over the table and kissed me, then whispered, "I'm glad your memory works."

"Everything works." I smiled back after the kiss.

She settled back in her seat. "I know, darling. I know everything works." She gave me that sexy little look, her lip slightly curled upwards. "So, let's hear it—our plan."

"Not yet, because I have no plan. How about you—you got a contribution to our plan?"

"No, I have no plan, but I have a surprise and a secret."

"I love surprises, but I'm nervous about the secret." I smiled.

"Don't be nervous, darling. The secret first. You know I used to play the piano when I was a girl. The secret is—I have been taking piano lessons and the surprise is that I learned a song. If I play, will you sing?"

"On a darkened stage with only a glass of champagne and you—what could be more romantic. What's the song?"

"I only learned one song—'My Romance' "

"Rodgers and Hart, the best. How about 'Our Romance'?" I said.

She walked the steps to the stage with very little assistance from her cane. She sat down and played the intro.

I sang softly, and slowly she followed.

I finished looking directly at her as she concentrated on the keys in front of her, finally hitting the last note and looking up at me. I sat down next to her on the stool and she put her head on my shoulder. We sat in silence for a few minutes, and returned to our table. I filled our glasses.

"Francisco, I've been thinking about all this and since Cuba seems to be the key, why not talk to Felix? He's a major person in the Cuban community."

"I was thinking along those lines. I'll do it in the morning. Now, let's go home. I have something else on my mind."

"Good idea," she said, smiling, drinking her glass of champagne in one slow sip.

The next noon I had lunch with Felix on South Beach in the open air. I told him what the Swamp Master had told me.

"I'll take all this under the client-lawyer privilege, and what I'm about to tell you I'll deny if I'm ever asked."

"Don't worry I'm not wired," I said with a smile.

"Francisco, everything the Swamp Master told you is true. Now I will tell you some things that are also true. Rumors of this have been around since the early 1980s. Be patient and listen carefully, perhaps we can connect all the dots."

We waited for our lunch to come. I ate my salad slowly and listened carefully, very carefully.

He started. "It all begins with the Cold War and Communism. It seems like a time long ago and far away. The idea was hatched in the late sixties when Cuba was locked in with the Soviet Union. The Soviets and Castro knew that drugs, cocaine in particular, were the 'tidal wave of the future' that could become an epidemic; a 'white plague.' It was also decided that it was a good way to corrupt and influence people including military people. This was later proved in Panama, where everybody in the local military knew Noriega was trafficking, but no one took any action—they were either corrupted or intimidated.

"By 1989 the DEA reported that drug consumption was up, out of control—drug trafficking, drug deaths, drug-related hospital emergencies. And the groups that dominated the retail drug trade were: Jamaicans,

Dominicans, Haitians, American black gangs, and the Mafia. The major wholesalers were the Colombians— what is not public information is that they were partnered up with the Cubans, to a very large extent.

"Then the defectors from Cuba appeared, first Florentino Aspillaga Lombard in 1987, a career Cuban intelligence officer; also in 1987 a major in Cuban intelligence named Jose Antonio Rodriguez Menier. He said that the then-chief of Cuban intelligence, German Barreros, bragged that 'drugs are the best way to destroy the United States.' We knew by then that their primary target was to undermine the American young people, corrupt them. Fidel has always viewed drugs as a very important weapon against the United States, because drugs demoralize people and undermine society. And this point of view rationalizes the money—my God, the money is incredible!

"Francisco, it was also proven to our satisfaction that Cuba was tied into the Sandanista Nicaraguan drug-trafficking operations. We have witnesses that place Raul Castro in Nicaragua in 1981, where he is said to have guaranteed the entry of Nicaragua into the world of drug trafficking—after all, we believe that the Marxist Sandinistas were under Castro's complete control. Frederico Vaughan was indicted for drug trafficking in Miami in 1986. You may remember he was deputy chief of Nicaragua's intelligence service.

"Finally, in 1989, the drugs got too hot for Castro; the world was waking up to his trafficking. So, he indicted General Ochoa and thirteen others in the Army and the Interior Ministry for trafficking in drugs. There was a speedy kangaroo-court trial and all these men were quickly executed by a firing squad, and that is how they claimed to the world they dealt with drugs in Cuba—swiftly and harshly.

"It was like a show for television as these men confessed in public to smuggling six tons of cocaine through Cuba in the late eighties—it was a complete success for Castro because some of these men were also dissidents in Fidels' regime—demanding changes in Cuba. General Ochoa was a commander of troops in Angola and was a severe critic of Fidel's. Fidel found an easy way to get rid of him. But we all knew it was a huge business for Cuba and they needed some political spin that they were taking action for then and now."

"I remember reading of that in the newspaper," I said.

"Francisco, General Ochoa's widow is on record telling a Spanish newspaper that Fidel and Raul were always aware of the drug traffic, and they promoted it as a good way to get money for the revolution and ruin the fabric of the United States."

"And then things quieted down," I added.

"Yes, everything stayed quiet in the world until April 8, 1993, when the *Miami Sentinel* broke a story that U.S. prosecutors had drafted an indictment. This was when Robert Martinez was the attorney general for South Florida. This is where it became a huge political hot potato. You see, Francisco, the proposed indictment would have named the entire government of Cuba, including his people in the Armed Forces and Interior Ministries, as a national Cuban criminal organization. Under the racketeering law the U.S. Government has a broad mandate to seize certain assets . . .

this would include Cuban boats, planes, and foreign bank accounts.

"And Raul would be named as the chief villain and would risk capture by U.S. agents whenever he stepped on foreign soil."

"An indictment would be the next closest thing to declaring war on Cuba," I said.

"Yes, and hence the political problems. You see, the U.S. Government has never brought a criminal indictment against an entire government or the head of state of a government. The closest we ever came was in 1988, when we indicted Noriega when he was charged as an individual along with his henchmen, but the Government of Panama was never named."

"But Felix, if we don't recognize Cuba—then we don't recognize the government—then we don't recognize the head of state—therefore we could arrest him," I said.

"Francisco, you could have been a great lawyer, very smart, but this current Administration is weak and they would never take Cuba on, you could imagine the headlines—U.S. Government trumps up drug charges as an excuse to invade Cuba, bring Castro down. U.S. imperialist monsters devour Cuba on false pretenses. The Cuban community of Miami also asked this same question, and the State Department says that the U.S. Government has for a long time had *'a tacit, informal, recognition of the Cuban administration'*—what the hell does that mean? Basically the United States does not have the stomach to take Castro on."

"Then Noriega's trial stirred all this again?" I asked.

"Precisely. The case against Cuba was formally introduced publicly for a second time by Noriega, and it has been bolstered by defectors from Cuba, jailed drug traffickers like Carlos Lehder, who was a major player in setting up Cuba as a drug haven. Lehder was on the stand for five solid days. We know Carlos Lehder began working for the Colombian Cartel in Cuba in 1979.

"It is at this time that Lehder met the famous American swindler Robert Vesco. Eventually by 1982, Lehder and some lower-level Cubans met with Raul Castro and the operation began. In return for millions in fees from the Colombian Cartel, the Cubans opened up friendly airspace with special radio frequencies and they allowed the Cartel planes to land. The Cubans were also able to warn the dopers of U.S. Coast Guard cutters and other drug interdiction operations. Cuban torpedo boats and cutters would escort the doper boats out of port and scan the way, set the course, into the United States to avoid the police, and they give the best course to the dopers. There is one undercover drug agent, a pilot, who says he flew his plane into the Varadero air base with a MiG-23 escort. These original services were later expanded into many other services that the Cubans provided, like housing, cars, security, and entertainment while the smugglers were in Cuba, like your friend told you."

"Robert Vesco was a part of the deal?" I asked.

"Yes, a player, a negotiator and organizer, financier, a brilliant man, still wanted by the Americans. He met the Colombians while he was hiding out from the U.S. Government in the Bahamas. And he remains in Cuba to this day."

"Then the Swamp Master was correct."

"Yes, the overall case against Cuba was finally all pieced together by Robert Martinez, and other U.S. attorneys, from old Miami drug cases; these cases all led to Cuba as the common thread, but they were just short of physical evidence, and documentation, that confirmed the Cuba connection. Martinez, the U.S. attorney, gave the case against Cuba the highest priority."

"Did your organization have anything to do with that?" I asked.

"We helped where we could," Felix said.

"I'll bet. Go on."

"The draft indictment claimed that Raul Castro along with high-ranking members of the Cuban Army and members of the Interior Ministry operated a pipeline into the United States that permitted the Medellin Cartel to bring at least seven and a half tons of cocaine through Cuba, for ten years between 1980 and 1990.

"The draft indictment also stated that the infamous 'Barba Roja-Red Beard' the director of Cuba's America's Department, whose job it was to travel the hemisphere fomenting Marxist revolution, actually was also organizing cocaine trafficking between the Medellin Cartel, and the Sandanista government of Nicaragua. He was Cuba's great spymaster for the Americas."

"So that's when it became international?"

"Yes, the Cuban government interceded for the Cartel and provided a coordinated smuggling program using Panama, Mexico, and Nicaragua. But the plum, the main target, was always the United States and the hub was Cuba."

"So, like always, cousin, you have your ear to the ground. I came to the right person." I smiled.

"Perhaps, but I don't know how we can help each other. Do you, Francisco?"

"Not yet, but maybe something will come to us. Is there any more?"

"To your history lesson? Maybe one thing. Cuba has progressed and expanded its business since the early nineties. Like your friend says, they have now gone into the aircraft business, stolen computers, gunrunning, stolen cars, but they have also become international in scope. Francisco, consider the location of Cuba and its resources as a shipping port. Boats come and go from every nation, particularly Russia and the Eastern Bloc. Ships cross the seas unnoticed, in and out of Cuba."

"A huge hub of smuggling . . . global gangsters!"

"Yes, warehouses, cargo planes, cargo ships, maintenance and warehouse facilities, qualified people, with huge financial connections, they still have banks in Panama and all over the Caribbean, the Caymans, and the Bahamas. They have an unlimited source of drugs pouring in from Colombia, Venezuela, Peru—all of Central and South America is a supplier of product. Just think of dope as any other product, a commodity, where there is a huge world-wide demand, and then apply sophisticated marketing, financial, and shipping applications using this high-tech world of instant communications. And Francisco—you want to know what is best of all for the Cubans?"

"Yes. The U.S. Government knows of this and can do nothing for two reasons—they are afraid of the political fallout and they have no will for controversy when it comes to Cuba."

"Francisco, don't be naive . . . the embargo is perfect

for them and they themselves are involved—the embargo means U.S. hands-off Cuba. Not the entire government, Francisco, just certain corrupt people inside the government. It is a perfect crime that can never be traced or prosecuted if you sit high on the political ladder. And you never have to get your hands dirty by dealing in drugs; all you have to have is political influence, deal in cash, and know how to keep the money offshore. Easy to do—any international lawyer or accountant can set you up with an unbreakable daisy chain of offshore bank accounts in twenty-four hours."

"Thanks Felix, I feel a lot better now that I know it's hopeless."

Felix smiled and sipped his ice tea. "Nothing is hopeless, you can always do something, *mi amigo,* unless you're dead."

"Well, we're not in that category yet. Felix, one last question. How high does this go?"

"We don't know for sure. We suspect that it goes high up in our own government, very high up in Washington. We're still working on it."

"I need to go now, Felix, and think about this."

We shook hands, and I drove home along A1A and followed the ocean. It was a slow drive. I needed to be near the ocean, calm myself, and think. I must think clearly here—overcome my anger, my outrage. How could I be in trouble, in this sea of corruption, when all I'd tried to do was the right thing? How could I get out of this and what was the Swamp Master's plan?

I must think. How deep did the corruption go? How big was the cancer? I drove up with the ocean to my right. I needed to calm myself. I took out my Tony Bennett tape and started singing along with Tony. It was very soothing, and by the time I got through South Beach I could feel that my body was relaxing. When I got home I would take a long run on the beach and cook Lillian a great dinner. I was gripping the wheel of my old Jeep softly now. I could feel the tension coming out through my hands and feet.

By the time I got just south of Golden Beach I was in much better shape. I was still singing along with Tony in full voice in the car when my mobile phone rang.

"Hello," I said, and turned down the Tony Bennett tape, which was blasting.

"Hello, Francisco."

"Who's this?"

"An old friend of yours, Bobby Day."

"A friend? You still my friend?" I asked.

"I never stopped being your friend. I got someone patched in on this line with me from a far distant place. It's a secure line."

A second voice came on the line. "This is Inspector Greene."

"What can I do for you?" I said.

"We know you must be angry, but we were taken totally by surprise. Our transfers came out of Washington and were given the highest priority that the FAA has," Bobby said. "We don't know how we can help you, but maybe we can do something," Inspector Greene added. "Of course, it would have to be done in the most confidential way. . . ."

I cut him off. "Bobby, how about the tape we took of these assholes, Harrison and the Frat House?"

"We gave it to the U.S. attorney and it's now gone, lost evidence. But it don't matter much; they got their own tapes of us and they just tell the story backwards, from their side and lie," Bobby added.

"How about you both testify on my behalf that I was undercover for you?" I asked.

"No can do, *amigo*," Bobby Day said. "We have been told that we can no longer be involved with this case, nor can we say anything about it because it is an active investigation and we will not be bought in from our new posts in Lower Siberia to testify."

"These orders evidently come from a very high level," Inspector Greene added.

"You know about Cuba, that planes have been flying in from Cuba?"

"We've known for years about a base near Guantanamo, but it is always covered with a governmental clearance, a *'special pass through'*—they say they are highly classified undercover operations—hands off," Bobby said.

"So, I'm fucked and you can't help me—but you want to help me? Is that it?"

"Look, Francisco, we know you're angry, but this is not the time to vent your anger," Bobby added.

"How do I know this isn't a new setup?"

"Use your common sense and your instincts, Francisco. If you don't want whatever help we can give you, then just say no," Bobby said.

"I'm so beaten up here it's not easy to think straight."

"Look, we can't keep this phone line for long, what would you like to do?" Inspector Greene added.

My brain was buzzing. "I want you both to call me

at four tomorrow afternoon, exactly at four, my time. Can you do it?"

There was a brief silence, then Bobby Day spoke. "It works for me."

"Me also," Inspector Greene added.

They hung up and I had four miles left to drive. I had to think of something, using the meager resources that I had, something to get me out of this mess. I had to get my mind up out of the quagmire of my own trouble. How could I have fallen into this, and why didn't I just let it go, forget about the goddamn Grumman Albatross and the fact that I was screwed on the airplane? Why did I file the civil suit against the government? Same reason I went undercover, because I thought it was the right thing to do. Well, doing the right thing had nothing to do with living a peaceful life, especially when it came to butting heads with a bunch of rogue government agents and whoever else was really standing behind the scenes pulling the strings on the puppets.

Think. Think. Think. Nothing came until I was only two miles from home. I turned Tony Bennett up, and did "I Left My Heart in San Francisco" with him full volume.

Then slowly the glimmer of an idea started to shape itself in my head. It was something that Felix had said.

Chapter Ten

I called Felix at his home the next morning. "Felix, I've been thinking about what we talked about yesterday; tell me how the United States could go down to Panama and rip Noriega, who was a head of state, off his pedestal. I thought it was against the laws of the United States to indict or remove a head of state."

"Simple, the U.S. said they never officially recognized him as head of state."

"Hell, they did business with the man for years; he claimed in his trial that the CIA paid him ten million dollars."

"Yes, Francisco, that is true, but the U.S. Department of Justice said it was really Guillermo Endara, an obscure politician, who was the actual president, the real elected head of state, and therefore Noriega was not the official head of state."

"And Castro?" I asked.

"In principle Noriega has the same status as Castro;

both men have never been recognized as the official head of state because the United States has always said the governments were illegal from the beginning."

"But different histories."

"Slightly. When Castro announced that he was an agent of the Communists, and in 1958 when he joined up officially with the Soviet Union, seized billions of dollars of American and foreign assets, he was declared an enemy—thus the embargo."

"Which is a godsend for the Castros and their smuggling business, since it keeps the United States out of any involvement with Cuba and allows him freedom to do as he wishes with the rest of the world," I said.

"Yes, and that may also be very good for certain American high officials who are personally benefiting from his actions through campaign contributions and bribes. Now, Francisco, I have to ask, where are you going with this?"

"Bear with me for a little longer, Felix."

"All right."

"Why hasn't the U.S. Government pursued this, exactly why?"

"The political line is that there has never been any substantiating documentation, no hard evidence, no documentation, to prove that Fidel and his brother Raul are probably the greatest drug lords the world has ever seen, and that Cuba is the undisputed commercial drug hub to the world."

"And what is the non-political line?"

"We don't really know. Robert Martinez was the U.S. attorney here in 1993 and according to the *Sentinel,*

Martinez was just about to indict Raul, and about seventeen of his henchmen."

"And?" I asked.

"When Clinton became president he asked for the resignation of every U.S. attorney in the country. He accepted Martinez's and then replaced him with Kendall Coffey, who was later removed from his office, accused of biting a stripper on the ass while she was dancing."

"Sounds like a great South Florida story."

"One of many—anyway, Francisco, the investigation of Cuba, after Maritinez was replaced and Janet Reno became the Attorney General, never resulted in any indictments. There is more, but I don't know if this is of interest to you."

"Try me," I said.

"All right, it gets a tiny bit confusing here. There are people within the Miami Cuban community, myself included, who believe that Raul is being groomed to take over for his brother. Raul has the Army under his wing and he was just given the sugar fields."

"He's younger than Fidel?"

"Yes, five years younger and in good health."

"And Fidel trusts him."

"Implicitly. Raul rises, and snaps his heels together when Fidel enters the room . . . literally, like an SS storm trooper, even to this day he does it. Raul is only a puppet in Fidel's hands, a total surrogate. We in Miami believe that in the future Fidel will concede certain political things to the United States, including his resignation with total immunity, but he will continue to rule through Raul; that is what many people believe, myself included."

"So, Fidel will never lose power or face. It will look like the U.S. has won. And if the United States indicts Raul, then Raul will never become the leader of Cuba."

"That's right, and perhaps this is what certain people in Washington want to happen—they want Raul in charge on the surface, but Castro will never lose control of Cuba as long as Raul is left to replace him."

"And Fidel is personally super-rich from the drug business," I added.

"That's right, and other thefts from the Cuban people, and getting richer. Now where are we going here, Francisco?"

"One last question. You're saying there has never been any documentation or hard evidence and that is what is holding this back, correct?"

"That's correct, but it may also be that certain corrupt people within the Administration do not want it revealed."

"Because they are making so much money from it."

"That's right, Francisco, that's right."

"All right, Felix. I'll get back to you very soon."

"Hey, *amigo,* you get me all worked up but no climax."

"Don't worry about the climax, just enjoy the foreplay," I said.

"Well, I'm left unsatisfied."

"I'll call you back today."

I hung up and went down to the Seven-Eleven to call the Swamp Master. I told him to meet Lillian and myself at the club at noon and to bring Mai Lynh.

The club remained closed. I had decided not to open it again until I had cleared up my personal situation. The Swamp Master and Mai Lynh arrived promptly at noon. I had ordered a pizza to be delivered for our lunch. We sat at the best table in the house, at the foot of the stage near the piano. I had a good bottle of California Merlot opened and out on the table when they arrived. I poured us each a glass and Lillian served up the pizza.

While we ate I filled everyone in on my conversations with Felix and my call from Bobby Day and Inspector Greene, offering their help.

"You trust 'em?" the Swamp Master asked.

"Yeah, I believe they were removed from the case and shipped out against their will. They both had houses and family ties in the community, which they had to leave. They could have screwed us and still stayed in Miami."

"How can they help us?" Lillian asked.

"Well, I got an idea, or should I say I have a half-assed idea," I said.

"Maybe it will line up with our half-assed idea," the Swamp Master said.

"Okay, Mr. Sawyer Pinder, you first."

The Swamp Master began. "I think somehow the answer is in the airplanes, not the dope. That we should try and follow the trail of the planes, and that will lead us also to the dope. I'm not quite clear in my own head about this, but I think we should follow the trail of the planes."

"Go on," I said.

Mai Lynh spoke next. "I know you know part of my

story from my husband, that I was a dancer and a hostess in Saigon at a club there when we first met. I had been there for two years when I met Sawyer." She reached over and held his hand as she spoke. "I will go into the Frat House as a dancer. I still look all right even though I have had two children."

"You look better than any of those sleazy dancers, babe," the Swamp Master said.

"Thank you, Sawyer, for the grand compliment. I will go in and learn what I can from the men inside. They will never suspect this and they do not know who I am."

"You sure you want to do this?" I asked.

"I'm sure, Francisco. I came to the United States for love and freedom. The actions of these men reminds me too much of my life in Vietnam with corruption everywhere. I would like to help—and I don't like that they tried to kill my man."

It was the first time she had ever said my name. She was a determined woman, and this was a way she could help her husband.

"I ain't fussy about her going . . ."

"Please, Sawyer, we know you do not like the idea of other men seeing me dance naked, but I do not care about this, so why should you?" She slipped her other hand across the table and took both his hands.

I knew it pained them both to do this.

"What exactly do you hope to find?" I asked.

"Nothin' exact about this, Francisco," the Swamp Master said. "We just both got a feelin' on this."

"When men drink and there are women around, they often speak of things they should not. This was true in

Vietnam, and it is true in Miami. We shall see what we shall see," Mai Lynh said.

I got the distinct feeling she could ask the right questions at the right time to get a man talking.

"Is that the plan?" I asked the Swamp Master.

"While she does that, I'm goin' back to the airstrip in the Glades and stake it out. Watch the hangar, see what planes they're working' on, and watch the airstrip for contraband planes landin' out there in the dead of night. I got an infrared camera system that I put together for still pictures, and a separate video camera."

"That sounds like a plan?" I said.

"It's a start," the Swamp Master said. "Whadda you got?"

"I have only elements and an idea, maybe we can work it out."

"What are the elements?" Lillian asked.

"The elements are what you two have in mind, plus Bobby Day and Inspector Greene, Felix and his Miami Cuban Connection, my connection with Jeff Bacon at the *Miami Sentinel*. Those are the elements," I said.

"Tell us the plan," Lillian said.

I paused before I spoke. It was an outrageous, bold plan, maybe a little bit crazy. I began. "My idea is to fly into Colombia, pick up what would appear to be a load of cocaine. Then fly on to Cuba and land at one of the Cuban airstrips, get evidence, and then fly into the airstrip in the Glades."

"Is that all?" the Swamp Master said. "Impossible, Francisco. And I thought I was a crazy person."

"Why impossible?" I asked. "You still have connections in Colombia."

"Maybe. What about a plane?"

"We could steal one out at Florida Private Planes in the Glades."

"What? What are you talking about?" the Swamp Master said.

"Look, since all the numbers, logbooks, etc. are already false, how can they report the plane stolen?" I asked.

"Maybe they will think one of their own stole it or a disgruntled dope dealer did it. The way they fuck people out there they'll have a huge list of suspects, certainly not us—they will never think we stole the damn plane," he said.

"Yeah, and if they bring attention to it, they have to go through all the paperwork. They're not going to do that," I said.

"Then what?" Lillian asked.

"Then we fly the plane to Colombia and we load up the plane, only not with dope, with sugar, and pack it in kilo packages so that it looks like dope. We take off from Colombia. And we head for Cuba."

"Cuba? How do we get clearance to land in Cuba?"

"You're dope dealing pals clear us for a landing to refuel and a pass-through. We pay the Cuban authorities with our own funds."

"And we record the whole thing on videotape?" the Swamp Master said.

"Yeah."

"It's a waste of time, even if we could do it. The spook and his pals will just discredit the tape as a put-up bogus job, and put a huge spin on it that you are under indictment. I'm a burned-out Vietnam pilot that used to be a undercover pilot because I got caught smugglin'. Francisco, it will never fuckin' fly—excuse my French, ladies."

"You're right, so that's why we gotta take along witnesses."

"Like?"

"Jeff Bacon from the *Miami Sentinel* and Bobby Day and someone from the Miami Cuban community."

"Like?"

"Like Felix," I said.

"Felix! You are totally nuts—he's your cousin! First of all, Bobby Day has done nothin' but fuck us, and second, Felix is a big-shot Cuban lawyer who probably wants to run Cuba when Castro and his corrupt brother finally leave. And Jeff Bacon—the closest he's ever come to danger is fighting over a parkin' spot at the mall," the Swamp Master said.

"You're wrong," I said with a smile. "Look, let's look to what motivates people, self-interest. I'll start with Felix. If we pull this off, Felix will be a bigger hero with the Cubans both here and in Cuba than Jose Marti—he exposes Castro and his brother as a drug smuggling monster to the Cubans in Cuba and Miami—while the Cuban people starve, Castro gets richer. And to both the Cuban-Americans and the Americans, Castro is exposed as a man who is personally poisoning the U.S.A. by flooding the country with the 'white plague.' "

"And Bobby Day? What about him? He's an FAA cop—the only thing to motivate him is to keep his job. And Inspector Greene, he's a clone of Bobby Day—two gutless wonders," the Swamp Master said.

"Maybe you're right, but they know what went down

in my case. And they were punished for doing nothing wrong—they were both posted, so they are now career-dead."

"That's it?" the Swamp Master asked.

"When I was undercover with Bobby, I saw the look on his face. He loved it, the action," I said.

"So, he may be like us—an action junkie."

"Like you." I smiled. "I'm no action junkie. I'm a singer in a Cuban nightclub."

"Yeah, right. It's not me suggestin' we fly into fuckin' Cuba," the Swamp Master said. "How do you get Inspector Greene to go along with this?"

"He doesn't have to know. I'll call Bobby on my own, after they both call me. I'll find out where he's posted and call him."

"Can he get us a 'pass-through' clearance from Cuba into the Glades airstrip?"

"I'll give it a shot." I smiled.

"So, I can see this is a nice, simple plan, Francisco," Lillian said. "You talk Felix into flying to Colombia, then into Cuba, and finally fly back into an illegal airstrip in the Everglades. At the same time you convince Bobby Day and Jeff Bacon to also risk their lives as well as their entire careers. This goes on while the Swamp Master and Mai Lynh are also risking life and limb? And all the while, you think these enemies of yours will be sitting quietly by?"

"Hey. Francisco, I'm up for the airstrip surveillance, but when the time comes I'm flyin' into Colombia with you, right?" The Swamp Master smiled, interrupting Lillian.

"Hell, you're stealing the plane," I said with a laugh.

The Swamp Master laughed also. "Oh, yeah, how could I forget about that?"

"Well, I have a lot of work to do," I said, pouring the last of the Merlot.

The call came at four from Bobby Day.

"I wanted to talk to you, Bobby, just you alone."

"Already I'm nervous. Lay it on me."

"Look, I don't know how much you know about Cuba, but I have reason to believe that there is an even bigger illegal plane operation in Cuba than at Opa-Locka, as well as a huge smuggling operation."

Bobby answered, "We know there is a lot of hanky-panky that goes on with Cuba. U.S. Customs and the FAA issue a lot of special 'pass throughs,' and it is confusing as to whether or not the planes are coming from the Guantanamo base or from the Cuban mainland. It's been going on for years, but I never heard they were doctoring planes and falsifying documents."

I paused. "Look, Bobby, I know you're a career law-enforcement guy."

"Just say it," he urged.

"All right. I'm organizing a plane to go down to Colombia, load up with kilos of sugar that look like cocaine, then fly to Cuba, land in Cuba, get serviced with fuel, and carry on. While we are there we will photograph the illegal plane operation and the drug operation."

"Oh, great! That's just great, Francisco, we fly down filing false flight plans and somehow we get clearance into Cuba and they let us land and then we get a 'pass-through' to fly into U.S. airspace and what . . . land in Miami?"

"No. Land in the Everglades at the FAA field."

"And why would I do this, risk my career on such a harebrained idea?"

"Because you are a patriot?"

"Well, I'm a patriot, but I have other alternatives than your scary-assed plan."

"Hey, Bobby, it was you and me that went undercover together because we thought we were doing a righteous thing. I get arrested and you get exiled."

"Give me a better reason," Bobby said.

"Don't you ever get angry at corruption? I'm not talking about a little drug smuggling and fucking with airplanes. I'm talking about a huge business in drugs and in stolen and modified aircraft. Cuba is perfect for warehousing, transshipping, and doing modifications to airplanes. Hell, they use American mechanics who get houses, hookers, and a big wad of spending money—what could be better?"

"Staying alive, for one."

"All right, how about your career. You hook it all together. Illegal planes, stolen planes, confiscated planes that are re-papered, doctored planes where engines and other parts are switched with no records. You would be the most famous FAA official ever. Cuba, the international chop shop for stolen aircraft."

"Francisco, that would be easy since there never has been a famous FAA guy."

"Well, that's even better—you would be the first!"

"God, you're too much!" he said.

"Look, I'll make you a promise. If I feel that it's too dangerous I won't go ahead with it."

"Please, Francisco, now you're truly bullshitting me. I think you're going to go ahead with this no matter what. I can tell by your voice."

"Look, Bobby, I'm out on a five-million-dollar bail. If I leave the country and I don't accomplish my mission, the five million is lost, and I go into jail with no bond."

"Francisco, everyone knows your wife is rich."

"Bobby, I'm telling you that the five million represents close to our entire net worth. Lillian has had severe financial problems with her husband's estate, and the restaurant has drained us of a lot of cash." I said this, not having really discussed it specifically with Lillian. If she was against the idea, I would abandon it.

"Christ, let me think about this. I'll have to let it sink in. When do you think you'll be doing this?"

"Don't know, but it will be soon. Can you get vacation time or a leave of absence?"

"Don't be closing the sale before the customer says yes," Bobby Day said.

"All right. Give me your home phone." He gave me the number and I hung up.

Jeff Bacon listened attentively as I took him through the details. We were in the bar of the Omni Hotel in downtown Miami near the *Miami Sentinel* offices. It overlooked Biscayne Bay and the causeway to Miami Beach.

He spoke when I finished. "When Martinez was the Miami U.S. attorney, we reported the Cuban drug story along with the *Miami Herald,* although they scooped us on it. So, Francisco, you want me to go along with you and shoot photos and write the story for the paper, even though I myself will be involved with breaking the law?"

"No law will be broken."

"Well. I counted a few while I was listening," Jeff said.

"We will get the necessary pass-throughs from the FAA. We will be carrying sugar, not cocaine; the Cuban government will know of our arrival and allow us in," I said. "It will be the biggest scoop of the decade."

Jeff Bacon was a seasoned crime reporter and a smart man. "How so? The story was already broken in 1993 by us and the *Miami Herald* and fell into obscurity."

"New twist, two new twists," I said with a smile.

"Okay I get that it's an international story now, but what's the other twist?"

"There are Americans helping them do it," I said.

"Will they be there, in Cuba?"

"The Swamp Master says there are always some Americans hanging around."

"You know what you're trying to do here, Francisco?"

"Tell me."

"You're trying to put together a mercenary team that does not carry guns. You are trying to form an intellectual media hit squad. A wild-assed pilot, a law-enforcement type, a crime reporter, a Cuban lawyer, and how do I describe you," Jeff said.

"A patriotic Cuban nightclub singer." I smiled.

"Great."

"Look Jeff, for Christ's sake. I need you all, it's the only way I can stop the media spinmeisters. I have thought of every spin that could be put on this. I concluded that if I did it alone I would be annihilated in twenty-four hours. The greatest media spin machine ever created exists today. Any regular citizen who goes up against the government is fucked."

"I'll tell you what. You get Felix Rodriguez on that airplane and you got me. But I need Felix to call me himself and tell me."

"You want the strength of the Miami Cuban community behind you," I said.

"No, I want a great lawyer behind me. But don't get me wrong—I already know there's a million Cuban patriots in Miami who believe Castro is a corrupt monster—I think we might need their support as well." Jeff smiled.

"Yeah, and maybe there will be a great newspaper behind us, both your English and Spanish editions."

"I never thought of that," he said with a smile.

"Francisco, you are crazy, totally insane, out of your mind. In fact, I can't believe you would suggest such a thing to me," Felix Rodriguez said. "And I'm supposed to call Jeff Bacon and confirm that I am going with you. First, to Colombia, then to Cuba, then to land in the Everglades at a secret airstrip.

"Francisco, I am married with three beautiful children. I have a successful law practice. I am a respected man in every part of the South Florida world. I would give all this up for a chance to be killed and disgraced?"

"You know it's a lot more than that, Felix," I said. "You have political ambitions—"

Felix interrupted. "Maybe. But why do you want to go off like James Bond, become a secret agent, underworld spymaster, and probably get everyone killed?"

"Felix, I'm no hero, but I'm mad. I helped the government by going undercover and we successfully busted an operation that literally was putting hundreds of airplanes back into civilian service—they were flying coffins! Only to learn that we had busted another government agency's corrupt undercover operation."

"Then it got complicated." Felix smiled. "The government started arranging testimony against you."

"Yes, so you tell me, Felix, should I just remain quiet, take my chances with the trial, with the system?"

"Maybe. I know the judicial system, I'm comfortable with the system. I—"

"That's just it, Felix—I think you're comfortable, and what I'm suggesting makes you uncomfortable. How old are you, Felix?"

"You know how old I am. Why?"

"Well, I just wondered if you wanted to make history while you're still a young man." I smiled.

"Does making history mean I wind up a footnote in the Castro story, just before he resigns anyway?"

"He resigns—Raul takes over—and your beloved Cuba stays in the arms, in the embrace, of the Castro brothers, strangling Cuba to death, and nothing changes. Ten million Cubans continue to get it up the ass, and you sit down in Little Havana playing dominoes and making idle threats that Fidel laughs at over his breakfast coffee," I said.

"Francisco, I don't play dominoes. You go too far."

"Do I? You got such a great life, Felix? Hell, I could spend the next two minutes and tell you the rest of your life story—it's totally predictable, a good predictable life. You could have made history. You could have helped release ten million people from the yoke of tyranny and oppression, but no, you prefer your mansion in Coral Gables, your hundred-thousand-dollar Mercedes automobile, your status in the community."

"Francisco, you really are going to far. Now you insult me."

"Felix, how could I insult you? You insult yourself by your inactivity. You have no temper, Felix?"

"For lawyers a temper is a luxury that usually leads right down the road to ruin."

"How about passion then? I've seen you talking about the Bay of Pigs and in 1966 the shooting down of the two Brothers to the Rescue planes by the Cuban MiGs—four loyal Cubans from Miami dead. I've seen you talk of the poverty and the misery of the Cuban people. That's great, Felix, but when it comes to action—you're all talk."

"Francisco, you think you can stir me up with all this rhetoric? I deal in legal words, spoken and written, and I use them as bullets for my beliefs."

"Well, come along with me and I'll give you enough bullets for a lifetime, a never-ending machine gun of words. The difference is that this time they will be backed up by action. Not just words, Felix, but action."

"Francisco, good luck to you, but I have no interest in going along with you on your adventure. I like my life, my wife, my kids, and my perks. So, no, thanks," Felix said.

"Okay, Felix, I understand."

He stared at me for a long while. Then I left.

Lillian sat quietly and listened to me. "So, Bobby Day is a maybe, Jeff Bacon is a yes, but only if Felix is a yes . . . but Felix is a no."

"Yeah, so it looks bad."

"You surprised?"

"Not really, maybe it's a dumb plan."

"It's big risk," she said.

"You thinking of the money—the bond?"

"Darling, it's five million dollars. You're not supposed to leave the country. They took your passport."

"I won't need a passport where I'm going," I said.

"Forget about the money. We can always make more. But it doesn't look like you're going anywhere." She smiled.

"Is that what you want?"

"I always love having you around. You know that. But I want you to do what you want," she said.

"You want me to cook dinner tonight?" I asked.

"Yes, and that's not all I want you to do," she said.

"What else did you have in mind?" I said with a smile.

"Oh, I don't know, maybe you could sing me a song after dinner."

"My pleasure." I said, humming to myself as I descended the stairs into the kitchen.

* * *

R. L. Smitten

The first call the next morning came from Felix. "Francisco, can you get to the restaurant in the Inter Continental Hotel in an hour?"

"Yes," I said.

"See you then," he said, hanging up.

I showered and drove the ten miles to Miami in ten minutes, and arrived almost perfectly on time. Felix had been given a corner table that overlooked Biscayne Bay. He was sitting with two other men. The two men wore sunglasses, one had a black beard. It was an ominous-looking table. They all looked up at me as I strode across the floor. Felix did not have to make the introductions. I knew these men.

I shook hands with Juan Rodriguez, my cousin and Felix's brother; then Ernesto Blades, a friend of both our families and a hero of the Bay of Pigs, rose to shake my hand.

Ernesto Blades had black sunglasses, a full black and gray beard, and black slicked back hair. He was an ominous presence. I shook hands with the men and sat down.

"Are you hungry?" Felix asked.

"Coffee would be good," I said.

Felix ordered the coffee and spoke. "Francisco, you know us. I see no need for small talk here. I have told these men what you told me about Castro and Cuba. I have broken no confidences, Francisco, because all that you told me was already known to these men.

"I have told them of your plan and I will let them speak for themselves. My friend Juan is a Cuban patriot who fought at the Bay of Pigs as a boy, and now he is the unofficial mayor of Little Havana." Felix smiled.

"I know your brother, Felix," I said.

"More like the landlord than the mayor," Ernesto Blades interrupted.

"That also," Felix continued. "And Ernesto Blades is the head of Omega 99. He was formerly a fighter pilot for Castro and flew his MiG-23 over here and landed at the Homestead Air Force Base. He was not shot down because of my brother Juan, who alerted the authorities of his arrival."

"I remember reading about it in the newspaper."

"Both Ernesto and I know of what you speak," Juan said. "Castro has many friends in high places in this country and his spies are everywhere. Many of these trained spies came into the United States with the Mariel boat lift in the late seventies, when that fool Jimmy Carter was President. They are here for three reasons, the drugs, the airplanes, and for general knowledge. You see, Fidel has used the embargo well, as an advantage. He blames the United States for all of Cuba's troubles. And he blames the Soviets for abandoning the Communist dream."

"He blames everybody but himself," I said.

"Yes," Juan continued, "that way he can carry on with his illegal activities and eventually make a deal with the United States."

"And the deal will be for Raul, or a Castro nominee, to replace Fidel as president when Fidel steps down," Ernesto Blades said.

"So, the Miami Cuban community will, in essence, be no better off than they are now," I said.

"That's right," Ernesto Blades said. "You see, Castro, through various agencies, has given a huge amount of

317

money to certain political people in this country both as political contributions and personal contributions."

"And they owe him," I said.

"And they love the cash flow," Felix said with a smile.

"We also have a network of spies in Cuba," Ernesto Blades said. "We know what you say is true. There are air bases in Cuba for the transshipping and warehousing of drugs. There are also hangars where airplanes are modified and refitted, false papers and ID numbers are placed on these planes, and they are flown into the United States and other places for sale. They are confiscated airplanes from several countries as well as stolen airplanes. This is all done with the cooperation of certain rogue agents within the U.S. Government."

"Like Michael Burton?" I said.

"A stone-cold killer and a high-ranking CIA official," Ernesto Blades said. "He is the most important man in the operation. He is also the most dangerous because he does not do this for money."

"Why does he do it?" I asked.

"He does it to funnel their share of the money to run various revolutions and support clandestine operations of all kinds that are not covered by regular budgeted money from the Congress," Juan said.

"So, let's get back to the point. It is obvious that if the Castro brothers can be exposed as major drug lords, with the United States as the target, they will be finished," I said.

"Yes, like a person standing on the edge of a cliff— the Castro brothers can be pushed over the edge or they can take a step backward to safety," Felix said.

"How can you help me?" I said.

False Witness

"We can help you get into Cuba, look around, and get out of Cuba. We cannot tell you how we are able to do it. We can only tell you what to do," Ernesto said. "Exposing the drug operation and the illegal aircraft could be the most important thing in Cuba's long history of trying to be free."

"What's the catch?" I asked.

"We want you to take Ernesto in with you. He knows the people. He knows the country. He will help you. You have the FAA agent and the newspaper person Jeff Bacon," Juan said.

"Jeff said he would only go if Felix went. He will be opposed to Ernesto," I said.

"Why?" Juan asked.

"Because Ernesto is a known anti-Castro revolutionary and the spinmasters will just say that it is all bullshit, an operation orchestrated by a known Castro hater, Ernesto Blades, and the entire operation will be identified, and it will be branded as a put-up job designed by the Miami Cuban community to bring down Fidel," I said.

"They will say the same thing about Felix," Ernesto said.

"No, they won't, and that's why Jeff is insisting on Felix, because he knows no one can break Felix's story. You see, the very reasons he does not want to go are the reasons he should go. He is a hundred-percent honorable, a moderate man of the Cuban community, a true patriot; he has no baggage like Ernesto here, who flew into the U.S in a stolen MiG, who everyone knows hates Castro and would do anything to bring him down," I said.

319

R. L. Smitten

"Anything else about my friend Ernesto?" Felix asked.

"Yes." I was getting hot now. It was my life on the line. "You Cubans fight amongst each other, always arguing. Felix represents *all* the Miami Cubans. If we go I want the entire American-Cuban community on my side. A million Cubans who all vote. That's what I want and Felix can provide that. Ernesto just provides for more arguing, because he's a radical. That's my final word on this," I said. "Felix comes or I will go without a member of the Cuban community. You three patriots say you want to free Cuba. Then get off your asses and stop these endless debates and do something."

There was a long silence at the table. Finally Felix broke the silence. "I will give you my decision tonight, Francisco."

"Okay," I said.

Felix smiled.

"What's so funny, Felix?" I asked.

"Well, how did we get from stolen aircraft to invading Cuba?" he asked.

"I won't tell if you won't," I said. "Besides, we're not hooked up yet."

I finished my coffee and left. On my drive home I tried to assemble my thoughts. The Swamp Master was checking out the airstrip in the Glades. His wife, Mai Lynh, was dancing at the Frat House. Bobby Day was thinking things over about how far he would go. Jeff Bacon would go if Felix came, and Felix had it all figured out that Ernesto Blades would come with us as a swap, while he remained safe in his Coral Gables mansion. And Lillian, she must have thought I was just plain crazy, and on top of it all, we had five million dollars on the line for my bond, not to mention my life.

And where was Michael Burton and that asshole Rick Jacoby these days? The thought of them sent a tremor through my body. I couldn't tell if it was anger or fear. Anyway, it wouldn't be long now until I would find out how the cards were going to fall.

When I got home there was a message waiting for me. The Swamp Master had asked me to call him from a phone booth at seven that night. He would be waiting for the call at his cousin's house.

I called him. His cousin answered, and put him over to me.

"Hey podner, we been busy. How 'bout you?" he asked.

"Yeah, I been busy. What's up."

"Can we meet?"

"Where?" I asked.

"How about the Denny's where you used to meet with Bobby Day, near the Opa-Locka Airport, on the Federal Highway."

"When?"

"Tonight at half-past midnight, I'll be with Mai Lynh. I'm pickin' her up at the Frat House around twelve."

"I'll bring Lillian."

"Good, any news on your end?" he asked.

"You'll be the second one I tell," I said.

"See you tonight."

I hung up, went up to the bedroom balcony, and sat down on the chaise lounge next to Lillian. She was sitting, letting the soft winds caress her face. She came out of her trance and smiled at me as I sat.

"Thinking?" I said.

"Wondering."

"About what?" I asked.

"What it would have been like to have just flown off that day and done what we set out to do," she said.

"It's not over yet," I said. "We're still standing."

"I'm standing better now," she said with a smile. "Francisco, I want you to know that I love your spirit."

"What?" I asked.

"Well, it's hard to explain. Most men . . . and women cave in when adversity comes their way. You stare it down, or maybe beat it down, or stomp it down. You always face things, confront things. It's one of the things I love most about you. I take strength from your spirit. I watch it and it makes me stronger," Lillian said.

"I think a lot of it is just out of desperation." I smiled.

"Right." She smiled back at me, and leaned over and kissed my lips. I held her in my arms for several minutes, and we listened to the soft sounds of the rolling ocean waves as they rumbled in from great distances traveled. I stood up and poured us each a cold glass of Pouilly-fuissé from the wine bucket that I had carried up from down stairs. We sipped slowly from our glasses.

"So, you want to tell me what's happening?" she asked.

For the next thirty minutes I filled her in, and also did a lot of thinking out loud. I was living up to my commitment and telling her everything, holding back nothing. "So, that's it," I said. "You want to take a drive with me to Miami tonight to visit with Mai Lynh and the Swamp Master?"

"I wouldn't pass up a chance for a meal at Denny's, you know that, darling." She smiled.

"Well, how about you come to the kitchen with me now and keep me company, and I'll make us a little something to eat before we go to Miami," I said.

"Okay." She stood and put her arms around my neck. "Maybe we could make a little detour first," she said, looking over my shoulder.

"I don't consider it a detour," I said, swept her off her feet, and carried her into the bedroom.

"They're on the move," the Swamp Master said. We were at a table in Denny's. "There's lots of activity."

"Like?" I asked.

"Like, planes are coming into the hangar there in the Glades and being turned around real quick. When I was workin' for 'em there was no sense of urgency. It kinda reminds me now of Nam when we were goin' on a major raid or a blitz somewhere. Now, you tell 'em, honey."

Mai Lynh sipped her orange juice and spoke. "Lots of the mechanics from Opa-Locka come into the Frat House. For the last three nights we have gotten a lot of party boys from Florida Private Planes, even John Harrison himself, and that Customs agent Rick Jacoby and his partner Michael Burton, although Burton never stays. They've all been flashin' a lot of cash, buying dances and drinks, and some of them have told me they got good bonuses. Some of them said they are ferrying planes to a place that is secret. I'm assuming it's Cuba."

"Why?" Lillian asked.

"Unclear, but I have a theory," Mai Lynh said. "I think perhaps they have been storing drugs in warehouses there for several months and they are going to send many planes off on the same night, not only to the United States, but to other places as well, like Europe. That's why they needed all these planes and pilots."

"Like an offensive," I said.

"Exactly. It's actually a great idea. They get pass-throughs for certain planes and they send in an armada of fuckin' planes on the pass-throughs. By the time anyone figures it out, the planes have entered the United States in Florida, Texas, California, the Carolinas, even Canada; they can fly on the pass-throughs anywhere they want to in the United States and Canada," the Swamp Master said.

"Or the world," Lillian added.

"Yes," Mai Lynh said. "These mechanics have told me that they have pushed through over twenty planes in the last month. Two pilots told me they flew down to Panama, across to Cuba, and took a commercial plane into Nassau on the return and back to Miami— never had their passports stamped once. They were each paid ten thousand dollars for the delivery and they are doing two or three planes a week."

"So, this could be the first time they have actually sent in an armada of airplanes full of dope into the United States," I said.

"Not just the United States, the world, Francisco, the whole fucking industrialized world. This is a form of globalization—Castro sees globalization in other businesses, why not globalize the dope business?" the Swamp Master said.

"I'm still not sure I understand. Why not bring the drugs in slowly like they have been doing?" Lillian asked.

"I have found out one other thing," Mai Lynh said. "Cocaine is a crop, like any other. They have had a huge crop in Peru, Venezuela, and Colombia, and the processing operations have all been increased. The drug lords doubled the price paid per pound on the coca leaves to the farmers, to counteract the slow eradication of the crops that the United States has been after for so many years. They have been shipping the processed coke in bulk straight to Cuba. It has been repackaged and warehoused there, until they could get fully organized."

"See, even if a few planes get busted, the numbers are so huge that it's worth takin' the chance," the Swamp Master said.

"Won't that hurt the future business for them?" I asked.

"I thought about that until one of the pilots told me that a Cuban pilot told him that Castro will be gone soon, and Castro knows it," Mai Lynh said.

"So, he ships off one huge last load out of Cuba, collects the money, and lives happily ever after," Lillian added.

"I think so, and the Cali Cartel knows Cuba will shut down for them as a shipping point when Castro departs," Mai Lynh said.

"So, why not one last great big shipment—pollute the United States, the Great Capitalistic Monster, and the rest of the world, and get paid a fortune for doing it," I said.

"Yes, it guarantees him plenty of money to carry on with or to leave a dynasty behind," Mai Lynh said. "It was drugs that corrupted the Vietnamese government, heroin. Now it is drugs that continue to corrupt this country."

"What's the timing?" I asked.

"Soon, I think," Mai Lynh said.

"I don't understand why Castro would take such a chance as this, just before Cuba does what the United States wants him to do. Wouldn't he ruin his chances for continuing power if it was ever disclosed what he did?" Lillian asked.

"Lillian, he would just say what he said the last time—some military radicals did this on their own. He would round up some military honcho-types, line their asses up against the wall, and shoot the bastards. He would have the trial and the execution on Cuban television and then say to the world—look how tough we are on dopers here in Cuba. When we find dopers operatin' we kill their asses, not like you soft-livin' American assholes, who give 'em long trials and put 'em in jail." The Swamp Master smiled his big broad grin. He was wearing his CAT hat and a T-shirt that said, WOMEN LOVE ME—BASS FEAR ME. I had to smile.

"So, you were right about the planes—follow the planes, you said."

"Yeah, Francisco, but I didn't know why I was right, until I seen all that activity in the Glades airport and Mai Lynh tipped me off about what was happening with these pilots and mechanics at the Frat House. Then it all come together."

"But we still don't know when. Any guesses?"

"Within a week," Mail Lynh said.

"Why do you say that?" I asked.

"Instincts," she said.

"Instincts come from somewhere?" I asked.

"Vietnam. I could always tell when the American soldiers were going to go out on a mission."

"How?" I asked.

"They drink too much. They talk too much. They spend too much, because they may not live to spend any more. They talk of their real girlfriends and their families, show us pictures. They talk of death and morbid things. They laugh too loud." Mai Lynh looked out the window of Denny's at the passing traffic on U.S. 1. "This is what stirs my instincts."

The Swamp Master put his arm around her, and pulled her close to him. She kissed his cheek.

"So the noose is tightening," I said.

"Yeah, podner, but around whose neck?"

"We'll know the answer to that in a little while." I smiled.

We finished our midnight breakfast, and returned to Golden Beach.

The next day I drove to meet with Felix in his office. I had asked him to confirm the Swamp Master's suspicions with his contacts, if he could. We met in the conference room with his brother, Juan.

"So, how does it look?" I asked.

"It looks like your friend was right," Juan Rodriguez answered. "There are reports of large movements of small airplane traffic into several Air Force bases hidden in the hills. The warehouses at the major base near Guantanamo have increased security as well. Also our people at the Havana airport have seen a good number of American people who they know are pilots flying into Cuba one way from Nassau and leaving from the main airport. These perhaps are the people that are being used to ferry in the small aircraft."

"Any feel about timing?" I asked.

"We have some people who are laborers at the warehouses, and they tell us the warehouses are almost full of the white powder," Juan said.

"So, Felix, how do you feel about it now?" I asked.

"I will go with you instead of my brother," Juan said. "I want to go with you."

"No, Juan, it is better if I go as Francisco says."

"No, Felix, I will tell you why it is better that I go. It is simple. Francisco and the people that go with him will need the help of the Cuban people who have been with us for years, waiting for a chance to expose Fidel and his regime. I know these people and I am known to these people as a moderate Cuban. I can also arrange for the clearances into Cuba and I can lead these people in assisting Francisco. Besides, I have military experience and I am in better shape than you, who only sits behind his desk."

Felix looked at him and thought. He finally smiled. "I know why you want to go with Francisco and leave me here."

"Why?"

"Because, Juan, you know you will need a good lawyer to get you out of jail if you get caught in Cuba or arrested here in the United States when you land." We all laughed.

"Francisco." Felix looked at me. "My brother is correct.

"Okay," I said. "But Felix, I need Jeff Bacon of the *Sentinel* with me and he says he will not go without you."

Felix smiled. "You leave Jeff Bacon to me. The publisher of the *Miami Sentinel* and I go back a long way and there are many favors owed on both sides."

I stood up. "All right, Juan, I have a feeling you will have very little time to get ready."

Juan stood up and shook my hand. "I'm ready now— I've been ready all my life for this."

He smiled, with a full set of white teeth against his handsome tanned Latin face. I believed him.

I had one problem left. On my way back to Golden Beach I made the call to Bobby Day. I got his answering machine. I then called him at his airport office, and his secretary told me he had taken two weeks vacation. It was around South Beach on my way home when my phone rang. It was Bobby Day.

"Hey, Francisco, can you hear me?"

"Barely."

"I'm in the cockpit of a C-130 that's flying into Key West. I'll be there in about two hours."

"Come to the house," I said.

"I'll see you."

Bobby Day arrived five hours later, and I set him up in the guest room. Later, at dinner in the dining room with Lillian, I asked him what made up his mind to come with me.

"I'm thirty-seven years old, Francisco, and I've been in the FAA for seven years. I've seen all kinds of stuff, but I never saw what happened to you. We break a major chop shop operation that puts hundreds of defective airplanes into the sky. We get rock-solid evidence, and it turns out that it's an undercover operation being run by Customs and we never got one conviction. Then they go right back in business like we never raided them."

"Where did the orders come from to drop it?" I asked.

"The orders came down from on high, from Washington."

"How high?" Lillian asked.

"Very high, is all I know. Inspector Greene told me that for an order like that, it would have to come from the top."

"So, that's why you're here?" I asked.

"Partly. See, it was that civil suit and the article in the *Miami Sentinel* that got your ass in trouble. But that isn't enough, there's more." He paused.

"Go on."

"See, one night I was out at Opa-Locka doing an inspection, and I saw a C-130 land. It was cleared with a pass-through because it skipped the Customs inspection. Well, I wandered up to the plane just as they were dropping the tailgate. Two vans moved up to the plane and I backed off into the shadows. The plane was packed with coke. They off-loaded hundreds of kilos and then turned around and took off."

"So?" I asked.

"So, the plane had flown in from the Guantanamo

area. I checked later. I wrote to the head of Customs and my boss and told them about it. But it got lost, on purpose, in bureaucratic bullshit."

"So, you knew about Cuba for a long time."

"Me and some others, but I let it go until now, when you told me that the Opa-Locka operation was all part of it. But Francisco, you know what really pissed me off?"

"Tell me." I said.

"What really pissed me off was that there were four Cuban soldiers on board that plane working with the Americans."

"How'd you know they were Cuban soldiers?"

"They spoke that special Cuban dialect of Spanish, and they had their Cuban Army boots on. Can you fucking believe the balls on these guys, that they feel so secure they can bring in Cuban nationals here to help them pollute our country? I guess I never got over that." Bobby Day finished his glass of wine and the rest of his pasta in silence with Lillian and me.

Well, I had my crew. All I needed now was an airplane.

Chapter Eleven

The Swamp Master lay next to me on a knoll of limestone that was covered with tall saw grass. The Glades airstrip lay in front of us. The Florida Private Planes hangar was a hundred yards to the south. We had came in close in an inflatable kayak, which we deflated and buried when we hit dry land.

The sun was setting, an orange ball of fire sinking into the endless waves of saw grass that swayed in rhythm with the southern trades blowing in off the ocean. The last few cars were departing from the hangar, carrying the remaining mechanics home.

"Security ain't shit anymore, 'cause there's hardly any planes left. Just the one outside guard, and an inside night watchman," the Swamp Master said. "Our plane's over there."

The Swamp Master pointed at a Grumman Albatross that was chocked and tied down on the tarmac fifty yards from the hangar. It was an identical plane to the one I had crashed. I could see beyond the plane to the boneyard of Grumman Albatrosses.

"Don't worry, Francisco, it's a good 'un." He smiled, and pushed back his camouflage floppy hunting hat. We were both armed with Glock automatics as side arms. "That there Albatross's my baby. I practically put it together myself, but I neglected to put a good one of these in the port engine." He reached in his pouch pocket and pulled out a fuel pump.

"How long ago were you thinking of stealing one of these?" I asked.

"Since the day I seen all those there Albatrosses layin' around in that boneyard."

"Why didn't they just replace it by cannibalizing a fuel pump from another Albatross?" I asked.

He smiled that big Swamp Master grin and said, "I took 'em all. I took every last goddamn one of them. And they ain't easy parts to find."

"So, you have to put that pump in the port engine," I said.

"Yeah, it'll take me about five minutes to make the switch."

"So, what's the plan?" I asked.

"The plan is we take that fuckin' Albatross sittin' over there."

"How?" I asked.

"Well, you take care of that guard in front, and I'll go make the switch on the fuel pump." He smiled.

"Simple as that, huh?" I asked.

"Yeah, this might help." He handed me a bottle of chloroform.

"Uncle Jed get this for you?" I asked.

"No, Uncle Barney, he's a pharmacist."

I lifted the top slightly and the pungent aroma filled the air. "Whew," the Swamp Master said. "You wanna ex-fix-e-ate me. Save that shit for when you need it." He handed me a clean white rag. "Use this, you gotta get up real close from behind and . . ."

"I know, I figured it out," I said.

"Just tryin' to help, that's all." He smiled. "And when you're done, don't wipe your nose with your hand."

"Let's go," I said.

"Don't be gettin' all antsy on me, Francisco. We'll go when they relax, after they finish their first rounds."

An hour later we made our move. The Swamp Master peeled off and made a beeline to the Albatross. I darted across the tarmac to the main hangar. I could see the small tower at the head of the runway. The lights inside were visible. I could see the silhouettes of two people moving around. I was on the corner of the hangar that faced the great swamp.

Inside the hangar there were two lights on. I peered through the window and saw the inside security sitting under the wing of an Aero Commander reading the newspaper laid out on the top of a desk in front of him. I watched him for several minutes. Eventually, he dropped his head into his arms on top of the desk, and I could see by the rhythm of his breathing, his back moving in sync with his inhaled and exhaled breaths, he was asleep. I saw the alarm clock in front of him; it must have been set on the top of the hour to wake him up so he could complete his rounds.

Good.

I made my way slowly around to the front of the

building, and spotted the outside security guard. He was sitting at a chair by a card table that was placed about twenty feet from the main front-door light. He was watching a six-inch color television set. As I inched my way up against the hangar wall toward him, I could see football players. It was the Miami Dolphins-New York Jets game on *Monday Night Football.* As I got near him, I could start to hear the commentators, and the roar of the crowd as the play intensified.

Suddenly, there was a clang, the sound of metal on metal. It must have been the Swamp Master, doing his thing on the Albatross. I flattened myself against the wall. The guard turned down the volume on the television, but left the picture on. He stood and hooded his eyes with one hand to see better in the blackness. He lowered his hand and stood dead still in the darkness. Then he moved to the head of the card table away from the light of the television screen. He just stood there motionless. He was a man in his forties, slightly overweight. He was over six feet tall, and I estimated his weight at two-thirty or so. He wouldn't go down easy. He wore a uniform from Badger Security, carried a Sig Sauer side arm, mace, a billy club, and a pair of handcuffs that were stuffed in a leather holder on his belt. This guy was a pro, not like the man inside—maybe police or military background by the way he moved. He picked up the two-foot-long tubular steel flashlight and started walking toward the Albatross.

Shit, he was a moving target now, in the open, much tougher to take down with the chloroform. You had to open the bottle, pour the fluid onto the rag, get it over his mouth, and hold it there for about five seconds. Not easy, with a 230-pound man who was trained to handle himself. Now, all I had left was surprise. But he was out in the open now, on his way to the Albatross, and there was a quarter moon up, so there was some light on the runway and the field.

I was still up against the hangar wall in the shadows. I had to do something fast. I saw a pair of headlights coming up the service road outside the security fence. They were moving parallel to the airstrip. They went under an overhead light, and I could see that it was a late-model Chevy Suburban, shiny black in the gray-black night.

Shit! Shit! Shit!

I had to move, and I had to move now. The guard was approaching the Albatross. I could see the strong beam from his flashlight flash on the planes that were tied down around the Albatross. I saw the Suburban's lights stop at the main guardhouse as I pushed off the hangar wall.

I stuffed the bottle of chloroform into my pocket and took off running across the grass field on the edge of the tarmac.

The guard was less than thirty feet from the Albatross when his flashlight picked up the cowling that had fallen from the port engine. I was running full tilt across the tarmac now.

The beam from his flashlight darted to the wing above the cowling. The Swamp Master's head and arms were now caught in the beam of light. The guard reached for his side arm and unholstered it in one motion. He aimed the Sig Sauer at the Swamp Master.

"Hold on there, podner," the Swamp Master said as

he moved out a little off the wing where it met the engine.

"Fuck you, asshole. You just stay there for a minute while I call this in." He placed the flashlight in the crotch of his arm, and reached for his two-way radio.

I was on him as he swung the radio up from his belt. I came up from his blind side. "No, it's fuck you, asshole," I said.

He was right-handed, and he swung to his right, like I hoped he would, bringing his gun hand around in an arc. I was waiting. I came down hard with a chop to his wrist. The gun flew and clattered on the pavement. I moved in closer toward him. We were facing each other now, but I was inside his arms, just where I wanted to be. I balled my fist, and hit him hard in the solar plexus, right on the bone that joins the rib cage together. I felt the entire rib cage compress inward from the force of my blow. I smelled his exhaled breath in my face, the smell of the rice and black beans he must have had for supper.

He collapsed at my feet. I reached in my pocket for the bottle of chloroform. As I did, I saw the Swamp Master catapult off the wing and onto his feet on the pavement. He swept up the fallen cowling and snapped it back onto the engine.

I poured the liquid into the white rag and covered the guard's face. I could feel his big black bushy mustache under my fingers as I pressed the rag into his flesh. I counted to ten, slowly. I wanted him out for a while.

The Swamp Master popped the door and turned to

me. "Get the chocks and the two tie-down clips." He disappeared inside the plane.

I kicked the chocks away and popped off the two tie-down cables. I followed the Swamp Master into the plane, but before I did I saw the black Suburban stop under the main light at the front door of the Florida Private Planes hangar. Two men jumped out of the front seat. I saw the red Hawaiian shirt flash in the glare of the light. The inside guard was awake by now and standing in the door. I saw him point our way. I jumped in the plane and slammed the door behind me. The Swamp Master was in the front seat.

I sat down in the copilot's seat. The Swamp Master was moving fast, clicking the toggle switches. He hit the start button for the starboard engine. It ground, then coughed, and finally spat into life.

"Is that who I think it is in that truck?" he asked.

"Yes."

"Shit!" he blurted as he hit the starter button for the port engine. The propeller whirred, but there was no sign of contact. "Where is he?"

I looked out the window and saw the men running back to the Suburban. "They're on the way," I said. The port engine whirred with no contact. "What's the matter?"

"No fuckin' gas. I didn't have time to prime it. And the battery is goin' to die."

He stopped the port engine and we both peered out the window. The Suburban was moving real fast toward us.

"They're gonna block us getting on the runway. They're cutting off the angle," I said.

The Swamp Master hit the start button again, and the engine whirred, then whined as the battery started to weaken. He switched it off and revved up the starboard engine, which turned us left in a semicircle so that the nose of the albatross faced the swamp. "We got one last chance with that battery, say your prayers!" he yelled over the noise of engine.

He hit the button, the propeller spun, whirred, then whined like it was going to die, and it coughed and sputtered into life. The Swamp Master worked the choke like a brain surgeon removing a tumor. He was trying to get the fuel-flow working. I did say a prayer, a Hail Mary. The port engine caught.

The Suburban was pulling in behind us to cut us off from the runway. "What now?" the Swamp Master roared.

"Hey, this is your plan," I said.

"We're fucked here, podner."

I looked slightly off to the right, just in front of us. It was the concrete ramp where they launched the airboats. "Go there, over there!" I yelled, and pointed. You didn't have to tell the Swamp Master anything twice when it came to danger.

He spotted the concrete launching pad, and pushed both engines full forward. The Albatross lurched forward toward the pad. "I hope it's deep enough, so the wheels don't get stuck in the mud," he yelled.

"Too fucking late now," I said. I could see the Suburban clearly. Michael Burton's face was visible in the headlights of the truck. Standing next to him was Rick Jacoby. They were confused, and couldn't see the launching pad in front of us that led into the great swamp. They thought we were trapped. Both men carried pistols. I did not see any automatic weapons. They stood dumbfounded, wondering what was happening.

The Albatross hit the airboat launching pad doing about thirty miles an hour. The wheels slipped down the concrete pad and into the water. They held firm.

"Francisco, it's concrete for about thirty feet, so they can haul out the airboats. Now just pray it don't shallow up, muck up on us in here, before we can retract the wheels."

I could hear the hydraulic grinding as the wheels climbed up into their wheel-wells. The throttles were full ahead. The plane lurched forward when it hit the water and dropped on the pad. The propellers dipped down, and for a second we thought they were going to hit the water and stop, but they cleared by inches and the plane righted itself. It slid from side to side as the hull straightened itself out.

They were shooting now. Burton and Jacoby stood at the edge of the water on the launching pad in the blackness. The red fire was spitting out the muzzles of their guns. We were skimming along on top of the water and the short-cropped saw grass. I knew it only drew about a foot of water when it was under speed.

"We're outta range, podner," he said with a huge grin. He pulled back about a quarter on the throttles as I pulled back on the wheel and we lifted. When we were fifty feet in the air, I banked us to the south toward Florida Bay. We had no running lights on and we were too low for radar.

"Where to now?" I asked.

"We gotta fill this baby up with fuel and hide it."

"I'm not going to ask how that's going to happen," I said.

"Best that you don't," he said with a grin. "I'll take that wheel now."

I left the Swamp Master deep in the Card Sound, above Key Largo. He was putting the camouflage netting around the plane when I left. It was the same netting I was sure they had used to hide the bales of marijuana they used to smuggle into the Keys in the late eighties. He would change the numbers while I was gone and update a logbook he had taken from his days at Florida Private Planes.

I borrowed his cousin's old Chevy Pickup and drove to Miami. I was committed now. There was no looking back from here.

We were to meet for breakfast in the Morro Castle restaurant on Eighth Avenue in Little Havana. I walked in at exactly eight, and went to the back of the restaurant to a wide circular booth. They were all there: Bobby Day, Felix, his brother Juan, and Jeff Bacon.

I sat and ordered some eggs Cubano, eggs and sausage, and *café con leche,* strong espresso coffee laced with hot milk.

"How'd it go with the plane?" Bobby asked. I had told them that we were going to use an Albatross that belonged to one of the Swamp Master's relatives.

"Great, real smooth, no problem at all," I answered.

"I got all the pass-throughs and this," Bobby said. He pulled his gym bag from the floor under his feet and unzipped the top flap. He reached in and pulled out a small electronic device about the size of a Walkman, with a six-inch antenna. "We stick this magnitized transponder on the plane and when I set the codes and activate this little beauty, the code comes up in the Miami war room as a pass-through pre-cleared by the FAA and Customs."

"How'd you do it?" I asked.

"Don't ask, so I don't have to lie."

"The Swamp Master has us cleared in Colombia," I said. "And Jeff, did you bring cameras?"

"Yes," Jeff Bacon said, "Al Baxter, the publisher, called me in and gave the okay on the whole assignment. He also sent me to the photo guys, and told them to fix me up with whatever I needed. I got four cameras, two videos-digital, and two 35-millimeters for still photos, one for day, one for night shooting."

He showed them to me. They were state-of-the-art cameras, worth thousands of dollars. I handled them as Jeff took them out of his bag.

"See, Francisco, they don't use films, they use disks, and the disks can be downloaded immediately to my computer." He waved his closed laptop at me. "And I can use a satellite to send in my story."

"You know how to operate all this stuff?" I asked.

"We'll find out, won't we?" he said, and we laughed.

I wondered what the favor was that Al Baxter, the publisher of the *Sentinel,* owed Felix—it must have been some favor.

We finished our breakfast and walked to the parking lot. Felix and Juan called me aside and into a van with darkened windows that was parked in the lot. Inside the van there were seats only for the driver and the passenger.

Juan closed the door behind us. There were two

metal boxes and a smaller wooden box. Juan flipped back the cover of one box. The box was full of weapons. "Compliments of Alpha 99, my brothers in arms. Choose what you want." He flipped back the cover of the second box. It was also full of weapons.

I chose four AK-47's and a dozen banana clips. I took an automatic shotgun, an Italian Speis model. I took four shock grenades, some smoke canisters, a LAWS rocket, five Mac-10's, five Glock 9-millimeters, all with clips and ammo. Juan and I put the weapons in the empty wooden box and padlocked it.

"Tell your brothers at Alpha 99 thank you. With all these weapons we could liberate Cuba ourselves," I said with a smile.

"We will liberate Cuba with brains, not brawn, and we will do it legally," Felix said.

"Don't worry. We will do it as legally as possible, my brother," Juan said with a smile.

"Said like a true Cuban patriot," Felix answered.

Juan and I wrestled the wooden box from the van and carried it to the pickup truck, where we put the box in the bed and covered it with the painter's tarp that was lying there.

"I will drive with you if it is all right, Francisco," Juan said. "Someone inside the restaurant right now will take the van."

"So, we had bodyguards." I smiled.

"A person can't be too careful, Francisco," Felix said.

"That's true," I said.

Bobby Day and Jeff Bacon followed us in their cars. I took the Turnpike to Homestead and then got on the Card Sound Road, crossed the concrete bridge to Key

Largo, passed the Ocean Reef Club entrance headed south, and ten minutes later we pulled into the PINDER CAMPGROUNDS AND FISHING CLUB. The property was made up of three mobile homes and twenty-two empty concrete pads and hookups for trailers. The family had made so much money smuggling in marijuana in the eighties that it just kept this property for a tax write-off. The property was grandfathered in as a commercial property before the moratorium on building in the Florida Keys; they kept all the permits and taxes up to date. The property appreciated in value every day it sat there.

The Swamp Master had finished painting the new numbers on the tail of the Albatross and had the plane well hidden under the camouflage netting. Days before, he had brought in a number of fifty-gallon drums of high-octane aviation fuel to fill up the tanks.

He came out of one of the mobile units wearing his painting overalls, a Miami Dolphins cap and a T-shirt that said, SAVE THE MALES. He was chewing tobacco and smiling like he was going to a party.

"How they hangin', boys?" he said.

I made all the introductions, and we got Juan, Bobby, and Jeff situated with a bedroom each inside the mobile units. He had the air conditioners up full blast.

"Nice and cool in here for you-all to sleep. We take off at nine tonight just after full sunset. Get as much rest as you can. I see some late nights in our futures."

He helped me load the crate of arms onto the Albatross. We opened the box inside the airplane. "Francisco, you goin' to war?"

"No, these are gifts from Alpha 99, backup tools in case we run into trouble," I said.

"Lot of firepower for one of them cerebral expeditions, ain't it, Francisco?" He spat his tobacco out the open door and smiled back at me. "Shall we go?" he asked.

I knew he was anxious; so was I.

We took the old pickup truck and headed down the Key Largo road to A1A; ten miles later we were in Tavernier. We turned off on the dirt road that led to the PINDER VILLAGE—TRAILER PARK AND R.V. CENTER. The gate was locked, and I could see the remote closed-circuit TV camera hidden in the tree above the gate. The Swamp Master saluted the camera and used his key to open the gate.

We drove to the furthest point, a tiny peninsula that jutted into the Atlantic and held a double-wide mobile home. He beeped the horn as he pulled in the ground-coral-stone driveway. Mai Lynh came out with both of his children. They ran to their father and jumped into his arms. Mai Lynh followed, and waited for her turn to move inside those big arms of his.

Behind Mai Lynh, Lillian stood in the doorway. She was dressed in a short white dress and had a thick black ribbon that spanned her forehead and ran through her blond hair. The band accentuated her high cheekbones and fine nose; her figure, which was well known to me, was outlined as the trade winds pressed her dress to her body. She smiled, that "I got a secret" smile with her lips that I loved. She moved slowly down the stairs. I moved to her and we were together, kissing, with the wind caressing us. I could feel the slight spray from the ocean and smell the salt and ozone in the air.

"Let's go," I whispered in her ear.

"I've been waiting all morning, darling," she said.

"Me too," I said.

We drove back out onto A1A and headed down to Islamorada and the Green Turtle Inn, an old elegant restaurant that had outlived hurricanes and other high winds and wild seas. It was twelve, and they had just opened for lunch. They sat us in a dark booth in the rear of the restaurant, where we would be alone. I ordered a bottle of Dom Perignon. We sat in silence as the bottle was opened.

"Are we celebrating?" she asked.

"L'chaim," I said. "A Jewish toast to—"

"Life." She finished my sentence. We sipped from our glasses.

"Yes, we're celebrating what we have, a rare thing, the rarest thing of all."

"We love each other."

"Yes, we love each other and we respect each other. There is no person I have ever met that has really loved me, and still allowed me to have my own life," I said.

"Francisco, you have done the same for me. You have shown me a new life, a real life. You know I don't want you to go on this flight, but I know I must let you go and do things your way. I respect you, my darling."

"You're wonderful."

"You know, Mai Lynh feels the same about her man. They give each other space, and they help each other."

"We don't have a lot of time," I said.

"Let's skip lunch, take this champagne and get a room," she said.

"Let's go," I said.

I paid the bill and we checked into the Holiday Inn on A1A. I set the champagne bottle down on the night table as we walked into our room. She shut the door behind us.

"Don't turn on the light, darling," she said.

I poured us each some champagne in plastic cups. We were quickly naked in bed.

"Francisco, would you just hold me in your arms for a little while and sing to me, please."

"Yes." I said, taking her in my arms. "What would you like to hear?" I whispered in her ear.

"Surprise me," she said.

I thought for a few seconds, then began one of most romantic songs I could think of.

When I finished, I felt her arms tighten around me, tighten like the arms of a lover seeing her love off to war. I turned her head to me and kissed her softly on the lips.

I dropped Lillian off at Pinder's at seven and picked up the Swamp Master. We did it quickly. It was hard for all of us to say good-bye.

We drove in silence until we got on the Key Largo road.

"Well, podner, you ready to rock and roll?"

"I've never been readier."

When the sun had set, the five of us removed the camouflage netting. Nobody asked why it covered the plane. Nobody wanted to know.

We waited twenty minutes for the afterglow to disappear and the dark to settle in. There was a quarter moon rising. We taxied out into the Card Sound when the Swamp Master's cousins signaled us that the skies were clear and that the water was clear of boats. We needed to taxi a half mile to get clear water to get airborne in our lumbering Albatross.

The Swamp Master had loaded the plane with one-hundred-kilo bags of sugar, wrapped with duct tape, the duct tape initialed so that it looked like a drug load. At the current wholesale price of twelve thousand dollars a kilo, it made the load worth six hundred thousand wholesale. We would fly directly to Barranquilla, Colombia, where we would touch down, refuel, and head out again to Cuba.

The Swamp Master faced us quickly into the wind and revved up both engines before pushing the throttles forward. I checked the gauges, and everything looked fine. I gave the thumbs-up and signaled for Jeff, Bobby, and Juan to strap themselves into their seats up against the bulkhead.

The Swamp Master looked at me and smiled. "Hang on to your jockstrap, Francisco, we're off."

The Swamp Master rammed the throttles forward, and I pulled back on the wheel and felt the big lumbering bird shudder as it fought to rise out of the water. At first it felt like a giant speedboat bouncing along, trying to get on a smooth plane; then the water was running under the hull of the airplane, the pontoons skimming the water as the wings dipped alternately with the rolling of the airplane. The engines were straining now as the prop speed increased. We were giving off a steady wake as the plane lifted and started to skim the water's surface. There was a slight chop on the water, which was helpful to us as we got up to speed—less water suction under the hull of the plane.

At the one-mile mark we were almost out of the water; then suddenly we popped up clear of the water and we were airborne. It was exhilarating to take this man-made creature of aluminum and steel that could walk on land, swim, and fly and put it through its paces. We were ten feet off the surface and rising when I heard the cheer from behind me. Three huge grins, three thumbs-up. I signaled back as the Swamp Master and I concentrated on the task at hand. We had to clear the Card Sound bridge, which was three miles ahead of us. The concrete bridge crossing the Card Sound rose eighty feet in the air to give the cruising sailboats clearance. It loomed ahead of us now like a strung bow across the water. There was little traffic on the toll bridge tonight, and there was nothing out of the ordinary for a seaplane to be using Card Sound to take off.

Fifty, sixty, seventy feet, registered on the altimeter, then seventy-five, then eighty, finally ninety feet as the span seemed only feet away from us, then a hundred feet as we slid over the top of the bridge, clearing it by twenty feet.

"How's that for a rush?" the Swamp Master yelled as we cleared the bridge.

"I don't need a rush," I said. "We cut that awfully close."

"No need to worry, we coulda always went under the bridge."

"Great," I said.

"We're in the clear now," he yelled.

We banked east over Key Largo, staying under a

thousand feet, out of the radar. The string of islands below us were mangrove-green, but looked coal-black at night. The Keys were connected by a ribbon of highway-bridges. At less than a mile out to sea, the Swamp Master banked again, changing our heading from east to southwest. We stayed under a thousand feet and parallel to the highway, heading for Key West. The traffic on A1A was light, no tourists this time of year. It isn't immediately noticeable if you're driving, but it's apparent from the air that the Keys turn westerly just above Marathon, and stay that way until Key West. That suited us perfectly. We would stay on that westerly bent for a few hours.

Forty minutes later Key West was under our starboard wing. My crew was busy. Jeff was already writing on his portable, while Juan sat at the rear of the airplane, where he had all the ordnance spread out on a canvas and was methodically checking all the weapons and loading them.

The lights of Key West disappeared behind us. We flew over the Sand Key light, the Marquesas, the Dry Tortugas, and then we were in the open ocean. There was a small glimmer on the ocean's surface from the quarter moon. We were flying at two thousand feet now, the slight chop of the ocean causing the whitecaps to flash in the moonlight. The engines were droning in an almost perfect harmony. The Swamp Master must have spent a lot of time on this plane's engines; they were operating well . . . humming.

It was almost hypnotic, the sound of the engines, the shine of the water, the rhythm of the breaking whitecaps, the blackness of the night, and the glimmering water. I looked over at the Swamp Master, who was concentrating on the instruments of both engines. He hummed to himself; he gave off a happiness that is very hard to explain. It happens when all your senses are maxed out, stretched, and there is danger in the air, danger around every corner, the unexpected monster of surprise lurking in the darkness.

" 'Bout three hours to the Yucatan Channel, Francisco," the Swamp Master said, looking up from his navigational clipboard.

"We're giving Cuban airspace a wide berth."

"Yeah, the U.S. flies those AWAC radar planes around here, but I think we're low enough so's they won't pick us up; besides, we're headin' in the wrong direction to bother with. Them Cubans got no money, so they don't send their patrol planes any further than they have to—we should be okay. I'm going to get some shut-eye if you can spare me for a few hours."

"Right." He unstrapped himself and nodded at the crew, who were still engaged in their activities. He yelled at them, "I'm getting a little rest while I can." They nodded. He walked down the far side of the one hundred kilos of sugar and stretched out on the metal floor. He used a life jacket for a pillow, and within minutes he was asleep.

I forced all thoughts from my mind. I have been in dangerous situations before. Speculation about danger is dangerous, because it can fog focus. You can lose the laser beam of concentration you need when the action happens. It was a key to my survival in Vietnam. My motto: "Don't worry about the things you have no control over; hesitation can mean death." My instructors taught me this before I went and knocked on the door to hell. "Don't anticipate you opponents' move—react to it—anticipation will slow you down." I have lived this way all my life when I was on the edge. I also subscribed to the credo of depending on your training and your instincts—they will never disappoint you.

I flew right down the middle of the Yucatan Channel, the Yucatan Peninsula off to our right, the home of the ancient Mayan civilization. A place that Lillian and I were going to explore together. The hours passed quickly. We were doing two hundred knots airspeed. I was fully alive behind the wheel as Mexico passed off into the night from the Gulf of Mexico, then into the Caribbean Sea, then Guatemala, Honduras, Nicaragua, Costa Rica, Panama, then finally, two hours after dawn, the coast of Colombia and the city of Barranquilla appeared.

"It's right there where it always is," the Swamp Master yelled beside me. "It's not like we're not old friends. Let me land this bird." He grinned, taking over control of the aircraft.

We had been flying at five thousand feet since we cleared the Yucatan. The Swamp Master banked us around in a slow westerly turn. We headed inland, flying over the ranches and farms of Barranquilla.

Twenty minutes later there was a black tarmac landing strip, almost a mile long. "This is us," the Swamp Master said. Two flatbed trucks carrying barrels of fuel sat on the edge of the strip.

"This is gonna be a little tight, gents," he said. Bobby, Jeff, and Juan were behind us looking out of the cockpit windows. "Better go strap yourself in."

They did as they were told.

The Swamp Master had a real feel for flying. He checked his gauges regularly, but he gave the impression that he really didn't need them. The strip was well positioned for the prevailing winds; there was a strong easterly wind today blowing in from the ocean. He banked around the strip until we were head on into the wind. He pulled back the throttles and lowered the flaps so we would start to drop. He had to put the wheels down just at the beginning of the tarmac. We would need it all. We were coming in a little too fast, so our rate of descent was not what it should have been. He pulled back further on the throttles and we dropped quickly, like a big dead bird. The ground was shooting up toward us, and it would be only a matter of a few seconds as to whether we landed in the dirt or on the tarmac.

He pulled the throttles back further, almost stalling us out as the blackness of the tarmac approached. The wheels hit and we bounced a foot or so off the runway; we hit and bounced again as he rammed the engines in reverse. I looked into the mirror and saw the legs of our crew bounce with the landing. They were strapped in X restraints against the fuselage that the Swamp Master had devised. He was no stranger to these wild and woolly adventures in flying.

He talked the plane in. "Hang on, baby, calm down, now just be a good girl and don't you be strainin' yourself here." The end of the runway was shooting up and the grass at the foot of the landing strip looked soft from the rains. We were loaded and would sink deep in the softness. The Swamp Master pumped the brakes.

We left little puffs of white smoke behind us as the wheels grabbed.

Finally the big bird settled down not more than twenty feet from the end of the runway. Four Colombians sat on the cabs of their fuel trucks, laughing and clapping as we came to a halt.

"You got the money, Francisco?" the Swamp Master asked.

I handed him three thousand U.S. dollars in fifties. Colombians were nervous about hundreds—counterfeiting hundreds was common.

He turned the plane around into the wind and turned the engines off. The trucks pulled up, one behind the other. We all got out and stretched our legs as the Swamp Master greeted the head man. They talked for a while, and the Swamp Master slipped him the cash. The trucks began the refueling; using fifty-gallon drums, they pumped the high-octane aviation fuel and topped our tanks off with five hundred gallons. This would give us enough range to reach Cuba and the United States, but we would take on two hundred gallons in Cuba for appearances.

We wasted no time on the ground. The Swamp Master knew the leader of the refueling and his crew from his smuggling days, but there was much unrest in Colombia with guerrilla warfare and rival factions everywhere. We all wanted to get out of there as soon as possible, and we did. It was a slow process with a hand-cranked pump. We were ready to leave an hour later. It had taken us thirteen hours to fly to Colombia, and it would take us five hours to reach Cuba from Barranquilla.

The fuel trucks backed away as the Swamp Master fired up the engines. He waited as one of the fuel trucks towed us back the fifty feet to the edge of the runway. We needed all the running length we could get.

When everyone was strapped in, and the engines were warmed up, he hit the throttles full forward and I had the wheel. We rumbled down the tarmac, avoiding the potholes, gaining speed. The speedometer rising slowly, twenty, forty, sixty—we lumbered along until we hit eighty—the runway disappearing under our wheels. Finally, at ninety, we lifted clear just as the tarmac ran out. We were in a valley that ran out to sea. It had been well selected by some ex-U.S. airmen and Colombian drug lords. The valley rolled by underneath us and the Caribbean Sea was now on the horizon. We were at four thousand feet when the ocean slipped under our belly.

We were Cuba-bound now. I said a silent prayer and looked over at the Swamp Master, who was concentrating on the instruments. And back at our crew, all three sitting silent, looking out in front of them.

It had been an accelerated life since the crash in the Everglades and our rescue by the Swamp Master, almost like fate wielding its unseen wand over my head. I couldn't let my mind wander or ponder those facts that had brought me to this place. I had to see it through now.

I would think about it later, if there was a later.

Chapter Twelve

At sunset we crossed over the Isle de Pinos, the 'Island of Pines', where Castro now kept the Cuban HIV-positive patients, in camps, isolated, like lepers. The MiG-23 had picked us up twenty miles off the coast of Cuba to escort us into Cuban airspace. This had been arranged by Juan and his Alpha 99 group, through their spies inside Cuba. We had a password ID. The tower said, "Viva," and we answered, "Viva Jose Marti." We knew our course bearing, and we tracked into the airport according to plan.

We had pre-clearance for a twenty-four-hour stop-over for fuel, rest, and advice as to where the U.S. electronic net was weakest around Florida. The cost was normally a hundred thousand for a hundred-kilo load, but we were being charged only twenty thousand, thanks to the agents within Alpha 99. It was important to our case that we would be charged, so we could record the payment to the Cubans in our case against them.

We passed onto the mainland near noon. The landing strip was only twenty miles from the Guantanamo military base. This meant that if "Fat Albert," the fifty-million-dollar surveillance blimp in Summerland Key, was up on its three-thousand-foot cable and the weather was clear, it would appear that the plane flew into and out of Guantanamo, causing more confusion in the Miami War Room, where they tracked the comings and goings from Cuba electronically.

The MiG peeled off as we approached the landing strip. The air traffic control was handled from a spindly wooden-legged tiny two-story tower with a small enclosed room with a red wind sock waving on the roof. A window-based air-conditioning unit stuck out from the side of the building. The small size of the air traffic tower belied the size of the installation. I counted six big hangars and a dozen major Butler buildings that I was sure were used as warehouses. Two four-story buildings were located on the perimeter. We had been told that these were called apartment hotels, but were primarily whorehouses.

As we approached, the air traffic controller's voice crackled into life. He spoke in English, as does every air traffic controller in the world. There was no traffic on the runway, and no other planes in the air, but you could tell by the many parked aircraft and the size of the installation that this was a busy place.

We hit the tarmac in the dark. The sun had set and the moon had popped up in the sky. The Swamp Master and I dropped the plane down out of the sky nice and easy; the wheels squealed a little, tiny puffs of white popped up when they made contact, and we rolled smoothly down the long runway. There were many skid marks from the planes before us.

A single man stood near the far hangar with two red and white flashlights raised in the air, signaling, calling us to him. The tower confirmed, and we headed toward the light. As we approached the man, a Cuban Jeep pulled out from under the tower with four men on board.

They pulled up to the door of the Albatross at the same time as the Swamp Master shut down the engines. Juan Rodriguez was first out the door, as we had agreed, we followed. There had been a code-word system developed in Miami by the Alpha 99 group.

"It's great to be in Cuba," Juan said in Spanish. We all stood on the tarmac waiting for the response, "That's because Cuba is great." We heard nothing.

The two men in the backseat of the Jeep stood up. They were armed with AK-47's and pistols in their belts. As they stood, their military jackets slipped off. One of them wore a bright red Hawaiian shirt. The other wore a T-shirt that said, MIAMI DOLPHINS KICK ASS. It was Rick Jacoby and Michael Burton. Their guns were leveled at us. The two men in the front of the Jeep stood. One was a colonel and the other man a sergeant. The colonel moved in behind the two Americans.

"Raise you arms, assholes, and stand side by side," Jacoby yelled. We did as instructed. "Isn't this fuckin' special—five assholes all together."

False Witness

Michael Burton stepped off the Jeep onto the tarmac, and told the Cuban sergeant to search us. He introduced the colonel. "This is Colonel Orlando Garcia of Cuban Intelligence. We are all here as his guests." The colonel nodded to us. A second Jeep pulled up with four armed soldiers. They dismounted the Jeep and formed a line, guns pointed at us.

Burton continued. "Let's see who's here on foreign, sovereign soil, on your soil, Colonel. First we have Sawyer Pinder, aka the Swamp Master, ex-smuggler and general renegade; next to him we have Francisco Cruz, currently out on bail for federal charges; next to him is Juan Rodriguez, a Cuban refugee, one of the leaders of Alpha 99, a bunch of fucked-up Cubans who can't get out of their own way; next is Agent Bobby Day—I remember you from the Opa-Locka airport raid. You're the one that worries us. And finally, who do we have? What's your name, boy?" he asked of Jeff Bacon.

"Bob Woodward. I left Carl Bernstein in Miami. He gets airsick," Jeff answered.

"You must be a journalist, or maybe a comedian. That's good," Michael Burton said, moving up to him as the Cuban searched him for weapons. "You're a funny guy." Michael Burton took his right fist and punched Jeff square in the face. His nose erupted in blood as Jeff slumped to one knee holding his face. Burton stomped down hard on Jeff's foot, collapsing his arch. Jeff rolled on the tarmac screaming in pain. "But see, this is no time to be funny."

"You're funny enough for all of us," I said to Burton.

Burton walked to me, stood inches from my face. "That's good, my Cuban nightclub singer genius, real good. You want to distract me away from the sissy reporter, who is now finally feeling something real that he normally writes about—*pain.* You want some pain?"

"Standing here looking at your ugly face is enough pain for all of us," I said.

"Another fuckin' comedian."

He went to stomp down on my instep. I moved it to the side, fast, and as his foot hit the tarmac I kneed him in the balls, hard as I could; he buckled forward and went for the rifle in his hands. But Jacoby was too fast. He swung his rifle butt in an arc, and it hit me in the shoulder, driving me down to me knees. I looked up, staring into the muzzle of his AK-47.

"Wanna be dead?" I looked into a pair of deadly psychotic eyes. Jacoby stood over me.

A hand appeared on his shoulder. It was Michael Burton, in pain. "Steady now, Rick, let's be smart here. This is a little complicated."

"What's complicated about death?" Jacoby asked.

"It's not death that's complicated—it's how you die," Burton said, still winded from the shot to his balls. He whispered, "And who the witnesses are."

Jacoby stepped back, and said to me, "Get up, asshole, today's your lucky day."

Jeff Bacon was back on his feet now. He had his hand to his nose with a white cloth trying to stop the bleeding. Two more Cuban soldiers wheeled up in a Jeep. They stepped out and looked to Burton for direction. "Use the plastic restraints on them," he said in Spanish. The soldiers moved in and tied our hands behind our backs, using the plastic strip handcuffs; the others held us at gunpoint. While this was being done, Jacoby climbed onto the plane and yelled to Burton, "Come on up here and look at this."

They both disappeared into the belly of the Albatross. Burton came out carrying one of our packets of sugar in his hand. He poured the white contents on to the ground. The two Cuban soldiers were mystified.

"What's the matter, you guys think the world does not have enough sugar? So, you have to import more?" Burton asked.

"Yeah, we thought we'd bring some sugar into Cuba, help the economy," the Swamp Master said.

"And weapons, you figured you'd break a major law here in Cuba and bring in guns." Jacoby walked out of the Albatross, his arms full of our weapons. He laid them down on the tarmac. "You guys are lookin' at twenty years for this alone—importation of arms into Cuba."

We stood in line, shoulder to shoulder, in silence.

"You, wonderin' how we knew you would be here? We been trackin' you on Cuban radar since you left Colombia. We got a call the minute that Colombian you got your gas from saw the Albatross. Right after you stole it, we put out a twenty-five-thousand-dollar cash reward for the first one that saw the plane. He called us in Miami, and we sent the AWAC plane over here for Customs. Then we gave the info to the Cubans, while we flew here. So, you see, you are a bunch of dumb fucks. How did you ever come up with this fucked-up plan in the first place? And then you steal the Albatross from us? We didn't know it was you, but it didn't take us long to figure it out.

R. L. Smitten

"I was mystified as to why you were in Colombia and getting refueled, but now it is clear to me, and it is actually quite clever. You might have succeeded if it wasn't for that Colombian informer. So, why don't you tell us exactly what your plan was; it doesn't matter to you now, anyway," Burton said.

"Anybody wanna talk?" Jacoby said.

We stood in silence.

"Well, I'm gonna put you in storage for a while, and think about what we wanna do next," Burton said.

We were marched in handcuffs over to a big hangar that was full of coke. We were taken into what was once a large meat freezer, but was obviously shut down now. It had not been well cleaned out, and it still smelled of rancid meat and flies were everywhere. When the door was opened, the odor almost knocked us over. We were shoved in, and as the door was closed behind us Rick Jacoby yelled, "This will help you to chill out."

As we slumped down against the walls, we could hear the whir of the fans as the cooling unit burst into life. The air, like a cold blanket, almost immediately began to flood in. It felt good at first against the Cuban heat, but I didn't like it, not at all. They'd taken all our credentials and personal property.

I had no watch, but I guessed it was midnight when the temperature was down to just above freezing. I knew it took about eight hours for exposure to overtake your bodily functions. By what I guessed to be four in the morning we were all shaking uncontrollably, shivering, teeth chattering, huddled together in a clump of human flesh for body warmth.

False Witness

By around eight in the morning we were almost frozen together in a cube of misery, and the moaning had begun. Only the Swamp Master and myself had refrained from the moaning and, in some cases, crying from the cold.

At nine in the morning the steel door was sprung open and I was pulled out. The door was slammed behind me, locking my friends in the freezing cold. It seemed ironic to be freezing to death on the tropical island of Cuba. Two guards dragged me out to the front of the hangar and dropped me on the blazing tarmac. I was still freezing as I looked up into the eyes of Michael Burton, Rick Jacoby, and Colonel Orlando Garcia.

"So, you cooled off now, Francisco?" Rick Jacoby said.

I was disoriented, on my back, still shivering, my hands still bound behind my back. I couldn't have done anything if I wanted to. I said nothing.

"Look, let's make this easy on all of us. Just tell us what this is all about Francisco," Michael Burton said. "Like who sanctioned this fiasco. The sooner you tell us the story, the sooner you wind up back in the good old U.S.A. and your stupid friends can get out of the freezer."

I shook my head, as if to shake the chill out of my brain. I was truly in trouble here, and I couldn't think, couldn't think at all. I went to speak, my lips moved, but nothing came out. No words, no sounds.

Colonel Garcia spoke for the first time. "Perhaps it doesn't matter what their agenda was, since they are now under our control. It has become our agenda, and after all, they are on sovereign territory and they have imported drugs here into Cuba."

"Sugar." I was finally able to speak. "We brought in sugar."

"No, my stupid friend. It is not sugar anymore—it has turned into *cocaíne—blanco morte*—the white death," the colonel said.

"See, Francisco, old boy, your sugar magically transformed itself into cocaine last night, and we are going to have the pictures to prove it," Rick Jacoby said.

Two Cuban soldiers carried Jeff Bacon's photographic equipment over to me and placed it front of me on the ground.

"We used this high-tech digital equipment to photograph the plane and the contents—it's cocaine, all right. Here, let me get some pictures of you," Rick Jacoby said.

I was starting to come into focus, trying desperately to conjure up a plan.

"All right, while you thaw out, let me tell you what we know, so it will make it easy for you to fill in the rest," Michael Burton said. "You stole the Albatross because you wanted to tie in Florida Private Planes.

"You have Bobby Day, who is operating on his own—I checked and learned that he is on vacation from the FAA.

"I'm assuming that Juan Rodriguez is here representing Alpha 99. Colonel Garcia has already arrested his contacts here in Cuba.

"Jeff Bacon is here with the permission of the *Miami Sentinel*.

"The Swamp Master is here to help you, and you are

here to get yourself out of the legal shithouse you are in. Now, my question is—have I missed anything?"

"No," I said.

"How is this mission financed? Maybe you want to tell me that," Burton said.

"I financed it," I said.

"We took all your money in the bail hearing."

"Not all. My wife helped me," I said.

Burton looked down on me, studying my face. It was a little after nine in the morning and the place was in full swing. I noticed a lot of aircraft on the tarmac. Some were being looked at by mechanics who looked American. The hangars were busy with aircraft being checked out. And there were a number of warehouses that were heavily guarded with Cuban soldiers and men armed but in civilian clothes. I assumed it was where the cocaine and the marijuana were held.

It was a month after the coca harvest in Peru, Venezuela, Ecuador, and Columbia and marijuana was an around-the-year crop. What Mai Lynh had told us was true. This was a major offensive. It came clear to me lying on the blazing tarmac. They were going to send in an armada of aircraft, a tidal wave of dope. They would find the holes in the electronic web that protected the United States and fly through, and I was looking at the two men who would supply the intelligence to the Cubans—Burton and Jacoby.

"That's it. It's that simple," I said. I would give them the truth. Burton had already figured it out. I would keep my story close to what he wanted to hear, and close to the truth. This would get my friends out of the freezer. "I will tell you the story on the condition you release my friends from the freezer. They are getting close to death—you don't want them to die like that in front of witnesses."

"Tell us first," Jacoby said.

"No, we can always put them back inside the freezer if we do not believe him," Burton said.

"I agree," Colonel Garcia added, and signaled two guards to go and open the freezer door.

I watched my friends straggle out, eyes jammed shut against the blazing sun, hands still tied behind their backs. First the Swamp Master, who crumpled in a heap a few feet from me. Bobby Day next to him. Jeff Bacon fell just outside the door onto the asphalt. Juan Rodriguez was next, trying to walk proudly, trying to open his eyes to the sun. He made it to me, slumped to one knee, then down to both knees, and he finally crumbled.

"All right asshole, talk," Jacoby said to me.

"This was my idea. These men came at my request. Juan came because he knew the terrain from when he had lived in Cuba."

"Don't start with a lie, Francisco. We know that Alpha 99 has people over here and he planned to use them. These men Colonel Garcia arrested are part of his cadre. We know this," Burton said.

"The other men came for the reasons you gave. Bacon to write his story. Bobby Day to bust the airplane scam, and the Swamp Master to help me," I said.

"To get even for us trying to kill him twice—that's why he came to bust our balls—to get even," Burton said. "So, you're telling me what I want to hear."

"I'm telling the truth. I can't help it if you already figured out most of it," I said.

"All right." Burton said. "Put them in the secure room in hangar two. They'll thaw out. Give them some water and we'll figure out what to do with them in a little while."

The guards helped us to our feet and walked us into hangar two. We were locked into a windowless room with no ventilation. It was stifling and stuffy. We went from one extreme to the other—standard torture technique.

The good thing was that they cut us loose from our restraints, the plastic handcuffs were removed. Our circulation slowly returned, and then we began to overheat. They left us with a few gallons of water—no food.

"Well, this is a fine mess you got us into, Francisco," the Swamp Master said to me with a grin. The others laughed. "Any ideas?"

"No. I'm still thawing out," I said.

"What's that old joke about the guy diving into the freezing water—dove in looking like Angus ran out looking like Agnes—that's how I feel. My balls are still frozen," Bobby Day said.

"Juan, that Colonel Garcia says he has arrested your contacts—you believe him?" Jeff Bacon asked.

"Perhaps my contacts . . ."

I grabbed his arm and put my finger to my lips. I was sure we were under surveillance. They all caught on right away. We stood and looked for fiber-optic lenses and mini-microphones. We found four mikes, but no cameras. I gave the signal it was all right to communicate with signals, but not to talk. We moved closer so we could use hand motion and talk. When someone wanted to communicate they whispered, while the others talked loudly to each other.

For the moment we were exhausted and everyone just wanted to rest. I fell asleep within the hour, and lay on the floor in my own sweat, dreaming fitfully, dropping into and out of sleep.

We had no windows and no watches, so we had no way of telling time accurately, but it was a long time before we heard from anyone again. Everyone was awake and sitting in a circle, silent, lost in their own thoughts.

The door suddenly popped open and Colonel Garcia stood framed in the doorway, looking down on us. Behind him was a major and three sergeants. They were in full combat gear. I went to speak, and the colonel dropped to one knee and put his hand across my mouth. He put his finger to his lips to indicate silence. He motioned for Juan Rodriguez and myself to exit the room with him. We went into the office that was outside.

"Listen to me, we have little time. They have a plan for you. They are going to put you all back on the Albatross, which they have now loaded with fifty kilos of real cocaine. They will use a Cuban pilot and land you in the waters twenty miles off Key West, and disable the plane. You will be picked up almost immediately by prearrangement with US Customs and Coast Guard—Jacoby will see to that. The Cuban pilot will be picked up by a speedboat. So, when Customs arrives, you will be in a plane with fifty keys of coke and you will all be arrested, discredited, and probably wind up in jail."

I looked at him in total bewilderment. The colonel looked over to Juan.

"He is with us—Alpha 99," Juan said.

"I thought they said you had arrested members of Alpha 99," I asked.

"I arrested my enemies and planted evidence on them. That's one of the reasons I am able to be here now, talking to you," Garcia said.

"Do you have a plan?" I asked.

"Yes, the Albatross is being made ready. At the right time we will come and get you and take you to your plane," he said. "We will take care of the guards and the tower so you will be able to get away."

"And you, after we leave they will execute you, all of you," I said.

The major standing behind Colonel Garcia leaned forward. "We are coming with you to Miami. We will escape with you in the Albatross," he said.

"Now we must move fast. You are scheduled to leave in thirty minutes. The surveillance microphones are turned off, but speak to your men out here. These two men will stand guard." The two sergeants took up their posts at the main door.

I slipped back into our cell and waved for Bobby, the Swamp Master, and Jeff to come on out. We huddled in the office and I told them what was going on. I watched as smiles crossed the faces of all but the Swamp Master.

"What's the matter?" I asked him. "Let me answer for you.

"You think the plan is too simple, that's what's the matter," I said. "I'm with you. I believe these guys, but I'm not nuts about the plan."

"Why?" Juan asked.

"Because the tower has to be taken out. They can relay our location from their radar and a Cuban MiG can be scrambled and turn us into dust in seconds. Also, there are too many Cuban soldiers around this camp—too much security, because of the shipment that's coming up," I added.

"What do we do?" Bobby Day asked.

I thought for a few seconds, then answered. "Let's swap clothes with four of these Cubans. Bobby, Juan, me, and the Swamp Master—Jeff stays. The colonel will come with us."

"Then what?" The Swamp Master asked.

"We get two aviation fuel trucks and we pump the fuel into the two hangars and the two warehouses from the rear of each building. We will need five hand grenades. One for each building and one for the tower. While the chaos is happening we will take off in the Albatross," I said.

Everyone was silent as they thought of what I had said. Finally, Juan broke the silence. "I will talk to the colonel."

We watched as Juan went over and huddled with the colonel. It was nine o'clock, and very dark. I had read the colonel's watch, and we could see the quarter moon out the office window. We had not eaten in a long time now, but we had water and our adrenaline was very high.

Juan returned. "The colonel says fine. He also tells

me that there is an American C-130 military transport plane on the runway right now, being loaded with dope—thousands and thousands of keys."

"So Burton and Jacoby are occupied?" I asked.

"Yes," Juan said.

"Lets rock and roll," the Swamp Master said with a big grin.

We swapped clothes as fast as we could.

I said to the Swamp Master, "When we break up I'll go with Juan and the colonel—you take Bobby." He nodded.

I next went to Jeff Bacon and stood with him next to the office window. "Look, the colonel will be coming back for you and walking with you. Jeff, when the place starts to light up, you go out the side door with these men and the colonel. Then cross the tarmac to the Albatross. If there is real chaos you can jog, if not, just walk in a regular pace. The colonel will be with you. There are plenty of guys in regular clothes around here, so just try and act natural."

"Sure, Francisco, sure I'll just act natural. What do I do about my hands shaking?"

"Keep them in your pockets. Look, these guys will be plenty scared so they'll be looking to you," I said. "Now by the time you get to the Albatross we should be getting there as well. So, keep an eye out for us."

The colonel was a good officer and smart; he had the message. He signaled us to join him and he opened the door. We walked out easily onto the field; there was swirling action around the C-130 being loaded. I could see Michael Burton and Jacoby supervising the loading. A fuel truck was parked under the wing topping off the tanks. The two hangars were open and the doors to one warehouse were open. Forklift trucks like laboring insects carried the pallets of coke out of the warehouse and into the belly of the C-130. The value of that load was astronomical.

The colonel had us follow him to the small shack that acted as the command post. We walked past it and into the trailer of an eighteen-wheeler. The tractor had been removed. It was used for ammunition and arms storage. It was locked. One guard stood sentry. We waited on the side as the colonel used his key to get the lock open. The sentry was only mildly interested. He had seen the colonel do this many times before.

When the colonel was inside, he called for Juan to join him. Juan climbed in. Minutes later they emerged carrying an ammo box, nothing else. The colonel locked the trailer and we disappeared into the shadows.

He whispered to us, "That soldier, the sentry, he is one of ours. I wish I could take him with us to Miami."

"Next time," I said.

"Next time Fidel will be a small footnote in a history book and we will be coming here for a vacation," Juan said.

The colonel handed us each two grenades. "I was lucky, these are incendiary grenades, phosphorous, that clings and burns, so after you throw them stay clear of the explosion."

"Okay, I'll take the far warehouse and hangar," I said to the Swamp Master. "You take the two nearest us. Give me three minutes to get the truck to the far warehouse before you move. We will meet at the Albatross."

"Right, podner."

I turned to the colonel. "You ready?"

"Yes. I will walk with you to the fuel dump and then give you a few minutes to get the trucks; then I will go gather up the men," the colonel said. "But first, I will stop at the tower and deliver these." The colonel patted the two grenades in his belt.

"Okay. Let's go," I said.

The colonel led Juan, the Swamp Master, myself, and Bobby Day, dressed in our Cuban Army uniforms, over to the fuel dump. Fifty-gallon drums were stacked next to the two-thousand-gallon tanks that stood on rails.

One lone sentry sat on a stool by the chain-link fence. The fence was unlocked waiting for the truck to return from refueling the C-130. Four trucks, all Russian models, stood just behind the fence. The keys were on a wooden board hanging inside the compound.

Juan walked up to the sentry, the Swamp Master behind him. The sentry, seeing the colonel approach, immediately stood to attention in front of his stool. Juan moved up, inches from his face. The Swamp Master circled behind and slipped his massive arms around the man and took him in a choke hold. The man hardly moved in his arms, finally slipping into unconsciousness. I tied the man's arms and feet with the telephone cord, after I pulled it from the interconnect box. I stuffed an oily rag in his mouth, while Bobby and Juan took the keys from the board and fired up two aviation fuel trucks.

The Swamp Master and I jumped into the back of our respective trucks. The colonel made his way back to Jeff and the Cuban soldiers.

Juan needed no instruction. He wheeled the Russian

truck out of the compound and behind the hangars and warehouses. Immediately I opened a slow flow from the hose on my truck. The drip would lead back to the fuel dump, a thin high-octane trail. We pulled up behind the warehouse. It was the open one where they were taking the dope to the C-130. The back door was locked, so I placed the nozzle up against the doorjamb and let the fuel flow.

I saw the Swamp Master. He was behind the other warehouse, right where he was supposed to be. The smell of the high-octane aviation fuel was pungent, like kerosene, and I didn't want to alert them inside the warehouse, so I put about half as much as I wanted to into the warehouse. I couldn't see it, but I was sure there was a liquid trail that snaked through the warehouse, under the pallets of cocaine. There were thousands and thousands of keys inside.

I moved quickly to the hangar. It had windows. I could see the planes inside, at least two dozen small to medium planes. I noticed one Gulfstream jet inside, and wondered if it was Fidel's. This door was sealed, so I broke a pain of glass and let the fuel flow into the hangar. The hose was pumping full-force now, and splashing on the concrete floor.

The Swamp Master had moved to the final warehouse. I could see him bent over the hose as the fuel poured in under the door. I heard them before I saw them. Four soldiers on sentry patrol rounded the corner not ten feet from me. It took them a second to figure out what we were doing. I dove behind the fuel truck as they opened fire. They reacted without thinking.

I yelled at the top of my lungs. "Juan, get out of the

truck." He had seen them as well, and was opening the door. I ran back toward the cocaine warehouse using the truck to shield me from the bullets. I looked over my shoulder. It happened so fast that it was like a blurr. A bullet sparked the fuel coming out from the open hose. The flames snaked in two directions. A bright red-yellow flash. One into the hangar and the other back to the fuel truck.

The truck exploded. I saw Juan's burning body catapult up into the air, flipping and spinning like a toy doll. The four Cuban soldiers all went up. They spiraled through the air, body parts blazing. I ran to the back door of the warehouse and shot off the lock with my Cuban Army 44. I threw the incendiary grenade as far as I could into the warehouse. There was a quick double-explosion. The grenade, then the aviation fuel. The building rocked, then turned into a massive fireball.

I had started to run back when I heard the second warehouse go up, then burst into flames. I kept running. The rolling waves of heat almost overwhelmed me. The sky was alight, blazing, like it was day. People were running everywhere on the tarmac. I ran past the far hangar just as it went up. It knocked me to the ground. I rolled and rose onto my feet. The second fuel truck went up. I was blasted off my feet onto all fours. I could smell my own hair burning, singed from the heat, sweat poured into my eyes.

I looked to my left when I heard the explosion underneath the control tower—the colonel had done the job. The tower turned into splinters and flying glass as the flimsy structure disintegrated—no tower—no radar. I was moving as fast as I could.

I ran past the hangar and near to the fuel dump. My little trail of aviation fuel back to the fuel dump had not worked. I ran toward the airfield and the Albatross.

I stopped long enough to hurl my last grenade into the fuel dump. It was the biggest explosion of all, and sent a huge heat wave out along the ground in every direction.

I was knocked off my feet again, but staggered back up. I was almost blinded by my own sweat, the dust, and the flashes from the explosion. I used my sleeve to clear my eyes. I ran as fast as I could to the Albatross. I heard the four engines of the C-130 as it took off down the runway. Skids of coke were flying out the open cargo door. I could see inside as it passed me. The cargo door was being raised hydraulically. The cargo hatch was lit. I could see Michael Burton as he helped to secure the door. Jacoby stood with him.

Just as the door was about to close we saw each other. Our eyes locked. He pulled his side arm, but it was too late. The lumbering C-130 was off the ground and the cargo door slammed shut as the plane banked toward the sea.

The colonel stood at the door to the Albatross. The men inside were throwing the kilos of cocaine out the open door, to lighten the plane.

"Where's Juan?" he asked.

"He's gone," I shouted, and dove through the open door, and almost got the last of the cocaine in my face. The colonel swung in behind me and secured the door.

I could hear the Swamp Master cursing in the cockpit. Bobby Day sat next to him. Finally, both engines fired into life. The four Cuban soldiers sat strapped in their safety harnesses to the bulkhead. The colonel stood looking out the porthole. We were already turned into the wind, but we would not have the full runway.

The plane lumbered out onto the runway. I grabbed the wheel. The Swamp Master pushed both throttles full-forward, trying to get as much speed as he could.

A Jeep was out on the runway behind us. It had a mounted M-60 on a tripod. I could see the muzzle red-spitting bullets and flame. I could hear the ping of bullets off the fuselage and wings. Little spots of light appeared as the bullets peppered the hull of the plane.

"Get down!" I yelled, and the men popped the X fuselage harness and hit the deck. I moved forward to the cockpit.

The plane skimmed along the runway. We were running out of runway and the Jeep behind us was closing in, fast. The runway disappeared below us and we hit on the hard earth. The wheels bounced in the dirt. The Swamp Master was yelling at the top of his voice, "Come on, you baby. Come on, you beast of an airplane. Come on you motherfucker-get-up-get-up-get-up."

Then the liftoff, the lightness, airborne, the end of the lumbering. The liftoff into smoothness. "I knew you would do it for me, baby. I love you. I love you. I'm sorry I called you a motherfucker. Please forgive me—you beauty," the Swamp Master bellowed as he eased the throttles back.

I took a deep breath and said, "Thank you, God." I moved back and looked out the porthole window. At thirty feet we could see the damage below us. It was lit up like daylight. The two hangars blazing, the cocaine warehouses lit up with flames, the fuel dump sending billows of black smoke skyward, two burning fuel trucks glowing red in the night, what a mess, and millions and millions of dollars worth of damage.

I thought to myself—incredible, four men, who knew what do—the damage they could wreak—incredible. I looked through the side cockpit windows at the fires below. The Swamp Master was staring at the instruments, as was Bobby Day. Their concentration was on flying this lumbering bird through the night, getting altitude. The mountains were ahead of us to our left. Straight ahead was the open ocean, and eventually the coast of Florida.

The glowing fires got smaller and smaller in our wake. After we cleared the mountains, we would fly low, about a thousand feet above the ground. We would keep at this level all the way across. Once we were over open water, the good thing about this plane was that if we got into trouble, we could simply land in the water and wait for rescue. And pray it wasn't the Cubans who got to us first.

As we approached the Atlantic, I could see Guantanamo to my right. The base was well lit and we could see the buildings and airstrip below us. There was little activity on the base. We passed well to the east so we would stay out of Guantanamo's airspace. I looked for the C-130, but there were no large planes visible on the landing strip.

"You guys all right?" I said to Bobby Day and the Swamp Master.

"Yeah," Bobby said.

"Yeah," the Swamp Master said. "That was some party."

"It'll go down in the record books as the most expensive party ever thrown in Cuba," I said.

"Where's Juan?" Bobby asked.

"He didn't make it. We were surprised by a Cuban patrol," I said.

There was a silence, only the droning of the engines and air noises. The Swamp Master spoke. "It's a bitch. He escapes Cuba, settles in Miami, and has the good life. And he dies on Cuban soil in a firefight."

"Felix will be crushed," I said. "They were very close."

I went and checked on the rest. Jeff Bacon was sitting against the wall, scribbling in longhand onto a pad, no computer now. The cameras were spread out at his feet. I pointed at them. "Thank the colonel," he said. "I shot the whole thing from the plane."

"You got it on film?"

"Yeah, most of it," Jeff said with a smile. The colonel was being attended to by his men, who were dressed in our clothes. He had cuts and bruises. I bent over to talk to him.

"You all right, Colonel?" I asked.

"Yes. Just some damage from when the tower went up. I'll be fine." I could see his men were all fine.

"Thanks for the cameras," I said.

"What cameras?" he asked.

I went back to the front of the airplane and squatted between the Swamp Master and Bobby Day, who was now flying the plane. "What now?" I asked.

"You're the boss here," the Swamp Master said. "We should be askin' you—it's your party."

"Right. How long until the coast of Florida?" I asked.

"We're almost in the electronic surveillance web right now; about three minutes from now and we're inside the net. We'll start beeping on the war room screen in Miami," Bobby Day said. "We still have the transponder, but I need to activate it before we enter."

"All right, let's activate it," I said. "How do you do it?"

"I set the code for today and I have to stick it to the outside of the aircraft," he said.

"We're flyin' for Chrissakes," the Swamp Master said. "And we can't put down in the water with all these holes from that fuckin' Jeep chasin' us."

"Go, get it, Bobby," I said. The Swamp Master took over the controls.

Bobby reached under his seat, and he brought it out. It was about the size of an alarm clock. He punched in a code and the digital numbers glowed red in the darkness. He flipped the protective cover over the flashing signal and held it up for us to see. "It has a very strong magnet on the underside that will stick to the fuselage of the plane."

"So, we open the door and you stick it to the fuselage," I said.

"Is that all?" the Swamp Master said. "No fuckin' problem, we are only moving at about a hundred and seventy-five miles an hour. We open the door—change the cabin air pressure. Somebody sticks their arm out and attaches the transponder to the fuckin' fuselage and we close the door—no problem what-so-fucking-ever. Except, I will have to hang onto the controls for dear life, and everybody inside this bird will have to hang onto their jockstrap and anything else they can find so we all don't go rolling around like bowling pins."

"Let's go," I said to Bobby. We were running out of time. "You get ready to slap it on the fuselage."

I moved back to where the colonel was and yelled for Jeff to come over to us.

"Look, we're opening this door for a minute. When we do, it will be like a wind tunnel in here and the plane will roll—real bad as the pressure changes. We have to do this so we don't get shot down by U.S. helicopters when we enter U.S. airspace. Strap yourself in, secure the cameras, and hang on. Tell the other men and take care of the colonel. You have thirty seconds," I said.

The men all scuttled away, scrambling to get themselves into the harnesses. They secured the colonel to the bulkhead wall and then harnessed themselves to the wall.

I released the lock and stood ready to open the door. "Ready!" I yelled to everyone, counted to five, and popped the door. The force of the incoming wind nailed me against the inside bulkhead wall. The plane started to yaw, first right, then left. I could see the Swamp Master fighting the controls. Bobby was hanging onto the bulkhead webbing, waiting for the cabin pressure to stabilize. I clipped the door open against the bulkhead with the metal door restraints. I moved closer to the opening, along with Bobby, who was holding the transponder with one hand and the webbing with the other hand. I was next to him, but closer to the open door.

"Give me that," I yelled. "I got a good spot here. Hold my belt! I'm going to reach out now."

He nodded. I moved through the opening. I had one hand on his belt as he held the cargo webbing. The air was streaming through the plane. Sugar was swirling from the bags that had been broken; odd bits of paper and flotsam were whirling around inside the fuselage of the plane. The plane was dipping from side to side like a drunken cowboy.

I heard the metallic *click* as the transponder magnetically glued itself to the fuselage. I pulled with all my might as Bobby also strained to help me re-enter from the open door. As I emerged, he yanked and I slammed against the inside bulkhead.

He nodded that he was okay and we sprang for the door, removed the restraint, and together pushed the door against the incoming wind. I looked below, and could see the ocean streaming by at less than fifty feet, the whitecaps breaking. Together, using all our might, we slammed the door into position and locked it shut.

We plopped up against the bulkhead and rested. The Cubans were all right. The colonel was looking whiter and whiter as shock set in.

"Inspector Greene has pre-cleared our pass-through code for a clearance into the United States. We won't be bothered by the AWAC or the patrol planes, or the Blackhawk helicopters. We're cleared in right now," Bobby said.

"Unless he forgot," I said.

"In which case we will be shot out of the motherfucking sky," the Swamp Master yelled from the pilot's seat. "And you guys are fucking welcome for me keeping us out of the ocean and crashin' and dyin'."

"Thanks," I said with a smile. "We were back there having a nice leisurely flight, enjoying our cocktails and peanuts."

We moved up to the front of the plane. I slid into the copilot's chair. Jeff Bacon moved in beside me.

"What now, genius?" the Swamp Master said.

"Let's head for the FAA strip in the Everglades," I said.

"The C-130," Bobby said.

"And those motherfuckers!" the Swamp Master said.

"Yeah, and those motherfuckers," I said.

"Finally, some action. I was getting sooo bored," the Swamp Master said with a big smile.

We came in west of Key West, and continued flying into Florida Bay, staying west of the Keys. We could see the lights of the cars going north up the Keys highway. The headlights sparkled in the night. There was only a slight reflection off the water from the quarter moon. The water rippled black and oily.

We flew into the Everglades Park just West of Blackwater Sound; Homestead passed underneath us and we moved into the center of the Glades. Finally, the Miccosukee reserve slipped under us. We were still flying low, now five hundred feet.

When we saw the Tamiami Trail, the Swamp Master raised the nose of the plane, bringing us up to a thousand feet. We flew over the Trail and into the Big Cypress Swamp.

The lights on the FAA runway dead ahead of us were

lit. We circled the runway from a thousand feet, and we could see the C-130 below us on the runway. We could see the headlights from six vans. They were nudged up against the cargo ramp of the C-130. Nobody had to explain what they were doing.

"I'm breaking radio silence," Bobby Day said.

The Swamp Master handed him the mike. Bobby located the emergency FAA frequency. He connected with Miami and got Inspector Greene.

"It's Bobby," he said.

"I've been waiting to hear your voice," Inspector Greene said.

"We're in the Glades and we got a code red," Bobby said.

"I understand, I got Felix here with me. He got a call from his homeland, said there was a fire."

My heart sank when I thought of Felix. Bobby looked at me. I shook my head—no, not now—don't tell him now.

"No time to talk now. How about you go into a full scramble, before the chicken flies the coup," Bobby said.

"Consider it done."

"That's it for now," Bobby said.

He looked over at me. "That should be that. We can just circle and watch the action," Bobby said.

"Well," I said.

"Here he goes, boys. Francisco can't take yes for a fucking answer and let them raid the joint and find a U.S. military plane loaded with dope, and at least one spook and a U.S. Customs agent on board. He's gotta do somethin'," the Swamp Master said. He turned to me. "I suppose you want to put down on the airstrip so we can get the shit shot out of us."

"Not exactly," I said.

"Enlighten us," Bobby Day said.

"Well, when we borrowed this plane, we launched it from that shallow lake beside the airstrip."

"You want us to land there?" Bobby Day said.

"Well . . ." I said.

"Francisco, we are full of fuckin' holes, or had you forgotten?" the Swamp Master said.

"How could I forget? The wind has been blowing through those holes the entire trip," I said. "I want to put us down on the lake and get us to the launching pad. If we sink, we sink. The water is only two feet deep," I said.

"Why?" the Swamp Master said. Then he paused. "Oh, I get it. You think that Jacoby and Burton will somehow slip away again, and we can maybe stop them?"

I said nothing. We all looked at each other, until finally the Swamp Master shrugged his shoulders. "Let's give it a try. I love walking around the swamp at night, with the fuckin' gators and the water moccasins and bein' shot at and chased. Sounds great."

I banked us around slowly to the east, and then turned again until we were flying due west. We came in parallel to the Tamiami Trail. The cars were off to our left. We could see the lake in front of us. It was really not a lake, it was a backwater of the ever-flowing Glades river. When the river of grass hits the Tamiami Trail, it slows down and backs up as it slips under the highway through man-made tubes.

We were dropping steadily when we saw Blackhawk helos come in over the runway. They hovered above the C-130. They turned their floodlights on and lit up the entire scene. We could see patrol cars—probably Florida Highway Patrol, because they were closest to the scene. They raced down the one road that led into the airstrip. Inspector Greene had done his job.

I looked ahead and dropped us to within ten feet of the water, then five; when we hit the water, we bounced up softly and then down again into the still swamp. I was running the plane a little faster than normal on a landing, so we could make it to the launching pad we had used to take off.

The water started to seep into the plane from the bullet holes. It squirted in like high-pressure hoses, driven by the speed of the plane. It didn't take long to get six inches of water in the belly, then almost a foot. The plane became suddenly sluggish. Like brakes on a car, the water inside the hull of the plane brought us to a stuttering stop.

The launching pad was only about ten feet in front of us when we stopped dead and sunk into the mire of the swamp. The plane's wing pontoons and the mushy bottom stopped us from sinking. I pushed the door open, and more water seeped inside the plane.

I stepped outside into the murky water and the gooey swamp bottom. The water level was halfway up my thighs. Bobby and the Swamp Master followed. Jeff Bacon was next; then we went back to help the colonel and the Cuban soldiers. We stripped off our military tops and were in our T-shirts. We slogged toward the concrete launching pad, which was only a few feet in front of us.

The military helicopters were still hovering above the plane, the airstrip was filling up with police cars, their red and blue lights spinning in the dark night. The three of us stood on the edge of the concrete pad, still in the water, watching the action. We heard a huge roar, and we all looked up together as a giant big-footed swamp buggy came up over the hill toward us, giant tires churning as they spun through the limestone, mud, and saw grass. They hit the pad with a mighty thud. I was looking into the eyes of Michael Burton. Jacoby sat next to him. They were strapped in.

I don't know who was more surprised as we saw each other. We all dove in different directions to get out of the way of the giant treaded, spinning big-foot tires as the swamp buggy tore over the pad, grinding, churning; then it slid into the swamp, kicking up mud, water, and grass as it hit the shallow lake. It swerved around the Albatross and headed for the deep swamp.

The Swamp Master and I rose out of the mud and saw grass together. He pointed at a small Park Service airboat sitting on a trailer to the side of the launch pad. We didn't have to say anything to each other. We grabbed Bobby Day and ran to the trailer. We jerked the hitch up and swung it around, and backed the trailer down the ramp until the hull of the airboat was in the water. The Swamp Master scaled the gunnels and jumped into the driver's seat.

I yelled at Bobby, "Go back to the Albatross and collect the guns and come back here." He took off. The prop swung slowly as the battery ground the engine.

The Swamp Master paused and pumped the choke on the engine. He tried again, and the engine roared into life.

I pushed the airboat off the trailer and into the water, and swung it around so the bow was pointing out into the open swamp. I hopped over the gunnel and into the passenger seat.

Bobby returned with his hands full. He had four 45 automatics and eight extra clips. He handed two 45's and four clips to me, and did the same with the Swamp Master. I rammed the guns in my belt and the clips in my pockets. Bobby gave us a final push and stepped aside. I buckled into the seat and looked up at the Swamp Master.

He had his hat on backward, and a big grin on his face. He was fully alive as he yelled at the top of his voice. The sound carried over the roar of the engine. *"Let's rock and roll, you motherfuckers—let's rumble!"*

I saw Bobby and Jeff Bacon heading for the airstrip and the police cars. The Blackhawk helicopters had landed; their nose lights, a million candlepower each, still blazing, had the scene lit up.

The propeller spun into life. The stern of the airboat dug into the water, then popped out as we moved forward, and we began to skim over the water. The Swamp Master headed across the small lake to the canal that ran alongside the Tamiami Trail. We had ground to make up, and he knew Burton and Jacoby would run close to the Trail looking for a place to get a car and disappear into the night.

I saw the buggy a half mile ahead of us. First the

lights, then the four huge tires acting independently of each other as the engine drove each wheel through the swamp. It looked like a monster crippled crab as it dipped and bounced, rising and falling, in the little moonlight that there was.

The Swamp Master popped us out of the roadside canal, and back into the tall saw grass. We would come up on them from behind, behind their ability to hear. We were going at least twice as fast as they were, and closing the gap rapidly.

I yanked the two guns out of my belt. I pulled the slide back, and popped a round in each chamber. We were directly behind them now, about a hundred yards from the canal. I looked up at the Swamp Master, who had found ear mufflers and goggles. He looked like a giant bug himself. I pointed to the guns and our fuel tank and held up five fingers. He got the idea and shook his head in agreement.

The swamp buggy fuel tank stood high above the seat. They still hadn't seen us behind them. I held the first finger up, then the second, the third, the fourth, and then the fifth.

We started blasting with both guns. Four automatics banging away. It was tough shooting, moving at this speed, but I could see sparks flying off the fuel tank. Then a liquid started to spray out on top of Jacoby, who was driving, and Michael Burton, who sat in the passenger seat. Burton was strapped in an X web belt. He turned his head, then hit the searchlight, bringing it to bear on us. He popped the belt, spun, and kneeled on the seat, hanging on with one hand. With the other he removed his weapon, but thought better of shooting, since a spark would blow them up.

We were out of ammo, and tossed the clips, slapping in new ones. The big-footed swamp buggy was starting to cough and spit as the fuel flow to the engine started to shut down. Jacoby swung the buggy hard left, and we went darting past, just missing the giant tires. This time they opened up on us.

The Swamp Master veered hard right, and started a snaking, serpentine path through the saw grass and shallow water. He made a wide arc and we got behind them a second time. They were approaching the canal. If they went in the deep canal, they would sink and they knew it. The engine was coughing, and both Jacoby and Burton were out of their harnesses, standing, guns drawn, but afraid to shoot at us behind them. They were running full speed for the canal. I was standing now, and turned to the Swamp Master. He knew what I was thinking. I turned and opened fire—both guns. He did the same.

The buggy came up on the canal and Jacoby and Burton jumped, just as the sparks started to hit the fuel tank. The buggy blew up, two giant tires flying off into the canal; one massive tire flew right over the highway, the Tamiami Trail, and the last just missed us by a few inches. The swamp buggy engine actually came off the bolts and tumbled forward, sizzling when it hit the water.

The Swamp Master pulled back on the throttle, and the hull lowered into the grass. I spotted Jacoby first. He was clinging to the bank of the canal, slithering out into the saw grass. Burton appeared next to him, and was doing the same. The Swamp Master moved in, positioning the airboat almost on top of them. I stood in the bow.

Burton still held a gun. He looked at me. I had both 45's aimed at him. The Swamp Master had Jacoby covered.

Burton moved his hand slightly toward his weapon.

"Wanna make my day, asshole?" I said.

Burton made a fast flicking motion with his wrist, and the gun flew over his shoulder into the canal. The airboat was too small for all of us to fit, so we towed them across the canal and tied them up on the bank near the highway. We threw our Cuban automatics, Yugoslavian-made, into the canal and waited for the Highway Patrol.

The next day we made the headlines of the *Miami Sentinel*. Special story by Jeff Bacon, complete with pictures. "Rogue American agents apprehended bringing in ten thousand kilos of coke in a U.S. military C-130 aircraft coming in directly from Cuba. Giant ring of international smugglers headed by Castro's Cuban Army chiefs—broken. Thousands of kilos of coke destroyed in Cuban warehouses."

Lillian and Mai Lynh met us after we were debriefed by Inspector Greene of the FAA and the head of Customs for South Florida. I had taken a shower at Customs and been given a military jumpsuit. The same for the Swamp Master.

The Swamp Master climbed into his truck and turned to say good-bye. "We're headed down to Key Largo to pick up the kids," he said with a big smile.

"How about you don't call for a couple of weeks,"

Mai Lynh said. "I want this man to myself; besides, he's had too much fun. I don't want him to get his blood up for this kind of stuff and start craving it," she said.

We watched them pull away, and we climbed into the car. I glanced back toward the Customs building in Miami and stepped out of the car. I stuck my head back inside. "Lillian, just a minute."

I walked over to the entrance. Felix was in the doorway, leaning against the wall. He looked at me with no expression as I approached. "Felix, I'm so I—"

He put his hand up in front of him, as if he was trying to ward off the pain. "Please, Francisco, say nothing."

I put my hand on his shoulder. He wouldn't look at me. I could see the tears streaming down his cheeks. He just shook his head. He spoke, low, quietly, measured. "This Cuba of ours—it sometimes is a cruel mother, it demands everything . . . everything."

I left him standing there, and got back in the old Jeep. Lillian was driving; we had the sunroof open. We crossed onto the MacArthur Causeway. The Miami skyline was lit up. The warm tropical air was like a cotton sheet, comforting, not confining. I held her hand. We drove in silence, holding hands, past South Beach.

I studied her face as she drove. The pure classic bone structure, the natural beauty, but this woman surpassed beauty. Her soul glowed through her skin. She had stood by me and never wavered. We had taken a mighty gamble and won.

The song drifted into my head but I remained silent.

My funny valentine, sweet comic valentine
You make me smile with my heart . . .

She smiled, but did not look at me. She squeezed my hand as if she knew I was singing to myself. Maybe we could go back to where we'd started now, and see the world together.

JIM DEFELICE
COYOTE BIRD

The president is worried—with good cause. Two of America's spy planes have disappeared. Soon he—and the nation—will face a threat more dangerous than any since the height of the Cold War. A secretly remilitarized Japan is plotting to bring the most powerful country on Earth to its knees, aided by a computer-assisted aircraft with terrifying capabilities. But the U.S. has a weapon of its own in the air—the Coyote, a combat super-plane so advanced its creators believe it's invincible. Air Force top gun Lt. Colonel Tom Wright is prepared to fly the Coyote into battle for his country—and his life—against all that Japan can throw at him. And the result will prove to be the turning point in the war of the skies.

__4831-0 $5.99 US/$6.99 CAN